The Shores of Midnight

BY THE SAME AUTHOR

Oriental Hotel
The Emerald Valley
Women and War
The Black Mountains
The Hills and the Valley
Inherit the Skies
Folly's Child
Daughter of Riches
Deception and Desire
The Eden Inheritance

THE SHORES OF MIDNIGHT

Janet Tanner

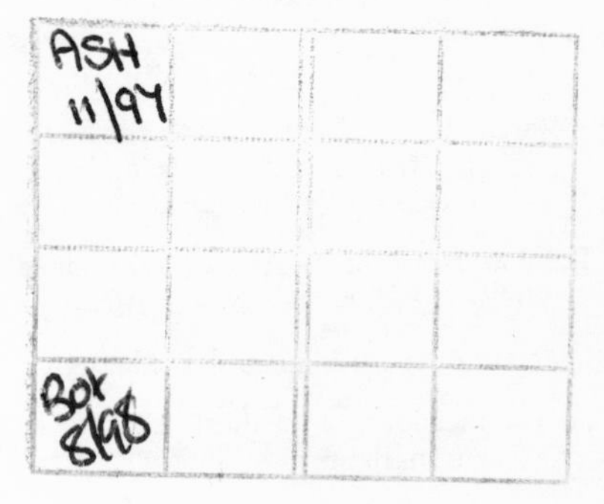

C

CENTURY · LONDON

First published by Century in 1997

First published in the United Kingdom in 1997 by
Century Ltd
Random House, 20 Vauxhall Bridge Road, London SW1V 2SA

Random House Australia (Pty) Limited
20 Alfred Street, Milsons Point, Sydney,
New South Wales 2061, Australia

Random House New Zealand Limited
18 Poland Road, Glenfield
Auckland 10, New Zealand

Random House South Africa (Pty) Limited
PO Box 337, Bergvlei, South Africa

Random House UK Limited Reg. No. 954009

A CIP catalogue record for this book is available from the British Library

Papers used by Random House UK Ltd are natural, recyclable products made from wood grown in sustainable forests. The manufacturing processes conform to the environmental regulations of the country of origin.

Typeset by Palimpsest Book Production Limited,
Polmont, Stirlingshire
Printed and bound in Great Britain by
Mackays of Chatham, PLC, Chatham, Kent

ISBN 0 7126 7831 X

Aye on the shores of darkness there is light
And precipes show untrodden green
There is a budding morrow in midnight
There is a triple sight in blindness keen

Keats

It was beginning again.

The cry took voice and echoed through the darkness. As she heard it with the ears of her soul the Wise One stirred.

The time had come. The time was now. She had known it would come again one day but it had been so long, so long. Now, once again, was the opportunity for old wrongs to be righted; once again the dreamers were awakening from their long sleep.

There had been other opportunities down the echoing years but they had been missed. This time there must be no mistake. This time the chance to make amends must not be lost for the soul trapped on the wheel of destiny, for if it was it would not occur again for more hundreds of years.

This time, with her help and guidance, it must be resolved.

THE HOUSE, very large [illegible]
on the outskirts of the village [illegible]
overgrown shrubs, was [illegible].
[illegible] illuminating a row of [illegible]
and [illegible] of [illegible]
[illegible] windows [illegible]
[illegible]

[illegible] Morris stood [illegible]
the [illegible] where the [illegible]
[illegible], flickering shadows [illegible]
the flashing blue strobe light [illegible]
[illegible] of game [illegible]
[illegible]

[illegible] always [illegible]
[illegible]. As [illegible]
[illegible] of being buried alive [illegible]
[illegible] it had seemed to [illegible]
[illegible]. Even pictures of [illegible]
[illegible] and she had [illegible]
[illegible] contact with [illegible]
[illegible] to take a [illegible]
[illegible] the thrill of horror [illegible]
[illegible] had ever experienced.

[illegible] twenty-six [illegible]
[illegible]. When [illegible]
[illegible] changed, it [illegible]
[illegible] there [illegible]
[illegible] that [illegible]
[illegible] and was likely to [illegible]
[illegible] lose control [illegible]
[illegible]

I

THE HOUSE, VERY large and very old, set back from the road on the outskirts of the village and half hidden by trees and overgrown shrubs, was burning furiously. Flames leaped from the roof, illuminating a row of garret windows under the eaves, and roared out of control behind the gaping holes which had once been first-floor windows but now yawned wide as screaming mouths.

Esther Morris stood at the rear of the knot of onlookers on the road outside where the hoses snaked slick and black in the dancing, flickering shadows, scribbling in her notebook by the flashing blue strobe light of the fire engine and trying to contain the feeling of panic which vied with an almost morbid fascination.

Fire. It had always made her feel this way, for as long as she could remember. As a child she had woken screaming from nightmares of being burned alive, or lain, too petrified to move, though it had seemed to her that the darkness was thick with smoke. Even pictures of fire in her books had reduced her to a quivering jelly and she had turned the pages quickly, her fingers shrinking from contact with the images, yet finding herself drawn, all the same, to take a quick peek a few moments later and feel again the thrill of horror that was more vitally real than any other emotion she had ever experienced.

She was twenty-six now, and a journalist with a large-circulation regional newspaper, *West Today*, but in the years between nothing had changed. If anything, the phobia had grown rather than lessened; now there was fear of fear itself, too, and the knowledge that, if faced unexpectedly with the object of her terror, she was likely to make a complete and utter fool of herself, lose control, faint, cry or be physically sick. In everyday life, of course, she encountered it less often. Hardly any houses had the open fires she had so feared as a child – nowadays it was central heating, with innocuous radiators and night-storage heaters – but Esther still felt uncomfortable in close proximity to a boiler. The roaring gas jets or hissing anthracite made her think of a wild beast, caged but not tamed, and the sick unreasoning fear would strike again, primeval and all-powerful. And try as she might to avoid them, there were always the occasions when it was impossible to escape being confronted by fire or its aftermath.

Tonight had been one of those occasions. Esther and her photographer, Martin Collins, had been driving the twenty miles back to town after covering a reception to mark the opening of a new stretch of privately owned railway when they had noticed a glow illuminating the night sky, and Martin had immediately turned off the main road in search of the scene.

'It's probably only a barn fire,' Esther had argued, trying to hide her apprehension. 'There were a lot round here last year. Let's get home – I'm dead on my feet.'

But Martin had ignored her, screaming round the bends in the narrow lanes in his usual imitation of a rally driver, and the feeling of dread, aggravated by his recklessness, had escalated to near-panic.

'For God's sake, Martin! Do you have to?' she'd snapped at him and he had glanced at her in surprise.

'What's wrong with you? There could be some good pictures in this – exclusives, even . . .'

And there would be. Undoubtedly there would be. Even a barn fire could have made spectacular photographs – this house, relic of a more leisured and affluent age, blazing into the night, would be the stuff front pages were made of.

The moment he had seen it Martin had been out of the car, camera at the ready, and it had been some minutes before Esther had summoned the courage to follow. It would be expected of her, she knew, to provide the copy, and Alec Vincent, her rather dour Scottish news editor, would be in no mood to accept what would sound to him like very lame excuses if she failed in her duty.

Now, as she noted down the information she had gleaned from some of the onlookers, her hands were unsteady, and she gripped her pencil grimly, concentrating on what she was doing, trying not to see the leaping flames and spark-studded smoke, trying to shut her ears to the roar and crackle, the sharp tinkle of breaking glass and the thud of falling timbers which not even the noise of the fire engine pumps could drown out.

The house, once owned by a veterinary surgeon and used as a clinic for small animals, was empty now, it seemed, and had been for some years. 'Brown the Vet' had died – of liver failure brought on by drink, if the locals were to be believed – and his executors had been unable to find a purchaser for the rambling monstrosity and its two acres of grounds. It had fallen into disrepair and what assets it had once possessed had long since been stripped – the magnificent staircase shipped out to a buyer in the USA, it was said, and the Adam fireplace removed one dark night by someone who had no right to it.

'We always expected it to be pulled down,' a fat woman in T-shirt and jeans told Esther. 'We reckoned they'd put up half a dozen executive homes on the site. Well, now this has happened, it'll come sooner rather than later.'

'Do you think it's arson?' Esther asked, trying to control her growing discomfort by concentrating on the job in hand.

'Very likely. We had a lot of barn fires round here last year . . . Little toads, I'd tan their backsides if I got hold of them.'

'It was my Geoff who rang for the brigade, you know.' Another woman, realising Esther was a reporter, joined in the conversation, her eyes beady with excitement. 'He saw the flames when he went out to shut up his greenhouse for the night. Geoff Scrivens, his name is – that's S-C-R— '

She broke off suddenly as a section of roof fell in with a crash, and almost against her will Esther's eyes were drawn back to the burning house. She stared, as if hypnotised, feeling the tension knotting her shoulders and arms and the sickness churning in her stomach, but quite unable to look away. It was as if all the nightmares of her childhood were hemming her in, flapping at her face like a flock of disturbed pigeons, filling her ears with the beating of their wings. Her breath was coming fast and shallow, her heart pounding with dread.

And then she saw it – a figure on the balcony that fronted the first-floor windows. For a few timeless seconds, which seemed to stretch into eternity, it remained there, silhouetted starkly against the flames. Then it was gone.

For a moment Esther was frozen by horror into immobility.

Then she felt her knees buckling and her breath, held for the duration, came out on a scream.

'My God! There was someone there!'

The woman who had been plying her with information turned, her face a picture of shocked disbelief.

'What?'

'There was someone there – on the balcony! Didn't you see her?'

'No. The house is derelict, my dear, I told you— '

'There was . . . there was!' Esther was weeping now, her breath, tainted by the smoke, coming in raw gasps. 'I *saw* her!'

'No . . . no, you're mistaken.'

'I'm not!' Her voice rose hysterically and as she lashed out wildly, as if beating off some unseen threat, the bystanders drew back, alarmed and embarrassed.

'Esther? Esther – what in the world is the matter?'

Martin! Oh, thank God – Martin! His voice seemed to be coming from a long way off, his face, like all the others, no more than a blur, swimming in and out of her vision. Esther felt her knees buckling beneath her and she was falling – no, not so much falling as sinking, in slow motion.

Martin saw her begin to sag and caught her round the waist, holding her for a moment like a sack of flour. Then he hoisted her arm around his shoulders, half carrying her across the road to where the car was parked. When they reached it he yanked open the passenger door and eased her into the seat, dropping down on his haunches beside her.

'All right now?'

'Yes – no – oh, Martin, there was someone there . . .' Her teeth were chattering so that she could scarcely form the words.

'What?' He sounded as shocked and disbelieving as the woman had done.

'There was someone on the balcony! Didn't you see them?'

'No.'

'But she was there when the roof fell in . . . and then she was gone . . .'

'Esther,' he said gently, as if to a child, 'I'm sure there was nobody there. You imagined it.'

'I didn't!'

'You must have. The place is empty – has been for years.

There's not even a staircase, so nobody could have got upstairs. And if they had done, someone else would have seen them. It was just an optical illusion, I expect. All those flames and shadows . . .'

'You really think so?'

'I'm sure of it. You had too much wine at that damned reception on an empty stomach.'

She laughed shakily, but without humour. Too much wine? Perhaps. She certainly felt nauseous. Giddy and nauseous and scared out of her wits. But in her mind's eye she could still see that figure, cowering back on the balcony . . .

'I'm sorry,' she whispered. 'I just lost it. And . . .' Her hands convulsed in her lap, feeling for something that should be there but wasn't. 'I think I've dropped my notebook.'

'All right, I'll go and look for it. You stay here.'

He pulled himself to his feet, a tall, whippy man in a bleached denim shirt and casual slacks. He had not pandered to the occasion by wearing a suit – he never did. It was his contention that if someone wanted a picture in the paper then they must take him as he was – and there were rarely any complaints about his attitude. Martin was too good a photographer.

Esther wrapped her arms around herself, wishing she could stop shaking and suddenly overcome with a wave of longing for Alain. His being here wouldn't have prevented her hysterics, of course – given that it was so totally beyond reason no one could have done that. But oh, it would be so nice to have him put his arms around her now, to have the scent of his very French aftershave in her nostrils instead of the acrid smoke, to have him whispering endearments in her ear, stroking her hair . . .

Stop it, for God's sake! She caught her lip between her teeth, biting it hard as the longing opened the floodgates of memory, made bitter-sweet now by the sense of loss. She would not think of Alain. What they had shared was over. He had deceived her and she had shut him out of her life. No man – not even Alain – was going to do what he had done and get away with it.

A few minutes later Martin was back.

'Got it,' he said, opening the driver's door and getting into the car. 'It's a bit wet, I'm afraid. There's water everywhere.' He held out the notebook, but on the point of taking it she drew her hand back sharply. 'What's the matter now?' Martin asked, a note of impatience creeping into his voice.

'Nothing.' Somehow she steeled herself to take the notebook from him, though her fingers still felt stiff and tingling. There was no way she could tell him the truth – that for a moment she had felt that the notebook, or indeed anything she touched, would be searingly hot. He'd think she was mad – *she* was beginning to think she was mad.

'I'm sorry,' she said feebly. 'It's just that I'm really funny about fire.'

'So I noticed.'

'I shall have to do something about it – see a hypnotist or something – before I make a complete fool of myself.'

Martin said nothing, but she read his mind.

Esther, you just did.

Aloud, he said, 'If you ask me, what you need is a break.'

She laughed shakily. 'I can't take a day off. I've got reams of stuff to deal with.'

'I'm not talking about a day off. I mean a proper holiday. You've had a pretty rough time of it just lately, haven't you, with one thing and another?'

Quick colour flooded her cheeks. So – he knew. They all knew. It was probably the talk of the newsroom when her back was turned.

No, that was just being paranoid. They couldn't possibly know the whole truth. Only she and Alain knew that she certainly hadn't told anyone. All they knew was that Alain had returned to France following a sudden death in the family. But they had probably noticed how upset and withdrawn she had been and come to their own conclusions. Always fiercely protective of her privacy, Esther hated the thought of her personal life being discussed and dissected.

'I expect I'll survive,' she said, trying to sound nonchalant and succeeding only in sounding bitter.

They lapsed into silence, Esther struggling to exercise some control over her shattered nerves as Martin covered the remaining distance back to town in his usual reckless manner.

'Will you be all right now?' he asked, pulling into a parking space outside the tall old house where Esther had a one-bedroomed flat.

'Yep.'

'Sure you don't want me to see you inside?'

'Sure. I'm going to make myself a hot drink and go straight to bed.'

'OK. I think I'll call in at the office and get these rolls of film developed. I want to see if they're any good.'

'I'll do my report in the morning.' She hesitated, half in, half out of the car. 'You really think I was imagining that person on the balcony?'

'I'm certain of it. Put a brandy in that hot drink, do you hear?'

'I will.'

She raised her hand in mock cheerful farewell as she crossed the pavement, fumbled in her bag for her keys and unlocked the door. Martin waited until she had it open before he pulled away; she turned to see the tail lights of his car disappearing around the corner and experienced a moment of desperate loneliness.

Her flat was on the second floor – one large light room which served as both sitting and dining room, a bedroom, a minuscule kitchen and a bathroom which might have been described by an estate agent as 'bijou'. The kitchen units had been almost new when she had taken over the flat, white melamine and too many floral tiles for her liking, but as yet she had not got around to replacing them. The bathroom she had treated herself to was new – a corner bath with a spa function, which would have been beyond her means had it not been included as a sweetener by the company who had fitted it, and a shower over. A shower was a necessity Esther had felt unable to do without – rushing for work in the mornings did not allow her time to soak in the bath. The rest of the flat she had furnished from auction sales and she was pleased with the result – the table, chairs, wardrobe and bed were old and solid without being antique, good-quality thirties and forties items which seemed to suit the room perfectly.

Esther liked her flat, liked the soft greens and russets in which she had decorated, adored the corner she had turned into a shrine of old family photographs she had rescued from her mother's and grandmother's homes, and her collection of household accoutrements from a bygone age – an old flat iron, a stone water bottle, a set of gaily coloured china milk jugs. She felt at ease with its comfortable homeliness accented by a few bright modern touches and, though it was far from being an interior designer's dream, it satisfied her in a way no show-house-like decor could have done.

Tonight, however, as she unlocked the door and stepped into the tiny dark hallway the loneliness came with her. She found herself remembering evenings such as this when she had come home from working late to find Alain waiting for her – the fresh flowers he had brought for her propped awkwardly into one of the china jugs – and wanted to weep.

She kicked off her shoes and went barefoot into the living room, switching on lights as she went. As she took off her jacket the pungent whiff of smoke that had impregnated the fibres wafted up to her and made her feel a little nauseous again. She would have a bath and wash her hair, she decided. Perhaps that way she would be able to get the horrible smell out of her nostrils.

She poured herself a brandy from the bottle she kept in the thirties-style sideboard and carried it with her into the kitchen, sipping as she went. Then, when she had filled the coffee maker, she went into the bathroom to start running the bath while it filtered. She liked her coffee black – caffeine never seemed to keep her awake, however late she drank it, though she was not at all sure how well she was going to sleep tonight.

The antique gold taps on her little corner bathtub cascaded scalding water on to her favourite musky bath oil and, as the perfume filled the tiny bathroom along with the steam, Esther felt her jangling nerves calming a little.

She stripped off her skirt and blouse and dropped them into the wicker laundry basket, catching sight of her image in the mirror as she did so. Her short thick wedge of light-brown hair was dishevelled, her face pale, and there were dark blue smudges beneath her eyes where her mascara had run.

'What a mess!' she muttered ruefully to her reflection and reached for a pad of cotton wool and bottle of cleansing milk.

A few minutes later she was in her bath, the glass of brandy and a cup of coffee standing side by side on a ledge within easy reach, slipping back to immerse herself completely in the bubbles. The corner bath was not long enough to allow her to lie out properly, and to get her head under the water she had to raise her knees and practically drape her legs over the edge. But it scarcely mattered. It just felt so *good* lying here.

'It's not really big enough for two of us,' Alain had complained when he had first seen the bath.

'It's not meant for two of us. And the bath at your house is big enough to hold an orgy in!' she had replied, teasing, but also slightly defensive.

'I don't want an orgy. I only want you . . .'

The memory hurt, just as all the other memories hurt. She sat up, reaching for the glass and the cup, sipping the brandy and coffee in turn and trying not to think about Alain. But it wasn't easy to forget someone who had meant so much to her. The only man I have ever loved or am likely to, Esther thought, and then snorted softly in a pathetic echo of her usual self-deprecatory humour. My God, she thought, that sounds like something from a bad romantic novel!

But it was true. For all that it was true. She had never before cared for anyone the way she cared for Alain, had never been able to allow herself to get close to anyone even. It had worried her sometimes, the way she had shied away from involvement. The moment a man showed a proprietorial interest something snapped inside her and any initial attraction she had felt was replaced by a feeling of panic, of being trapped. A part of her had longed desperately for a normal loving relationship, shared dreams, a family eventually, yet she had secretly begun to doubt her ability to achieve it.

And then Alain had come into her life and suddenly it was quite different.

She had met him when she was detailed to interview him for a feature which was to form part of a two-page advertising spread in her newspaper, and before setting out she had studied all the information in the files.

Alain Lavaur was a Frenchman who had set up his own business exporting wine from his home region – Languedoc and Roussillon – and he was now in the West Country to establish the English end of the operation. There was a photograph clipped to the file; the black-and-white newsprint showed a darkly handsome man, unmistakably of Mediterranean origin, with features that could almost be described as aristocratic. But it had in no way prepared her for the effect he would have on her.

Faced with the man whose deeply tanned skin was emphasised by the crisp white of his shirt and whose handshake was firm and cool, she had reacted, she thought, like a moonstruck schoolgirl. But there was nothing schoolgirlish in the instant feeling of affinity which lent depth to the attraction. Esther had felt instinctively that here, at last, was a man she would not run away from. As he talked she found herself almost hypnotised by the dark brown eyes with a hint of yellow around the irises, and the beautiful voice, silky and dark brown to match the eyes, with an appealing accent overlying his near-perfect command of the English language.

At the end of the interview he had invited her to have dinner with him and she had agreed with such alacrity it had startled her. Usually she made a point of keeping her business and personal lives separate. Now, she only knew she wanted to see him again more than she had ever wanted anything. That night, when he had taken her home after a romantic candlelit dinner, she had known she wanted him to stay. It didn't seem too soon – it simply seemed right. Already she felt as comfortable with him as if she had known him all her life, as intrigued and seduced by her own emotions as she was by Alain himself.

In the weeks that followed nothing had happened to change that. Their affair had been both tempestuous and wholly satisfying. Alain was a wonderful lover, considerate as well as passionate, and given to the sort of romantic gestures that filled her with delight and made her feel warm and cherished. In the flush of love the smallest detail of her life had taken on new significance – she sang in the bath, she laughed as she walked in the rain with her face upturned to catch the drops.

She knew he had been married but it did not seem important, except that it was a part of his life in which she would never be able to share. He had assured her it was over and she had believed him. Fool that she was, she had believed him.

And then, without warning, her world had fallen apart.

She had stayed the night with Alain at the big old house which he was renting in an exclusive area of town. They had been to the theatre and returned to enjoy a supper of French bread and salad, washed down by a bottle of one of Alain's best red wines, before they had fallen into bed and into each other's arms. After a night of lovemaking they had slept heavily

– too heavily – until the shrilling of the telephone had shocked them awake.

'Who can that be at this time of the morning?' Alain was pushing back the sheets and reaching for his robe. 'I must get a phone put in up here.'

Esther licked a finger and rubbed her eyelids. Last night she had forgotten to take off her mascara; now her eyes felt gummy. Broad daylight was streaming in through the gap in the curtains and when she glanced at her watch she sat bolt upright in shock. Eight fifteen! Thank heavens the telephone had rung or she would have been late for work!

She got out of bed and slipped into Alain's spare robe, which had been hanging behind the door. A quick shower, a cup of tea if she was lucky, and she might just make it in time for the morning conference of the news team, irreverently known as 'prayers'.

As she went along the landing to the bathroom she could hear Alain on the phone in the hall downstairs but she could not hear what he was saying and did not try. She closed the bathroom door and turned on the shower, climbing into it without waiting for the water to heat up. It cascaded over her, cold enough to make her gasp. She unstoppered Alain's shampoo, lathering it into her hair and using the residue to soap her body, not even wondering any more who it was who was ringing Alain.

She was out of the shower, reaching for a towel, when the bathroom door opened. Alain stood there and she knew at once from his expression that something was seriously amiss.

'What is it?' she asked sharply.

'I've just had some terrible news. That was Hélène on the telephone.' His voice sounded odd. For a moment Esther could not think who Hélène was, then she remembered. Alain's ex-wife. She wrapped the towel around herself, shivering a little.

'What?'

'It's Thierry. Her brother – you know? My partner. He's dead.' He said it tentatively, as if he couldn't quite believe his own words.

'Oh no! How?'

'There's been an accident. It seems his car plunged over a ravine. He went out for a drink last night, Hélène said, and didn't come home. They found the car this morning – burnt out. It must have caught fire when it crashed. Thierry . . . well, it sounds as if he never stood a chance.'

'That's terrible!'

'How the hell did he manage to do it?' Alain was shaking his head in shocked bewilderment. 'Some of the roads through the mountains are treacherous, of course. Narrow, with hairpin bends, and the ground just falls away . . . But there are safety rails at most of the worst places and Thierry knows those roads like the back of his hand. I just don't understand it.'

'Was there another vehicle involved?' Esther asked.

'I don't know. Hélène didn't say.'

'Perhaps he swerved to avoid something.'

'He'd been drinking, more likely,' Alain said savagely. Then he bowed his head, running a hand through his hair distractedly. 'Oh, I shouldn't have said that. Not with the bloke dead. Christ! I can't believe it!'

'Oh Alain, I'm so sorry.' Esther went to him, putting her arms around him. Water from her wet hair was running in rivulets down her neck and over her bare shoulders. 'What are you going to do?'

'Well, I shall have to go home, obviously. I'll ring the airport, check on flights. I hope I can get one today. There are going to be a lot of formalities to attend to. I suppose the body will have to be identified for one thing . . .' He closed his eyes briefly.

'Isn't there someone else who could do that?'

'For Christ's sake, Esther, he's my partner – and my brother-in-law! It's for *me* to do. And I certainly don't want Hélène having to worry about arrangements. She's in a terrible state. She lives on the edge of her nerves at the best of times. Something like this and she'll go to pieces. If anyone starts pressuring her to make decisions about arrangements, God knows what she'll do. I have to get over there – fast.'

'But she's not your responsibility now, surely.'

The moment the words were out she could have bitten off her tongue. Under the circumstances it was an unforgivable thing to say.

'Well, you are divorced, aren't you?' she added lamely.

He looked guilty suddenly. 'Not exactly.'

She stared at him. 'What do you mean – not exactly?'

'I mean – legally Hélène is still my wife. It's a difficult situation

– there's the business to think of, and besides, we are both Catholics.'

'But you told me it was over!'

'It is. Hélène and I split up before I came to England. It is over.'

'It doesn't sound that way to me!' The sense of betrayal was overwhelming. 'It sounds to me as if you've been deceiving me, Alain!'

'You knew about Hélène,' he said defensively.

'But not that you were still married to her! How could you keep something like that from me?'

He shrugged miserably. 'I suppose I was afraid you'd take it badly.'

'And you were right!' The hurt of knowing that every precious moment they had shared was now sullied by his deceit was spawning blazing anger. 'I don't play around with married men, Alain. Especially ones who think they can get away with a bit on the side when their wives are on the other side of the Channel!'

'It wasn't like that . . .'

'Wasn't it? I expect that's what they all say. Well, at least now I know where I stand. What a fool I've been!'

'Esther – please – don't be like this . . .' He reached out to touch her arm; she jerked away.

'How could you do it? How could you lie to me about something so important? Well, that's it. I can't be doing with it, Alain. Just – leave me alone, all right?'

For a moment he looked shocked, then he turned away with an angry shrug.

'If you're not going to listen to me I haven't got time to stand around here arguing. My business partner is lying dead, in case you have forgotten. And I have to make arrangements to go home.'

Hurt and anger stifled the brief stab of guilt.

'Yes, go home, sort out your affairs, look after your wife! I think that's what you should do. Now if you don't mind, I'd like to get dressed. I'm going to be late for work.'

She slammed the door in his face and threw on her clothes. She was shaking from head to foot and perilously close to tears. As she emerged from the bathroom, still fastening the clasp of her watch, he was on the landing waiting for her.

'Come with me,' he said simply.

She stared at him. 'To France?'

'Yes. I love you, Esther. I don't want to lose you. Not like this. Not at all.'

She almost weakened.

'It will be for the best if it's out in the open,' he went on. 'It will prove to you that I wasn't playing games, and my family will realise they have to accept that my marriage to Hélène is over.'

'So they haven't realised it yet?' She was angry again. 'Well I really don't think that's the sort of situation I want to walk into. It's up to you to sort things out first. If and when you do, well . . . maybe . . . but I rather doubt it. I feel cheated and used, Alain, and that is going to take some getting over.'

'Esther . . .'

'I have to go to work, Alain. Please let me pass.'

That had been the last time she had seen him. The first shock had hardened into cold fury at his deception and the shadow it cast spilled darkly over everything they had shared. If he had told her the truth she wouldn't have liked it, but perhaps she could have learned to accept it. But he hadn't told her. That was what she couldn't forget or forgive.

In the three weeks since he had left he had phoned several times, but she had hung up on him, and when a letter arrived she dumped it unopened in the wastepaper basket. She honestly didn't see how she could ever trust him again. But still she couldn't forget him, and she knew that in spite of everything she still loved him with that fierce, almost obsessional love that had startled her with its intensity in the beginning.

She wasn't getting over him. On the contrary, he was constantly on her mind.

Lying in her bath, aching with loneliness and longing, Esther wondered if she was being a fool to herself to stand by her principles so stubbornly. Alain had, after all, asked her to go to France with him. He would never have done that, surely, unless his marriage really was over? So who was she hurting but herself by refusing to give him another chance?

She sat up abruptly, reaching for a towel, and noticed a red weal on the inside of her forearm. Puzzled, she touched it – and winced. It was surprisingly tender. But how had it happened? She must have scalded it on the hot tap when she was drizzling in the bath oil, and not realised it. Strange! But she had been in rather a state . . .

Don't start that again! she chided herself. Think about Alain and what you are going to do.

She towelled herself fiercely. She was weakening, she knew. Talking herself into getting in touch with him. And already the prospect was making her feel better, elated almost.

Yes, that was what she would do: telephone and see what his response was. If he hadn't changed his mind then she would arrange some holiday and go to France. She was still hurt and angry with him but there was no getting away from it. In spite of it she loved him too much to give up on him so easily.

Glowing from a sense of purpose as well as from the hot bath and the brandy, Esther went to bed. But when she slept it was to dream not of Alain, but of fire – fire that roared through a cavernous old house, creating illusions with the flames; fire that had destroyed a car in a mountain ravine and with it a man's life. And the dreams were the echoes of all the other dreams which had haunted her throughout the years, unexplained, inexplicable.

2

ALAIN LAVAUR REPLACED the telephone receiver and remained motionless for a moment, his hand still resting on the pale grey Bakelite. Then he sat back, massaging his aching neck with his fingers and wondering how on earth he was going to sort out all the problems confronting him.

What the hell were you thinking of Thierry? he asked silently. It was a question he had asked a hundred times since he had come home after his partner's death and discovered that the thriving business he had left behind when he had gone to England six short months ago had deteriorated into a morass of unpaid bills and angry creditors. Just what did you think you were doing?

But the question was more rhetorical than puzzled. Alain thought he had a very good idea what was behind the jumbled accounts and doctored ledgers, and the spat of anger and frustration he felt now was directed as much at himself as at his dead partner.

He should have known better than to trust Thierry. Once a gambler, always a gambler.

In the years when they had been growing up together – the years between boyhood and manhood – he had often seen Thierry risk sums that had horrified him on the turn of a card or the spin of the wheel and there had followed that period when Thierry had disappeared from the scene and Alain suspected he had gone completely off the rails.

If he was honest he knew he had only himself to blame for what had happened now. He had been wrong to leave Thierry in charge of the French end of the business. Wrong not to have kept a closer eye on what he was up to. But he had honestly believed Thierry had put his youthful indiscretions behind him – and besides, he had had his own personal reasons for wanting to put some distance between himself and his homeland. They had coloured his judgement, blinded him to everything but what he had chosen to see: a reformed character as eager to make a success of the business as Alain himself was.

Now he found himself facing a situation that could mean only one thing. Thierry had not changed at all. He had been milking the business of such huge sums that it was now on the point of collapse. Thank God Alain had realised what was happening now, before things went any further! But even so, the problems were so serious that he was beginning to doubt that he could resolve them.

He rose from the padded leather chair and crossed to the window, moving with the easy grace of the athlete he had once been. Even now, worried as he was, he somehow conveyed the impression of a man in control of his destiny. It oiled his path, that confident demeanour, combining as it did a brimming enthusiasm for whatever venture he undertook with the subtle suggestion of inner strength and iron will. Few were aware that the apparent confidence was something of a charade, nurtured and developed over the years as a defence against a basic desire for approval. Alain scarcely ever admitted as much, even to himself. He had almost become the persona he had devised for himself. Those he met in the course of his business dealings found him charming and efficient, apparently highly principled and not afraid to take a risk here and there while at the same time giving the impression that it was not really a risk at all – that, with his flair and expertise and the star of good fortune that seemed to shine on whatever he did, nothing could possibly go wrong.

In the last few weeks, however, that star seemed to have deserted him in both his private and business lives, and Alain feared it had gone for good.

He stood now at the window, trying to draw some spark of hope from the unchanging panorama spread out before him.

To his left lay the village, red tiled roofs and centuries-old sunwarmed stone, crowned by the tall old clocktower where the bell chimed the quarter-hours with comforting regularity. Beyond it, and stretching across his middle vision, the Pyrenees dominated the landscape, rising from the *garrigue*-covered foothills and pine forests to purple-clouded heights, while to his right the distant blue of the Mediterranean sea merged with the blue of the sky in a shimmer of heat haze. Closer in the plains and stony hills were green with vineyards – tens of thousands of grape-bearing bushes arranged in orderly rows to cover acre upon acre of land, much of it owned by the Lavaur family.

The wine from these vines – and those grown by the better cooperatives in the district – was the lifeblood of Alain's business, and its success had come because of a change in government policy. For centuries Languedoc and Roussillon had produced vast quantities of *vin ordinaire*, the rather indifferent wine which washed down everyday meals in homes and bistros the length and breadth of France but was of little interest to the connoisseur. But in recent years the government had given up trying to persuade the *viticulteurs* to replant their vineyards with asparagus and instead encouraged them to change the variety of grape to those which would produce superior wines. Nowadays much of the region's wine was very good indeed and Alain had seized the opportunity it offered. He had formed an export company and the venture had proved even more successful than he had dared hope. The local cooperatives were only too glad to allow him to promote their produce and the English wholesalers and wine merchants, hard hit by the lifting of duty restrictions, snapped up the reasonably priced but very drinkable wines he was able to offer them.

As the business took off he had first brought Thierry in to assist, then entrusted him with the day-to-day running of the French end while he crossed the Channel to organise the import distribution network and expand the market. In England he had set up contracts worth thousands of francs and even persuaded two national supermarket chains to allow him to supply them with wines which would be marketed under their own label. Lavaur Wines, it seemed, was going from strength to strength.

Now all that was in jeopardy. The books and accounts showed huge discrepancies, vast amounts had apparently disappeared, and creditors had not been paid. The telephone call Alain had just taken had been the latest in a line from irate *viticulteurs* asking when they could expect what was due to them and it had taken all his powers of persuasion to talk this one into giving him a little longer to sort things out. But in all honesty he did not know how he was going to do it.

Damn Thierry! he thought, looking out at the sundrenched countryside and seeing it all dark edged with the threat of impending ruin. And damn himself for not checking up more thoroughly on his partner. How could he have been so stupid as to allow this to happen? Because contact with home had made him uncomfortable, perhaps, especially after he had met Esther. Thierry was, after all, Hélène's brother.

Alain had thought he was too much the businessman to allow personal problems to impinge on his professional judgements but he had been deluding himself. And he had reckoned without the curse of the Rousseaus. What was it about them that they managed to create such havoc? And why had he and his family fallen into the trap of allowing them to do so time and time again?

Some of the answers he thought he knew. But not all of them. Some things are never discussed within a family, however close. Some questions are never asked. They are simply accepted as a fact of life. It had always been so with the Rousseaus.

For as long as Alain could remember, Thierry and Hélène Rousseau had been around – almost as much a part of his world as his own sisters, Simone and Valerie. In some ways he had been even closer to Thierry than to his own sisters. He and Thierry were almost exactly the same age and as both were the only boys in their families they had become companions and friends in spite of the differences in their backgrounds.

Odette Rousseau, Thierry and Hélène's mother, worked for the Lavaurs as a domestic. She was a pretty, vivacious woman – no mean achievement considering the hard life she led. Every day she walked the two miles from the village to Le Château Gris to clean, sew and help the cook with the preparation of the vegetables, and when the children were not at school they came with her – to keep them from under the feet of their father, Isobelle, Alain's own mother, said.

Alain had always looked forward to the days when Thierry came to the château. He was a magnetic character with his sultry good looks and irresistible charm on the one hand, and a wild streak on the other. Thierry was always ready to take a risk, always determined to do exactly as he pleased and the devil take the consequences, and he had no respect for rules and authority. He was everything Alain wished he dared be – and besides, he was tremendous fun. Every day spent with Thierry was an adventure.

Through the long hot summers they were out from dawn

to dusk, tracking each other through the pine forests and the scrubby, sweet-scented *garrigue*, or weaving fantasy action games into the crumbling walls of the ruined fortress on the hill behind the village. They picnicked on peaches and apricots, great lumps of locally produced cheese and bottles of freshly made lemonade. They swam in the river pools. And their lives stretched out before them marred by nothing more than the long evening shadows or the prospect of a scolding if they tore their clothes or became so immersed in their games that they forgot the time and missed the curfew hour.

In those days, of course, Alain had scarcely noticed Hélène. She was just a little girl who played with dolls and cried if she fell over and skinned her knees – tiresome, not worthy of a moment's thought. It was later, much later, when he had looked at a tip-tilted nose, china-blue eyes and soft shoulder-length hair bleached to a golden brown by the sun and felt as if a giant hand were squeezing his heart. Much later, long after circumstances had changed and Thierry and Hélène were no longer visitors to the château but part of the family.

Alain had been eleven years old when the Rousseau children had been orphaned. Their father, Maurice, whom Alain had often heard Isobelle refer to as 'a drunk and a waster', had died some years earlier – 'They'll all be better off without him,' Isobelle had said – but now Odette too was dead.

Her death had shaken Alain to the core. It was the first time anyone he knew well had died, and for it to be someone so young, so full of life, made it doubly shocking. He couldn't believe it at first when he learned what had happened and even now, more than twenty years later, he could recall every detail, indelibly etched in his memory as it was.

It had been a beautiful June morning when the haze that would later disperse to let the hot sunshine through was still hanging over the valley, wreathing the tops of the trees with streamers of fine lace and hiding the distant blue peaks of the Pyrenees. He had been up with the dawn, letting out the dogs and whooping through the dew-wet grass while they charged about, sniffing excitedly at the fresh early-morning scents. He had gone farther than he intended and by the time he got back he was ravenously hungry. He unlatched the kitchen door and the smell of fresh coffee and croissants that greeted him made him hungrier than ever.

Simone and Valerie, his sisters, were seated at the table, but neither of them was eating. They were both looking puzzled and worried, both craning towards the door that led to the hall and drawing room, as if they were listening.

'What's wrong with you two?' Alain asked.

'Shh!' Simone hissed at him, and Valerie whispered, 'Something's happened.'

'What?'

'We don't know. The phone rang. Maman answered it and she called Papa and they've been in the drawing room talking ever since.'

'Papa's still here?' Alain said, beginning to share their alarm. A glance at the clock confirmed that his father should have left for his office long ago.

'Yes.'

Alain helped himself to a croissant, stuffing it into his mouth and positioning himself close to the door.

'I can't hear anything.'

'We could just now, couldn't we, Simone? Maman sounded very upset.'

'So what was she saying?'

'I don't know. I couldn't hear. But I think she was crying.'

Maman – crying! That was even more disturbing than Papa's failure to leave for the office on time. Maman never cried.

'You don't know that, Valerie,' Simone said, very much the older sister.

'I do! I could tell . . .'

The door opened so suddenly that Alain almost fell through it and his father, Henri, came past him as if he was not there. His handsome face was very drawn, very grey. Maman followed.

'Alain, what do you think you're doing? Don't you know it's very wrong to eavesdrop on other people's conversation?' Her voice was sharp, but although she too looked pale and worried her eyes didn't have the puffy red look of someone who has been crying.

'I wasn't!' Alain said defensively.

'What's happened?' Simone asked.

'Something very sad,' Isobelle said.

She didn't sound sad, Alain thought, just fraught. She took her silver cigarette case from her bag, which was lying on the counter, extracted a du Maurier and placed it, unlit, between her lips.

'What?' Valerie asked. 'What is it, Maman?'

'It's Odette. I'm afraid she's dead.'

'Dead!' They stared at one another, uncomprehending.

'She can't be!' Valerie said.

'She was here yesterday,' Alain said.

'I'm afraid it's true,' Isobelle said in the same hard voice. 'She died in the night.'

'But why?' Alain burst out. 'Why did she die?'

For a moment neither of his parents answered him, but Alain saw a look pass between them. Then Isobelle said, 'You children ask too many questions. Isn't it enough that she's dead, without you having to ask why?'

She reached for her lighter and Alain saw that her hand was trembling.

'These things happen sometimes,' Henri said. It was the first time he had spoken. His voice was gruff, unlike his usual mild tones.

'But . . .'

'Poor Thierry! Poor Hélène!' Valerie was crying.

'What's going to happen to them?' Simone asked. 'They've got nobody, have they?'

'That's what your father and I have been talking about,' Isobelle said, drawing deeply on her cigarette. 'If no relative comes forward, we have decided to give Thierry and Hélène a home.'

'Live here? With us?' Simone said.

'We can hardly let them go to an orphanage, can we? We do have a responsibility to see that they are looked after,' Isobelle said.

'Why?' Simone asked. She was looking at them intently.

'What do you mean – why?' Isobelle snapped. 'Odette worked for us, didn't she?'

'Well yes, but – '

'We have plenty of room,' Henri said. 'It won't inconvenience you children at all.'

'It'll be great!' Alain said, too excited at the prospect of having Thierry around to notice Isobelle's tight, disapproving look, forgetting momentarily even his shock that pretty laughing Odette was dead.

It was only later that he remembered, and kept remembering, so that each time he thought of it it shocked him again like the ripples following an earthquake; and much later that he had asked the same question as Simone: why had his mother and father been so ready to offer Thierry and Hélène a home? But somehow he had never asked, never even talked to Simone about it, though he felt she knew something he did not. Instinctively he knew that some questions are better left unanswered, some things better left unsaid.

'Of course – a relative might turn up,' Isobelle said. 'If so, naturally the children will go with them.'

But no relative had turned up. Thierry and Hélène had moved into Le Château Gris. And Isobelle and Henri had accepted responsibility for them.

It hadn't always been easy – especially where Thierry was concerned. Living under the same roof, Alain had discovered a side of him that had not been apparent before. Traits that had seemed attractive in a holiday companion took on a different hue when exposed on a daily basis. Thierry could be devious and sly, stopping at nothing to get his own way, and his buccaneering good humour had a dark side. And then there were the times when he tried to make Alain take the blame for the things he had done, staying silent while Alain was castigated for things that had not been his fault because he was too proud, too honourable, to 'split'.

Alain made allowances for him, knowing Thierry had just lost his mother and trying to imagine how he would feel if it were Isobelle who had died.

They still enjoyed each other's company between the fights but as Thierry entered his middle teens he became increasingly wild – drinking, gambling, smoking, seducing an eager stream of local girls – and the distance between them grew.

Alain couldn't quite understand the ambivalent feelings he had towards Thierry. On the one hand he longed to be like him, to cock a snook at authority and live life to the full; on the other he was appalled by Thierry's excesses and angry at the way he abused the privileges Henri and Isobelle had given him.

'Thierry is his father all over again,' Alain once overheard Isobelle say to Henri. 'He has bad blood in him.'

Yet still they made allowances, still they took him back. More than once, Alain knew, Henri had made a visit to the *mairie* to get Thierry out of trouble. They wouldn't have done it for him, he thought resentfully. They were always preaching the importance of taking responsibility for one's actions, and he could imagine his mother telling him that he had to learn his lesson. But since he was always law-abiding there had never been any occasion to put this theory to the test.

As for Hélène, both Isobelle and Henri adored her. She was exquisitely pretty – far prettier than either Simone or Valerie – full of fun, at times precocious and winsome, at others loving and almost naive. When she was in a good mood Hélène could charm the birds from the trees, but she had her black moods too – times when an impenetrable darkness would descend and nothing anyone could say or do could help. Her small-featured face – so like her mother's – would go glum, her china blue eyes lost their sparkle and she seemed to retreat to a world of her own. Sometimes Alain would hear her crying in her room, soft, heartrending sobs that made him realise that she, too, was suffering from the trauma of having her world torn apart. Then, just when it seemed it never would, the mood would lift and Hélène would be her usual sunny self.

He was nineteen when he realised he was in love with her and it had hit him like a bolt from the blue. One day, it seemed, she was a child he wanted to protect, the next she was a woman inspiring in him a fierce desire to possess. He could remember the moment of revelation exactly.

It had been a hot summer's day, a day when the air was still and heavy with the threat of thunder, and even the bees and crickets seemed to have been lulled to silence. He had thought about going to the river for a swim, but couldn't be bothered to make the effort to get there. Instead he had taken a book into the garden, looking for a shady spot. The lawns were too close to the house for his liking, the rose garden too exposed. He went through a trellised arch and into the orchard beyond.

And then he saw her. She was lying underneath one of the apple trees, arms spread wide, eyes closed. She was wearing a loose cotton skirt over a one-piece swimsuit, but the skirt was rucked up, laying bare her long slender legs, and she had slipped off the straps of the swimsuit and pushed it down to her waist.

The grass around her was quite long but it did nothing to hide her. He froze, embarrassed for her – for both of them – yet quite unable to tear his eyes away. He had never seen a woman's breasts before. Pictures in magazines, yes, but not in the flesh. His fumbling encounters with the girls he had been out with had never allowed him to see more than a quick tantalising glimpse, although he knew the feel of firm yielding flesh beneath his eager seeking fingers. Now he looked down at the sweet creamy curves with their rose-tipped areolae and felt the breath catch in his throat. She was so beautiful and he had never realised it! How could he have failed to notice those breasts growing beneath the cotton frocks she wore? He looked at her and felt an erection growing, but more than that, more than the purely physical, was a tenderness, a glow of warmth quickly fanning to a fire.

For long timeless moments he gazed, consumed by emotions too confused and turbulent to be identified. Then he turned and crept away. Hélène slept on, unaware that he had been there. But Alain never managed to read a single word of his book that afternoon.

From that day on he had never looked at Hélène in the same way again. He wanted her, with a fierce longing that made living under the same roof so difficult as to be impossible.

She was still young, of course, still only thirteen years old, and he was on the threshold of life. He had left home to go to college but the years did nothing to dim the flame of desire that had been lit that summer afternoon in the orchard and given a whole new dimension to the protective love he had felt for her for a very long time.

Later, when she was older, he had allowed her to know, and discovered that she returned his feelings. They had laughed when he had told her of his first glimpse of her, he a little embarrassed still, she delighted and amused.

When they had told Isobelle and Henri they intended to marry, Isobelle at least had been delighted. She had already grown to love Hélène as a daughter. But Henri had reacted strangely.

'Are you quite sure?' he had asked. 'Are you sure she's the one for you?'

'Quite sure. But why . . . ? I thought you loved her.'

'Oh I do, I do. But she's so much like her mother . . .'

Alain had looked at him, puzzled, all the unspoken questions suddenly there once more like silent spectres at the feast. But the habit of the years was too strong to break and he had not asked them. Besides, already Henri was showing the first signs of strangeness that would soon develop into fully fledged Alzheimer's disease. Better not to confuse him or even to attribute too much to his reaction. Enough that Isobelle was happy with the match; enough that Hélène was going to be his wife.

It was over now, of course. All the passion spent, all the love eroded by the years between. There came a point when it was just too much effort to try any more, just as it had been too much effort to cycle to the river that long-ago summer's afternoon. There came a point when the hurting each other was just too much to bear.

He and Hélène had parted and an era had come to an end. And now Thierry was dead and it was another ending. Even now Alain found it as difficult to believe as he had once found it difficult to believe that Odette was dead. Perhaps it would have been easier to accept if he had actually seen the body. But he hadn't. By the time he had got home to France identification formalities had already been completed and, considering the manner of Thierry's death, there had been little point in seeing him for the purposes of paying his last respects.

The phone shrilled again, breaking into his thoughts and making him start.

What the hell now? he wondered with the weary resignation of a man beginning to anticipate the blows. More problems? Another creditor threatening action if the money he was owed was not forthcoming immediately? Whatever, it couldn't be good news. There simply was not any good news these days.

He moved back to his desk, steeled himself to sound confident and optimistic, and lifted the receiver.

'Hello. Alain Lavaur?'

There was a tiny pause, accompanied by a faint hollow sound, a little like an echo in the narrow passage of a cave. Then a woman's voice which he recognised instantly said, 'Alain? It's me – Esther.'

Isobelle Lavaur laid down the magazine she had been reading, removed her spectacles and allowed them to dangle with casual grace from her long, well-manicured fingers. But the look she gave her son was sharply penetrating and her voice, when she spoke, was chilly and disapproving.

'I'm sorry, Alain, I'm not sure I follow you. Are you telling me you have invited an English friend to stay with us?'

'Yes, that's exactly what I'm saying.' Alain's tone was slightly aggressive, and, realising it, he made a conscious effort to control himself.

Why was it that his mother invariably had this effect on him? He could handle difficult business deals, negotiate and argue with perfect strangers and never for one moment allow his self-possession to be disturbed. But when his mother looked at him in that discomfiting way of hers he became a little boy again, desperate for her approval yet at the same time determined to exert his independence. The conflict of emotion made him angry and resentful. He did not understand it and liked it less and almost always their confrontations ended with his saying something he later regretted. Hélène had always maintained the trouble arose because he and Isobelle were too much alike, and certainly there was something in what she said. Without a doubt he and Isobelle shared a cool outward demeanour and an inner intensity coupled with a streak of stubbornness and a desire to have things their own way at whatever cost. But Alain knew it was more than that. He had never admitted to Hélène that he was actually a little afraid of his mother; to have done so would have diminished him in his own eyes, if not hers. But in his heart he knew it was true all the same. And knowing it made him react violently to her advice and criticism.

'Well, I must say you surprise me.' Isobelle reached for the Gauloises Blonde she now smoked, and her lighter, which lay on the patio table beside her. 'I would have thought you had far too many problems at the moment to be able to entertain visitors.' She flicked the lighter and drew on her cigarette, treating her son to another reproving glance.

'It's true I have a lot of sorting out to do,' Alain said, helping himself to one of the Gauloises and lighting it. 'But Esther isn't exactly a visitor and I am sure she will understand if I explain there are things I have to do.'

'I see.' Isobelle's lips tightened a shade. 'I take it what you are trying to say is that this Esther is something more than just a friend.'

'As a matter of fact, yes, she is.'

'I thought so.' She drew on her cigarette. 'And what is Hélène going to think about that?'

'I don't suppose she'll like it very much. But I am afraid that is neither here nor there. Hélène and I are separated, Maman. Our marriage is over.'

Isobelle glanced away from him sharply. She did not much like Alain calling her 'Maman'. When her son and two daughters had been small children, of course, she had found it quite charming. Now it simply made her feel dreadfully old. It was worse, in some ways, than being married to a man suffering from premature senility. She could always convey the impression she had been a child bride. But there was no escaping the implications of being called 'Maman' by a man of thirty-six.

Neither did she like what Alain was saying.

'I had hoped you and Hélène might have another go at making your marriage work,' she said tautly. 'But I suppose that's between the two of you. Where is this Esther going to be staying?'

Alain's eyes narrowed. 'Well, here, I thought. We have plenty of room.'

'I see.'

'Isn't that convenient?'

'Not entirely.'

'Why not?'

'Beatrice is getting old. She finds it harder now to cope with looking after us, especially since she moved out to live with her sister in the village. She's already asked me if she can work fewer hours and I have agreed.'

'I can't believe one house guest would make that much difference.'

'Then there's your father to consider. We never know from one day to the next how he's going to be.'

Though he was only sixty-five years old, Henri's Altzheimer's was now very advanced. His behaviour could be unpredictable, but he was harmless and sweet-natured, and Alain knew his mother was making excuses.

'I can't see that Father poses a problem either, but it's clear you don't want Esther here, so I'll make arrangements for her to stay at an hotel. It is your house, of course, and I shouldn't have presumed. In fact, I'll make a reservation for myself at the same time.'

'Don't be ridiculous, Alain.'

'I'm not being ridiculous, Maman: I am trying to be considerate. I must be making extra work for Beatrice too. I'm sorry. I hadn't realised.'

He saw the flash of concern in the dark eyes with the yellow irises, mirror images of his own, and knew that for the moment the advantage in their power game had shifted his way. Isobelle liked to dominate and castigate, but she also wanted him here.

'This is your home, Alain,' she said fiercely. 'I would prefer it if you were still living with Hélène, of course, but since you are not your place is here. Besides, where else could you have gone under the circumstances? No, I won't hear of you moving out.'

'And what about Esther?'

'Of course, she must come here too.'

'Are you sure? I don't want you making her feel unwelcome.'

'You should know me better, Alain, than to think I would be rude to a guest.'

'I mean it, Maman. I'll willingly book us both into an hotel.'

'No.' She thought, but did not say aloud, that if the girl was here, under her roof, at least she would be able to keep an eye on her and perhaps even influence events a little. 'I was taken by surprise, that's all. Of course she must come here.'

He nodded, satisfied. But the altercation had made him realise how restrictive it was to be back under his mother's roof. As soon as he had sorted out his immediate problems he would look for a home of his own.

With some regret he thought of the house he had bought when he and Hélène had married. Rambling, secluded, picturesque, with a stable block he had intended to fill with horses, it had been everything he had ever wanted. But there was no point in dwelling on that now. He would just have to find something else – if he could afford it!

'When will your friend be arriving?' Isobelle was asking.

'The day after tomorrow. I've suggested she should fly into Gerona, and I'll drive down to meet her.'

Gerona, in Spain, was a little over an hour's drive away.

'The airport there is open now?'

'It opened for the summer season last week and it's much more convenient than Perpignan from the point of view of flights from England. No need to change in Paris.'

'Oh Alain, Alain . . .' She hesitated, choosing her words, not wanting to resurrect the argument but unable to keep silent. 'I really hoped that now you have come home you and Hélène . . . Why have you never mentioned this Esther before?'

'Because since I came home, Maman, I have had other things on my mind.'

It wasn't the whole truth, but it was certainly part of it. Dealing with Thierry's death – and its aftermath – had occupied him almost exclusively. But in many ways that had been a relief. He hadn't wanted to think about Esther, especially after he had tried phoning her and she had hung up on him. It seemed she had meant what she had said that last day about wanting him out of her life. Keeping busy was one way to avoid the pain of knowing he had lost her. And equally he had been glad of the excuse to keep his distance from Hélène. When he'd seen her, pale, tear-streaked, her pretty laughing face pinched and tragic, his first instinct had been to take her in his arms and comfort her, just as he always had in times of trouble. And Hélène had wanted it too, he was sure. But he couldn't do it. It would open doors that were best left closed. He didn't want to give her the idea that he was ready to try again – he wasn't. He couldn't face going back to the way things had been, and in any case it simply wasn't fair on either of them when Esther was so much on his mind. Short as their relationship had been compared with the years he and Hélène had shared, it had been a passion too powerful, too all-consuming, to forget so easily. But he had made up his mind that forgetting was his only option and given over all his energy to trying to save his business.

Now, out of the blue, she had telephoned. She was coming to France!

In spite of all his problems – and the new ones Esther's arrival was sure to create – Alain felt his spirits lifting. He even managed to smile at his mother, who was looking at him in that quizzical, faintly reproving way she had.

'Maman, I know you would like to see me and Hélène back together, but it's no use. We were only tearing each other apart. Esther . . . well, she makes me happy. Isn't that enough for you?'

Isobelle sighed. 'Of course I want your happiness, Alain. But there are some things . . .' Her voice tailed away; she seemed to be lost in the past. Then she drew herself up. 'Let's not talk about it now. Why don't we have an aperitif? It's almost lunchtime.'

Alain nodded. The moment of confrontation had passed again, and he was feeling better than he had for days – weeks.

'That sounds like a very good idea, Maman,' he said.

Simone Lavaur pushed her word processor keyboard away from her, leaning her elbows on her desk top and burying her face in her hands. Her eyes were aching and she felt a little shaky from exhaustion. She had been at her computer too long, she knew, but she had been anxious to complete the chapter she was working on before switching off and going to bed.

Simone – Alain's senior by two years – was a writer by profession. Those meeting them for the first time often commented on how alike they were, and there was indeed some truth in this. They had the same dark hair, the same brown eyes with a hint of yellow around the irises, the same slightly hooked and rather prominent noses and angular chins. But the features that made Alain handsome were a little too masculine to flatter a woman, a little too pronounced, and at an inch or two taller, and without the slightest inclination to bother with what her mother called 'making the best of herself', she gave the impression of being almost gaunt.

The similiarity, in any case, ended with the purely physical. Whereas Alain enjoyed good food and fine wines, Simone scarcely ever bothered to cook and never drank alcohol. While he threw himself energetically into the business of making money, her passion was reserved for the rich and troubled history of the beautiful country that was her home and the scholarly writing from which she earned her living. Simone would never make a fortune from the books she wrote, but money did not interest her either. She considered herself lucky to be able to spend her time doing the things she most enjoyed – writing and researching – and was mildly surprised that she should be paid for it.

For as long as she could remember, Simone had been fascinated by the civil war which had raged here in Languedoc and Roussillon almost eight hundred years ago, and the Cathars, a gentle but ill-fated heretical sect which had been persecuted out of existence by fire and the sword. The Church of Rome had sent crusade after crusade in an effort to destroy those who rejected its teachings, and finished the task with the cruellest of inquisitions. The Cathars and those who protected them had died terrible, violent deaths and they had met them willingly rather than renounce the faith in which they so fervently believed.

As a child Simone had loved to visit the remains of the old fortresses where the Cathars had taken refuge from the Crusaders. Some, like the one on the hill behind her family home, were no more than crumbling walls and untidy mounds of fallen stones, weathered by the centuries, covered with lichen, and half lost in a forest of undergrowth and saplings. Others, such as Queribus, last refuge of the Cathars, and Carcassonne, the walled city, had been partially or wholly restored. But it was almost impossible to travel far in Languedoc without being confronted by one of these castles, clinging impossibly to a craggy mountain peak.

Simone had at first explored, then studied. Her thesis on the Cathars had been published and she had found a ready market for the books that had followed and now filled a shelf on the bookcase beside her desk. The titles were evidence of the way she had managed to bring history to life: *The Tragedy of the Cathars*; *Martyrs in the Sun*; *Faith, Fire and the Sword*; and several others.

At present she was working on a biography of Simon de Montfort, military leader of the crusade against the heretics, and a giant of a man who had been as cruel and ruthless as he was a brilliant soldier. But the events of the past weeks had seriously disrupted the rigid timetable she had set for herself. Though she was due to deliver the manuscript to her publishers in just a few weeks' time for publication early in the new year, Simone had been forced to put Simon de Montfort on the back burner while she helped sort out the formalities and lent her support to Hélène, who was utterly devastated by her brother's death.

Under any circumstances Hélène would have been grief-stricken, Simone knew. She and Thierry had always been close. But as things were, the situation was doubly difficult. When Hélène and Alain had separated Thierry had moved in with his sister – to look after her, he had said, though privately Simone suspected that the fact that he could live in luxury and not have to pay a penny for the privilege was an added attraction.

With Thierry's untimely death, Hélène's chief prop had been snatched away from her, and Simone had felt she had no option but to invite her sister-in-law to stay with her during the traumatic early days, at least. She could have gone to Le Château Gris of course, but Simone did not feel that was the right environment for her. In spite of her fondness for Hélène, Isobelle had never been the warmest of women and Henri was unpredictable and sometimes disconcerting. Besides this, Simone had known Alain would be bound to be coming home. Although like the rest of the family she hoped that one day he and Hélène might reconcile their differences, something Alain had said to her on the telephone one day had made her suspect he was seeing someone else, and she was practical enough to realise that the tensions that would be bound to arise if he and Hélène were under the same roof would only add to Hélène's distress.

With Hélène wandering distractedly around her tiny cottage, Simone had been unable to do any work, and though she had risen early and stayed up late, trying to write while Hélène was in bed, she had found concentration impossible. Yesterday, however, Hélène had gone to stay with friends in Perpignan for a few days, and Simone had snatched at the opportunity for peace and quiet to try to make some progress. Hélène had said she would be going back to her own home on her return from Perpignan, but she might yet change her mind, and Simone knew that, even if she did not, once Hélène was back she would still feel responsible for her.

When her alarm had woken her, Simone had got up at once and taken orange juice and a pot of strong black coffee on to the patio at the rear of her cottage so that she could watch the sun break through the early-morning mist while thinking herself into the next chapter of her book. Then she had settled herself at her word processor and tried to pick up where she had left off. At first it had been difficult and Simone had felt as if she was still swimming in thick black treacle, but eventually the prose had begun to flow. Anxious not to lose the muse again, she had worked on and on without a real break, leaving her desk only to check a reference here or there or to make fresh coffee and pick herself an apricot from the tree in her garden. But now her fingers were sluggish on the keyboard and she was aware she was making mistakes. Time to stop, or tomorrow morning she would only find herself having to scrap what she had done.

She rubbed her prickling eyes and massaged the nape of her neck with her fingers before straightening up and reaching for the switch that would cut the power supply to her computer. Then she frowned, staring at the screen in puzzlement.

It is beginning again.

The words leaped out at her, garish yellow on black. Simone gave her head a small shake. Why on earth had she typed in that sentence? It made no sense at all and certainly had no relevance to the paragraph that went before. She must have been falling asleep without realising it, she supposed, and her mind had begun to wander. That happened sometimes when she had worked for too long. The difference was that she did not usually actually write the words that came into her head in that drowsy state. More often they were no more than the expression of an illusion, the wonderfully satisfying certainty that she had solved whatever problem had been blocking the flow of her prose. But inevitably when she returned to full wakefulness it was to be faced with the realisation that the solution that had seemed so obvious a few minutes earlier was no solution at all, and the sentences that had seemed to have the ring of genius were nothing more nor less than utter rubbish.

Not that this was rubbish exactly, just . . . inexplicable. She couldn't remember having even thought the words, much less tapped them into the machine. But for some reason they made her uneasy, as if a forgotten idea was lingering on the edges of her consciousness like the echo of an unexplained fear.

'It's time you went to bed,' Simone said aloud – like most people who live alone she often talked to herself.

She put her forefinger on the 'delete' button and depressed it, watching the cursor devour the meaningless phrase. But for some moments their pale orange shadow remained, clearly visible against the black background, and Simone's feeling of unease remained too.

When the shadow had faded and disappeared Simone saved the unedited text that went before to her hard disk, turned off her word processor and went into her little kitchen with some idea of making herself an omelette. The draining board was piled high with unwashed cups and glasses, the legacy of a day when washing up had been the farthest thing from her mind, and the coffee grounds sat in the sink, soggy brown heaps in their discoloured filter bags. She opened the fridge – no eggs and only a small piece of cheese growing mould on two sides. So much for the omelette. Well, she was too tired to be bothered to cook, anyway, and certainly too tired to eat.

She mustered the energy to open a tin of cat food and put it down in readiness for Félix, her tabby, who had not put in an appearance all day. Félix was probably out hunting, she thought, and would no more want his supper when he came home than she did. But she couldn't bank on that.

She went back to check that she had shut down the computer properly. The screen stared back at her, blank and lifeless. Then she went upstairs, slipped out of her clothes – a sarong-style skirt and baggy overshirt which disguised her long angular frame – and dropped them in a heap on the floor before falling thankfully into her old-fashioned bed, unmade since she had left it early this morning.

But tired as she was, her mind was still racing, and in the darkness she seemed to see again the lingering shadow of that meaningless phrase on the screen of her computer.

It is beginning again.

3

'WELL, I MUST say there's nothing in the South of France to compare with a pint of good English beer!' Bob Slater set his glass down on the table, wiped the foam from his moustache with the back of his hand, and grinned contentedly at the younger man who sat on a leather-topped stool facing him.

'Oh come on, Dad, I'm sure it has its compensations!' Andrew Slater returned amiably. 'Everybody knows ex-pats live the life of Reilly. Retiring on a good pension to a place in the sun with nothing more taxing to worry about than how many bottles you'll need for your next lunch party, or what flowers to plant in your patio tubs, has to be a pretty good option.'

'Well, it certainly beats being a copper these days,' Bob admitted. 'There was a time when I loved the job – felt proud of it – and got a real sense of satisfaction out of clearing all the villains off my patch. But it all went sour. The villains got nastier, the courts went soft, the authorities swamped us with paperwork and stifled us with petty restrictions, and society's attitude changed. How the hell the police force is supposed to do a good job without the support of the magistrates and judges or the respect of the public beats me. We're caught between the devil and the deep blue sea these days. Up salt creek without a paddle!'

Andrew laughed. He'd heard it all before.

'You're still a gourmet when it comes to metaphors, I notice – and your soapbox is in pretty good shape, too. Drink up – I'll get you another pint before this place is invaded by the luncheon-voucher brigade.'

'You mean it gets worse?'

'Much worse. Another half-hour and you won't be able to get near the bar.'

'Oh well, in that case . . .'

The central London pub was already reasonably full with

office workers taking an early lunch break and out-of-town reps studying notes for their next port of call over a glass of expense-account wine. The constant hum of conversation and the chink of glasses and knives and forks hung in the air with the haze of cigarette smoke. Ties had been loosened, and suit jackets were draped over the backs of chairs.

Andrew stood up and a trio of miniskirted girls at the next table glanced at him appreciatively, seeing a man in his late twenties, built like a rugby player, with a face a little too craggy to be handsome, and thick fair hair which was beginning to recede slightly at the temples, and liking what they saw. Andrew did not even notice their attention. Part of his undeniable attraction for the opposite sex was that he was supremely unaware of it.

'Do you want something to eat?' he asked his father.

'What's on offer?'

'They do a very good hotpot.'

'No fish and chips?'

'Well, I expect so, but not the sort you're thinking of. Breaded plaice or scampi – not cod in batter wrapped in paper and swimming in fat and vinegar.'

'Pity. Fish and chips is another of the things I really miss in France. I think I shall have to open a good old-fashioned chip shop.'

Andrew laughed: the vision of his father in a white overall beneath a sign proclaiming 'Frying Tonite!' was an amusing one.

'Do you want me to see what's on the "specials" board?'

'No. Hotpot will do me fine.'

Andrew crossed to the bar, thinking how good it was to see his father. They had always shared a good rapport, and though his parents' marriage had broken up while Andrew was still in his teens, his relationship with his father had not suffered. The divorce had not been a shock to him – he'd seen it coming for years. The uncertain shift pattern his father worked as a policeman, the long hours that came with responsibility as he moved up through the ranks, the dedication to his job, had resulted in a private life marred by broken arrangements and spoiled meals. Andrew had heard his mother complain, known exactly what she was complaining about, and still wanted to side with his father, though of course he never did. Taking sides when parents argued was not a good idea. To his relief the break-up, when it finally came, had been almost without rancour – mainly because no one else was involved, he had always thought.

Later, of course, both his mother and father had married again, but once again his father had won out in the popularity stakes. Diana, Bob's wife, was warm, generous and kind, not to mention glamorous in a smooth, plump, older-woman way, whilst Bert, his stepfather, was dour and set in his ways, with a resentment of Andrew which he did not bother to hide. Andrew had left home as soon as he could afford the rent on a bedsitter because of Bert, refusing to move in with Bob and Diana only because he knew that to do so would hurt his mother's feelings. But he had always seen a lot of them, even after he had left his native Bristol to move to London, and, when Bob had retired from the police force and he and Diana had sold up and gone to live in the South of France, Andrew had missed them more than he would have imagined possible. He was always delighted when they came to England for a few days as they invariably did twice yearly – when Diana visited her English dentist and her Harley Street doctor for check-ups, shopped at Marks and Spencer for underwear, and stocked up on all the various oddments she had taken for granted in England but was unable to buy in Languedoc. At the moment she was keeping an appointment with her favourite hairdresser, getting the perm and tint which kept her hair golden and immaculate between her biannual visits, and Andrew had taken an hour or two off to have a drink, a spot of lunch and a man-to-man chat with his father.

He returned to the table now, setting down the fresh drinks and returning his wallet to his pocket before settling himself on the stool once more.

'So.' Bob took a pull of beer. 'How is the business of crime looking from your angle?'

Andrew pulled a face.

'Damn near as ugly as it looked from yours. Probably more so, if the truth be known. It's just that I'm not as jaded as you yet.'

'At your age I should hope not! Give it a few more years, though, and I expect you'll change your tune.'

'Probably.'

As an investigative crime reporter for a mass-market Sunday paper, Andrew felt there were already times when he had seen enough of toe-rags and fraudsters and unscrupulous men-on-the-make to last him a lifetime.

They were his bread and butter, those unsavoury characters, and, generally speaking, he got along with them well enough. With his blunt uncompromising manner and his ability to talk their language when it mattered he had established a network of informants who, for the most part, trusted him where they despised so many of the gentlemen of the press. They provided him with the tip-offs and leads he needed to operate in his particular line of work, not to mention a couple of scoops which had made his name. But just occasionally the seediness of it all got to him and he yearned for the days when he had been a jobbing reporter on a respectable regional daily back home in Bristol.

Then he would remember with affection the interviews with a retired council worker who had come into a fortune by way of a treble-chance windfall, the grand old lady who had been given a balloon ride to celebrate her eightieth birthday, and the owner of a cat that had turned up after having been missing for almost three years. These, and all the others, were the ordinary human-interest and animal stories that had characterised those hectic yet somehow charmingly innocent days when he had been cutting his teeth and learning his trade, and the extent of his connection with crime had been limited to visits to the Crown or magistrates' courts.

His colleagues, too, had been of a different ilk from the hard-bitten go-getters he now shared an office with. Some had been older men who had spent their entire working lives on small-time newspapers covering nothing more controversial than local derby football matches; others, like himself, had been fired with the ambition to see their bylines on the front pages of the national press.

Those were the days, he sometimes thought, as he waited for an informant in some less than salubrious dive, a wad of notes for the pay-off in his pocket alongside his microscopic tape recorder. Those were the days – shouting a pint in the local at lunchtimes and in the evenings after the paper had been put to bed, discussing stories, laughing about gaffes, cursing the editor and the subs, bemoaning the fact that a story that had been destined for the front page had been relegated to a couple of paragraphs on page seven because some more newsworthy item had grabbed the headlines.

But the nostalgia was usually short-lived. Andrew knew that he was far too addicted to his adrenalin-charged world of triumphs and frustrations to be able to go back. When the time came, when he could finally take no more of headless torsos and scheming wives with murder in their hearts and crooked politicians and ruthless tycoons, he would, like his father, turn his back on crime. But when he did he would turn his back on journalism too. There was no way back to the cosy world for him. He had crossed too far to the other side for that. And retirement, as yet, was a long way off.

'We had a bit of excitement in our neck of the woods the other day.' Bob broke off, watching the barmaid deposit a dish of steaming hotpot on the next table. 'Hey – that smells good!'

'It is good – I told you. Go on, what excitement?'

'A local man was killed when his car went off the road into a ravine and burst into flames late one night. They didn't find the car until the next morning and the poor fellow had been burned to a cinder. I knew him, too. The local police put it down to an accident, but I can tell you if it had happened on my patch I'd have asked a few more questions.'

'You mean you don't think it was an accident?'

'Let's say I think it's a bit suspicious to say the least. Thierry Rousseau – the man who died – had been drinking in a local bistro that evening and rumour has it he'd had a pretty violent argument with another man who joined him while he was there. They left the bar together, still arguing, and drove off together. But when the car was found, only this Rousseau chap was in it. If it was me, I'd have wanted to know who the man he was arguing with was and what happened between the time they left the bar and the time Rousseau went over that ravine.'

'You mean you think he was murdered.'

'I'm not saying that. Just that I'd like to know a bit more to convince me it was an accident. As far as I can make out the official line is that Rousseau simply lost control of the car after he'd dropped his companion off somewhere. And there's no doubt that he'd been drinking. But he knew those roads like the back of his hand and I knew him as a man who could hold his drink. He had a pretty chequered past, by all accounts, but drunkenness, as such, no.'

'So why didn't the local police follow it up?' Andrew asked.

'Good question. Perhaps they didn't listen to the rumours – or didn't want to. They can be a bit slapdash in these country areas sometimes. They simply treated it as an open-and-shut case. And the family is very influential in Languedoc. Very likely the last thing they wanted was for Thierry's past to be raked up all over again. As I see it, they were probably pressing for a quick release of the body – what was left of it – and the police didn't want to upset the apple cart. It had to be identified by way of personal effects, as far as I can make out, so I don't suppose it would have been easy to find out much about the cause of death. But all the same, I wouldn't have been so easily satisfied.'

Andrew smiled to himself. He knew his father had had something of a reputation as a dogged investigator – a trait he had inherited.

'I'm surprised you could resist asking a few questions yourself!' he said.

Bob chortled. 'You must be joking! I finished with police work when I handed in my warrant card. But it's interesting, all the same.'

'So who are the family that they have the local police in their pockets, then?' Andrew asked.

'Thierry Rousseau's relations by marriage – the Lavaurs. A very old, well-respected family locally, not quite nobility but the next thing to it. Thierry was in business with his brother-in-law, Alain. I know him well. In fact, you could say I played my part in the setting up of their operation.'

'You?'

'Me. Don't look so surprised. Your old man has hidden depths, you know.'

'I don't doubt it! Go on – what did you do to become a business tycoon?'

'Hardly that! No, as I say, I know Alain Lavaur socially. When he decided to start up this company exporting Languedoc wines to England we were chatting about it at a drinks party. He hadn't decided where to base the English end of the operation and I suggested Bristol.'

'That figures.'

'Well – it's ideal, isn't it? Port, airport, good road network, two hours from London and Birmingham . . .'

'And home.'

'Sure. Anyway, Alain looked into it and agreed with me. Must have rather liked the old place, too. He took off to see to that end of the operation himself and left Thierry to run the French end. A mistake, if you ask me, but then, that's his business. Alain was actually in England at the time of the accident.'

The barmaid arrived at the table with the hotpot in individual earthenware dishes, side salads and cutlery wrapped in paper napkins. For a few minutes the two men ate in silence.

'So,' Bob said, wiping a spot of gravy from his tie and tucking the paper napkin into his shirt front, 'when are you coming over to see us?'

'Oh, I don't know. I've got a fortnight's holiday coming up, but I promised Mum I'd spend at least part of it in Bristol. Apart from the odd weekend I haven't been home for months.'

'I would have thought a weekend was about all anyone could take of Bert.'

Spearing a chunk of meat, Andrew glanced at his father. Did he detect a slight jealousy? But Bob's face was expressionless.

'I don't know how your mother puts up with him,' he added blandly. 'The man's a crashing bore.'

'But at least he's *there*,' Andrew said. 'I dare say she's glad of someone who gives her his wholehearted attention.'

The criticism flowed over Bob without raising so much as a ripple.

'She got what she always wanted then,' he said, without the slightest hint of rancour, and Andrew was forced to agree.

Certainly Bert, who liked to adhere rigidly to regular mealtimes and asked nothing more from an evening's entertainment than to watch every game show, sitcom and football match that his twenty-four-inch television could throw at him, was Bob's opposite in every conceivable way.

Bob was certainly right, too, when he said a weekend in Bert's company was enough for anyone. If he was honest, Andrew wasn't even sure he could stand his mother's fussy attentions for much longer than that.

It was always a treat initially to have morning tea brought to him in the bedroom that had once been a red-and-white shrine to Bristol City Football Club and was now decorated in Laura Ashley florals; to rise late to a cooked breakfast which he had scarcely had time to digest before lunch was on the table –

old-fashioned lamb roasts with mint sauce and peas fresh from the garden, home-baked apple pies and sponge puddings with lashings of custard. But all too soon the loving care could become claustrophobic. In spite of his determination to be grateful, Andrew very quickly became irritated by the way his shirts were whipped away for washing the moment he took them off, and by the electric blanket his mother insisted on switching on mid-evening to warm his bed for him no matter how often he asked her not to. She surely wouldn't do that in June – would she? But she would find a host of other ways to pamper him all the same, and Andrew was not sure how much of it he could take without losing patience and saying something that would upset her.

'Why don't you come over to us for a bit?' Bob suggested. 'Have a weekend with your mother, leave your car in Bristol and fly out – the service from Bristol to Gerona starts in June, and Gerona's only just over the border from us, as you know. Then you could spend a couple more days with her when you get back. Break it up a bit. If you haven't got anything else planned, that is.'

'No, I haven't. Karen and I were going to take off somewhere, but as you know we've split up.'

'Yes, I was sorry to hear that. Karen was a nice girl.'

'Too nice for me,' Andrew said lightly. He and Karen had been together on and off for almost two years, but his job was no more conducive to a settled relationship than his father's had been, and Karen no more understanding than his mother when it came to broken arrangements. Six weeks ago he and Karen had agreed to go their separate ways and Andrew was only glad he'd resisted her efforts to get him to put a ring on her finger; it would never have worked. But he missed having her around, all the same.

'So, apart from your mother there's nothing to stop you coming to France,' Bob persisted, warming to the idea. 'Sun, sea, good food and wine – what more could you want? You could even do a little sniffing around in the mystery of how Thierry Rousseau died. You might even end up with a scoop on your hands.'

Andrew laughed.

'You know, you missed your vocation, Dad. You should have been a travel agent or a time-share salesman, not a policeman.'

'Saints preserve us!' Bob scooped up the last of his hotpot with a chunk of bread, wiped his mouth on his paper napkin and rolled it into a loose ball. 'Think about it, anyway. We'd love to have you.'

'You're sure that goes for Diana too?'

'What do you think? Diana is never happier than when she's got guests.' He glanced at his watch. 'Speaking of Diana, I think I'd better make a move. I promised to pick her up from her hairdresser, and you never know if you're going to get stuck in London traffic. That's another good thing about Languedoc – all those empty roads.'

'Where a car can go over the edge of a ravine and not be found until next morning,' Andrew said thoughtfully. 'Yes – well, I guess I'd better be getting back to my desk, too. I've got a lot of work to clear up before I can take a holiday.'

'So you'll think about it?'

'I'll think about it. I'll see you again before you go back anyway, won't I? We'll talk some more about it then.'

But already he thought he had made up his mind. The thought of a week or ten days in Languedoc was a tempting one; even more tempting was the prospect of a possible story to divert him if he got bored – as he was sure he would – with simply lazing in the sun. Andrew disliked being idle for long. He got his kicks out of investigative reporting. Combine an interesting lead to follow up with all the other attractions Languedoc had to offer and it presented an irresistible cocktail.

Of course, it wasn't likely there was anything in the story beyond local gossip. His father had been around crime so long he saw it everywhere. But all the same . . .

Andrew smiled to himself. If he could square things with his mother – and he was quite certain Bert would be more than ready to help him do that – he was definitely going to spend at least part of his holiday in France.

4

LATE AFTERNOON SUN, yellower than the scorching white brightness of midday, bathed Gerona airport in a golden glow and turned the windows of the small modern building to a score of mirrors, each reflecting a pool of fire. As the Britannia 757 taxied on to the apron Esther rescued her bag from beneath her seat, hunting in it for her sunglasses. The sun had been shining when they had left Bristol, less than two hours ago, but not with this intensity. This was Spain, baking in the blazing heat of summer-come-early, and without so much as setting foot on the burning tarmac or feeling the hot heavy air there was no mistaking it.

The jet was a charter flight and the majority of those on board were holidaymakers bound for the Costa Brava. In the seats next to Esther's a young couple clad in jeans and T-shirts juggled with a ghetto blaster and two huge straw hats, and immediately behind her a toddler screamed as he had done for almost the entire duration of the flight. She tried to ignore him now as she had done for the past two hours, but the shrill sound grated on her all the same and eventually she gave in to the urge she had so far resisted to glance censoriously over her shoulder at the young mother who seemed content to allow the screams to continue unchecked. Quite unabashed, the mother returned Esther's glare with a smile in which resignation was tinged with pride – as if she was inviting admiration for the child's lusty lungs and small hammering fists, Esther thought in exasperation.

She glanced out of the aircraft window again, towards the airport buildings, and wondered if Alain was waiting for her inside. He had said he would be – no, correction, he had said he would meet her, but she supposed that amounted to the same thing.

At the thought a small spasm of nervousness constricted her throat, and she realised, not for the first time, that now the moment of reunion was almost upon her she was more than a little apprehensive. So much longing, so much loving, so many sleepless nights of heart-searching, and all leading to the moment when she would walk through that bright white building and come face to face once more with the man she had told herself she would never see again.

What would it be like, that moment of meeting? she wondered nervously. Did he even want her here now? He had asked her to come, yes, but it seemed to her now that the invitation had been issued in another lifetime by a man who had become more of a romantic dream than a flesh-and-blood lover in the long weeks between. He had been so distant when she had phoned him. But he had sounded pleased too.

'I was thinking of taking you up on your invitation,' she had said, trying to sound cheerful and casual. 'That is, if you still want me to come, of course.'

He had not hesitated – at least, she didn't think he had hesitated. With the distance between them and the strange echo on the line it was difficult to be sure. And there was always the possibility that whatever he had said in the surprise of the moment he might have had second thoughts afterwards. Hadn't she wondered herself about the wisdom of what she was doing, unsure whether she wanted to confront the Alain she had known on her own terms in the context of his home setting – the man with a background, a family, a wife?

But she had come anyway, because, if the truth were known, she couldn't stay away. Whatever happened, she owed it to herself to give their relationship another chance.

The doors of the airliner were open now, the warm air billowing in to meet the holidaymakers who crowded eagerly into the aisle. Esther remained in her seat for a few minutes, letting them go ahead. There was no point in rushing: if Gerona had anything in common with the other Mediterranean airports she had visited it would be some time before the baggage was unloaded and the carousel began turning. The sun seemed to have a soporific effect on those who lived in it and Mediterranean baggage handlers never hurried their work any more than they hurried any other aspect of their lives.

When the crush in the aisle thinned to a trickle Esther slung the strap of her bag over her shoulder and slid out of her seat.

Then she followed the tail-end of the queue of passengers down the aircraft steps.

Alain was waiting in the half-empty reception area.

Esther saw him the moment she walked into the baggage hall and her heart leaped just as it had the first time she had met him. She waved and he waved back, raising his hand with the sort of laconic grace that was typical of him. As she waited for her bag to appear among the jumble of suitcases, holdalls, pushchairs and parcels on the carousel she kept glancing at him, impressed all over again by his elegant good looks. He was wearing sunglasses and a white shirt which emphasised the darkness of his skin, bronzed by the southern sun to an even deeper shade than when she had last seen him.

Her bag rolled towards her on the carousel. She grabbed it, hoisting it off and heading for the customs post. The officers glanced at her, looking more at the slim figure revealed by well-cut linen trousers and short-sleeved shirt than at the luggage she was carrying, but she scarcely noticed. She had eyes only for Alain, who was coming to meet her.

'Hi.' She knew she sounded slightly breathless.

'Esther.' He did not sweep her into his arms as she had imagined in her wilder dreams he might, but kissed her warmly on both cheeks in the French fashion. 'You came then. I was so very afraid you might change your mind.'

'Of course not. At least I'd have let you know if I had.'

He took the bag from her.

'Is this all the luggage you've got?'

'Yes.'

She read his mind: one holdall was not indicative of a very long stay.

'It holds more than you'd think,' she added weakly.

'Sure. I'm parked just outside.'

He ushered her out of the glass doors, which opened automatically at their approach, and across the airport road, where several taxis lingered hopefully and a coach disgorged a load of sunburned holidaymakers, to the broad parking area beyond.

'Did you have a good flight?' he asked, as formally polite as if he were one of those taxi drivers making conversation with a fare-paying passenger.

'Not bad. There was a child who kept screaming when he couldn't do exactly as he liked, but at least it wasn't for long. An hour and forty minutes. The air hostesses had to work like stink to get everything done and they still didn't manage to finish the duty-frees. Just as well I wasn't panting for a bottle of cheap gin.'

'You see? I told you it wasn't far.' He smiled at her and her heart lurched again.

How could he do this to her? She should, by rights, still be angry with him. Yet a glance, a smile, that momentary meeting of eyes and she went weak inside, prepared to forgive him anything. Nobody had made her feel this way since she was fourteen years old and in love with the captain of the school cricket team. Even when he had asked her best friend out she had still secretly adored him.

But in spite of the way she felt there was still an air of awkwardness between them and she knew instinctively that it was not just she who had been apprehensive about this meeting. Alain was on edge too. Something would have to be said to clear the air, but she was not sure how to go about it.

In the event it was Alain who took the lead.

When they were installed in his red BMW, windows wound down to let in some air, he made no attempt to start the engine but instead turned to her, sliding his arm along the back of her seat.

'So – does this mean you are ready to forgive me, Esther?'

She hesitated, thrown by the directness of his question.

'I don't know.'

'You mean you are not ready to forgive me?'

His rueful look made her go weak all over again. All she wanted was for him to kiss her the way he had used to. But she knew that would solve nothing. Rather, it would confuse the issue.

'It's not a question of forgiving you,' she said steadily. 'It's not that simple, is it?'

'Why not?'

'Because . . . well, because of all the things I said before you left. You have a wife, Alain – at least, I presume nothing has changed in that direction.'

'I have a wife, yes. But my marriage is over to all intents and purposes, as I told you.'

'That's not the point.'

'I think it is. I love you, Esther. I'm crazy about you. And I think you feel the same way. Why would you be here otherwise?'

She could not deny it.

'I've missed you dreadfully. And I do think we have something very special. I've tried to forget you – God knows, I really have tried. But I couldn't. So I thought maybe if I came to France we might be able to work something out.' She hesitated. 'I mean, when I found out you were still married to Hélène I was too shocked and angry to be able to think straight. And then you'd gone, so we couldn't talk any more, and I got . . . well, stubborn.'

'Yes. You can be very stubborn, Esther. You can be like a dog with a bone.'

His eyes were teasing her; she could feel the power of his charm. She had intended to say that nothing had changed except her willingness to give their relationship another chance, that in the final analysis she would still insist on upholding her principles and that if he wanted her enough he would have to divorce Hélène. But she knew now that this was not the right moment for ultimatums. The closeness they had shared would have to be re-established first.

'I know I can be pig-headed,' she said weakly. 'It's just that . . .'

'Yes. What?'

His arm had moved from the back of her seat to her shoulders. She could feel his fingers playing with the slim gold chain she wore around her neck, brushing lightly against her moist skin.

'I think you know.'

'Yes. I know. If you had a husband I think I would kill him.' The fingers tightened suddenly, pressing against the tendons, then relaxing again. 'But I wasn't lying, Esther, when I told you my marriage is over. Hélène and I separated before I came to England. It was one of the reasons I was anxious to get away – put some distance between us. Everything was getting very complicated.'

'But if your marriage was over, why didn't you get a divorce?'

'I don't know really. For one thing we are staunch Catholics – or at least, my family is – and we're old-fashioned in that we don't treat divorce as lightly as some people seem to these days. For another . . . well, it really wasn't an issue. There was no one else involved – just me and Hélène deciding we couldn't live together any longer. It was only when I met you that the situation changed. I spoke to Hélène then on the telephone – suggested we should formalise things, but . . .' He broke off, staring into middle distance.

'Yes?' Esther prompted.

'She . . . wasn't agreeable.' His tone gave the impression of something left unsaid.

'You told her about me then?' Esther asked.

He avoided answering the question directly.

'She was . . . having one of her depressions. She gets them sometimes. She can be . . . very fragile. I thought it best to leave pressing the question of divorce for another time. And then of course Thierry was killed and . . .'

So she still doesn't know about me, Esther thought. She could imagine what had happened. Alain had failed to find the right moment to broach the subject just as he had failed to find the right moment to tell her that he was still married to Hélène. But she didn't want to begin an argument about it now. Hélène would find out soon enough now that she was here. And if things worked out the way she hoped, Alain would do what he had shrunk from doing before and file for divorce.

Another thought struck her – one that had nagged her from time to time.

'There aren't any more surprises in store for me, are there?' she asked.

'What do you mean?'

'Well, you don't have any children, do you?'

'Of course not!'

'That's all right then. I just wondered . . .'

'No, we have no children.' Again his tone, final, curt almost, gave her the distinct impression of something unsaid.

Why not? she wanted to ask. Was it a case of not wanting them – or not being able to have them? There was still so much she did not know about Alain.

But she was glad to have the confirmation that that complication, at least, did not enter the equation. Divorce was always so hard on the children.

Alain leaned towards her.

'We can talk about all this later, can't we? For now . . . oh, Esther – I am just so glad you came.'

'Me too.'

His fingers slid along her jaw, turning her to face him, and she felt herself melting.

The problems were still there, they hadn't gone away – but at least she and Alain were together again. And together they would work them out.

I love him, Esther thought. I can't care about anything else.

His lips were on hers, the faint musky scent of his aftershave in her nostrils, her hands pressed tight against the long hard muscles of his neck and shoulders.

For the first time in weeks, Esther was utterly, completely happy.

Andrew Slater crossed the car park outside the airport, unlocked the small red Renault which he had hired, and tossed his bag on to the back seat. Then he fished in the pocket of his jacket for the directions his father had sent him and studied them closely. They were clear and concise, as was Bob's style, and illustrated with a little sketch map showing the border post, motorway toll booths and the turn-off Andrew needed to take. It looked simple enough, Andrew thought, and added the cynical rider: famous last words! But even if he did get lost he had a tank full of petrol and all the time in the world.

He started the engine, turned out of the airport and made for the motorway that would take him into France.

The road, three lanes of well-maintained carriageway, far less busy than its English equivalent, ran arrow-straight through countryside that was sunbaked yet verdant. Alain's BMW sped along it, stopping only for the border post and the motorway toll booths, heading towards the Pyrenees, which dominated the skyline.

Esther looked at them in awe, layer upon layer of mountain, which rose from the green foothills to the misty blue peaks beyond, and was reminded of a child's model or a three-dimensional theatre backdrop. Heat haze hung in the air and the farthest peaks were shrouded in cloud.

'I love the mountains,' Alain said simply.

'They're beautiful.'

'More than just beautiful. They are majestic. And they give one such a sense of timelessness, don't you think?'

'Yes.'

Was that what it was – timelessness – this wonderful feeling of dreaming that had descended on her? She had thought it was happiness, but perhaps Alain was right and it was more than that. The countryside seemed to be drawing her in, filling her with a contentment born of yearning satisfied, a sense not of being in a foreign country but of having come home. She settled back against the sun-warmed leather, shading her eyes with one hand while her other elbow rested on the open window of the car.

'You see that old fortress over there?' Alain said.

Esther looked to her left and saw a tower rising jaggedly from a hummock of mountain on the skyline as a pointing finger might rise from a clenched fist.

'What a desolate looking place! It must be very old.'

'It is. Twelfth century, probably. You'll see a lot like it hereabouts, and all built on the most inaccessible peaks. Some are in ruins, not much more than a pile of stones; others have been restored. Most of them were Cathar strongholds at one time.'

'Cathar.' Esther had heard the term but was hazy as to its exact meaning.

Alain glanced at her.

'You don't know about the Cathars? No, I suppose you wouldn't. Not many English people do unless they have visited this area. The Cathars don't exactly get equal billing with the Maid of Orleans when it comes to teaching French history to English children. But to us they are a very important part of our heritage. You can't come to Languedoc and not learn something of the Cathars.'

'So – educate me.'

'My sister Simone is really the one you should be asking. She's an authority on the subject – makes her living writing about it, as a matter of fact. But since she's not here I'll do my best. How much do you already know?'

'Not much,' she admitted. 'They were some kind of religious sect, weren't they?'

'They were heretics. They didn't hold with the sacraments and they denied the divinity of Jesus Christ. Their beliefs were based on a very old religion known as "dualism" – the two worlds – and they had some very strange ideas. Of course, the thing was that in the early Middle Ages the priests and bishops hereabouts were a pretty lax lot. They didn't do their job properly. In fact they got the church a very bad name, and a lot of the people got disillusioned with them and turned to Catharism. I can't think why, though. Can you imagine what would attract a person to a religion that tried to outlaw every kind of pleasure known to man?'

'You mean – ?'

'The Cathars believed everything in the material world was evil. They weren't allowed to eat meat or anything resulting from procreational activity, such as eggs, though for some reason fish was all right. And they certainly were not allowed the pleasures of the flesh themselves. Sex was definitely taboo. Only a minority lived up to these standards, of course. They were known as "Perfects" or "Good Men" and they formed the priesthood. The ordinary believers continued to live fairly normal lives and only renounced their pleasures when they were on their deathbeds and unable to partake any more anyway. Then, when they had received what was called the *Consolamentum*, the purification rite, they generally starved themselves to death.'

'That's a bit harsh!' Esther laughed, then glanced back at the ruin, silhouetted on the skyline. 'Why did they need fortresses, though?'

Alain pulled into the centre lane to overtake a large tanker.

'I'm coming to that,' he said as he completed the manoeuvre. 'When the Pope realised what was going on, and how many Catholics were straying from the fold, he sent a legate to try and show them the error of their ways. The legate was murdered for his pains and of course that left the Pope no option. He raised a crusade to wipe out the heresy, and I'm afraid things got a bit bloody, as they tended to do in the Middle Ages. An awful lot of people died rather nasty deaths – Catholics as well as Cathars, it has to be said.'

'Why Catholics?'

'Because they refused to give up the Cathars in their midst. They looked on them as neighbours – misguided, but harmless enough – and Simone would tell you that it wasn't just amongst the peasants that Catharism was rife. Plenty of middle-class professional people, doctors and the like, were amongst their ranks, and even some of the nobility. But, as I say, the *laissez faire* attitude of the non-Cathars cost a great many of them

s. It's said that twenty thousand people died in the t at Béziers alone, and most of them were Catholic. a very famous story about that massacre. When the nder of the army asked the church leader how he could tell which of the people were Catholics who should be spared and which were Cathars, the churchman told him to kill them all – the Lord would know his own. When the slaughter began many of the people took refuge in the Church of the Madeleine. The crusaders set fire to it and they were all burned alive.'

Esther shuddered.

'That's horrible. Sheer barbarity. And anyway, what had any of them done to warrant a death like that?'

'The Cathars were heretics. To the Church of Rome heresy was a cancer which had to be cut out before it spread out of control. Actually, it was already out of control in Languedoc. The whole area was infected with it. But to get back to the fortresses. When the crusaders came the nobles, whether they were Cathars themselves or not, gave refuge to the heretics. There were many famous sieges. Most people think the last one was at Montsegur – "a fortress for the victors, a temple for the defeated" – but actually it wasn't. The very last Cathar stronghold was Queribus.'

'And this went on . . . how long?'

'About forty years. Incredible, really, considering the horrible way most believers died.'

'You mean – like the people in the church at . . . where was it?'

'Béziers. Well, yes. Fire was the top favourite when it came to dealing with heretics. Thousands of them were burned at the stake. You'd have thought, wouldn't you, that when they realised where their so-called religion was leading them they'd have given in and returned to the fold. But they were a stubborn lot. A bit like you, Esther.'

He glanced at her with that same teasing smile but this time she found it impossible to smile back.

Some of the brightness seemed to have gone out of the day, the long shadow of past atrocities reaching down across the centuries to blot out the sun like the cloud that hung thick and impenetrable over the mountains.

Sensing her change of mood, Alain reached across to cover her hand with his.

'Anyway, it all happened a very long time ago. As a result of the crusade Languedoc became part of France – most of its conquerors came from the north and were loyal to the king. As for Catharism, it died a natural death.'

'I'd hardly call it natural!' Esther said.

'Well, perhaps not. I'm referring to the pockets of it which remained after the crusades. When most of the leaders were dead it simply petered out and the people returned to the Church of Rome. Nowadays Languedoc is almost totally Catholic.'

'As you are.'

Alain smiled faintly. 'My family have been Catholic for generations. I can't imagine any of them going along with that kind of nonsense – though I have a sneaking suspicion Simone's sympathies might lie with the Cathars.' He paused. 'And Valerie – my younger sister – is a bit of a deviant, too, come to think of it. She's fascinated by the supernatural. Even believes in reincarnation – or so she says. When she was at college she made friends with a girl who was into all that kind of thing. It caused quite a furore when Valerie brought her home for a holiday – Maman was not amused. Actually she went on to become quite a famous medium – goes by the name of Aurore.' He lapsed into silence and Esther found herself thinking how ironic it was that, while both his sisters had strayed from the faith they had been raised in, Alain still seemed to be influenced by its teachings. If he was to be believed it had played a part in his reluctance to divorce Hélène. Or was that the whole story? Esther remembered her feeling that he had left something unsaid when he had been explaining the situation and felt a moment's misgiving, which she quickly thrust aside. She wasn't going to worry about that now. It would keep for later. Right at this moment she didn't want anything to spoil her joy at being with Alain.

Isobelle Lavaur was in the drawing room of the large old country house that was her home. She stood beside the window, holding the telephone receiver beneath the hair which had been carefully coiffed to hide the tiny tucks left by her latest facelift, and listened to the shrilling of the bell at the other end of the line.

She was about to give up and replace the receiver when the bell stopped abruptly in mid-ring and a woman's voice, light, almost girlish and a little hesitant, spoke.

'Hello?'

'Hélène. You're back from Perpignan, then.'

'I got back this afternoon. How nice of you to ring, Isobelle.'

Hélène never referred to her mother-in-law as 'Maman'. Long ago, when she had been a little girl, Isobelle had been Madame Lavaur to her, later she had invited Hélène to call her by her Christian name.

'How are you today?' Isobelle asked now.

'Oh, all right, I suppose.'

'Being with your friends was good for you then?'

'It took me out of myself while I was there. But now I'm back . . . oh, the house is so *empty*, Isobelle!'

'I'm sure it's dreadful for you, *chérie*,' she said.

'Yes, but . . . I'm hoping . . .' Hélène hesitated. 'How is Alain? Is he at home?'

Isobelle's eyes narrowed. Hélène wanted Alain back. She was almost sure of it. She had suspected it for some time but wondered if it was only her own wishful thinking, but now she detected the note of eagerness in Hélène's voice and was certain she was right.

If it weren't for this wretched English girl, I believe there might be a chance they'd get back together, she thought. It made what she had to say doubly painful.

'He's not here at the moment,' she said, transferring the receiver from one hand to the other. 'Hélène, there is something I have to tell you. Alain has invited a friend to stay. He has gone to the airport now to meet the plane.'

'A friend? What sort of friend? You mean someone connected with the business?' Hélène sounded puzzled.

'No. It's someone he met while he was in England. A woman.' She heard the swift intake of Hélène's breath, and went on swiftly, 'I'm really sorry to have to tell you this, but I thought you should be warned. I didn't want you to turn up unprepared and find her here.'

'No – no, of course not. You mean . . . she's staying with you?' Hélène sounded strained, as if she were making a tremendous effort to conceal what she was feeling.

'Yes. Hélène— '

'Who is she? What's she like?'

'I don't really know. I haven't met her yet. Her name is Esther

Morris. It's all very difficult. You know how much Henri and I want to see you and Alain together again. I really don't know why you parted in the first place. I can only hope . . . Hélène, are you still there?'

'Yes, of course I am. Isobelle, you don't think . . . that he— '

'I really don't know, Hélène. But it seems to me that unless you want to lose Alain for good you should do something about it – and quickly.'

'Oh yes?' Hélène laughed, a short brittle sound that was closer to a sob. 'And what am I supposed to do?'

'Well, that is up to you. You're the one who was married to my son – if you don't know how to get around him I don't think I can tell you. But surely there must be something you can salvage?'

There was a small silence, then Hélène said, 'I honestly don't know that I can try any more. I'm just so sick of trying. It was bad enough before, and now – with Thierry gone – I'm tired, Isobelle, tired of everything. There's no point, is there? In the end, what is the point of it all?'

Her voice was thick, as though she might be crying, and Isobelle felt a twinge of alarm. She knew Hélène's dark moods of old, and she had had a terrible time recently, enough to push a much stronger person than she to the brink.

'Hélène!' she said fiercely. 'You wouldn't do anything silly would you?'

'Like I did before, you mean? That was an accident, Isobelle. I thought you knew that.'

'Yes, of course, but— '

'I feel like it sometimes, I must admit. But no, I won't do anything silly.'

'All the same,' Isobelle said, 'I don't think you should be there on your own. You should have stayed with Simone. I'll telephone her, ask her to come over and be with you.'

'No!' Hélène said sharply. 'You mustn't bother Simone. She's very busy with her work and I've taken up too much of her time already.'

'Very well. But take care of yourself, Hélène – and think about what I've said. If you don't want to lose Alain, then you really must make some effort to patch things up between you before it's too late.'

She put down the phone feeling anxious and annoyed. It should never have come to this. Hélène and Alain had had their problems, she knew, but they had given up far too easily. Young people did nowadays. They had none of the staying power of her own generation. There had been plenty of times, goodness knew, when she had felt like walking out on Henri, but she had not done it. He had had his mistresses and she had had her lovers and it had all been perfectly satisfactory. Well – most of the time, anyway. Her lips tightened as she remembered the occasion when it had not. But that was all in the past now. Henri was ill, aged before his time, so that sometimes he scarcely knew who she was. There would be no more mistresses for him, and no need for subterfuge on her part if someone suitable happened along. Why Alain and Hélène couldn't have come to some similar arrangement was beyond her.

She sighed and looked out of the window again. They would be here soon, Alain and his friend. She would have to be polite to her, she supposed, but she did not feel like being polite. What she felt like doing was telling the wretched woman to get on the first plane back to England and leave her son and his wife to try to mend their broken marriage.

Hélène stood with her arms wrapped around herself, tears streaming down her cheeks.

So Alain had found someone else. She shouldn't be surprised, she supposed. She should have known when he phoned to ask her for a divorce that he had a reason. But she hadn't wanted to allow herself to believe it. She'd been so sure that if only he would come back to France she could win him over, just as she always had. He loved her – didn't he? – and she loved him. Beside that one fact all their differences would pale into insignificance. Things had been difficult between them, it was true, but it was mostly her fault. Her unwillingness to have a child, for one thing, her terrible black moods for another.

She could be impossible when those moods descended on her, she knew. She had suffered from them ever since she was a child, when her mother had died, but she could find no reason for them now. They came without warning, filling her with darkness and dragging her down into a pit of despair, making her strike out at anyone close to her, say things she did not really mean, do the most unreasonable things. In their black shadow everything became distorted like images reflected in a fairground hall of mirrors and there was no escaping the swirling fog that closed in around her.

Once, unable to stand it any longer, she had tried to kill herself. She had told everyone afterwards that it had been an accident, just as she had told Isobelle so just now. But it hadn't been. She had looked at the bottle of tablets and seen a way of escape, the only escape, because then, as now, she was tired, too tired to fight any more.

She wouldn't do it again, though. Having her stomach pumped hadn't been a pleasant experience. And besides, whatever she might say, she wasn't ready to give up on Alain. She loved him, she missed him, she *wanted* him – oh dear God, how she wanted him! From the moment they had separated she had known she had to get him back somehow, and now, with Thierry dead, she wanted him more than ever.

When he had come back to France she had told herself it was only a matter of time. There were reasons why he hadn't come back to her immediately. He was terribly busy trying to sort out the mess Thierry had left; they were both distraught at his death; everything was too upside down for them to get together and sort out their differences.

Now she realised there was another reason. Alain had found someone to take her place. Time had run out. Isobelle was right. If she was not to lose Alain for ever she must do something – and quickly.

Hélène made an effort to pull herself together. She dried her tears, poured herself a large stiff drink and lit a cigarette. As the neat spirit began to take effect the cloud of depression lifted a little and the spark of determination fanned to a flame.

She refilled her glass, took it into the still-sunny garden and sat down beside the peach tree which Alain had planted for her to decide on a plan of action.

5

'SO – HOW LONG are you planning to be here, Esther?' Isobelle asked.

Dinner was over – a delicious meal of chicken roasted in the French manner and garnished with grapes in a light wine sauce. Now Henri, Alain's father, had gone to bed and Isobelle, Alain and Esther had taken their coffee and the remains of the bottle of wine on to the patio.

The heat had gone out of the day but the air was still pleasantly warm and a breeze, lighter than the Mistral, which sometimes blew down from the Rhone Valley, or the cloud-bearing Tramontane, rustled through the trees on the wooded slope below the patio.

Esther glanced at Alain's mother and wondered why she made her feel so uncomfortable. She had been charm personified, every inch the perfect hostess, yet Esther could not help feeling it was a surface charm only and there was no warmth beneath that apparently welcoming manner – no warmth for her at least. Perhaps it was asking too much that there should be. It was only a few hours since they had met for the first time. But Esther tended to trust her first impressions – and all her instincts were telling her that Alain's mother did not want her here.

'I have a fortnight off from work, but Alain and I haven't really talked about how long I should stay,' she said, deciding on a policy of honesty. 'It depends mostly, I guess, on how long you are prepared to put up with me!'

'Oh really! Any friend of Alain's is welcome for as long as he wishes it – he knows that.'

But Esther had seen the slight hardening of the tiny lines around her eyes.

'It really is very nice of you to have me here – and to look after me so well,' she said swiftly. 'But the last thing I want is to impose. You must promise to tell me if I'm becoming a nuisance. I can always book into a hotel.'

'I wouldn't hear of it. No, I simply wondered what you would find to do with yourself. Alain is terribly busy at the moment trying to sort out his business affairs. I don't suppose he will have the time to show you around.'

And you're not about to offer! Esther thought wryly.

'Esther can use the old Saab,' Alain said. 'I'm sure she will enjoy pottering around and exploring. And I can't work *all* the time, Maman.'

'It seems to me that unless you can sort things out rather quickly you won't be working at all,' she returned tartly. 'Neither will you have a car – or anything else for that matter.'

Esther turned to look at him, saw that his expression was worried rather than outraged, and felt a qualm of concern. Alain had intimated that there were problems, but from what Isobelle had said it seemed they were much worse than she had realised. Yet the business had seemed to be going so well in England!

'We don't want to talk about that now,' Alain said firmly. 'To be honest I don't even want to think about it. As to how long Esther will be staying, I hope it will be a very long time.'

He reached out and took Esther's hand, but her feeling of pleasure was marred as she noticed the way Isobelle's mouth tightened and the swiftness with which she averted her eyes.

'Perhaps I should leave you two alone,' she said drily. 'I'm sure you have a great deal to talk about.'

'Don't be silly, Maman. There's no need for that.'

'Well, if you're sure . . . I think I'd like some more coffee if there's any left, Alain.'

He reached for the pot, dutifully refilling her cup, and Esther experienced a stab of irritation. There was nothing she would like more than to be alone with Alain.

'So, you are a writer too, I hear,' Isobelle said. 'My elder daughter writes – in fact she is a very successful author. Perhaps Alain has told you about her.'

'Yes. I'm not in her class, I'm afraid.' Esther laughed apologetically.

'No, Simone does have a very special gift, I must agree. She brings history to life, doesn't she, Alain? Not that we always see eye to eye with her interpretation of it, of course. But

I suppose one does not have to agree with everything one's children do.'

Another double-edged barb! Esther thought.

'Simone does tend towards sympathy for the Cathars and she doesn't always show the church in a very good light,' Alain said. 'Maman finds it hard to accept that, don't you, Maman?'

'The church simply did what it had to do to put down a heresy. It took a harsh line, perhaps, but things were different in those days.'

'Oh I don't know that I agree with you. A lot of terrible things have been done in the name of religion over the centuries – are *still* being done in some parts of the world.'

'You can't blame the church for that. There will always be zealots and madmen who latch on to religion to further their own power-crazy ends. A great many of the atrocities that occurred here during the crusade were carried out by soldiers and mercenaries who killed because it gave them pleasure— '

'And the church gave them licence to do it,' Alain cut in. 'Not only that, but rewarded them handsomely. The Cathars were no threat to anyone, except perhaps in a theological sense, and they were brutally butchered for their beliefs. Simone simply wants to set the record straight.'

'Simone, I am afraid, is not a very good Catholic.'

'There I will agree with you,' Alain said, and Esther breathed a silent sigh of relief. She had the feeling this argument had taken place many times before and that the differences between mother and son were something of a ritual. That Isobelle was passionate in her defence of her church she had no doubt, but she wondered whether Alain was not perhaps enjoying the role of devil's advocate. He was, after all, as staunch a Catholic as his mother, only perhaps less blinkered. While she was unwilling to accept that the church of her faith could ever have been in the wrong, he was prepared to look at history with a less prejudiced eye.

'Some of Simone's beliefs are totally alien to everything she has been brought up to believe in,' Isobelle was saying. 'I simply don't know where she gets them from . . .' She broke off, cocking her head. 'Is that a car I hear?'

'Probably. We do have them, Maman, even here in the country.'

'Don't be facetious, Alain. I meant I thought it sounded like a car coming down the drive.'

She was still listening; the others listened too.

'You're right. It does sound as if it's coming here.' Alain glanced at his watch. 'It's late for visitors. You're not expecting anyone?'

'No. Are you?'

'No.' The engine note grew louder, then died, and they heard the slam of a car door. 'Perhaps it's Simone or Valerie. They knew Esther was arriving today. They've come over to say hello.'

Footsteps on the path; obviously whoever it was had guessed they would be on the patio and was coming straight round.

'It probably *is* Simone or Valerie— ' Alain broke off. 'Oh! No it's not.'

A young woman had rounded the corner of the house, small, slightly built and wearing a simple cream sundress, her light-brown hair falling loose to lightly tanned shoulders in a way that made her look almost ridiculously young. She hesitated for a moment, as if unsure of herself suddenly, and into the silence Alain said, 'It's Hélène!'

'Hélène, my dear, how lovely to see you!'

Isobelle rose, kissing her daughter-in-law on both cheeks, twice.

'What on earth are you doing here?' Alain asked abruptly.

Hélène looked from one to the other of them, then her hand flew to her mouth in a small defensive gesture.

'I'm sorry – I'm really sorry . . . I didn't know you had company . . .'

'It's quite all right, Hélène. You know you are always welcome,' Isobelle said, hiding a smile of satisfaction. 'Let me introduce you to our guest. This is Esther – a friend of Alain's from England. Forgive me, Esther, I don't think I know your other name . . .'

'Morris,' Alain said. 'I'm sure I told you, Maman.'

'Did you? That's the trouble with getting old – one does forget! And Esther, this is Hélène, Alain's wife.'

'Esther – what a pretty name . . .' Her tone was bright with false friendliness and a little breathless from nerves.

'Why are you here, Hélène?' Alain asked abruptly.

Pink colour tinged her fair cheeks.

'It's too silly really – but my lights seem to have fused. Not only the lights – I've got no power for my fridge and things either, and in this heat . . . well I thought maybe Alain could do something for me. It is only a fuse, I'm sure, but you know how useless I am with things like that . . .'

'Why didn't you telephone?' Alain asked, his voice curt with embarrassment.

'I tried to but you didn't answer. I know Beatrice doesn't hear very well any more, or perhaps she's gone home, and I guessed you'd be outside, so I just came over. I'm sorry . . . I really am sorry . . .'

'Do stop apologising, Hélène!' Isobelle said. 'For heaven's sake, you have enough troubles without losing your electricity on top of it. Of course Alain will come over and have a look at it for you. If he'd had the house rewired properly when you moved in it would never have happened.'

'There's nothing wrong with the wiring,' Alain said crossly. 'As Hélène says, it probably is just a fuse.'

'Then it wouldn't take you a moment to fix it, would it?' Isobelle said smoothly. 'I suggest you go straight away, before it gets too dark to see.'

Hélène gestured helplessly.

'But I'm interrupting your evening. Your friend— '

'You can't possibly be alone in that great house with no electricity,' Isobelle said firmly. 'Esther and I can have a chat and get to know one another, can't we Esther? Go on, Alain, go with Hélène. We'll be fine.'

Alain hesitated, undecided, then he got up abruptly.

'Is the fuse wire still where I used to keep it, or will I need to bring some?'

'I don't know. It should be there. I haven't touched it.'

'I'd better take some in case it's not.' He glanced at Esther. 'I'm really sorry about this.'

'It's all right,' she said, but her voice was tight.

'I won't be gone long. Promise.'

She thought he would kiss her goodbye but he did not. Strangely, that hurt more than the fact that he was going. He had no real choice, she could see that. But she would very much have liked him to demonstrate to both his mother and his ex-wife that *she* was his woman now.

* * *

'What are you playing at, Hélène?' Alain asked shortly as they rounded the corner of the house.

'What do you mean?'

'Coming here tonight. You know very well what I mean.'

'The lights fused. I told you. I didn't know what to do.'

'Oh come on! You came because you knew Esther was here. Who told you – Maman?'

'Alain! Do you have to be so horrid? Why should I make something like that up?'

'I didn't say you made it up. But I do think it's very convenient.'

'Convenient! Having my lights go?'

'The timing of it. Oh – I don't know . . .'

He shrugged helplessly. How was it Hélène could make him feel this way – infuriated, exasperated, yet still oddly protective? It was impossible, he supposed, to have loved someone, lived with them, for so long, and not feel a sense of responsibility for them, even if the relationship was over. But she had created a highly embarrassing scene and put him in an impossible position especially given the delicate situation between him and Esther at the moment, and he was angry with her.

'Alain . . .' She put a hand on his arm, seeming to make up her mind, looking at him in that appealing way that had once turned his bones to water. 'You're right, of course. I did know that . . . woman was here. And I just couldn't bear it. Thinking of you, with her. I had to come.'

'Oh Hélène . . .' He shook his head.

'It is so awful without you,' she rushed on. 'I miss you so much. I'm all by myself in that great house . . .'

'Is it worse than living the way we did the last couple of years?' he asked harshly. 'You know we were at one another's throats most of the time. We both agreed it was best we should part.'

'I know. But it wasn't always like that, was it? We were good together, weren't we, you and I? We should never have thrown it all away.'

He swallowed at the pang of nostalgia and regret that rose, unexpected and unwanted. Yes, they had been good together. And yet they had ended up tearing each other apart. Remembering the confrontations, the arguments, the hellish confusion of loving and hating all mixed up together, was painful, even now.

She couldn't seriously want it all to begin again? He didn't think he could have faced it, even in the confused state he had been in when he had fled to England. Too many arguments, too much hurting, too many hopes that this time things would be different dashed. In the end he had felt only a sense of relief that it was over. He had wanted some peace, and the chance to get on with his life. Oh yes, he had loved Hélène, but living with her had been hell. He hadn't thought he could ever be bothered with another woman ever again. And then he had met Esther. And wanted her so much he had forgotten all his doubts, forgotten Hélène.

Now, with the memories of the good times, the old spark of attraction stirred again treacherously, but it made him only angry.

'It's too late, Hélène,' he said. 'We had our chance and we blew it.'

'Oh, don't say that, Alain – please . . .'

He steeled himself. 'Is there really anything wrong with your lights, Hélène?'

'Yes, of course there is!'

'Then we'd better do something about it. Look, you drive your car and I'll follow you in mine. I'll do what I can, but then I'm coming straight back here.'

'All right.' She nodded, as if conceding defeat. But she had seen what she wanted to see – that tiny spark of hesitation that he was trying so hard to conceal. 'If that's the way you want it.'

'It is.' He turned abruptly, heading for where his car was parked on the broad turnaround in front of the house.

Hélène got into her own car and started the engine. As she drove slowly down the dark drive she saw the reflection of his lights in her mirror as he followed her and heard herself giggling softly, uncontrollably, a reaction partly of the release of tension and partly of a heady sense of exhilaration. Alain might say it was all over between them but she didn't think it was the whole truth. There was no way it was ever going to be all over between them, not completely. He still felt something for her, she was sure, and if she played her cards right, she thought she could still win him back.

Andrew Slater stretched his long legs luxuriously and settled himself back against the cushions of the low wickerwork sofa.

He had just enjoyed a delicious meal of fillet steak and salad, followed by apricots poached in liqueur and topped with lashings of crème fraîche; now, with a cup of strong coffee and a glass of cognac within easy reach at his elbow, he felt replete and glowing, at peace with the world.

From the tiny kitchen which led off the sitting room came the clatter of crockery and the murmur of voices interspersed with the occasional burst of laughter as Bob and Diana cleared up together after the evening meal, and Andrew could not help comparing their easy cameraderie with the rather stiff old-fashioned relationship his mother had with Bert, his stepfather.

Bert would never dream of picking up a tea towel to dry a plate – and his mother probably would not want him to, Andrew thought wryly. She enjoyed making a martyr of herself – it seemed to provide her with a reason for living. But Andrew found it galling, all the same, to see Bert slumped in front of the television set idly flicking the buttons on the remote control while Andrew's mother slaved over a hot stove, a sinkful of washing-up or a pile of ironing. During the four days he had just spent with them Andrew had offered to help out with the chores, as much to make a point as anything, but his mother had refused all his offers, just as he had known she would, while Bert had stared stonily into space, turning a deaf ear to the remarks Andrew had made about his mother needing to take things more easily.

He had offered to help Diana with the washing up tonight too, and like his mother she had refused.

'You're on holiday, Andrew. Go and sit down! Bob will give me a hand with the dishes, won't you, darling?'

And he had. That was the difference. Listening to their banter coming from the kitchen as he sipped his cognac, Andrew thought that theirs was what a relationship should be: a partnership between equals who enjoyed each other's company. Not for the first time he wondered if his mother had been partly to blame for the way Bob's career had monopolised his life during the years of their marriage. Make yourself into a doormat and sure as hell you'd be treated like one!

'Well then, my lad, you've left some brandy for me, I hope!' Bob appeared in the doorway. He was wiping his hands on a tea towel and when he finished he tossed it back on to a working surface, causing Diana to admonish him.

'Bob! Spread it out, can't you? It won't dry there!'

Bob did as he was told, then returned to the living room, grinning.

'Women! She's a slave driver, that one!'

'And you love every minute of it,' Andrew said with a smile.

'Well, yes, it's not such a bad life.' He poured himself a brandy. 'You all right?'

'Fine, for the moment, thanks.'

'Good. Don't want you regretting that you came out to see us.'

'I can't see myself doing that.'

'Your mother wasn't too upset that you broke your visit to her, I hope?'

'I don't think so. She's pretty well occupied looking after Bert. And in any case I'll be going back there for a couple of days at the end of my holiday. It's all planned out very well really.'

'Well, I'm certainly glad you made it.' Bob glanced at Diana, who had appeared in the doorway. 'Can I get you a drink, sweetheart?'

'No thanks. I'm going to have a nice long soak in the bath and leave you two to your men's talk.' She crossed the room, a plump, casually elegant woman in a brightly coloured shirt worn loose over wide pyjama-style trousers of cream silk, and Andrew saw his father's eyes follow her approvingly.

Yes, they definitely had something going for them, Andrew thought. He only hoped when he was his father's age he would be as lucky.

'So – have there been any developments in the Mysterious Case of the Deceased Languedoc Businessman?' he asked.

'Ha!' Bob looked at him over the rim of his brandy glass. 'Now we're getting down to the real reason behind your visit, are we? I whetted your professional appetite. All this "Good to see you, Dad" is just flannel.'

'Not at all!' Andrew protested. 'But I was intrigued by what you told me. I can't help having a nose for a story.'

'It's all right – you don't have to make excuses. But I'm afraid I haven't got any more for you. I told you – my days of investigating crime are over.' He sipped his drink, then went on reflectively, 'I did hear one thing, though – or, rather, Diana did. There are rumours the business is in trouble.'

'The business?'

'Alain Lavaur's wine exporting company. The one the late unlamented Thierry Rousseau was supposed to be looking after here whilst Alain was in England. Word is that a lot of local *viticulteurs* are owed a lot of money.'

Andrew's eyes narrowed. 'Really?'

'That's what we heard. Interesting, eh?'

'Very,' Andrew said thoughtfully. 'I suppose if I pursue this story, though, you and Diana really will think it's the only reason I'm here.'

Bob Slater got up to draw the curtains against the deepening dusk.

'Does it matter what Diana and I think? Come on, lad, if you weren't interested in your career you wouldn't be your father's son, would you? Get out there and find your story – it'll do you a damned sight more good than sitting around here all day drinking my brandy!'

Andrew laughed, relaxed in the easy rapport he and his father shared. Whether there turned out to be a story in Thierry Rousseau's death or not, he was sure he was going to enjoy his holiday.

'Would you think me very rude, Isobelle, if I were to go to bed? It's been a long day.'

More than an hour had gone by since Alain had left with Hélène and Esther was growing increasingly uncomfortable in his mother's company.

'Of course you must be tired,' Isobelle said. 'I'm sure Alain will quite understand you didn't want to wait up for him.'

She sounded almost smug, and it reinforced Esther's distinct impression that she was an unwelcome visitor. Isobelle would like to see Alain and Hélène together again, Esther realised.

'You know which is your room, don't you?' Isobelle went on. 'And the bathroom is just along the landing.'

'Thank you.'

'Sleep well.'

'I'm sure I will.'

But she knew she would certainly not sleep until she knew Alain was home, and perhaps not then. She felt far too strung up. It was one thing to accept that Alain still had a wife, even that given the circumstances he still had to be in contact with her, and quite another to have her appearing on the scene as she had. And it had disturbed Esther more than she cared to admit.

Like the rest of the house, the guest room to which Alain had shown her earlier was decorated in the Catalan fashion – dark wallpaper with a design of overblown cabbage roses, dark paintwork and heavy dark curtains. It was, Esther thought, faintly oppressive, and as unlike the bright modern apartments she had encountered on previous visits to the Mediterranean as it was possible to imagine. But at least the windows gave on to a small balcony which offered stunning views of the Pyrenees, and when she threw them open the sweet haunting perfume of night-scented stocks wafted in on the warm evening air.

She stood for a moment drinking it in and listening for the hum of a car on the drive which would indicate Alain's return, but there was no sound in the soft darkness but the chirping of the crickets, the intermittent distant barking of a dog and the chime of the village clock striking the quarter-hour. She had noticed the tower which housed it earlier, rising high above the cluster of houses; now, in the quiet of the night there was a haunting quality to the sound of the bell, stirring elusive emotions and long-forgotten memories. Esther tried to catch them, but they slipped away from her, leaving only an overwhelming poignancy.

She turned away from the window, removed her holdall from the bed and folded back the patchwork coverlet and single woollen blanket, leaving only the cotton sheet. Then she took her toilet bag and made her way along the landing to the bathroom. When she emerged ten minutes later, she stood for a moment at the head of the stairs, listening for the sounds of conversation. There were none – obviously Alain had still not returned. What on earth was he doing? Surely he should have sorted out the problem with Hélène's lights by now?

A row of books supported by carved wooden bookends stood on top of the old-fashioned chest of drawers, and Esther ran her eye along them, looking for something to distract her. A couple of thick tomes bearing Simone's name, a novel, a book of verse . . . Esther knew her French was not good enough to cope with any of them. But there were also some guide books, filled with pictures of the area. Esther selected two or three, got into bed and propped the pillows up behind her.

She flipped through the first, tilting it towards the bedside lamp and admiring the panoramic views of mountains and plains, rivers and vineyards, and experiencing again some of the pleasure and soporific contentment she had felt as Alain had driven her through the beautiful Roussillon countryside this afternoon. But now, as then, it was the stark images of the ruined Cathar strongholds, rising unexpectedly from the mountain peaks, which fascinated her the most, and she thought she must try to find out more about the people who had taken refuge in them. They were Alain's forebears, their history was his heritage, yet until this afternoon she had scarcely even heard of them. Now, however, they seemed to call to her across the centuries, their romance and their tragedy stirring lost chords in the symphony of time.

How harsh life must have been in those windswept fortresses! Yet enduring the bleakness of their surroundings had presumably been a small price to pay when one considered the alternatives. Esther turned a page, came face to face with a picture of a simple stone monument erected in a field where more than two hundred Cathars had perished at the stake, and shivered violently. Death by burning. She could imagine nothing more horrible – couldn't bear even to think of it. She closed the book sharply and dropped it on to the bed beside her as if the pages had suddenly become searingly hot.

The clock bell chimed another quarter, its mournful knell echoing eerily across the valley. What on earth was Alain doing? Esther lay, tense and anxious, wondering about the wisdom of having come to France, trying to find some comfort in the things Alain had said and failing dismally. They were, after all, just words. The reality was that he was not here now, but with his ex-wife. No, not even his ex-wife. His wife, who still had the right to call on him if she needed to.

Then, quite suddenly, lights arced through the darkness, tyres crunched on gravel and a door slammed. He was home! A stair creaked, then the handle of the door turned and Alain's voice, very soft, whispered, 'Esther? Are you awake?'

'Yes,' she whispered back.

'Sweetheart – I'm so sorry. I could cheerfully murder Hélène for that.'

The sight of his tall form, shadowy in the moonlight, made her heart turn over.

'She does know how to pick her moments,' Esther said. 'What was wrong with her lights? Did you manage to fix them?'

'Eventually. The trip switch had cut in for some reason and the whole house was off. It took a while for me to sort it out.'

'Yes, it did, didn't it?' She didn't know why she'd said that.

'Esther – I said I'm sorry. Don't let's quarrel again. Here – these are for you. Roses and lavender. I picked them in the garden as a peace offering. You like roses, don't you?'

'Oh, Alain!' The perfume of the flowers was in her nostrils, soothing yet heady. 'What colour are the roses? I can't see.'

'Red, of course. Red roses to say I love you.'

'Thank you. They're beautiful. But they'll die if we don't put them in water.'

'Oh Esther, always so practical! We'll put them in water if it makes you happy.'

He reached for the carafe on the bedside table, easing the stems through the narrow neck. Then he sat down on the edge of the bed, pulling her into his arms.

The touch of his hands on her bare shoulders was electric. He pushed aside the sheet, caressing her, and she wound her arms around his neck, loving the feel of his firm muscles, melting at his whispered words of love. No reproaches now, no questions, no ultimatums. Nothing mattered beyond the fact that they were lying together as close as two people could be and still wanting only to be closer, closer . . .

Afterwards they lay in each other's arms, unwilling to let go the magic. Esther felt her eyelids growing heavy with a delicious languor. She turned her face into Alain's shoulder and fell asleep with the salt taste of his skin on her tongue.

Beside her Alain slept too, and as they moved together in a deep unconscious embrace the weeks of separation melted away as if they had never been.

6

SIMONE HAD BEEN at her word processor all day. Her neck and shoulders felt tight, her head was aching and she knew that the time when she should have stopped working had long since come and gone. But today things had been flowing well and the compulsion to carry on had been strong. Just one more sentence . . . just one more . . .

Now, however, exhaustion was catching up with her. She moved the mouse to 'save', clicked the button – and then went cold with horror. The screen had gone blank. What on earth had she done? Oh, please God, she couldn't have lost it, could she? Not all that work! How long was it since she had saved? She couldn't remember.

In utter panic she stared at the blank screen, rolling the mouse with small jerky movements. There *was* something there – a line half-obscured at the very top. She pulled it down and stared again, this time in disbelief.

It is beginning again.

The same phrase she had seen before, only this time there was more.

What happened before must happen again.

Simone rubbed her aching eyes, moved the mouse again, and as suddenly as they had appeared, the phrases were gone. For a moment the screen was blank and then her text came flooding back, paragraph after paragraph exactly as she had typed it. Relief coursed through her, followed immediately by bewilderment. She hadn't tapped in the words this time, of that she was quite certain. It must be something in the program, but the word processor was far from new and such a thing had never happened before. She'd have to call the engineer out to have a look at it – she couldn't afford to have the wretched machine pack up on her when she was under such pressure to get her manuscript completed and dispatched to the publishers.

Simone gave herself a small shake, coaxing her stiff muscles to life. Then she switched off the computer and eased herself out of the chair. As she padded to the kitchen her bare feet made small sucking sounds on the tiled floor. She should eat, she knew, but it was too late now to bother. Instead she poured herself a glass of ice-cold milk.

When he heard the click of the refrigerator door, Félix came streaking in from the patio to rub pleadingly round her legs. Simone poured some of the milk into a saucer for him and opened a tin of tuna fish as a treat – a change from his usual cat food.

'Poor old Félix,' she apologised to him. 'Your mealtimes aren't very regular when I'm working, are they?'

But Félix looked well on it anyway. Simone had rescued him as a small starving kitten three summers ago; now he was sleek and well fed, his eyes bright and his fur shiny.

Simone pulled the patio door closed but did not bother to lock it. She seldom did. Burglary was almost unheard of in this peaceful rural area. Leaving Félix hunched purposefully over his dish of tuna, she went back to switch off the lamps beside her desk and collect a notepad, pencil and a couple of reference books. It was her habit to take work to bed with her, the notepad in case inspiration struck during the night, the books so that she could read herself to sleep.

The bedroom was little more than an attic, with a sloping roof, low beams to catch the unwary, and shuttered windows. They were wide open now and had been all day but there was still a heavy airlessness in the room and a slightly oppressive feel as if there might be thunder on the way. Simone undressed and lay down, stretching luxuriously. At least the cotton sheets felt deliciously cool, but she wouldn't read for too long tonight. When the bedroom was this hot even the sixty-watt bulb in the bedside lamp seemed to give off heat equivalent to a small radiator.

She reached for one of the books – a glossy-covered paperback devoted to the city of Carcassonne and its turbulent history.

Once upon a time Carcassonne had been a Roman fortress, long before that, in the sixth century BC, cob and wattle huts and a hill fort had stood on the site, overlooking one of the great trading routes between the Atlantic and the Mediterranean. In the Middle Ages its walls, towers and moats had encompassed a count's castle, a cathedral and dwellings, as well as two satellite settlements, St-Michel and St-Vincent. Nowadays it had been restored as a tourist attraction as well as a monument to the past, and the publication Simone turned towards the light of her reading lamp had been produced for the millions of visitors who flocked there. Though far less scholarly than most of the books she used for reference, it was full of clear and beautiful photographs, maps and diagrams which detailed La Cité as it had once been, and it presented a précis of Carcassonne's history which helped to clarify in her mind the myriad facts her researches had accumulated.

Carcassonne had figured in Simone's books before. Its capture by the crusaders in 1209 had been one of the earliest triumphs in the campaign against the Cathars. But this time it had special significance for her. It had been Simon de Montfort, on whose biography she was now working, who had laid siege to the city with the blood of the people of Béziers fresh on his hands, and when he had finally forced its surrender he had been rewarded by being granted its lands and titles. After his death in 1218 de Montfort had been buried there, and though his earthly remains had later been removed and taken to his ancestral home near Versailles, his tomb could still be seen in the church within the city, Eglise St Nazaire.

Simone disliked the way Carcassonne had been commercialised – she much preferred the more inaccessible and unspoiled ruins where the peace of the years had settled on the mounds of weather-worn stone along with the moss and lichen. But the careful reconstruction of the past made her job easier, providing a bridge to span the centuries.

Now she laid down the book, settling herself back against the pillows and picturing the towers and battlements, sunbaked and golden beneath the deep unbroken blue of the sky. It had been August, and the height of the southern summer, when de Montfort had led his armies up the hillside to the fortified settlements. Raymond Roger Trencavel, Viscount of Carcassonne, though himself a Catholic, had provided a safe haven for the Cathars of the surrounding villages and the siege had lasted three long weeks until the garrison and the people who had taken refuge within the city were so weakened by thirst, starvation and the rampant fever which came from inadequate sanitation that they could no longer resist.

How terrible it must have been for them, holed up like rats in a trap and in mortal fear of the fate that would befall them if they were forced to surrender to the Crusaders!

Simone reached out and switched off her reading lamp. Drowsy now, she let her mind drift, imagining what it must have been like to be hungry, thirsty and terrified, unable to escape the constant noise of the raging battle. In the silence of the night she could almost hear it – the pounding of missiles fired from the trebuchets as they peppered the walls and battlements, the whistle of arrows, the screams of men and horses.

'Don't die, Mother! Please don't die!'

The voice, that of a distressed child, was loud in her head, closer than the noise of battle.

Puzzled, she opened her eyes. They felt heavy, as if she had been deeply asleep for a very long time. Soft moonlight was playing in through the half-open curtains, deepening the shadows under the sloping roof and investing the familiar room with a quality of unreality. Simone shifted restlessly. Her throat was burning, her head swimming, but though she desperately wanted a drink she could not summon the energy to move her aching limbs enough to reach for the carafe of water she always kept on her bedside table.

What on earth was wrong with her? She'd been fine when she'd come to bed – tired, but otherwise fine! Now she felt really ill. And what on earth was that awful smell? Sewage? Rotting meat? Yes . . . but something else too. The smell of fear, sweet and rancid.

'Mother?' It was the child's voice again, softer this time, just a mere whisper. It seemed to be coming from the corner of the room.

There was a figure in the shadows, indistinct, transparent almost. As she looked it became clearer and she realised there was not just one figure but two. A boy, perhaps four or five years old, with a shock of red hair and light-blue eyes, and a girl, several years older. Like the boy she was painfully thin, but her hair was a darker shade of reddish brown and her eyes a deeper shade of blue.

Simone screwed up her own aching eyes, wondering how it was

that she could see them so clearly with no illumination but the faint light of the moon – and why the room no longer looked like her familiar attic. The walls around her now seemed to be rough untreated stone and in the corner of the room a ladder led up to a kind of mezzanine. It was, she realised, very like the sleeping quarters in medieval cottages which had been known as the '*solier*'. But what was she doing there? It was all so confusing.

In the cloying heat flies buzzed ceaselessly. Simone felt one settle on her face but she could not summon the energy to brush it away.

'She is very sick.'

Another voice, this time a man's, but gentle and sad. It came from right beside the bed. Through the haze of sweat which was clouding her eyes, Simone became aware of a gaunt figure robed in black bending over her.

'The fever is upon her. 'Tis rife in the city.'

Of course! she thought, relieved, that was where she was! Carcassonne. La Cité. How could she have forgotten?

But the relief at remembering that much was short lived. For the other memories were tumbling in now, filling the void, making her sweat with fear and dread.

She was here because it was where they had taken refuge when the soldiers came – she and Jeanne and little Pons.

Oh, sweet Jesu, the soldiers!

It was more than a week now since the messenger had ridden into St-Vincent, the village that lay in the shadow of the walls of Carcassonne. She had been in the tiny patch of garden behind their *ostal* picking figs from the tree which grew there when her daughter, Jeanne, who had been to fetch water from the spring, had come running home to tell her of the man on the lathered horse who had galloped through the streets. Jeanne had not known the reason for his fevered ride, only that she thought it meant trouble, but soon afterwards Guillemette Martin, her neighbour, had come bursting in with the news.

'There's been a terrible massacre in Béziers. All the people are dead. The crusaders mowed them down in the streets and then set fire to the Church of the Madeleine. There were six hundred souls taking refuge in the church alone, it's said. They were all burned to death!'

'Sancta Maria!' she had whispered, horrified.

She had heard the rumblings, of course – they all had – that the Pope had joined forces with the King of France to raise an army to eliminate the heresy of Catharism and restore the lands of Languedoc to the Catholic Church, but she had hoped the stories were nothing more than rumour and scaremongering. She couldn't see how ordinary people like them, going about their business and practising their simple faith, could possibly be of the slightest interest to the King and the Church. But the Perfects – the priesthood of their Cathar sect – had warned that it might not be so. The Pope was concerned at the spread of the heresy and Philippe Auguste was eager to add the lands of Languedoc and Roussillon to the Kingdom of France. A crusade would mean deadly peril for all who opposed it, the Perfects had said. Now, trembling with dread, she realised they had been right.

The lamb stew, simmering in an earthenware *olla* on the open fire, had boiled up to spit and hiss on to the coals, and she had reached out distractedly to pull it aside.

'Word is that the crusaders are on their way here now,' Guillemette had gone on. 'The Viscount Raymond Roger is gathering as many knights as he can to defend us, but all the knights in Christendom wouldn't be enough to hold the suburbs against Simon de Montfort's army. I tell you, Helis, that man is the very devil!' Guillemette crossed herself.

'What are we to do?' Helis had asked, her voice shaking.

'We must take refuge in the city. At least the walls and moat will afford us some protection. But for how long . . . who can say? Raymond Roger thought Béziers was safe enough and look at what has happened there!' She shook her head, impatient suddenly. 'I don't know . . . you Cathars! Why can't you see that by your heresy you bring trouble to us all? Why should the rest of us, who are good Catholics, be burned in our beds when we have done nothing wrong? If they do the same here as they've done at Béziers, they'll kill us all first and ask questions afterwards.'

'Sancta Maria – not in front of the children!' Helis had said sharply. 'We've been neighbours a good many years, Guillemette. Don't let's quarrel now.'

Guillemette had sighed.

'No, you're right – I don't want to quarrel, Helis. You've done me no harm, and you'll go to hell soon enough for refusing the sacraments. But all the same . . . lambs like this one . . .' She reached out to stroke the carroty hair of little Pons, who had come running in and was now cowering into his mother's skirts, frightened by the tension in the air. Guillemette was very fond of Pons. 'I'm going home now to get my things together and you would do well to do the same.'

She was right of course, Helis knew. They had no choice but to take refuge within the city walls. But she hated the thought of leaving her little *ostal* with its neat garden and her handful of scrawny chickens to the tender mercies of the crusaders. Perhaps if they retreated to the city they would escape with their lives, but what would become of them if the soldiers looted and burned everything they possessed?

Still, she mustn't think of that. The most important thing was ensuring the safety of Jeanne and Pons, her children.

That night the three of them had joined the straggling procession of women and children making for the safety of the city. For the most part the menfolk were remaining in the village to try to defend their homes, but Helis had no husband to leave behind. Jacques, the children's father, had died soon after Pons had been born, and Helis had had to take on the business of wine seller in order to scrape a living for herself and the little ones.

The city was overcrowded with refugees; they thronged in the narrow cobbled streets, mingling with the garrison the Viscount had assembled, and crowded into the *ostals* of those willing to take them in. Helis and the children had found shelter in a cramped cottage where the family already numbered seven, and their only bed was a rough blanket spread out on the flagged floor. When two days had passed with no sign of the crusaders, Helis had dared to hope they had gone elsewhere. But of course it was simply that an army made up not only of knights but also a ragged band of foot soldiers travelled much more slowly than a messenger on a fast horse, especially when they had also to transport the war machinery needed to attack a fortified city like Carcassonne.

It was ten days now since the army had been sighted making its way across the plain, and the ordeal had begun in earnest. The suburb of St-Michel had fallen quickly, its old walls too weak to withstand the onslaught, and the troops had rampaged through the streets before turning their attention to St-Vincent. When that, too, had fallen, and the black pall of smoke from the fired buildings blotted out the clear blue of the sky, Helis had thought the worst moment had come. But she had been wrong.

Simon de Montfort, who did not want to see Carcassonne reduced to ruins as the suburbs had been, had laid siege to the city. Day after day it echoed with the pounding of missiles from de Montfort's trebuchets, and the shouts of Raymond Roger's men as they hurled rocks and blocks of wood from the ramparts at the attackers who were digging away at the foundations.

With the city surrounded there was no longer any way to reach the River Aude or the fountains in the suburbs to draw water, and with the garrison and the thousands of refugees to be fed, food supplies were dwindling at an alarming rate. In the fierce heat fever had broken out, spread by the flies that swarmed about the open sewers and the rotting carcasses of animals slaughtered for meat but not yet salted.

When Helis had first begun to feel ill she had tried to tell herself and the frightened children that it was nothing.

'I'm as strong as an ox,' she had reassured them. 'I'll be all right.'

But she had not been all right. Her cheeks had grown more flushed and her throat more ragged, as if a fire was burning inside her. Yet in spite of the cloying heat she shivered uncontrollably, spasm after spasm shaking her thin frame. All night she had tossed and turned, drifting between wakefulness and horrid nightmarish dreams and in the morning when she tried to rise she fell back again on to the blanket, too weak to stand.

Renée Renaud, the woman of the house, a kindly soul and herself a Cathar believer, had brought a straw palette to make her more comfortable and Jeanne hovered fearfully, moistening her mother's lips with drops of precious water and trying to comfort Pons, who clung whimpering to her. Renée had also sent for the Perfects – the Good Men – and now they had arrived. Hope had flared briefly in Helis's fever-bright eyes as she recognised Raymond, who was not only a Perfect but also a doctor. He would be able to do something to make her better, surely? He must be able to! She couldn't die! Who would take care of the children then? But in Raymond's sweet face she saw only sadness as he bent to take her hand in his.

'Can you hear me, my child?'

She tried to answer him, but her lips were parched. With an effort she managed to nod her head.

'You are very sick, Helis. I can offer you little hope. I think it would be best if you were to be consoled.'

The congestion which was already making breathing difficult tightened so that it felt like an iron band around her chest.

Sweet Jesu, he was offering her the *Consolamentum*! To the ordinary Cathar believer that meant one thing and one thing only: that death was imminent. Once a Cathar had been consoled it was necessary for him to enter into the *Endura* and refrain from eating or even drinking again, for this way lay salvation. The evils of the material world must be renounced in order to ensure safe passage of the spirit to that other world, where all was goodness and light.

'I can't!' she whispered. 'The children . . .'

'My dear, you must. If you should recover, we won't hold you to it, of course. But for the sake of your eternal soul you must be ready in case the worst should happen.'

She sobbed weakly, too sick to move. But at least she was lucid now. She watched as those who were not Believers left the room, taking Pons with them. The table was set with a clean white cloth and a few drops of precious water were used to symbolise the washing of hands. Raymond the Perfect bent low over her, speaking the holy words, and touching her elbow with his copy of the Gospel According to St John – though they differed from the Catholic Church on many points of dogma, the Cathars were also Christians.

At last it was over, and after offering her a few more words of comfort, Raymond and the other Good Men left. In spite of her sickness, a sense of peace had come over Helis – a still, sad peace unlike anything she had ever known, for her fear had left her and she thought she could glimpse joy beyond the pain. But there were some things that had to be done before the fever tightened its grip again.

'Jeanne . . .' With her failing strength, she stretched out her hand to the child who hovered, eyes enormous in her thin face, then fumbled at the neck of her gown for the roughly fashioned locket she always wore. 'The Star of the Domus. You must take care of it now and give it to Pons when he is old enough.'

'Mother . . . no!'

'Yes. Unfasten it for me . . .'

Trembling, the child obeyed, and stood holding the locket reverently between her hands. Inside it were some clippings from her father's nails, pared away after he had died, and a lock of his hair. The Star of the Domus – the charm which afforded protection to the house of Marty. Passing it down from father to son was a superstitious custom, disapproved of by Cathars and Catholics alike, but in some matters, despite her faith, Helis, like many others, adhered to the old ways.

'Take care of it, my child,' Helis whispered. 'And take care of Pons, too.'

'I will, Mother.' Jeanne's voice was frightened but resolute and Helis sank back on the pallet, satisfied. Her head was beginning to swim again and though she fought against it the darkness was closing in . . .

Simone shifted restlessly. The pictures were fading, so that she seemed to be looking into an abyss, and the voices and the noise of battle, so clear a moment ago, were fainter, as if they were coming from a long way off. As she drifted she became aware of another sound which she could not place. The village bell? No, too sharp and loud, too insistent – it didn't fit somehow, didn't belong.

Simone's eyes snapped open. The telephone. The telephone was ringing. For a moment she lay, utterly confused, unsure of where she was or what was happening. But the bell was still shrilling, and she struggled into a sitting position. Her head was throbbing dully and her whole body ached. She fumbled with the coverlet, pushing it aside, but when she swung her legs to the ground they felt weak and shaky.

To her muzzy senses the telephone had the ring of urgency, reminding her chillingly of the morning she had been woken by a call from Hélène, telling her Thierry was dead. She stumbled along the landing, groping at the walls for support. But by the time she reached the top stair it had stopped and the silence was as loud and threatening as the insistent bell had been.

She hesitated at the head of the stairs, half expecting it to begin again, and when it did not she sat down where she was, burying her face in her hands.

God, she felt ill! And the dream she'd had . . . The aura of it still surrounded her, every detail startlingly clear, not slipping into a muddy meaningless quagmire as most dreams did, so that it somehow seemed more real than the shadowy moonlit world of her own house.

It had been looking at the book about Carcassonne as she fell asleep that had done it, she supposed, but she often read herself to sleep and she could never remember such a thing happening before. She hadn't even thought she was asleep when it began; she could clearly remember turning her head on the pillow and seeing the two children in the corner of the room before the scene had changed and become an *ostal* in Carcassonne. And the woman whose persona she had seemed to inhabit – Helis? – where had she come from? She was Simone's own vision of one of Simon de Montfort's unfortunate victims, obviously. Yet there had been something hauntingly familiar about her, and Simone had identified with her with the comfortable ease of slipping on an old shoe.

Simone frowned suddenly as a memory teased at her.

Many years ago when Valerie, her younger sister, had been a student, she and a college friend whom she had brought home to stay for the holiday had persuaded Simone to take part in what they had rather grandly called a 'psychic experiment'.

When they had first suggested it, Simone had refused. She knew that Isobelle, a strict Catholic, would be furious if she found out what they were doing, and for once she thought she agreed with her mother. Valerie seemed to be totally under the influence of her new friend, Aurore, but Simone considered her slightly weird with her strange light eyes, flowing hair and hippy style of dress. The two of them were spending a good deal of time in Valerie's room, burning candles and joss sticks – Simone couldn't think why Isobelle hadn't noticed the smell of them wafting about on the landing, but perhaps she had not realised what it was.

Though she thought the whole psychic scene was nothing more than superstitious nonsense, it also made Simone vaguely uneasy. Dabbling with that sort of thing, whether there was anything in it or not, could be dangerous, she felt, and she did not want anything to do with it. But Valerie had refused to take no for an answer. She had always known how to get her own way, and she had added logic to her own particular brand of charm.

They couldn't do the experiment without a third person, she had explained – and, if Simone thought it was all nonsense anyway, what harm could it possibly do? Surely there was no need to be so stuffy about it? After all, Aurore was a guest, and it was up to them to make sure she enjoyed her stay.

At last, reluctantly, Simone had given in to her sister's persuasion, although afterwards, thinking about it, she had had the oddest feeling that it was not so much Valerie's cajoling as the way Aurore had looked at her that had broken down the barriers of her objection. Aurore had said not a word, but there had been something oddly compelling in those piercing eyes of hers . . .

'You can be the first subject,' she had said when they were ready to begin.

'Oh, I wanted to be first!' Valerie complained, but Aurore had been insistent.

'No, I think your sister should be. After all, she has agreed to help us when she didn't want to. And I think she may be in for a surprise . . .'

And so Simone had found herself lying on the floor, her head resting on a cushion, whilst Valerie massaged her feet and Aurore gently stimulated what she called 'the third eye' – a spot just above the bridge of Simone's nose.

'Just float,' Aurore had urged her. 'Through the ceiling, up, up, above the rooftops . . . Now, look down and tell me what you can see.'

At first there was nothing – she had known there wouldn't be. Then, as she relaxed, too bored and sceptical to do anything but simply lie there, she had begun to picture lush green grass dotted with buildings of golden stone and a wooded hillside stretching away to the mountains, purple-blue in the distance – the familiar landscape that surrounded her home, except that it was somehow subtly different.

'What can you see?' Aurore had asked.

'Nothing much. Just the countryside.'

'What are you wearing?'

'I don't know.'

'Look down – look at your feet. Can you see them?'

'Yes. I'm wearing slippers – no, not slippers, boots – soft boots . . . and my skirt . . . it's long. Brown. Very rough . . . like sacking . . .'

As if from a long way off she had heard Aurore's swift intake of breath.

'What is your name? Do you know your name?'

And without the slightest hesitation she had replied, 'Helis. Helis Marty.'

It was all imagination, of course. She'd thought it then and she thought it now. Somewhere, sometime, she must have come across that name – in a story book when she was a child, perhaps – and it had lodged in some unconscious part of her mind.

But why should it have reoccurred to her now, some twenty years on, in a dream? The mind is a mystery, Simone told herself. It plays the strangest of tricks. But she felt disconcerted now, as well as ill.

With an effort she picked herself up and went back to bed.

7

SOFT MORNING SUNLIGHT creeping in at the gap in the curtains woke Esther. She came to slowly, stretching out her hand for Alain and encountering nothing but the expanse of rumpled sheet.

For a moment she felt bereft and ridiculously disappointed; then, as she smelled the soft crushed perfume of the flowers he had brought her, the happiness was back, suffusing her in a rosy glow. Last night they had been together again, as close as two people could be, and it had been wonderful. Beside that one fact the heartache of the past weeks and the still unresolved problems paled into insignificance.

She pushed aside the sheet and got out of bed, reaching for her cotton wrap. Then she padded barefoot across the stained-board floor, which was scattered with brightly patterned rugs, and drew back the curtains.

The view she had admired on her arrival was breathtaking in the freshness of morning – the village, with its mosaic of tiled roofs, nestling in the valley, and unspoiled countryside stretching away beyond it to the backdrop of the Pyrenees, mist-shrouded and mysterious. A wood pigeon clattered noisily from the trees beneath her balcony, wheeling clumsily away over the clustering branches, and the village clock began to strike the hour. Once again the sound of it called to her, awakening the same feeling of poignancy she had experienced yesterday, haunting as a forgotten dream.

She leaned on the balcony for a moment, testing out the unfamiliar emotions which filled her, then she turned back into the room, collecting her toilet bag and heading for the bathroom.

Someone was on the landing rummaging in a carved wooden chest which stood in an alcove and Esther recognised the tall spare figure of Alain's father.

In spite of the early hour he was immaculately dressed and his mane of snow-white hair was neatly brushed.

'Good morning,' she greeted him.

He straightened, a puzzled expression clouding his bright blue eyes. Then his mouth pinched, deepening the lines in his olive-skinned face, and his expression grew indignant and accusing.

'Who are you? What are you doing in my house?'

'I'm Esther – we met last night, don't you remember?' Esther said, taken aback by his hostile tone.

'I most certainly do not! How dare you wander about upstairs?'

'But I'm staying here!' Esther protested.

'Staying here, eh? That's what they all say! Well, I'm sorry, but it won't do. You'll have to go. This is private property, you know, and you are trespassing. Who are you, anyway? Not that I suppose you'll tell me. What are you doing in my house?'

Esther hesitated, wondering how to deal with this tirade. Pointless to simply answer him again – they were just going around in circles. But plainly Alain's father was distressed by her presence. She couldn't just ignore him – and in any case, he was barring her way to the bathroom. She decided to humour him.

'It's all right, monsieur. Don't be upset. I know this is your house. I'll go, I promise. Just let me past.'

For a moment his hawklike features softened and she saw the indecision in those very blue eyes. Then he drew himself up to his full height and took a step towards her.

'You think you can trick me, do you? Oh, I know you – don't think I don't know who you are! You're here to make mischief again, aren't you? You're here to upset my son! Well, I won't have it, do you hear?'

Esther was beginning to be alarmed. The gentle man whom she had met last night, who had kissed her on both cheeks in a traditional greeting, who had eaten his meal with scarcely a word and gone off to bed obedient as a child, seemed to have undergone a personality change, and she had no idea how to deal with it.

'Please, monsieur, don't be angry. I want to help . . .'

'Help? You?' He roared the words at her, glaring furiously. 'You won't help! You'll make matters worse! I know you of old! You are— '

'Father? What's the matter? What are you shouting about?' Alain called from the hall below.

He came up the stairs at a run and stared in dismay when he saw Esther.

'Father! You're not shouting at *Esther*, are you?'

'I'm afraid he was,' Esther said, embarrassed. 'He seemed to think I was a trespasser.'

'Father, really!'

'Oh, I don't know . . .' The old man looked confused now. His aggression had vanished and he resembled nothing so much as a guilty child. 'You shouldn't let them wander about up here, Charles,' he protested mildly.

'I'm not Charles, Father, I'm Alain. Charles is your brother – remember? And this is Esther. She is a friend, and I should think you frightened the life out of her with all that shouting.'

'I wasn't shouting!'

'Oh yes you were. Now, are you going to come down to breakfast? It's all ready, and I'm sure you are hungry.'

His face brightened. 'Breakfast? Oh yes! I'd like that!'

'Come along then.' Alain took his arm. 'I don't know what we are going to do with you, Father.' He glanced over his shoulder at Esther, shaking his head in perplexity. 'I'm sorry about all this, chérie.'

'It's all right.' Esther was overcome with pity, both for the confused man and those who had to cope with him. 'I'll be down as soon as I've dressed.'

'Don't hurry. There's nothing to spoil.'

He turned to smile at her. Her heart warmed and she continued her interrupted journey to the bathroom.

In the big sunny kitchen, Esther and Alain were lingering over breakfast. Isobelle and Henri had long since finished, leaving them alone, and Esther was enjoying the feeling of cosy domesticity which came from sharing the remains of the hot croissants and black cherry jam while making a fresh pot of coffee. But she couldn't quite ignore the pile of letters which Alain had brought in and dumped unopened on a corner of the dresser and which she suspected were his day's business mail.

'Are you sure I'm not keeping you from something you should be doing?' she asked.

'Sure.' His tone was clipped. 'Work can go hang today. Anyone who wants to threaten to sue me will have to wait until tomorrow to do it.'

For a moment she thought he was joking, then realised with a sense of shock that he was not.

'What are you talking about?' she asked, concerned. 'The business isn't in trouble, is it?'

He did not answer, simply picked up a spoon, turning it over and over between his fingers, but his expression, set and bleak, was reply enough.

'I don't understand,' she said. 'I thought you were doing so well.'

He put the spoon down with a clatter.

'I don't want to talk about it, Esther. I don't even want to think about it.' He looked up at her. 'What would you like to do today?'

'I don't know . . .' She couldn't think of anything but the bombshell he had just dropped. 'Alain – don't shut me out, please. Tell me what's wrong.'

He sighed, then shrugged impatiently.

'Oh, Thierry left a few problems, that's all. I expect I'll sort it out eventually.' But the weariness of his tone belied the confidence of his words. 'Look, I mean it, Esther. I do not want to worry about it today. This is the first time we've been together in weeks and you are on holiday. I thought I'd take you somewhere nice, so which would you prefer – countryside or sea?'

She tried to match his determined change of mood.

'Oh – the sea.'

'All right, the sea it is. I suggest Collioure. It's a fishing village set in a beautiful bay. And we can call in on Valerie on the way.'

Valerie. Alain's younger sister. Esther felt she almost knew Valerie already – Alain had often talked about her. He often talked about both his sisters, in fact, but Esther had the feeling that if Alain had a favourite, it was Valerie.

Valerie was, he had told her, widowed. She had married young – to a wealthy businessman who was many years her senior. The family, concerned by the age difference, had disapproved, but it had been a love match and against all their expectations, a very happy marriage. Valerie had been heartbroken when François had died suddenly of a massive heart attack. But at least he had left her well provided for. Valerie had inherited three houses, a small vineyard, stocks and shares in some of the best gold-chip investments and a healthy bank balance.

With no children ('I think my mother believes she is fated never to have grandchildren', Alain had said) and no need to work for a living, Valerie had been able to indulge her artistic talent. She painted – delicate ethereal watercolours which seemed almost to belong to a bygone age – flowers and butterflies and peaceful rural scenes, all in muted shades and with softly blurred focus. It was Valerie's dream that one day her paintings would be hung in exhibitions and galleries, but so far, though she sold the odd painting, success on such a grand scale had eluded her. And it probably always would, Alain had predicted. Her work was far too lacking in controversy to please the critics.

'We almost pass her door on the way to Collioure,' Alain said now. 'And I'd like you to meet her.'

Esther reached for the coffee pot.

'Are you sure she'll want to meet me?'

His eyes narrowed. 'What do you mean?'

She hesitated. 'Well, your mother doesn't approve of me being here, does she?' He began to protest, and she smiled wryly. 'Oh, she doesn't, Alain. Don't try to pretend otherwise.'

'What has she said?' he asked sharply.

'Nothing. She's been perfectly charming. But she doesn't need to say anything – I can feel what she's thinking, all right. Why should your sisters react any differently?'

'Oh Esther, if my mother has made you feel uncomfortable then I apologise on her behalf. But Valerie's not a bit like that. She's not one to judge – after all, she's quite unconventional herself.'

'Her painting, you mean?'

'Yes . . . and other things . . .'

'What other things?'

'Oh, she has some unusual ideas . . . and some of her friends are a bit on the odd side . . .' He gave a short embarrassed laugh and glanced at his watch. 'Perhaps we ought to think about making a move if we're to make the most of our day. And in any case, I'd like to get out of here before that damned phone starts ringing.'

Esther smiled. 'Ready when you are.'

But, though visiting relatives implied a pleasing permanence in their relationship, she couldn't help wishing they were simply going to spend the day alone.

The village where Valerie lived had been built on a mountainside. From a roundabout which was a floral masterpiece in shades of pink and mauve the the road wound upwards, past a parish church with its impressive tombs and obelisks to a mishmash of dwellings, very old and very picturesque. Narrow cobbled alleys branched away from the main street lined with terraces of ill-matched houses, some as many as three storeys tall, with flights of stone steps leading up to stable-style doors, others small and squat with cellars below ground level where the rubbish gathered in windswept mounds against the peeling paintwork. All had shuttered windows and the occasional balcony jutted from the bulging walls. Outside one a mangy dog stretched out in the sun, another was brightened by pots of dusty scarlet geraniums. High above the valley the road erupted into a small square where a postman sitting astride a motorised bicycle chatted to a wisened old woman outside what appeared to be a small shop, though no wares were visible beyond a stack of gas cannisters and a tray of fresh ripe peaches, and in one corner of the square a modern telephone booth jarred oddly against the ancient mellowed stone.

Alain drove slowly over the cobbles and selected a parking spot.

'We'll walk from here.'

The sun was already hot; as she got out of the car Esther felt it beating down on to her bare arms and legs. No wonder Alain was so tanned; she would have to be careful or she would burn before she realised it. She took his arm, loving the way it felt against her own, and quickening her step to keep up with his long strides.

Valerie's house stood on the corner of one of the streets which sloped away from the square, tall and narrow, reached by way of its own gate – something of a rarity here! – and a little path on each side of which marigolds and geraniums, big as small bushes, flourished.

Alain rang the bell, but there was no answering sound of life within the house.

'Perhaps she's out,' Esther suggested.

'I doubt it. She's probably in the garden painting.'

He rang the bell again and after a few moments the door was opened, not by Valerie, but by a man, barefoot and wearing only a pair of cut-off denim shorts which he was buckling at the waist with one hand.

'Oh, it's you.' His tone was offhand to the point of rudeness, and his eyes, an unusual shade of tawny brown, were dismissive and scornful.

'Yves! I didn't expect to find you here at this time of day,' Alain returned, equally coolly. 'I didn't think you got up until lunchtime.'

'I don't, unless I'm disturbed.' The implication was obvious – he had spent the night here. 'You want your sister, I presume.'

'That was the general idea, yes.' Alain was bristling, his antagonism almost tangible. 'Is she in?'

A young woman in a floral silk wrap appeared in the doorway behind the man. Her feet, too, were bare, and her long dark hair mussed into a cloud around an unmade-up face.

'Alain – what a nice surprise! I didn't expect to see you this morning!'

'That's obvious,' Alain said stiffly. 'I brought Esther to meet you, but if it's not a good time . . .'

'Oh don't be so stuffy, chérie! You sound like Father before he went gaga. Come in . . . don't mind the mess . . .'

She led the way into a bright chintzy room where the clutter of at least one day's living spread across the furniture like the flotsam left by an ebb tide. She gathered up a few magazines in an ineffectual attempt at tidying up, changed her mind and dumped them again on a low coffee table.

'So – you're Esther. It's lovely to meet you at last. I've heard such a lot about you.' Her smile was bright and welcoming without the slightest hint of censure. 'How about some coffee? Or lemonade, perhaps? I've got some freshly made in the fridge.'

'Lemonade would be lovely,' Esther agreed.

'Good.' Valerie fetched a glass jug covered with a small beaded cloth. 'We'll have it on the patio. Bring the glasses, will you, Alain? You know where they are.'

'You don't expect me to drink that stuff, do you?' Yves grumbled, throwing himself down on the cane sofa.

'No, darling, I don't. And I know your poor eyes can't take

the sun this early in the day. So you can stay here and read your paper in peace,' she returned sweetly.

The patio was an attractive paved area brightened by pots of begonias and yet more geraniums, and overlooked a sloping patch of orchard. From here, as from almost everywhere in the area, the Pyrenees dominated the horizon. As she crossed to the white-painted balcony to enjoy the view Esther heard Alain hiss at his sister, 'What's *he* doing here?'

'Yves? What do you mean, what is he doing here?'

'Well – is he staying? He hasn't moved in, has he?'

'I don't know,' she said carelessly. 'One never does with Yves.'

Alain shook his head, his disapproval apparent.

'Well, it's up to you, I suppose.'

'That's right, it is.' She smiled at Esther. Come and have your lemonade and tell me what you think of Languedoc.'

'Sunny,' Esther said, joining them at the patio table. 'Although it was actually quite hot in England when I left. It will probably be dreadful when I get home – I expect I shall have missed the only two weeks of summer.'

'So she's making the most of it,' Alain said. 'We're on our way to Collioure. Your favourite bay.'

'Collioure! Oh yes, it's wonderful. You'll love it, Esther.'

They chatted for a while longer, then Alain got up.

'We'd better be going.'

'Yes, you want to catch the best of the day . . .' But Valerie sounded regretful.

They went back into the house. Yves was still sprawled on the sofa, flicking through a newspaper. A glass containing what looked suspiciously like whisky stood at his elbow. Alain passed him without so much as a glance in his direction.

'How's business then?' Yves asked. From his tone it was obvious he knew things were far from good and was enjoying the fact.

'Oh, ticking along,' Alain replied shortly.

'Missing Thierry, are you? No, I suppose not. He's no great loss, is he?'

'Yves! That's not a very nice thing to say!' Valerie chided him. 'I thought Thierry was a friend of yours.'

Yves snorted derisively and returned to his newspaper.

At the door Valerie kissed both Alain and Esther.

'I'm so glad you came to see me. Are you going to see Simone?'

'Not today. She'll be working.'

'We must have a get-together, all of us. Come for drinks. I've found the most wonderful new aperitif. If I drink the lot myself I'll end up with liver failure.'

'I'm sure Yves will help you out with it,' Alain said drily. 'In any case, you should come to us. You haven't been to see Papa for ages.'

'I know.' Valerie pulled a guilty face. 'I will come, Alain, honestly. This evening, perhaps.'

'Do, Valerie. In his condition . . .'

'Yes, yes – there's no need to go on about it.' She waved them goodbye, then went back into the house and closed the door.

'Well,' Yves drawled from the depths of the sofa. 'So Alain has found someone else! There's a turn-up for the book.'

She crossed to the window and perched on the ledge beneath it.

'What did you think of her?'

'Esther? Very tasty.'

'Oh, you've got a one-track mind! Well, I thought she was nice. But I don't suppose Hélène will think so. She's not going to be very happy about it, is she?'

'If you ask me, she'll put up quite a fight.' Yves tossed his paper aside without bothering to refold it. 'And I wouldn't want to put money on which of them will win, either. Esther might look the favourite at the moment but Hélène is a dark horse with a lot of staying power. With odds like that it would be all too easy to lose your shirt.'

'And you should know all about that!'

'Did I hear you telling Alain you'd go over to Le Château Gris this evening?' he asked.

She sighed. 'Yes, and I'm not looking forward to it. Do you think Simone would come with me? She's very good with Papa.'

'Surely you don't need Simone to hold your hand?'

'Of course not!' It was too close to the truth for comfort. 'But Simone hasn't met Esther yet – it would give her the chance. I think I'll give her a ring later on.' She got up. 'Do you want something to eat?'

'No.'

'Neither do I. I think I'll go and do some painting. Unless, of course, you have other ideas.'

As she passed him he reached for her, pulling her down into his lap.

'Now what would make you think I might have?'

She giggled.

'Because, Yves Marssac, you always do!'

8

SIMONE HEADED HER ancient Citroën north, sitting resolutely in the inside lane, refusing to dice with the lorries ferrying fish and fruit inland from the balmy Mediterranean coast and wondering what on earth had possessed her to make this journey today.

For one thing she should be working, trying to make up some of the time she had lost over the last weeks; for another she really did not feel at all well. It wasn't anything she could put her finger on, just a general malaise, as if she were sickening for something, or had been very ill and was just beginning to get over it. Perhaps she had picked up a bug, she thought. Certainly last night she had felt very peculiar and the vivid unsettling dream with its overtones of delirium seemed to point to that too. At least this morning she just felt weak with a slight lingering headache, but she hadn't been able to bring herself to work, and instead she had given into the overwhelming compulsion to go to Carcassonne, the setting for last night's dream.

Chugging along the road that ran parallel to the coast, Simone thought how odd it was that every detail was still etched so clearly in her mind. Usually dreams faded to a blur with the coming of morning, leaving nothing but disjointed fragments and a lingering aura. But this one was still startlingly real to her.

Once, during the night, she had even thought it was going to begin again. After going back to bed she had tossed and turned, dozing, waking uncomfortably hot and sticky, dozing again, and in one of those interludes between sleeping and waking she had thought she heard the sound of wailing, the sort of wailing which had once been customary when someone had died, and glimpsed again the rough stone wall of the cottage and the shadowy figures. But they had slipped away from her and, peaceful at last, she had fallen into a deep sleep, which had lasted until morning.

The feeling of unreality was still with her now, however, as she drove, following the coast road northward, and the name of the woman in the dream – the woman she had seemed to become – repeated itself over and over inside her head like a mantra.

Helis Marty.

Carcassonne dreamed in the hot June sunshine. Simone found a parking space and walked up the steep rise towards the ancient fortress. Outside the city walls a children's merry-go-round tinkled Victorian fairground music and tourists milled about or sat in the shade of the dry moat eating ice creams.

Simone went in through the entrance beneath the great portcullis, past the stalls of the official tour guides, and into the narrow cobbled streets. These streets were lined now with souvenir shops, and bistros and *crêpéries* spilled plastic furniture and brightly coloured sunshades into the ancient squares, yet somehow the spirit of the place remained, every stone so steeped in history that it survived in spite of the garish modern-day trappings of the tourist trade which had been foisted upon it.

She wandered through the winding alleyways to the church – the Eglise St Nazaire – and stood for a few minutes in the cool gloom looking at the tomb of Simon de Montfort. Then she lit a candle to the Blessed Virgin before making her way back into the sunlight.

It was lunchtime; the cafés and bistros were busy. Simone selected one, ordered a lemon pancake and sat down at a table shaded by an umbrella to watch the world go by. She was beginning to feel very distant again, and the thronging crowds had the aura of unreality. Making the long journey had been a mistake – she knew that now. She was going to have to drive all the way home again and she didn't know how she was going to manage it. Just at the moment she couldn't summon up the energy to move so much as a muscle.

She slumped in her chair, looking down the narrow cobbled way which led out of the square. No sun there – the tall buildings that lined it on either side cast it into deep shadow – yet the air seemed to shimmer with heat haze. Simone blinked and for a moment her vision cleared, then the shimmer was back, a kaleidoscope of dancing molecules which seemed to obscure the postcard stands and the dump bins of Carcassonne pens and

Carcassonne badges. Even the tourists idling along the street seemed to be swallowed up in it, as a sea mist rolling in blots out everything in its path.

The molecules danced again, rearranging themselves. And then, quite suddenly, she saw them – shadowy at first, ethereal ghosts materialising from the mist and gradually taking on substance – the girl in the rough brown gown holding the hand of the little boy with flaming red hair and leading him up the cobbled street. The children from her dream! Here – now! Simone caught her breath in surprise, and, as she did so, she heard the little girl's voice.

'Come on, Pons, don't drag your feet so! We'll never get anywhere.'

The boy looked up at her tearfully, rubbing his face with a grimy hand.

'I'm hungry!' he wailed.

'I know you are. So am I. Crying won't help.'

'But I want to go home!'

'You know we can't.'

'Mother . . . I want Mother . . .'

'Oh Pons, stop it! Be a good boy for me, please!' She tugged at his hand again, close to tears herself.

It was five days now since Helis had died, slipping into a coma from which she had failed to wake, and still the siege continued.

The noise of the battle was at the city walls now. Stones from the trebuchets – the giant catapults – thudded into the ramparts and the steady onslaught of the men working beneath their cowhide-covered chariots to weaken the foundations rumbled like thunder. From the battlements the defenders rained down logs and fire, but even as they did so they knew that it was hopeless. With little food and water to be shared among the thousands who had crowded into the city, and with the fever spreading like wildfire through the sewage-ridden streets, weakening and killing even the strongest of them, how could they possibly hold out for much longer?

But what was the alternative? Surrender would, they feared, mean one thing and one thing only: another massacre as bloody as the one at Béziers.

For Pons's sake Jeanne had tried very hard to be brave.

But it wasn't easy, and, dearly as she loved him, his constant whimpering only made things worse. He had refused to leave her side for even a moment since Helis had died. Now, Jeanne feared that with him slowing her down she would never be able to find the water and scraps of food she had left the *ostal* to search for.

'Would you like me to take you to Guillemette for a little while?' she suggested. 'She'll look after you.'

Instantly Pons brightened. He liked Guillemette, who had always been kind to him. He did not notice the shrewish voice which so irritated Jeanne; he only knew that he felt safe with the woman who had been a part of the old carefree life.

Guillemette was standing in the doorway of the *ostal* where she had lodging. When he saw her, Pons ran to her, burying his face in her skirts.

'Hello, my lamb,' she greeted him.

'Can Pons stay with you while I go for food and water?' Jeanne asked. 'I won't be long. But he holds me up so.'

Guillemette nodded. 'Take as long as you like. He'll be all right with me.'

'He keeps crying and saying he's hungry.'

'Aren't we all? But I have high hopes the siege isn't going to go on much longer. I was talking to a man just now who says that Raymond Roger has gone to the crusaders' camp to negotiate a truce.'

'A truce?' Jeanne wasn't sure what that was.

'He's going to try to make peace. The Blessed Virgin alone knows what terms Montfort will demand, but we can't go on like this much longer. If Raymond Roger succeeds, some of us, at least, will be able to leave the city.'

Jeanne felt a thrill of fear. All very well for Guillemette to be optimistic – she was not a Cathar but a Catholic.

'Off you go, then, child!' Guillemette said and Jeanne guessed she was impatient to have Pons to herself. Guillemette had no children of her own; Jeanne had once heard her mother say that Guillemette was barren.

She started down the winding cobbled street, heading for the Count's Castle. Sometimes scraps left over from the nobleman's table were brought out to the hungry people. Without much hope, Jeanne sat down in a doorway to wait. She had heard that there was scarcely enough food now to go around even in the castle and the leavings were likely to be more meagre than ever.

The sun was hot, and, tired out by her restless nights on the hard floor of the *ostal*, Jeanne began to feel sleepy. Desperately she tried to force herself to stay awake. She didn't want to miss out on the scraps when – if! – they came. But despite her efforts her chin drooped on to her chest and Jeanne dozed.

The clatter of horses' hooves on the cobbles disturbed Jeanne and she started, opening her eyes. Soldiers were riding through the streets – not Raymond Roger's troops, but men wearing the cross of the crusades! Instantly she was wide awake and trembling with fear. What were the crusaders doing inside the city?

Terrified, she watched as the crusaders clattered past, their swords drawn. They were going into the Count's castle and the guards were doing nothing to stop them! Sancta Maria, what was happening? She waited, hardly daring to breathe, and after a little while the nobility began streaming out, the knights and older men clad only in their shirts and breeches, the ladies and damsels falling over their trailing skirts in their haste.

Jeanne grabbed the arm of an elderly village man standing near by.

'What's going on?'

'The Count has surrendered. We are all to leave the city and take nothing with us. But at least we won't be massacred like those poor souls at Béziers.' He crossed himself and Jeanne realised that unlike her he was a Catholic. So – the Catholics were to be spared. But what of the Cathars in their midst? What of the likes of her and Pons?

Pons! Jeanne's heart came into her mouth with a sickening thud. She must get back to Pons! She should never have left him for so long!

She gathered up her skirts and began to run up the winding street, weaving her way through the thronging crowds. Her heart was beating a tattoo and her breath came in harsh tearing sobs.

The planks that provided a rough door at the *ostal* where Guillemette had lodgings had been drawn aside. Jeanne darted in, then stopped, staring around in bewilderment. Where was everyone? She dashed through the *ostal*, calling their names, then ran back outside. For all the people hurrying hither and thither she could not see one face she recognised, and the cottage next door was empty, too, though belongings were still scattered about as if the occupants had left in haste.

Sobbing and breathless, she made her way to the *ostal* where she and Pons had been staying. Perhaps Guillemette had taken him back there. But their *ostal* too was deserted. Once more she ran out into the street, once more she was buffeted by total strangers.

A crusader on horseback was cantering down the street, the crowds drawing back to let him through, but Jeanne, overcome with panic, scarcely noticed him. She darted blindly out, almost under the flying hooves, and as the crusader reined in with an oath someone reached out and dragged her from the horse's path.

'What are you trying to do, child – kill yourself?' the crusader bellowed at her. 'Get going! Follow the others!'

An elderly woman took Jeanne's arm. She had a wisened face, leathery and lined from sixty or more years of Languedoc sun, but her eyes were kindly.

'Don't be frightened. Just do as he says.'

'I can't! I can't!'

'You have to. If we leave the city they won't harm us. That's the promise. But you can't stay here. De Montfort is going to make Carcassonne his headquarters.'

'But . . .' Jeanne was almost beyond words.

'Where's your mother?' the old woman asked.

'I haven't got a mother. She's dead.' Jeanne could feel the tears welling up in her eyes. 'And I can't find my little brother. I don't know what's happened to him.'

'He's safe, I'm sure,' the woman comforted her. 'Nobody has been harmed.'

'But I must find him!'

'He's not here, my dear. The people are all leaving. You come with me. You'll find him later.'

Jeanne allowed herself to be propelled along the street. As the procession made its way towards the city gates she still looked around frantically but with hope fading. She would never find Pons in this crowd – never! He must have left with Guillemette, but where had they gone?

As they passed through the city gates into the charred ruins which had once been the suburbs a fresh wave of horror washed over Jeanne. There was nothing left now of the *ostal* which had once been her home – nothing but blackened ruins.

'Where are we going?' she whispered.

'I don't know, my dear. We'll find shelter somewhere.'

Down the hillside, baking in the heat of the sun, through the bristly *garrigue*, into the shelter of a small wood. Jeanne glanced behind her in desperation, saw the procession splitting and going in different directions and made up her mind. If she simply went on with this kindly woman she would never find Pons. At least if she stayed near the place where she had last seen him there was a chance. It was a vain hope, she knew, but it was all she had left, and Jeanne was almost beyond reasoning.

As the woman let go her arm to negotiate a bramble, she took her chance, darting away. The woman called to her but she ran on, her skirts catching on the undergrowth. She would stay here, hidden in the thicket. At least then she could watch the column of refugees as they passed and she might catch sight of Pons among them. Or Guillemette might return this way, looking for her.

Shaking, bewildered, frightened out of her wits and half crazy with despair, Jeanne crouched out of sight in the bushes.

At daybreak on the day after Carcassonne had surrendered Philip Bertrand saddled up his horse and rode out of the city with a handful of men-at-arms.

Early sun glinted on his helmet and chain mail and the red cross of the crusader stood out boldly against the battle-stained white of his tunic. But Philip could no longer feel pride in the wearing of it. In the six short weeks since he had ridden with Count Raymond of Toulouse to join the crusade he felt he had aged thirty years, for the high ideals with which he had set out had been burned with the heretics and the Catholic townsfolk in the Church of the Madeleine at Béziers.

God's teeth! How could they have done such a terrible thing? Philip had asked himself over and over again as he lay, exhausted from the fighting, yet with sleep eluding him, in his tent. He could scarcely believe that the outrage had been committed in the name of the Catholic Church, still less that he had been a party to it. But it had – and he was. There had been no choice. Abbé Arnaud-Amalric had decreed 'Kill them all' and the vagabonds and mercenaries who made up the bulk of de Montfort's army had been only too ready to comply. He had watched the massacre and felt his stomach turn. This was not what he had joined the crusade for, this vicious and merciless annihilation of helpless people, guilty and innocent alike.

As a staunch Catholic he had longed to be old enough to fight for God and the King in the Holy Wars. He had been raised on the tales of the chivalry and valour of his grandfather, who had fought with King Louis VII in the Second Crusade against the infidel, the Muslims who threatened the Holy Lands. But never for one moment had he envisaged that for him a crusade would mean participating in the senseless slaughter of his own people.

Philip Bertrand's home was in the plain of Toulouse to the north of the region in which he now found himself. He was the third son of a nobleman, and there had been other reasons besides his desire to fight in the name of Christ which had tempted him to join the crusade. As one of a large family he had little prospect of inheriting lands of his own, for the laws of the south decreed that his father's estates should be divided equally among his heirs. Philip was ambitious and the King had promised the grant of lands and titles to those who joined the noble cause. To this bribe the church had added its own inducement – absolution from mortal sin to any knight who gave of his services for forty days. Philip was a young man of normal healthy appetites, which had caused him to find himself in the confessional on more than one occasion, and the prospect of absolution had been attractive to him.

But how, he asked himself now, could he justify the terrible events in which he had participated? How could wholesale slaughter secure the redemption of his immortal soul? And how could he ever take advantage of lands granted to him as a result of deeds that sickened him? It was one thing to fight the infidel cleanly and bravely, quite another to stand by and see Catholic priests cut down with the sacrament in their hands and watch innocent women and children burned to death in the sanctuary of a Christian church.

After Béziers Philip had had no more stomach for the fight but his forty days were not yet up. He had followed Simon de Montfort to Carcassonne because there was nothing else he could do, and he had been glad of every moment's delay when the crusaders' progress was hampered by the lesser nobles who came to meet them to pay homage and avow their allegiance to the cause. At least the massacre of Béziers had achieved something, he conceded. Men who would otherwise have fought de Montfort's army had realised the consequences of resistance and capitulated readily, thus preventing more gratuitous loss of life. But still he could not find it in himself to see what had happened as anything but an outrage. And he was determined that whatever lands might be offered to him he would not take them, stained as they were with the blood of his fellow countrymen.

Philip had feared the massacre at Béziers would be repeated at Carcassonne, but thankfully that had not happened. The siege had ended peacefully, with Count Raymond Roger surrendering himself into the hands of Simon de Montfort. Philip suspected Raymond Roger had been double-crossed – he would never have willingly entered the crusaders' camp to treaty if he had suspected he would be taken prisoner – but at least it had meant that the lives of the people of Carcassonne had been spared. Left leaderless, the garrison had opened the gates to de Montfort who, not wishing to see the mighty city which he wanted for his own reduced to ashes, had simply driven out all those sheltering within and installed himself in the count's castle.

Philip had little sympathy with Raymond Roger. Whatever difficulty he now found himself in he had brought upon himself by giving safe haven to the heretics. But for all that Philip had had enough of fighting his own countrymen. The forty days he had promised to the Pope and the church had elapsed; now, with the mission completed, he was going home.

A glorious sense of relief filled Philip as he urged his horse down the hillside, leaving behind the walled city and the charred ruins of the suburbs.

The path through the *garrigue* gave way to thicket; quite suddenly the scorching heat of the sun was shut out by the branches of trees, growing closely together, and he slowed his horse to a walk as he picked his way through the thick undergrowth. He was alert now, and watchful, all too aware that the thicket could provide cover for the enemy if any of them had remained in the area. The knights who had been driven out of the city had, of course, been disarmed, but Philip knew that countryfolk could sometimes be dangerously cunning, and he told himself he must be careful. A handful of crusaders on unfamiliar ground would be an easy target, and the people of Languedoc had much they would wish to avenge.

Even as the thought crossed his mind the quiet was shattered by the cracking of a twig, followed by the noisy rustling of the bushes as a startled bird took flight. Instantly Philip was bolt upright in the saddle, looking around him sharply.

Someone was there – he was certain of it. Though all was quiet again, he could almost feel eyes watching him and hear hushed breathing with the ears of his mind. Philip's hand closed over the hilt of his sword.

'Who's there?' he called out. 'Show yourself, you coward!'

Another bird flew, rattling the branches, but the bushes were still. Philip hesitated, unwilling to turn his back on whoever, or whatever, was hiding there watching him. He did not want an arrow between his shoulder blades. He could be mistaken, of course. Perhaps it was the thickness of the trees all around making him nervous. He was about to motion his men to ride on when the undergrowth rustled again, faintly yet unmistakably. Philip turned towards the sound, sword drawn, and as he did so a figure broke cover with such suddenness that his horse shied.

The figure was a child, a girl of eight or nine years old, in peasant garb. She stood for a moment, staring in terror, trapped between the thick bushes and the rearing horse, then darted away, plunging through the ferns and down the forest path. For no good reason, Philip went after her. She ran swiftly, her feet flying over the rough ground, but he caught up with her easily, cutting her off. Again she darted into the thicket, but this time her toe caught in a bramble and she stumbled and fell headlong.

As he reined in his horse, she scrambled into a hunched position, looking up at him fearfully but with a touch of defiance. Her hair, he noticed, was tangled and matted with burrs and twigs, her thin face stained with the juice of wild berries. But besides being dishevelled she also looked ill. Her cheeks were flushed, her eyes unnaturally bright.

'Are you alone?'

The question was a defensive one: for all he knew there might be other refugees hiding out here in the woods, who would pose a far greater threat to him than a small defenceless girl.

She nodded, then quickly shook her head, as if realising that to admit to being alone rendered her vulnerable, but somehow he was inclined to believe her first unconsidered response. Besides, the thicket *felt* deserted but for the two of them. No sense now of unseen eyes watching him, only the eyes of the child, round and frightened, fixed on his face.

'Don't be afraid,' he said. 'I won't hurt you.'

Still she shrank away and he realised that if she had heard the stories of what his fellow crusaders had done he must seem to her to be a monster in human form.

'Are you from Carcassonne?' he asked.

She nodded again, an almost imperceptible jerk of her head, and her matted hair fell across her flushed face. It was an unusual shade of dark reddish brown and her frightened eyes were a very deep blue, the colour of the sky at twilight.

'Where are your mother and father?' he asked.

She did not answer, but he saw her lip quiver before she caught it swiftly between her teeth.

'Aren't you with them?'

Her head went back; she dashed a thin brown hand across her mouth.

'God's teeth!' he expostulated, irritated because his awareness of his own possible danger was being overtaken by concern for this frightened child. 'Haven't you got a home to go to?'

'No!' she burst out suddenly in a voice that sounded hoarse and rasping. 'You burned it. My mother and father are dead and I can't find my little brother. I hate you! I hate you all!'

He stared at her, shocked into the realisation that for some the absence of killing at Carcassonne had been scant comfort.

'What's your name?' he asked, more gently.

'Jeanne Marty. You . . . you haven't seen Pons, have you? He's four years old, with red hair and— ' She broke off, as if realising the impossibility of her question.

'No,' he said. 'I haven't seen him.'

'He was with Guillemette. I don't know where they've gone.' A solitary tear rolled down her nose.

Pity filled him, and a sense of shame knowing that it was he and his fellow crusaders who were responsible for the child's plight.

'There must be someone you can go to!' he said angrily.

She straightened her shoulders.

'There isn't, but why should you care?'

He could not answer that, could not explain that his concern was common humanity mingled with guilt. How many innocent people were homeless and bereft as a result of this wretched crusade? How many, like this child, were orphaned and alone? He looked at her helplessly, wondering what to do. He could not restore her parents to her or find her brother, who might be anywhere the refugees had scattered. He couldn't rebuild her home from the ashes or put her shattered life together again. But he could not leave her here either, lost, frightened, with no food save the berries on the trees, no shelter, no human company.

Philip hesitated for only a few moments, then he reached down, stretching out his hand to her.

'Come on, I'll give you a ride.'

She cowered away.

'Don't come near me! Don't touch me!'

'I won't harm you. Come on.'

She looked around wildly as if about to flee again, then suddenly all the fight seemed to go out of her. He saw her sway, saw her eyelids hood over her too-bright eyes. As her legs gave way beneath her he leaned down, grabbing her thin arm and, with a sure movement born of long practice in the tilt-yard, hoisting her into the saddle in front of him. Her head lolled forward, revealing a sheen of perspiration on the nape of her neck.

'You can't stay here,' he said aloud, though he knew she could not hear him.

He touched the horse's sides with his spurs. As he regained the path the men-at-arms eyed him with curiosity and he shrugged impatiently.

'She's sick from hunger and exhaustion.'

'But what will you do with her?' the oldest of the men-at-arms asked gruffly. 'We can't take her to a settlement. For all we know she could be the bait for a trap.'

'I know that. But if we leave her here she will surely die.' Philip turned his horse. 'Ride on!'

They looked at him as if he were mad. And perhaps he was, Philip thought. He only knew that if he left her here, alone in the woods, with Montfort's blood-crazed armies roaming the countryside, he would have her on his conscience for ever. There was nothing else for it. He was going home – and he was going to take the child with him.

* * *

Someone was speaking, someone not in the vision, but close by.

'Mam'selle! Your crêpe, Mam'selle!'

The scene was fading, changing again from thick wooded country to the busy square, with its plastic tables and brightly coloured sunshades. Simone looked up and saw the waiter, jeans-clad, with a tea towel tied apron-fashion around his waist, standing beside her.

'Oh yes – thank you . . .'

He set down the plate on the table and stood waiting. In a daze Simone fumbled in her bag for money to pay him.

She couldn't believe what had happened. She must have dozed off, of course, but to have continued with last night's dream . . . She couldn't remember such a thing ever having happened to her before. And once again it had been so vivid, so detailed! Only one thing was different. Last night it had been as if she had actually been Helis Marty, the woman who had died of the fever. This time she had felt oddly detached, an onlooker. She hadn't actually identified with any of the people. And yet she had been there. From some vantage point she had followed the child, Jeanne, and shared in her agony.

Simone pressed her fingers to her lips. They were trembling.

What on earth was the matter with her? Was she having some kind of breakdown – escaping into a fantasy world?

You are being quite ridiculous! Simone scolded herself. And falling asleep at a restaurant table in the middle of the day is more indicative of physical illness than mental.

Though she was no longer hungry she managed to eat the pancake but decided against following it with anything else. Suddenly she was very anxious to get home. There was something very claustrophobic now about the centuries-old fortress, as if the smells and the noise and the fear of her dream hung in a cloud over the sunwarmed stones. More than anything in the world she wanted the comfort and security of her own four walls around her. More than anything she wanted to get away from Carcassonne.

9

HÉLÈNE WAS CRYING.

She sat on the bed in the room that had been Thierry's, surrounded by his possessions, which she had spread out around her. In her lap lay a pile of photographs: Thierry with his friends, laughing, glasses raised in a toast, Thierry with a pretty girl on each arm, Thierry in the driver's seat of his beloved car – the one in which he had crashed to his death. He looked handsome and totally carefree.

Oh Thierry, why did you have to die? Hélène wept.

She lifted a jersey from the pile of clothes beside her and buried her face in it, trying to recapture the essence of him from the soft cashmere to which the scent of his toilet water still clung faintly.

He had been her only brother and she had loved him so much! Oh, he had been wild, yes, especially in his youth. He had not always done the things he should have done and very often he had done all kinds of things he should not have done, but that made no difference to her feelings for him. If anything it had only made her love him more. When others were angry with him for his fecklessness she had felt that she alone understood him and accepted him for what he was. And he had understood her and been there for her. In the terrible dark days after their mother had died, whenever her fear and grief threatened to overwhelm her, he had been there. 'We'll be all right,' he had said. 'I'll look after you.' And he had. When the black moods came it was Thierry alone who could tease and cajole her out of them. Not even Alain had understood her as he did. For Thierry was her own flesh and blood. However infuriating she might be – and Hélène knew she could be infuriating – Thierry had never judged her. She was always certain of his unconditional love and support.

Now he was gone. Never again would she hear his laughter, never again be able to turn to him for comfort in the bad times or share her happiness when things were going well, never giggle over shared memories of childhood pranks. The realisation was almost more than she could bear.

And just to make things worse the hope of getting Alain back was fading. Only yesterday she had been so optimistic, so determined. It had taken all her courage to deliberately turn off the electricity and go to Le Château Gris to ask for his help, but for a little while she had thought it was worth it. She had been so sure, when they had talked, that whatever he might say, he still cared for her. But he had seen through what she had done. 'The switch was tripped,' he had said. 'It's never done that before, has it?' 'I don't think so,' she had said, but she had felt the guilty colour rush into her cheeks, and she had known he had guessed the truth. He had become very cold, then, very angry, and nothing she could say got through to him.

The depression that had plagued her since her childhood, but which seemed to be much worse lately, had begun then. It closed in around her, a thick impenetrable cloud darker even than her grief and more frightening. At least grief was understandable, not like those other suffocating emotions that made her feel she was losing her mind. But it was terrible, nonetheless. The same overwhelming sense of helpless loss she remembered from her childhood, when her mother had died. Only worse. Then, she had at least had Thierry. Now she had no one.

Hélène gathered the photographs together and put them back in their envelope. Then, still clutching the cashmere jersey, she began to wander round the room, touching Thierry's scattered belongings with reverence while the tears gathered in her eyes and slid down her cheeks.

Sometime she would have to clear the room and dispose of his things, she supposed, but not yet . . . not yet. So far she had not even allowed Francine, the daily woman, to strip the sheets from the bed. Thierry had slept in them; when they had been laundered something else of him would be gone for ever. Besides, Thierry had refused to allow Francine into his room when he was alive; to ask her to attend to it now, when he was dead, would be the final betrayal.

Hélène ran her fingers along the books on the shelf above the bed, pulling one out and opening it at random. A paperback spy story – typical of Thierry's unsophisticated taste. She read a couple of paragraphs, then the words were blurring before her eyes and she replaced it on the shelf, tucking it neatly into line.

Thierry's desk stood in front of the window – a small oak bureau with pigeonholes and drawers of differing shapes and sizes. When he had moved in, Hélène had suggested the desk could go in one of the downstairs rooms, but Thierry had preferred to squash it into his bedroom – further evidence of his desire for privacy. Not that he had conducted company business from here, apart from the odd piece of work he had brought home with him, and Hélène had wondered sometimes why he had the desk at all. But then, Thierry had been something of a play-actor; perhaps to him the desk had been a piece of set dressing, representing an integral part of one of his fantasies.

Sorting out the desk was another task she was not looking forward to. She had already leafed through the papers that lay beneath heavy glass weights in the main compartment and found nothing of any great interest. But there were still the drawers, one of them locked, and the pigeonholes, to be gone through. To Hélène it seemed akin to rifling the pockets of a corpse, intrusive and somehow obscene. But sooner or later she – or someone else – was going to have to do it. Hélène wanted it to be someone else even less than she wanted to do it herself. At least if she came across anything which she felt Thierry would not want the world to see she could destroy it and no one would be any the wiser.

On the window ledge beside the desk was a box file, slightly battered, the title sheet on the spine grubby but unlabelled. Hélène took it over to the bed and sat down to open it.

Apart from Thierry's passport, which lay on top, the documents inside looked almost as frowsty as the file itself – dog-eared papers dating back many years. But, buried among the yellowing papers was a printed will form, filled out in ink, which looked much newer. Hélène examined it, and gasped. Thierry's name on the form . . . Thierry's will! She could scarcely believe it. She hadn't known he had made a will – in fact he had always joked that since he had nothing to leave there was no point in doing so – and obviously he had not been to a solicitor. This was a do-it-yourself document. Hélène began to read and as she did so her eyes filled with tears once more. Thierry had left everything to her. Except, of course, that there was nothing to leave.

Or was there? Attached to the will with a paperclip was a manila envelope. Hélène opened it and slid out what appeared to be an insurance policy. As she scanned the legally couched phrases her eyes widened. Unless she was mistaken, Thierry had insured his life in the sum of five hundred thousand francs!

Trembling a little now, Hélène read and reread both the will and the insurance policy. She was stunned; he had never mentioned any of this to her and she had had no idea the documents existed. But the will was legally signed, though the names of the witnesses meant nothing to Hélène, and, like the insurance policy, bore a date immediately following the break-up of her marriage.

Oh Thierry! Hélène whispered, beginning to understand.

He must have been more concerned for her than he had ever admitted; feeling she could no longer rely on Alain for her security, he had insured his own life and made certain that she would be the one to benefit should anything happen to him. But why hadn't he told her about it? It was possible he had thought it would upset her, of course – and so it would have done. But why hadn't he gone to a solicitor? Why had he kept it all secret? It didn't make sense. But it was very typical of Thierry and his way of doing things. He distrusted lawyers – perhaps because his rackety lifestyle had brought him into contact with so many crooked ones – and he liked to play his cards close to his chest. And of course, it would never have occurred to him that he had so little time left.

How could people ever have seen him as all bad? Hélène wondered. This proved how thoughtful and caring he could be. He had wanted to make sure she was provided for, and in so doing he had made her a rich woman.

She froze suddenly as the enormity of her inheritance got through to her. Five hundred thousand francs! A small fortune! Enough to clear all Alain's debts and put the business back on its feet! She'd phone him right away and tell him. He'd be so relieved!

She ran downstairs, then with her hand on telephone she stopped suddenly. In her excitement she had quite forgotten about Esther. Alain was with Esther now. It was Esther, not she, who would sink or swim along with Alain. A hard knub of jealousy and hatred formed in Hélène's throat. She would willingly give Alain every penny she had if it would make him happy. But not . . . *that woman*. Why should she benefit from Thierry's bequest?

For long moments Hélène stood motionless, torn between wanting to tell Alain this very moment that she had the wherewithal to save his business and reluctance to share any of it with him while he was with Esther. Then a thought occurred to her, a germ of an idea which blossomed and grew as she examined it.

Could she not use the money as a weapon in her fight to get him back? Not a very nice thing to do perhaps – but she was past caring about such niceties. And how to do it? She couldn't come right out and bribe him. She just couldn't *do* that – and besides, however much Alain might want the money to save his beloved business, his pride would never allow him to agree. But supposing he were to find out by accident – supposing he didn't even know she knew about the money – then it would give him the chance to pretend *he* didn't know either. That way they would both get what they wanted without any loss of face.

It was a risk, of course. Alain might choose to remain with Esther even if it meant financial ruin for him. And if it came to that, Hélène supposed she would use the money to bail him out anyway. The mess he was in was, after all, of Thierry's making, and in any case she loved Alain too much to want to see him ruined.

But first she was going to try to make the situation work for her.

Hélène went back upstairs and slipped the documents back into the box file with Thierry's passport on top of them.

She knew exactly what she was going to do.

The first thing Esther and Alain saw as they turned into the drive of Le Château Gris was Hélène's car, parked on the broad gravel turnaround outside the house.

They had spent a wonderful day at Collioure, an idyllic fishing village where high cliffs encompassed a bay which sparkled in the sunshine. With the fishing boats drawn up on the beach and the artists at work in cool shady spots along the harbour walls,

Collioure had reminded Esther of St Ives, Cornwall – except that this was unmistakably the Mediterranean.

They had wandered hand in hand through the narrow streets and then picnicked on crusty bread and cheese, huge juicy peaches and a bottle of local wine which they bought at one of the little open-fronted shops on the waterfront. It had all been perfect. But now Esther looked at the little Renault gleaming in the afternoon sun and felt her heart sink.

Hélène and Isobelle were in the drawing room. On a small table between them were teacups and a plate of biscuits and small fancy cakes.

'Ah – Alain. I'm glad you're home. Hélène is here,' Isobelle said, rather unnecessarily.

'I can see that, Maman.' Alain's tone was short. 'There's not some other problem, I hope, Hélène.'

'No, I brought you something, that's all – a box file I found in Thierry's room. I thought there might be something in it you might need.'

There was something different about her this afternoon, Esther thought. Still fragile, still vulnerable, yet at the same time more self-possessed, more positive. The combination was oddly attractive – even Esther, resenting her, felt it, and she realised with a pang how much more potent the effect would be on Alain. Already she could sense he was softening towards Hélène.

'You mean it's business papers.'

'I think so. I haven't been through it – I couldn't bring myself to – but that's what it looks like.'

'Well, anything that can throw light on what's been going on in my absence would be helpful,' Alain said. 'Thank you, Hélène.'

She smiled briefly.

'I won't say it's a pleasure. But you know what I mean. If I can do anything to help sort things out you know I will. I feel dreadful that Thierry has left you in this mess. I just can't understand it. I'm sure there must have been a reason . . .'

'Oh I'm sure there was,' Alain said drily.

Hélène flushed slightly.

'I know it's stupid, but I almost feel responsible. After all, he was my brother . . .'

'Hélène, whatever Thierry did was not your fault. I'm the one who made him a partner in the business. I have only myself to blame.'

'But I can't help feeling you did it because he was my brother.'

'Oh come on, you know better than that.' Alain glanced down at the occasional table. 'Is there any tea left in that pot? I could drink a cup, and I'm sure Esther could too.'

'I must go,' Hélène said, getting up.

'Really? So soon?' That was Isobelle.

'Yes, really. I've got things to do. And by the look of it there's a storm brewing. I'd like to get back before it breaks.' It was there again, that new purposefulness. She smiled at Alain. 'If I find anything else I'll let you know.'

'I'd be grateful.'

As she picked up her bag the first thunder rumbled in the distance. Already the air was beginning to grow heavy and oppressive.

The storm would be here soon.

It broke almost without warning as Simone drove home from Carcassonne. One minute, it seemed, the sky was clear and blue, the next, the sun had disappeared behind towering cumulonimbus and the ribbon of road ahead of her shimmered in the strangely incandescent light. Thunder rumbled. Then, with a sudden crack, the heavens opened and rain lashed the windscreen and bounced off the yellow bonnet of the Citroën.

Simone cursed and slowed to a crawl. She could have done without this! Her wipers were a bit temperamental, certainly not up to coping with such a downpour. For a few minutes she limped on, peering through the cascading water. Then she spotted the sign indicating a picnic area, and, relieved, pulled into it, choosing an open area well away from the trees.

The picnic area was all but deserted. Simone pushed her seat back and tried to relax. She didn't care for thunderstorms. It wasn't that she was afraid of them exactly but they made her edgy and nervous – because the sudden ferocious unleashing of the elements made one realise just how helpless and insignificant one was in the vastness of the universe.

With the windows rolled up and the fan no longer blowing cold air it was soon hot and muggy in the car. Simone gazed into middle distance, watching the lightning flicker and flash above the trees that surrounded the picnic area to the south. But it didn't look as though it was raining there: sunlight was filtering through the branches and making dancing patterns on the hot hard earth. Simone frowned. The edge of the cloud, presumably. It happened sometimes. But the division was not usually so marked.

A horse and rider were coming through the trees. Simone experienced a twist of surprise. A horse and rider – here, in a picnic area whose only access was from the motorway? And what on earth was the rider wearing? White. But not only that: something that glittered silvery in the bright rays of the sun – someone got up in fancy dress. A player from one of the pageants which were held during the summer in small towns all over Languedoc, perhaps.

The wind that had risen with the storm blew a flurry of rain against the windscreen of the car, turning the glass opaque, but somehow Simone could see the rider even more clearly than before – his white tunic with its bold scarlet cross, his hauberk of chain mail, and, in front of him on the saddle, a brown bundle.

No, not a bundle: a child!

In spite of the heat Simone was suddenly cold and clammy, her head swimming, her vision blurred. Oh dear God no! she thought in panic. Not the dream again – especially not here, when she was certainly not asleep! She tried to open the door of the car. If only she could get out, feel the rain on her face instead of that burning sun, then it would stop! But just as before she was unable to move. There was a peculiar sensation in her stomach, as if she was being drawn, very fast, through a vortex, and then she was there in the sunshine with the knight and the child. *Her* child – Jeanne Marty . . .

The track led over heathland and through forests of beech and chestnut and it seemed to go on for ever. Dimly, Jeanne was aware of the jolting of the horse and the sun beating down on her bare head and burning her face, but it seemed vaguely unreal, a nightmare from which she could not wake. She was ill, she knew – perhaps with the fever that had taken the life of her mother and so many others. Her throat was so dry and sore that she had difficulty in swallowing and her eyes pricked as if they were full of the grit the horse was kicking up on the dusty path.

With her head drooping forward so that she could see nothing but the wild thyme and yellow broom which edged the track, and even that was made misty by the perspiration which trickled into her eyes. She was drifting now, in and out of consciousness. She was not aware of passing through the city of Toulouse, nor the village which lay in the shadow of Montaugure Castle and shared its name. But when the horses stopped at the gates of the fortress the clanking of the great portcullis as it was raised to let them through roused her a little, and she heard the shouts as men came running into the courtyard to greet them. Weakly she sagged against the arms which held her in the saddle.

'God's teeth, Philip, what have we here?' The voice was a deep bellow which echoed through the mists of fever.

With an effort she raised her head and saw a man in a surcoat of deep rich blue. Tall and broad, he made a commanding figure, and his eyes, blue as his surcoat, seemed to blaze with anger.

'Who is this child?' he demanded.

'I don't know, Father. I found her hiding in the woods after the siege. I think she's sick.'

Chain mail chinked as the knight dismounted and Jeanne clung to the horse's mane so as not to fall off. Strong arms were lifting her; her head rolled against his shoulder and the sharp metallic hauberk grazed her cheek. Dimly she was aware that he was carrying her across the courtyard and up a flight of steps. Then the mists closed in and Jeanne knew no more.

When she opened her eyes the first thing Jeanne saw was a high ceiling of saxe blue which seemed to descend and recede again. She was lying on a wooden-framed bed, softer than any she had ever known. Once, it must have been canopied and curtained, for the supports for hangings still rose bare and straight from the four corners; but now there was nothing to impede her view of the ceiling or the ochre stone walls, which were decorated by an elaborate fresco depicting knights on horseback, their swords unsheathed, and dark-skinned men cowering beneath the flailing hooves. Jeanne turned her head, following the figures in the fresco, and realised she was not alone.

A woman was sitting beside the bed. She wore a rose-pink gown and veil topped by a fillet of a deeper shade of rose, but her head was bent and Jeanne could not see her face. Alarmed, she tried to sit up, but the movement sent a sharp pain through her temple, making her gasp.

'Sancta Maria!' The woman laid down the embroidery on which she had been working. 'So – you are awake, my child!'

Jeanne swivelled her head on the pillow. The pain darted again, though not so sharply, and she found herself looking into a pair of clear blue eyes in a face so sweet and serene that she forgot to be afraid. The woman stretched out a hand to smooth Jeanne's hair away from her face. Her fingers felt cool and gentle and the soft fabric of her sleeve as it brushed Jeanne's cheek was scented faintly with lavender.

'It's good that you have come back to us,' she said. Her voice was deep and husky for a woman's, and her words puzzled Jeanne.

What did she mean – 'come back to us'? And who was she?

'I don't know you,' she said.

The woman smiled.

'No, you don't, but I certainly feel I know you! I have sat beside your bed for five days and nights since my nephew Philip brought you home to Montaugure. I have been very worried about you, especially last night when the fever reached its crisis. But I can see now that you are feeling much better. I am right, aren't I?'

Five days and nights? It wasn't possible! Then, as memory began to return, Jeanne struggled to sit up.

'I have to go! I have to find my little brother!'

The woman's face softened with pity, but she lay a restraining hand on Jeanne's shoulder.

'My dear, you cannot go anywhere.'

'I must – I must!'

But she was still weak and her head was hurting again. Jeanne sank back against the pillow, her eyes filling with helpless tears.

'Don't upset yourself. You need all your strength to get well, Jeanne,' the woman said gently. 'It is Jeanne, isn't it? That's what you told my nephew you were called when he found you.'

The horse and rider in the woods . . . running from them but not being able to escape . . . the terror as he scooped her up . . . Oh yes, it was all coming back now.

'Am I your prisoner?' Jeanne asked with a touch of defiance.

'Prisoner? Oh, my dear, of course not!'

'Then why can't I go?'

'For many reasons. As I say, you are still weak from the fever. But even if you were not, where would you go?'

'Home, of course!'

And then she remembered. She had no home. It had been burned by the crusaders. Tears welled once more.

'You see, my dear, it is not so simple. Besides, you are now a long way from where Philip found you. It was foolish of him, perhaps, to bring you here, so far from your family, but he was afraid for your safety. Bad things were happening – very bad. Many people had died.'

'Oh, I know!' Jeanne burst out. 'But I have to find my little brother!'

'When did you last see him?' the woman asked gently.

'In the city. He was with Guillemette, my mother's friend . . .'

'Then most likely he is with her now. The people of Carcassonne were all spared, weren't they? Perhaps when you are strong again some of our knights can take you south to look for your brother. But not yet, my dear. You have been very ill. If it had not been for the physicians – and my own special potions – you would have died. It is very easy to die of the fever.'

'My mother died of the fever,' Jeanne whispered. 'She was sick, and then the Good Men came – '

The woman's face clouded and she laid a finger across Jeanne's lips.

'Hush! You must not talk of such things here. It's not safe. Now, I am going to get you something to drink. You'd like that, wouldn't you?'

Jeanne nodded. Her throat was indeed parched.

'Lie still and rest then. I shall not be long.'

A few minutes later she was back with a goblet, which she placed to Jeanne's lips. The tisane tasted unfamiliar but not unpleasant, and it soothed the rawness of her throat a little.

'You will sleep again now,' the woman said gently. 'When you wake you will feel much better, I promise.'

Jeanne nodded. Already she could feel her eyes growing heavy.

'What do I call you?' she asked.

The blue eyes were full of sadness and pity and the wisdom of the ages.

'My name is Agnes Bertrand,' she replied gently.

She took the child's hand in hers. The saxe-blue ceiling was floating and receding once more. Jeanne closed her eyes and slept.

The rain had stopped, the storm passed. One moment Simone seemed to be looking at the saxe-blue ceiling, the next it had become sky, clear of cloud, intense yet shimmering as the sun caught the droplets of moisture in the air and turned them into prisms of light.

Shaken, she sat for a moment with her hand pressed to her mouth. She didn't understand what was happening to her; didn't want to think about it, even. She only knew she was more desperately anxious than ever to get home. She was not at all sure that she was in a fit state to drive. Supposing the dream started again when she was on the motorway. But what choice did she have?

Dazed, trembling, Simone turned the key in the ignition and pulled out of the picnic area.

Simone had been home for about half an hour when the telephone rang. It was Valerie.

'Oh, you're there now then! I rang earlier, but there was no reply.'

'Yes, I'm here.' To her own ears her voice sounded strained and slightly shaky, and Valerie, too, noticed it.

'Are you all right? Did I interrupt you?'

'No. I've been out.'

'Oh.' Valerie sounded vaguely offended. As if I had no right to a life of my own beyond my work, Simone thought, irritated. Then she went on: 'Alain brought his new lady to visit me today. Have they been to see you?'

'No.' Anything more than a monosyllable was beyond her.

'Ah – well, anyway, Alain mentioned that I haven't been to see Papa lately. I thought I ought to go over, and I was wondering if you'd like to come with me.'

Simone groaned inwardly. She knew only too well that Valerie put off visits home whenever possible because not only was she uncomfortable with her father's condition but also she usually managed to end up falling out with her mother, who differed sharply with her on almost every score. Valerie now wanted Simone along when she made the duty visit to act as a buffer.

'When were you thinking of going?' she asked wearily.

'What about tonight?'

'Oh no, not tonight,' Simone said quickly. 'To be truthful, I don't feel very well. I think I've picked up a bug or something.'

'In that case then I suppose you'd better not. We don't want you giving it to Papa. What's wrong, exactly? A tummy upset?'

'No – more fluey. I ache all over and feel very far away. And I've been having these really weird dreams – the sort you get when you're feverish. Very vivid – a bit nightmarish, really.'

'Oh how horrid!'

'It is rather. And these . . . well, they are really odd. They're like a story – one picks up where the other left off.' She hesitated, feeling a sudden need to talk about it, yet at the same time reluctant to admit, even to herself, just how disconcerted she was by what was happening.

'What are they about?' Valerie asked.

'Oh, the siege of Carcassonne, the Cathars . . . all the stuff I spend my life studying. But it's as if I'm there – really there – not asleep at all. I must be, I suppose, but I could swear I'm not. They just kind of . . . *start*.' She hesitated again. 'Do you remember when we did that third-eye experiment all those years ago with your friend Aurore? It's sort of like that, more like being in a trance than dreaming. In fact, in some ways it feels just the same. I seemed to be fantasising then about a Cathar woman named Helis Marty – and that's just how these dreams started.' She broke off with a small embarrassed laugh.

'Really?' Valerie was all ears suddenly. 'Simone, how exciting! I remember doing that third-eye thing – you were jabbering on for ages. I was really jealous because I was the one who wanted to do it but I couldn't get anywhere. Aurore said it was because I was trying too hard – and I probably was. But you were well into it. Aurore was very impressed. She was convinced you were regressing.'

Simone felt her skin creep suddenly.

'What on earth are you talking about?' she asked, too sharply.

'Regression. Reincarnation. We have all been here before, you know? Regression is one of the things that can happen if you put yourself into a trance. You can go back – see yourself as you were in another life – remember all the things you have forgotten in the mists of time . . . It doesn't always work, of course. Proper deep hypnosis is the best way. But sometimes out-of-body experience like the third-eye thing can open the pathway too. Aurore was sure that's what happened to you.'

'What utter rubbish!' Simone snapped.

'There you are,' Valerie said philosophically. 'We knew you'd say that. That's why we didn't tell you at the time. We knew you'd put the damper on it.'

'And so I would. Reincarnation – really!'

'I don't know why you are so sceptical about it. There have been plenty of recorded instances.'

'Faked!'

'I can't understand why you are so sceptical about it, when Aurore reckoned you would be more psychic than any of us if only you would let down the barriers,' Valerie went on, ignoring the interruption. 'As I said, she was convinced then that you were regressing to a former life. Well – perhaps now you're doing it again!'

'I am not psychic!'

'So you keep saying.' They had had this argument many times before. 'But just think: maybe once you were this – what was her name? – Helis Marty, and the dreams you are having are glimpses of something which happened to you then. Maybe that's why you've always been so interested in the history of the Cathars – because in another life you were one!'

'Twaddle!' Simone said shortly. 'More likely it's the other way around – it's because I'm interested in the Cathars that I'm having these dreams. As to the name, I've read that somewhere and remembered it. In any case, it was only in the first dream that I seemed to identify with Helis – and then she died of the fever – but the story is still going on. That proves it can't be regression. If it were and I was once Helis Marty – which I don't for one moment believe anyway – how could I see things that happened after my death? I couldn't possibly know about them, could I?'

Valerie was silent for a moment.

'I don't know, Simone. I can't explain that.' She sounded subdued.

'Exactly. Because you are looking for some deep and devious meaning in my dreams to fit in with your own theories. And there isn't one. As I already said, I know a great deal about that period

– I almost live it for my work – and for some reason I am simply dredging it all up from my memory bank. It's just imagination – very weird, I can tell you, and very unsettling. But I can't believe there's anything supernatural about it.'

'All right, have it your own way.' Valerie sounded slightly hurt, and Simone regretted her tirade.

'I'm sorry. I just don't believe it, that's all. Now – about going to see Papa . . .'

'Yes. Do you think you'll be fit to come with me if I leave it until tomorrow?'

'I certainly hope so. I'll talk to you again in the morning. How's that?'

'Fine.'

Simone replaced the receiver. Her hand was trembling a little. What utter bilge Valerie talked! How could she actually believe anything so unlikely? Yet she did, and always had, at least since she had come under Aurore's influence, and maybe even before. Reincarnation indeed! A nice idea, in some ways more attractive, perhaps, than the Catholic doctrine she had been raised in, which allowed each soul only one chance at getting things right before the Day of Judgement. It could be argued that it was more fair and certainly more demanding if one believed that every act of wrongdoing had to be attoned for at some time in the future before the slate could be wiped clean, every karmic debt paid rather than simply overlooked provided it was confessed to and absolved. But it was nothing more than fantasy for all that – pure romantic fantasy for the gullible.

For just a moment Simone found herself wondering why she rejected the theory so forcefully – she thought she was fairly open-minded about most things. But reincarnation! Even thinking about it evoked a violent response quite alien to her usual easygoing response to the world around her. Could it possibly be that deep down she was afraid that she was wrong and Valerie was right? That reincarnation was not a fantasy at all but a reality and she was indeed reliving a former life as Helis Marty through these strange, vivid dreams?

Simone shivered violently and pushed the thought aside. This was really getting to her! But there was a simple explanation, there must be – most probably that this stupid bug she had picked up was giving her delusions. She would make herself some supper and go to bed, and tomorrow, hopefully, she would be well enough to get down to work again. The old routine would soon banish all this nonsense from her mind.

But the sense of unease and uncertainty was still there, hanging over her, and with it a shadow of something that might have been apprehension, or even fear.

10

'IS IS ALL right if I use the phone, Dad?' Andrew asked. 'I thought I'd give Alain Lavaur a call.'

Bob Slater glanced up from his morning paper and pulled a wry face.

'Yes – sure. But you won't get much out of him. He's not the chattiest of men at the best of times, and he sure as hell won't talk to a newspaper reporter.'

'Well, I'm hardly likely to put my cards on the table quite that plainly!' Andrew said with a laugh. 'Give me credit for a bit more ingenuity than that, Dad!'

'Ah!' Bob folded his newspaper and laid it across his knees, bare, tanned and sinewy beneath his faded khaki shorts. 'Under-cover work! I see.'

There was relish in his tone and Andrew smiled to himself. All very well for his father to pretend he was no longer interested in investigating suspicious cases; just show him the hare and the old instincts were still there, just below the surface, waiting to be reawakened.

'You could put it like that.' He took a ripe peach from a pottery bowl which stood invitingly on the stripped-pine dining table and bit into it. 'I've been thinking about what you said about Lavaur Wines being in trouble, and it occurred to me that if they are, Alain Lavaur might be interested in selling out if the opportunity arose.'

'If the debts are as heavy as I've been led to believe, nobody would be stupid enough to make an offer,' Bob suggested. 'They'd just sit back and wait until things are so bad they could pick up the whole operation for a song.'

'For all we know they are that bad already.' Juice from the peach was trickling through Andrew's fingers; he dived into the kitchen to finish eating it over the sink, then came back talking while his mouth was still full of the last succulent piece. 'I'm interested to know what Lavaur's reaction would be to an offer. And I'd like to stir things up a bit, toss a few balls in the air and see how they come down. I can do that at the end of a phone line without giving anything away.'

'Surely the fact that you're English will seem peculiar?'

'I don't see why. The operation has a base in Bristol, after all. Plenty of British shippers would like to get their hands on an enterprise like this one. It's been very well received in England, I can tell you. I did a bit of homework before I came over, and I can promise you some of the people Lavaur has been negotiating to sell to would be only too pleased to cut out the middleman.'

'Well, if you think you can get away with it . . .'

'I can't see what I've got to lose.'

'Apart from a lot of money you haven't got if he should take you up on your offer!' Bob joked. He got up and crossed to the window to alter the rake of the venetian blind, through which the morning sun was pouring in slanting bars. 'Go on, then, there's the phone, and the directory is on the shelf underneath. You don't mind if I listen in, do you?'

'Help yourself – but keep one ear open to make sure Diana doesn't come barging in and wrecking everything. She's got a highly recognisable voice, if you know what I mean.'

Bob chuckled. 'I certainly do!'

Andrew leafed through the directory. An office number was listed under Lavaur Wines but no private line; Alain Lavaur's home number must be ex-directory, he guessed. He dialled, and while waiting for the line to connect he glanced at his father, lurking conspiratorially in the doorway, and winked. Then a woman's voice was on the line, and Andrew gave his father a thumbs-up sign before turning his back to concentrate on what he had to say.

'Alain Lavaur, *s'il vous plaît.*'

'I am sorry, Monsieur Lavaur is not in the office today,' the voice said in French.

Andrew just about understood her, but doubted his own ability to converse in French.

'*Parlez-vous Anglaise?*' he asked hopefully.

'Of course!'

Yes, of course, he thought. A receptionist for an import-export company would almost certainly be bilingual.

'It's very important I speak to Monsieur Lavaur,' he said. 'Could you tell me where I can contact him?'

'In what connection do you wish to speak to Monsieur Lavaur?' Her voice was prettily accented; Andrew found himself wondering what she looked like.

'I'm afraid I can't discuss that with anyone but Monsieur Lavaur,' he said crisply. There was silence at the other end of the line and he added, 'It is extremely urgent.'

'I see.' She sounded worried now. She hesitated and he could almost hear her brain ticking over as she wondered what she should do. 'Well, I can give you a number where you might be able to contact Monsieur Lavaur. I can't promise anything, of course. He might be away from home.'

'Ah – this is his home number, is it?' Andrew asked, pleased. If Alain Lavaur was a friend of his father's, Bob would almost certainly know the ex-directory number, but without a legitimate source for Andrew to attribute it to, Lavaur's suspicions would be aroused.

'His home, yes. I wouldn't normally disclose it, but he has been working from home as well as the office since . . .' The girl broke off, obviously afraid she had said too much. 'Since he returned from England,' she finished tactfully.

'Of course.' Andrew wondered if he could push her a little. 'Monsieur Rousseau's death must have come as as great shock to you all,' he ventured.

'Oh yes – it was a terrible tragedy. Terrible!'

'Surprising, too, since he knew the roads so well.'

'Yes.'

'But then of course he liked to drive fast, didn't he?'

'You knew Monsieur Rousseau?' she asked, sounding a little surprised.

'We met. He struck me as a man who liked to take risks.'

'He could be like that, yes. But all the same, to meet such a terrible end . . .'

'It must have been a great shock to all his friends, too – especially the one he was with that night. Oh goodness, I've forgotten his name . . .'

'I'm sorry, I don't know what you're talking about.' The girl's tone had become guarded. Andrew realised he would get no more from her and did not want to risk arousing her suspicions.

'Never mind. The number you were going to give me was . . . ?'

She told him and he jotted it down, reading it back to her. Then he thanked her, depressed the cradle and dialled again.

'Calling his home number,' he said to his father over his shoulder.

This time the telephone rang for some while, and Andrew was beginning to think that Alain Lavaur must indeed be away, when a man's voice, deep and very French, answered.

Andrew felt his pulses quicken.

'Monsieur Lavaur? I'm sorry to trouble you at home but I wanted to speak to you urgently and your office tell me you are not expected in today.'

'That is correct. To whom am I speaking?'

Andrew had already decided on a cover story.

'I represent a worldwide marketing organisation for wines and spirits. A few weeks ago a colleague of mine contacted your partner, Thierry Rousseau, and I'm now in France, following up his visit. I was wondering – '

'I'm afraid Thierry Rousseau is no longer with us,' Alain said.

'Ah. You mean he's left the company?'

'Thierry Rousseau was killed in a road accident. I am now dealing with the side of the business that was his responsibility. How can I help you?'

Andrew made a great play of feigning shock.

'I'm so very sorry . . . I had no idea . . .'

'Of course not. Perhaps you'd like to tell me what it was your colleague talked to Thierry about.'

'Well yes . . . under the circumstances . . . Could I make an appointment to see you, Monsieur Lavaur?'

'At the moment my diary is pretty full. This is a difficult time, as I'm sure you can appreciate. But if you could give me some idea what it's about . . .'

Andrew paused briefly. He had hoped to get the appointment without having to explain first.

'Very well. I'll put my cards on the table. My company is very interested in Lavaur Wines. Very interested indeed.'

'In what way?'

'We believe that an arrangement with yourselves would be of benefit to both of us.'

'You mean you want to buy wine from us.'

Andrew thought quickly. If Lavaur Wines was indeed in the sort of trouble his father had suggested then it was possible they wouldn't be able to meet orders. But Alain Lavaur might be amenable to the suggestion of an injection of cash . . .

'A little more than that, monsieur,' he said. 'As I said, we are a worldwide organisation, with considerable resources. We talked to Monsieur Rousseau about the possibility of using some of them to help Lavaur Wines to reach their full potential and Monsieur Rousseau was of the opinion it was worth looking into. That's where I come in. If we could meet . . . talk— '

'Pardon me, monsieur. But if you are suggesting what I think you are suggesting, then the answer is no. Lavaur Wines is a family-run company. We would never be interested in selling out.'

There was a finality in Alain's tone which told Andrew he had overplayed his hand. He was surprised. He would have thought Alain would have grabbed at any lifeline offered to him.

'We certainly wouldn't want to do anything which would affect the running of the business,' he said hastily. 'Monsieur Rousseau— '

'M Rousseau had no authority to have even a preliminary discussion on such an important issue,' Alain said. There was a clipped note now in his tone, and Andrew realised what it was that was eating him. Not so much the suggestion that he might lose effective control of his company as the fact that he believed Thierry Rousseau had been doing some negotiations behind his back. *That* had been his mistake. He should have left Thierry out of it.

'Please, let me come and see you and explain,' he began soothingly, but Alain interrupted.

'I've told you, my diary is very full at the moment. If you would like to telephone my office and leave your number with my secretary, then I'll get back to you when I have the time.'

There was nothing for it. He was up a blind alley and there was nowhere left to go.

'I'll call you again, Monsieur Lavaur.'

* * *

'Well?' Bob said from the doorway as he replaced the receiver. 'How did you get on?'

'Not too well, I'm afraid. He's very touchy on the subject of Thierry Rousseau and not responsive to the idea of selling out, either.'

'Perhaps he thought you'd heard rumours about the business and were trying to pick off a bargain. He's a proud man.'

'Perhaps. Whatever, I'm afraid I'm not going to get to meet him.'

'Who do you want to meet?' Unnoticed by either of the two men, Diana had come back into the house from the garden where she had been watering the geraniums before the sun became too hot. Now she appeared in the doorway, pushing her sunglasses up into her neatly coiffed hair and stripping off the cotton gloves she wore for gardening.

'Andrew Lavaur.'

Diana laughed shortly.

'Oh that's easy! Why didn't you say so last night? I'll have a lunch party and invite him.'

Bob gave her a straight look.

'I know Alain is a friend, but he never comes to our lunch parties. They are strictly for expats . . .'

Diana smiled smugly.

'Well, he's got an English girlfriend staying with him, hasn't he? What would be more natural than to ask her over to socialise with some of her fellow countrymen?'

Bob shook his head in bewilderment.

'How do you know that?'

'Oh . . . the grapevine. You should know it's impossible to keep anything quiet around here for long. Once one of the girls gets to hear something it goes around like Chinese whispers.'

'The point of Chinese whispers is that the information gets distorted,' Bob chided. 'God knows how much truth there is in the things you hear, Diana.'

'Well this is certainly true. They were seen together yesterday in Collioure, and apparently she is young and very attractive. I'd love to know what Hélène thinks about it! Yes, I'm definitely warming to the idea of getting the chance to look her over myself. I'll call round a few friends and then you can phone Alain and invite him and his girlfriend along.'

'Why me?' Bob protested.

'It would come better from you.'

'I'm not so sure about that,' Bob said. 'He might think I'm after this girlfriend of his if she's so attractive.'

'Rubbish! He knows you prefer older women.' She pinched his cheek playfully.

'Well, there you are then, Andrew – looks like you'll get to meet Alain Lavaur if Diana gets her way. And she usually does!' Bob said with a grin. 'I hope he doesn't recognise your voice, though. That could be embarrassing!'

'I shouldn't think he will.' Andrew gathered his notes together. 'The telephone can be pretty distorting, and in any case, to a Frenchman I expect all Englishmen sound alike, a bit the way we all look alike to Chinamen! Well done, Diana, I'm looking forward to this.'

She shook her head, looking bemused.

'I think I must have missed something here. What are you talking about?'

He told her.

'I thought you were supposed to be on holiday, Andrew,' she chided him, but she was smiling. 'I must say I'd like to know the truth about Thierry Rousseau, though. How exciting, having two investigators in the family.'

'One!' Bob corrected her. 'Andrew is the only seeker-out of deep dark secrets these days. I've had enough of it to last a lifetime, but he still gets a kick out of it, don't you, lad?'

'Afraid so,' Andrew agreed.

It was true: he did enjoy his work enormously. As for the 'deep dark secrets' his father had referred to, he had long since learned that almost everyone harboured them. Sometimes they were harmless, of no concern to anyone else, and when that was the case he was content to let them remain hidden. He had no wish to punish the innocent or the merely foolish. But sometimes unearthing them and using the power of the press to make them public meant that justice could be done. And where the guilty were concerned, Andrew felt no compunction at all.

As yet, he did not know which category Alain Lavaur fell into. But his reporter's nose was telling him that there were certainly circumstances surrounding Thierry Rousseau's death which warranted investigation.

* * *

Alain replaced the receiver and sat staring at it, deep in thought.

Perhaps he'd been too hasty in dismissing this offer – if such it was – so arbitrarily. With things as they were, someone buying in might just be the answer. But in reality he had no bargaining power. Perhaps the man who had called didn't know that yet – Alain realised with a shock that he hadn't even asked who he represented – but Alain himself was all too aware of it. He had had a sudden vision of just what it would mean to him to lose control and it had made him see red. Lavaur Wines was his baby. He couldn't give it up without a fight. Never would have done, unless it had become so large and successful that he could no longer manage it without going public or selling out. And as for Thierry having discussions about it behind his back . . . that had been the last straw.

Alain sighed, glancing at his desk, at the pile of files and papers awaiting his attention. He wished he could get down to them straight away, sorting things out and working on a possible solution to his problems. But he had promised Esther he would take another day off and he did not see how he could disappoint her.

No, it would just have to wait. And the man who had called would have to wait too.

Trying without much success to put his worries out of his mind, Alain went in search of her.

'This is sheer heaven,' Esther said.

'I'm glad you like it.' Alain smiled briefly at her before relapsing into silence.

They were at Port Argelès, sitting beside the marina where luxury yachts bobbed at anchor in the azure water, their white-painted hulls and expanses of chrome and perspex gleaming and shimmering in the hot afternoon sun. Earlier they had explored the town and the golden beaches which ran end to end along the coast like a string of beads. They had eaten fresh shellfish in a café at the water's edge and taken a short boat trip around the bay. But for some reason, although all the ingredients for a day of shared pleasure were there, the rapport they had enjoyed yesterday was missing. Alain was preoccupied, distant . . . different.

'I just wish I'd brought my swimming costume,' Esther said,

making another effort to break the silence. 'The water looks really inviting.'

Alain said nothing.

She glanced at him, sitting there as if he were carved out of stone, finely chiselled profile set, eyes staring into the middle distance.

'Hello? Is anyone there?' she quipped.

'Umm?'

'I said, is anyone there?'

'Oh, sorry.' He smiled briefly. 'I'm not being much company, am I?'

'Aren't you enjoying it?' she asked.

'Yes . . . yes, of course. But I've got things on my mind.'

'I can see that. Is it the business? I know you're worried about it, but I'm sure it will work itself out.'

He sighed. 'I wish I could believe that. Things are very serious, Esther. Thierry got things into one hell of a mess. I have my work cut out to try and rescue it.'

'And you're thinking you shouldn't be wasting time sitting here in the sun looking at boats.'

'Something like that.'

'Oh Alain, I'm sorry!' She reached out and twined her fingers in his. 'I've come at a very bad time, haven't I? But you mustn't feel you have to entertain me, you know. I'll be perfectly all right on my own. It's enough for me that I'm here – that we're together again. I don't want to be a hindrance if you have more important things to do.'

He squeezed her fingers.

'You know you are quite a girl.'

'Not really. Just one who loves you. Honestly, Alain, I mean it – you mustn't let the business suffer because of me. I'd like to be able to spend every minute of every day with you, of course – but not at the expense of something so important to you.'

He nodded a little guiltily.

'Actually, there is something I ought to do right now – a phone call I should make. I've been thinking about it whilst we have been sitting here. Would you mind?'

In spite of what she had said about not wanting to keep him from more important matters, her heart sank.

'You mean you want to go home?'

'No, no. There's no need for that. I'm sure I can find a public telephone. You can stay here and enjoy the scenery.'

He stood up, quickly and decisively, without waiting for her agreement. 'I won't be long.'

'Oh . . . right.'

She watched him walk away across the parking area in the direction of the road, chewing at her lip and fretting over the insecurity she still felt where Alain was concerned. With her head she could understand that he was worried about what was happening to his business; in her heart she still doubted the depth of his commitment to her and ached for continual reassurance. Never before had she felt so vulnerable – but then, never before had she cared for anyone as deeply as she cared for Alain. The fact that he seemed to be shutting her out today was deeply hurtful and she felt helpless, trapped by circumstances and by her own emotions.

But of course it wasn't just his preoccupation with his business that was upsetting her, she realised. It was also because Hélène was so much part of his life here in France. It wasn't healthy, the way she kept popping up like the proverbial jack-in-the-box, and although Alain displayed apparent irritation at her continued intrusion into his life, Esther couldn't help wondering if he minded her attentions as much as he said he did. Perhaps he found it flattering to have her running to him for every little thing; perhaps it was more. Did he still care for her? Esther wondered, and felt the raw pain of jealousy which came from knowing that even if their marriage was over, this woman who was still his wife had once shared his life far more completely than she did. He said he loved her, but he had married Hélène. Could what they had shared ever be completely forgotten? Esther burned with the desire to possess not only Alain's present and future, but also his past. She was being ridiculous, she knew, but knowing it could not change the way she was feeling. She couldn't bear to share any part of him with another woman.

What the hell has happened to me? Esther asked herself suddenly. The girl who had gone out of her way to avoid commitment had totally disappeared and been replaced by a woman obsessed. She could think of no one but Alain and nothing seemed of the slightest importance unless it concerned him. If this was being in love – this agony and ecstasy and involvement to the exclusion of everything else – she could do without it! Unfortunately, she had no control over her emotions any more: they were too powerful to be disciplined. In fact, she seemed to have no control over her life, full stop!

Esther sighed, reaching into her bag for a tube of sun-screen cream, and massaged some into her arms and legs. But the feelings of frustration and misgiving remained, undermining the memories of moments of love satisfied and taking some of the brightness out of the day.

Hélène was in the garden painting.

It had been Valerie who had first encouraged her to take up the hobby and though she knew she had no particular talent she quite enjoyed it. Splashing paint on to paper could be quite therapeutic, and when she was in the right mood her work had an ebullient gaiety which echoed the bright, unsophisticated side of her nature. There was something almost childlike about the bold shapes and primary colours, the 'people' with round smiling faces and chunky limbs, the simple spare still lifes – a kind of cross between a Beryl Cook and the efforts of a primary school fourth-year. When Hélène was happy her happiness was infectious – and it showed in her paintings. No one would ever call them art, but they induced a warm glow in anyone who looked at them.

Today she was painting a street market scene – stalls piled high with cheeses and fresh fruit and vegetables, presided over by jolly-looking country men with ruddy faces, and as she worked the glow of optimism she was feeling spilled out on to the paper.

Suddenly she became aware that the telephone was ringing, the sound of the bell carrying out through the open kitchen window. She dropped her brush into its pot and leaped up, almost knocking over her easel in her eagerness.

Perhaps it was Alain!

She ran up the path to the house, wondering how long the telephone had been ringing before she had heard it, afraid it might stop before she reached it.

She flew across the kitchen and grabbed the receiver from its wall housing.

'Hello?'

There was silence at the other end of the line, a split second of silence, and then the empty tone of disconnection.

Hélène groaned in frustration. Too late. If only she hadn't been in the garden! If only she had reached it seconds earlier! It might *not* have been Alain, of course, but somehow Hélène was sure that it was.

She replaced the receiver and hovered within reach of it, wondering if he would try again. Well – hardly, if he thought she wasn't there! She wandered outside, wandered back indoors again, unsettled now. Her eye fell on the aperitif bottle, standing in the midst of the clutter on the kitchen table. She'd had a drink at lunchtime and forgotten to put it away afterwards. Perhaps she would have another now.

She fetched a glass and half filled it with the sweet golden wine, sipping at it thirstily as if it were lemonade. It was rather too warm from having been left out, but it still tasted good. Hélène enjoyed the syrupy feel of it on her tongue. She poured the rest of the wine into her glass and put the empty bottle down beside the kitchen bin, ignoring the stack of other empty bottles which was erupting from the corner like some insidious amoebic growth. Then she lit a cigarette and took it, and her glass, back outside.

She was halfway across the patio when the telephone began to ring again. She turned to rush back inside, slamming her glass down on the kitchen table so violently that wine slopped over the rim and made a sticky pool on the unvarnished wood.

'Hello?'

No one answered her.

'Hello?' she repeated. 'Who is it?'

Still no answer. Just that echoing silence. Then there was the click that told her the line had disconnected and once more nothing but the dialling tone.

'What's going on?' Hélène said aloud. She was puzzled, disappointed and also a little disconcerted.

She had been quite certain there was someone on the other end, listening to her. A wrong number, probably. But all the same . . .

Hélène snatched up her glass and drained it. Then, leaving it on the kitchen table, she went back into the garden.

But she was no longer in the mood for painting, and her earlier efforts suddenly looked hopelessly amateur to her. What a load of rubbish! She wrenched the sheet of paper from the easel and screwed it up into a crumpled ball. Her throat was aching with unshed tears and in spite of the brightness of the sun, the dark cloud of depression was hovering over her again.

In the house, the telephone began to ring again.

11

THE SUN WAS dipping towards the Pyrenees and the swifts wheeling and swooping in the clear evening sky as Simone drove through the winding lanes to pick up Valerie and take her to visit their father. She was feeling better today, apart from the suggestion of a headache lingering somewhere behind her eyes, and she had even managed a little work.

Valerie was waiting for her, sitting on the low stone wall outside her cottage, and together they drove to Le Château Gris and walked around the house to the back door, which was invariably left open behind its beaded mosquito curtain.

'We're in the salon!' Isobelle called when she heard their voices, and Simone led the way through the cool dim hall with Valerie a step or two behind as if even now she was putting off the moment when she would be in her parents' company.

The family had obviously not long finished their evening meal and were lingering over coffee – Isobelle, elegant as always, smoking a cigarette, Henri, picking ceaselessly at the piping which finished the upholstery of his chair and staring into space, Alain lounging carelessly on the sofa, one leg crossed over the other with ankle resting on knee. Of Esther there was no sign.

'How nice to see you both,' Isobelle greeted them. 'I thought you were locked away with your computer, Simone. And Valerie too! We are honoured!'

Valerie flushed slightly; Simone knew that already Isobelle had succeeded in putting her on the defensive.

'It was Valerie's idea to come over this evening,' she said swiftly. 'And I thought I could do with a break.' She dropped a dutiful kiss on Isobelle's upturned cheek and crossed to hug her father. 'How are you today, Papa?'

He looked up at her, his eyes puzzled.

'Maman? What are you doing here?'

'No, Papa, I'm not Maman. I'm Simone, remember?'

'Simone? No – you are teasing me! Simone is just a child!'

'I'm sorry, Papa, but Simone hasn't been a child for a very long time. It is me, look!' She dropped on to her haunches beside him, bringing her face close to his.

'Oh, I don't know, I'll have to believe you, I suppose. Everyone tells me such stories these days. I don't know why they do it!' he complained.

'Never mind your father, Simone,' Isobelle said, a touch acerbically. 'He's getting worse and worse. There's no point trying to have a sensible conversation with him any more.'

'But that doesn't mean you should ignore him.' Simone touched his face tenderly. 'Don't worry about it, Papa. You don't have to understand.'

'He doesn't – believe me! You should be with him all the time, then perhaps you would realise how irritating it can be,' Isobelle retorted sharply. 'It's all very well to come here and lecture me on how your father should be treated – you are not the one who has to put up with him.'

Simone rose. 'I'm sure you are right, Maman. It just makes me sad to see Papa this way. When I finish my book he must come over and stay with me for a bit. It would give you a break, and I'd love to have him.'

'That would be very nice, Simone,' Isobelle said, but her dry tone indicated that she did not expect Simone's offer ever to become a reality.

'Hello, Papa.' Valerie hugged her father as Simone had done, but she straightened more quickly, looking around. 'Where's Esther?'

'She has just gone to the bathroom.' Isobelle's tone was disapproving, as if she could hardly believe her daughter could be so impolite as to ask such a question. Then, at the sound of footsteps on the stairs, she narrowed her eyes at Valerie in a warning glance. 'Here she is now, I think.'

The door opened and Simone saw a young woman in a long russet-coloured skirt and matching waistcoat over a cream silk blouse, who was obviously a little taken aback at finding two more people in the room than when she had left it.

'My daughters, Valerie and Simone,' Isobelle said swiftly.

'Oh yes – Alain took me to see Valerie yesterday.' Esther smiled at Valerie, then turned to Simone. As their eyes met a slight sense of shock jarred through Simone. She took a half-step forward, her face puzzled.

'Do I know you?'

Even as she said it she knew she was mistaken; this girl with her hazel eyes, thick wedge of light-brown hair and slightly puzzled expression was a stranger to her.

'I don't think so.' The English voice was unfamiliar too, and somehow slightly out of place, as though it didn't belong to her at all, Simone thought, confused.

'No, of course not. But just for a moment I thought . . . It must be someone else, someone who looks like you . . .' But she knew it wasn't that either. She couldn't think of anyone she knew who looked even vaguely like Esther.

'And I've certainly told them all about you, Esther,' Alain said, covering the slight awkwardness of the moment. 'Besides which, you and Simone have a lot in common. You are both writers.'

'Simone is an author.' Isobelle's tone somehow managed to insult them both with the simple statement of fact.

'I know.' Esther smiled ruefully. 'I'm not in your league, I'm afraid, Simone. I don't think I have the talent or the dedication to write a book – certainly not a string of them!'

'Oh, it's just a knack,' Simone said modestly. 'Personally I'm full of admiration for anyone who can survive the pressure of deadlines day after day. Once a year is quite enough for me.'

'How is it going, Simone?' Alain asked. 'Nearly finished?'

She pulled a face. 'I wish! I've been finding it a terrible struggle since all the upheaval over Thierry.'

'Oh don't let's start getting morbid again.' Isobelle feigned a shudder of distaste. 'Now, what can we offer you girls? Liqueur? Cognac?'

'A large crème de menthe frappé,' Valerie said promptly.

'Alain can deal with that. The ice is in the freezer. And you, Simone – will you have the same?'

'No thank you, Maman. You know I don't drink alcohol.'

Isobelle laughed lightly. 'Oh, of course you don't. How silly of me to forget! Goodness, I'm getting as bad as your father!'

But Simone knew she had not forgotten at all. For some reason it gave her pleasure to goad her daughters while indulging her son. Once upon a time, when she had been a child, Simone had thought it was only she who suffered at her mother's hands. She had been convinced that she was the ugly duckling, unwanted and unloved, for in those days Isobelle's barbs had revolved around the fact that, while Valerie was a delightfully pretty child, Simone was undeniably plain.

'Simone is the clever one,' Isobelle would explain on introducing her to friends. 'We can't expect beauty and brains can we?' And privately she would berate her: 'Can't you at least try to smile, child? Heaven knows, there's no way to make a silk purse out of a sow's ear, but at least it would improve matters.'

Simone had wept bitter tears, staring at her reflection in the mirror and wishing with all her heart that she was as pretty as Valerie, not only for her own sake, but for Isobelle's, so that she would no longer be ashamed of her. It was only much later that she had realised that the remarks about beauty and brains were double-edged barbs, aimed as much at hurting Valerie with the implication that she was stupid as they were at highlighting Simone's shortcomings. She had ceased to care that she was not beautiful and refused to allow Isobelle to needle her. But Valerie was less equable. She still reacted badly to her mother's slights and criticisms – probably because deep down she longed for her approval, Simone thought.

'The coffee is still quite fresh,' Alain suggested now. 'Or there's Perrier in the fridge.'

'Perrier would be nice.'

'OK – one Perrier, one crème de menthe frappè.' He went off to the kitchen and Simone sat down on the pouffe, resting her back against a bookcase.

'So – have you been doing much painting, Valerie?' Isobelle asked, and as the two made somewhat stilted conversation, Simone found her eyes drawn once more to Esther, who was now sitting opposite her on the sofa next to the vacant space Alain had occupied.

What was it about her that was so familiar? Simone simply could not put her finger on it, yet still the impression persisted – a feeling not so much of having seen her somewhere before than of having known her all her life.

Becoming aware of Simone's intent gaze, Esther looked up. She smiled, and again something within Simone responded, as if that smile had plucked some deep hidden chord. – What *was* it about her? She settled back against the bookcase, watching Esther surreptitiously now. The voices of the others washed over her, a background hum to which she was no longer listening, and the room, viewed from behind her half-closed lashes, appeared slightly blurred.

Strange – it didn't really look like the familiar salon any more, and Esther, too, looked subtly different, her features indistinct. The village clock began to strike the hour and the sound, carrying clearly in through the open window, sounded haunting and oddly compulsive. Simone found herself counting the strokes: seven, eight, nine, ten . . . Surely it wasn't ten o'clock already? And still the bell continued. Puzzled, Simone listened to the next stroke, and the next, wondering vaguely what had gone wrong with it, and yet at the same time sure she knew the answer, if only she could remember.

Of course! It wasn't the clock at all, but the church bell calling the faithful to prayer! She almost laughed aloud, wondering how she could have been so silly as not to recognise it. But the laugh was buried deep within her and no sound came. And in the dim light, flickering faintly before her half-closed eyes, she saw Jeanne.

From her hiding place in the stables Jeanne heard the indistinct tolling of the bell and drew farther back into the dim passage between the stalls, her face setting stubbornly.

She should be answering its call, she knew, and joining the others for the celebration of Mass. It was All Saints' Day, an important one for Catholics, and Viscount Bernard Bertrand would expect her to be in the family pew with the other members of the household. But she did not want to go to Mass. The service, conducted in a language she could not understand, bored her, she found the pomp and ritual repellent and slightly ridiculous, and the smell of the incense made her feel nauseous. It was all so different from the simple worship she was accustomed to, and though in the beginning she had tried to accept it out of gratitude to the Viscount for giving her a home, her dislike of the religion in whose name her family had been destroyed had festered to fierce hatred. This morning, when she should have been preparing to attend the service, she had slipped away to hide in the stables in the hope that they would go to church without her.

A warm nose nudged Jeanne's shoulder and she turned, laughing out loud in surprise.

'Braida – you monster! You made me jump! And it's no good poking me with your nose like that. I haven't got anything for you.'

The horse continued to nuzzle her anyway and Jeanne rubbed her nose, loving the scratchy feel of the coarse grey hair beneath her palm and the soft snuffling noise that came from the great nostrils. Braida was one of the good things about life at Montaugure!

It was almost three months now since Philip Bertrand had brought her here, at death's door from the fever which had claimed her after the fall of Carcassonne. The crusade against the Cathars was continuing, but safe within the haven of the castle walls, Jeanne knew little of what was going on. Agnes, Philip's aunt, concerned for Jeanne's fragile health, had insisted it should not be discussed in her presence, and she had heard nothing of the death of Count Raymond Roger Trencavel in a prison cell – from natural causes, supposedly, though it was whispered that there was little natural about it – or of the fall of Limoux, Albi and several other Cathar towns to Simon de Montfort's army. Nor did she hear the discontented rumblings of the nobles of the South as they saw their lands taken over by the church and the state. Her greatest concern was that she still did not know what had happened to her little brother, and since there was nothing she could do at present to find him she occupied herself exploring the castle that was her new home.

What a vast place it was – the great hall, with its minstrel gallery and the dais where the family ate, the countless rooms and chambers linked by echoing passageways, and the spiral stairways of stone leading up to balconies and turrets high above the green expanse of the Plain of Toulouse.

Even now at the end of the long hot summer a chill emanated from the thick walls, but it was the sight of the double portcullis with its great iron-barred door between the grilles which made Jeanne shiver. All very well for Agnes to assure her she was not a prisoner; the portcullis made her feel like one. Neither did Jeanne care for the chapel, with its prie-dieu and statuettes and the white-clothed altar lit by four candles, where the aroma of incense lingered in the honey-coloured stones. But the stables, on the far side of the courtyard, drew her like a magnet. Jeanne loved the horses and felt no fear as they poked their great heads over the doors of their stalls to greet her.

Used as she was to a whole family sharing one small cottage, Jeanne could hardly believe the vast number of people who lived in the castle – the squires and ladies-in-waiting, the serfs and the serving wenches, the ostlers and the priest who was Bernard and Agnes's brother. Bernard must be very rich, she thought, and she was surprised when Agnes told her he was in fact a vassal and held his castle and lands by feudal tenure on condition of homage and allegiance to the Count of Toulouse.

The family consisted of the Viscount Bernard and Cecile, his wife; Father Benet, the priest; Bernard's sister Agnes and his four sons. But Oliver, the youngest, was squire to one of the Knights of Toulouse, and consequently she saw little of him, and the two older sons, Martin and Raymond, were married and no longer lived within the castle walls but with the families of their wives. Though Viscount Bernard treated her kindly enough she could not help being a little afraid of him, and Cecile was haughty and hard-faced, showing her resentment of Jeanne in a million small ways. Jeanne had once overheard Cecile berating Philip for bringing her here, and thereafter she avoided Cecile whenever she could, just as she avoided the black-garbed Father Benet, though for different reasons. Only with Agnes and Philip could she feel truly comfortable. The goodness of the woman who had nursed her so tenderly made it impossible not to love her, and as for Philip, now that her first fear of him had faded, he had become a hero in Jeanne's eyes.

Philip, more than anyone, made a great fuss of Jeanne – at first from a sense of responsibility, then because he was growing genuinely fond of the serious little girl who had borne so much so bravely. Jeanne felt her heart lifting when he was around, just as she felt comforted by Agnes's serene presence. But nothing could prevent her grieving for her mother or longing for the familiar countryside which surrounded Carcassonne, and nothing could assuage the raging guilt which overcame her every time she thought of how she had lost Pons. In all likelihood Agnes was right and he was safe somewhere with Guillemette, she told herself. But Guillemette wasn't his family. She was – the only one he had left. And one day soon she would persuade Philip to take her south to look for him.

Every night she prayed fervently that she and Pons would be reunited. But when Father Benet took her to the chapel to instruct her in the Catholic faith and pray with her, no words would come. As for the Mass, when the sacrament was distributed, she felt actual physical discomfort.

'You must eat the body of Christ so that you may have everlasting life,' Benet had instructed her solemnly, but Jeanne knew different. How could anyone escape hell so easily, especially when salvation was offered by a priest who was no better than those he sought to save, living off the land and keeping a string of concubines? Not that Father Benet had a concubine as far as she knew, but there were plenty who did, unlike the Cathar Good Men, who lived pure and spiritual lives. And she could not forget what Helis had told her once when she had asked about the Catholic Mass: 'It's nothing but sorcery and superstition, Jeanne, and sorcery is wicked. Never, never meddle with sorcery.'

Today the family were going to celebrate Mass not in their own private chapel but in the Church of St Marguerite in the village, and the sound of the bell summoning the congregation carried up the hillside and into the stables. When it stopped, Jeanne thought, she would be safe to leave her hiding place – though she was not at all sure she wanted to. It was nice in the stables.

Voices in the courtyard outside made her start and her heart sank as she realised it was Philip. If he was here when the bell was summoning him to Mass it must mean he was hunting for her – and had a good idea where she could be found! Jeanne looked around in panic. It was dim here in the stables, but not so dim that he would not be able to see her easily enough.

The voices were closer now and Jeanne made up her mind. There was one place where she would be out of sight when Philip entered the stable! Swiftly she slid back the bolt on the door of Braida's stall and slipped inside, pulling it closed after her. The horse shied slightly in surprise and stamped uneasily, but Jeanne knew no fear.

'Braida – hush!' she whispered, wriggling past her and crouching down in the heap of straw at the rear of the stall.

The light became marginally less dim as the door was opened fully; by it Jeanne could see the huge fetlocks, level with her nose, and the hooves pawing the ground restlessly. Then she heard footsteps in the passage and shrank back into the corner, wrapping her arms around her knees.

'Jeanne?' It was Philip. She had been right – he was looking for her. She crouched still as a statue, hardly daring to breathe. Surely he wouldn't guess where she was? But a moment later his voice came again, this time from directly outside the stall. 'Jeanne – come out this minute! I know you're in there.'

He sounded stern – Jeanne had never heard him use that tone before. She remained motionless, still hoping he was bluffing and would go away, yet very afraid he would not.

'Are you coming out or do I have to come in there and get you?'

She knew then that it was useless. She got to her feet and wriggled back past the horse. As she emerged Philip caught her arm as if he was afraid she might bolt again, holding her firmly while he secured Braida's stall.

'What in Christ's name do you think you were doing?' he demanded angrily. 'Surely you know better than to go into a horse's stall like that?'

Jeanne stared at him, mute with surprise. She had expected a scolding, for missing church, but not from Philip – and certainly not for being in a horse's stall. Why, at home it was common practice for farm folk to share their home with the animals.

'Don't you realise you could have been kicked or trampled?' he went on more gently.

'Oh, Braida wouldn't hurt me!' she replied confidently.

'Well, not Braida, perhaps, although if you had startled her she is as capable of kicking out as any of them. But I dread to think what might have happened if you had chosen any of the other stalls for your hiding place. It was a very foolish thing to do, Jeanne.'

Her face set mulishly. She did not like Philip talking to her in these stern tones.

'How did you know I was there?' she asked sullenly.

'For one thing the stall was unbolted on the outside. A groom would never leave a stall unbolted – or if he did he would be punished most severely. And for another, there was this.'

He pointed to a scrap of fabric which had caught on a sharp splinter and Jeanne gasped in horror. Her new gown which Agnes had sewn for her! She must have caught it when she dashed into the stall! Anxiously she twirled the skirts back and forth trying to see where it was torn.

'Never mind that now. We're going to be late for church and Father will be furious.'

'But I don't want to go to church.' She looked up at him pleadingly; she could usually get her own way with him. 'Don't make me, please. Say you couldn't find me.'

'You are asking me to lie to my father? And go to Mass with that sin unconfessed – on All Saints' Day too?'

He sounded so shocked she hung her head in shame. It was wrong to tell lies, of course, but all the same . . .

'I don't want to go, Philip. I'm not a Catholic. I'm a Cathar.'

He looked around sharply, afraid she might have been overheard.

'You must not say that, Jeanne. You are not a Cathar. You are a Catholic like us – or you will be when your instruction is finished.'

She pursed her lips, glaring at him defiantly.

'Never!'

He sighed. 'Jeanne, you must come to church or Father will be angry with both of us.' He looked around and sudden inspiration struck. He couldn't carry her to church kicking and screaming as he had brought her here, but he could use his powers of persuasion.

'You like horses?' he asked.

'Oh yes! They're wonderful. Especially Braida.'

'Then I'll make a bargain with you. Come to church like a good girl and I will teach you to ride. You'd like that, wouldn't you?'

'Oh!' Her eyes went wide; she could scarcely believe it. 'Could I ride Braida?'

He hesitated. 'Well, she's a bit big for you really, but I suppose she is gentle enough. Yes, I should think you could ride Braida – with Father's permission, of course.' Her face fell and he added, 'One thing is very certain, Jeanne. He will not give it unless you come to church.'

He knew he had won. She followed him out into the sunlight, where he brushed the straw out of her skirt and her hair. The tear in the gown, fortunately, was hidden in the folds of fabric.

'Come on then, we'd better make haste,' he said.

The bell was still tolling as he took her hand and hurried her across the courtyard.

The *Aves* and the *Pater Nosters* and all the other unfamiliar and meaningless words drifted unheard above Jeanne's head as she sat in the pew reserved for the Bertrand family. Not even the smell of the incense bothered her today, for her nostrils were still full of the scents of the stable, and excitement bubbled deep inside her each time she thought of Philip's promise.

They had arrived just moments before the service had begun. Viscount Bernard had given her a very stern and serious look and Cecile had pursed her lips angrily and looked away. Jeanne ran her eye along the pew, seeing Philip's brothers and their wives, fat demure Louise and flighty Bernadette. Even Oliver was here, looking pale and pasty with a rash of angry red spots on his chin. But of Agnes there was no sign. Jeanne screwed up her face, puzzled. How was it that Agnes, a baptised and confirmed Catholic, could escape church when she, a Cathar, could not? But she was not going to worry unduly about that now. She had other, more exciting things to think about.

Jeanne peeped through her fingers at Philip, who knelt beside her.

Oh, how handsome he looked in his scarlet surcoat, caught at the waist by a leather belt studded and buckled with gold! His hair was golden, too, gleaming in the sunlight that slanted in through the high vaulted windows. How could she ever have been afraid of him? Now she thought he was wonderful, looking forward to the times when she could be with him and afterwards remembering and relishing every moment. Even her memories of the nightmare ride when he had brought her here had taken on a different perspective now, and a tiny thrill ran through her when she remembered the horse's strong neck between her thighs and Philip's arms around her waist, holding her when she almost fell.

And now he was going to teach her to ride – and on Braida too! What more could she possibly wish for? Braida and Philip, all to herself, and both at the same time! Oh, it would be worth enduring church services every day in order to have that!

Jeanne felt a surge of joy and love more powerful than anything she had ever known – except perhaps on the day when she had asked him slyly why he did not have a sweetheart and he had replied, 'Why should I need a sweetheart, Jeanne, when I have you?' Oh, she loved him so much! So much!

'One day, Philip, I am going to marry you,' she vowed silently. 'I will be your wife and we will have a stable of horses all our own – except that perhaps Viscount Bernard will give me Braida as a wedding gift. And we will ride every single day, galloping like the wind, racing one another. And sometimes, just sometimes, you will lift me up on to the saddle in front of you, just as you did that first day . . .

Her childish dreams danced like dust motes in the shaft of sunshine. But the emotions in her heart were anything but childish.

'Your Perrier, Simone. Simone?'

She blinked, uncomprehending, still seeing the handsome face and golden hair of the young knight. Then the features blurred, swimming before her eyes, and as she struggled to bring them into focus she saw that the eyes looking down at her with obvious concern were not blue at all but dark brown. Alain. It was Alain. How could she have thought for even a moment that he was someone else?

'Thanks.' She took the Perrier from him. Her hand was trembling.

'You were miles away.'

'Yes, I was . . .' Miles away. Centuries away. Dear God, I *am* going mad . . .

'You look half asleep to me,' Isobelle said acerbically. 'You've been working too hard again, I expect.'

'Probably.'

She sipped the Perrier and the cool clean taste of it revived her a little. No time at all seemed to have passed in the real world – Alain would have taken only moments to fetch the Perrier and the ice, which he was now scooping into Valerie's crème de menthe frappé, and Isobelle was still talking to Valerie about her painting. Yet Simone felt as if she had been absent from the room for a very long time.

She cupped the glass between her hands, wishing desperately she could excuse herself and go, and knowing she would have to stay for another hour at least. Her mother would be offended if she dragged Valerie away so soon after their arrival. Her father – if he remembered they were there at all – would be upset, and the others would think it very strange. But at least she didn't feel ill this time, just very, very distant.

And frightened. Not only for herself, for the peculiar things that were happening to her, but also, for some inexplicable reason, afraid for Esther.

She looked at Alain's English girlfriend and was overcome with an enormous wave of anxiety and a sense of impending danger. Simone shivered suddenly and violently. As the others talked on, she sat nursing her glass between her moist palms and wondered what on earth it all meant.

'Are you all right, Simone?' Valerie asked.

It was an hour and a half later; they had said their good-byes, and Simone was turning the Citroën on the broad gravel turnaround.

She glanced at Valerie; in the dusk it was impossible to see her sister's face clearly, but from her tone Simone knew it was anxious.

'Not really,' she said with a small nervous laugh. 'It happened again.'

The leather seat creaked as Valerie shifted to look at her.

'You mean . . . your dream?'

'Yes. It just . . . started. One minute I was listening to you all talking and the next . . . well, I was somewhere else.'

'In Carcassonne?'

'No. It's moved on from there. To a castle near Toulouse called Montaugure.'

'Were you there? As the woman – Helis, wasn't it?'

'No, I told you – she died in Carcassonne.' Simone's tone was slightly impatient, but she was unaware that the retort gave away the fact that subconsciously, at least, she had accepted far more of the story than she was prepared to admit. 'I was just looking on again, like watching a play, except that it's more than that. I seem to be aware of things that have happened that I haven't actually seen and I can read the minds of the characters. This time it was all centred around Jeanne – Helis's daughter. Philip Bertrand took her home with him to Montaugure and she's got a tremendous crush on him.'

'Philip Bertrand?'

'Oh, he's a knight. Young, handsome. He found her hiding in the woods after Carcassonne fell. It's funny. I could see him so clearly . . . When Alain gave me my Perrier I was still so far away that I didn't recognise him for the moment. I thought he was Philip!' She broke off, shivering at the recollection. 'It's really getting to me, Valerie!'

Valerie was silent for a moment.

'When did it start – tonight, I mean?'

'Oh, when Alain went to fetch the ice. I was just sitting there, looking at Esther and wondering why I thought I knew her, and . . . well, that was it, really. I heard the village clock striking the hour but it just went on, like a church bell. And suddenly I was there – at Montaugure.'

'Esther!' Valerie's tone was thoughtful, yet with a sudden edge of excitement. 'You recognised her, didn't you?'

Simone laughed shortly. 'I didn't recognise her. I've never met her before.'

'All right – not recognised. But you did feel you knew her.'

'Yes,' Simone agreed reluctantly. 'She was sort of . . . familiar.'

'More than just familiar. I saw your face, Simone. You looked as if you'd seen a ghost.'

'Oh Valerie, you do exaggerate! What are you getting at, anyway?'

Again Valerie was silent, staring out into the deepening twilight as Simone negotiated the narrow lanes.

Then she said a little tentatively, 'You don't think she might be one of the people in your story?'

Simone's flesh crept suddenly. She jerked the car violently around a bend in the lane.

'Oh for heaven's sake, don't start that again!'

'But she could be,' Valerie persisted. 'Suppose these dreams of yours *are* regression and she is a reincarnation of someone you knew in another life? It's very likely you would recognise her, isn't it? Not as Esther Morris, of course, but as someone else. Someone from that other life. Simone – listen to me. I've been thinking about it a lot since we talked yesterday and it occurred to me to wonder if since you feel you're not actually there – not any more, at any rate – it might be that what you are seeing is a sequence of events so traumatic that they have been trapped in the ether. You know, the same way an atmosphere clings to places where terrible things have happened, only even more vividly. We've all heard of motorists being convinced they've knocked someone down only to find there's no one there and finding out afterwards that an accident happened at that very spot sometime in the past. Well, I wondered if something similar was happening to you, only the replay was much longer and more detailed because somehow you'd tapped into the whole story. But what I couldn't understand is why it should have started now. I mean – I've always said you were psychic, but you've lived here all your life and it's never happened before. Now I'm beginning to wonder if it's because of Esther. I mean – *she* wasn't here before, was she? She is the one factor that's different. Esther has come into our lives – a stranger you feel you know somehow – and suddenly this story from the past is being revealed to you.'

Simone laughed nervously.

'This is getting more and more ridiculous!'

'But supposing I'm right!' Valerie was very excited now. 'Supposing Esther is one of the people in your story and she lived here in Languedoc in the thirteenth century. Supposing something really awful happened to her – and now she's back it's all begun to happen again – Simone – Simone!' Her voice rose an octave suddenly to a frightened shriek. 'Look out! What are you *doing*?'

Simone braked hard and swung the steering wheel to the left just in time to avoid the curving bank which was leaping up at them in the light of the headlamps. As she rounded the bend, swaying but safe, Valerie laughed shakily.

'I thought you were going to have us in the hedge!'

'Mm.' Simone was trembling violently. It had been a close thing. She'd totally lost concentration for a moment. Valerie's remark about the past happening again, echoing as it did the words which had appeared unbidden on the screen of her word processor, had shaken her rigid. 'Look, do you think you could just stop talking nonsense at me for a moment and let me get you safely home?'

'Perhaps I'd better!' Valerie agreed. 'We're nearly there now, anyway. You really are a dreadful driver, Simone!'

Simone did not reply. With an enormous effort she concentrated on the road and Valerie sat beside her in silence as she nursed the car up the steep hill to the village.

Valerie's cottage was in darkness; presumably Yves was either out or in bed. Out, in all probability. Bed was not something he thought about until the small hours, except in quite a different context. Simone put on the handbrake, leaving the engine running, and Valerie turned to her.

'I'm sorry if I upset you, Simone, but it's all so exciting! Nothing like this has ever happened to me before.'

'No,' Simone said drily. 'Nor to me.'

'But it has! That third-eye experience, for one – and now this! You've got to go on with it, Simone, and see what happens!'

'It's not a question of "going on" with it. I haven't sought these daydreams, I promise you.'

'Oh, you know what I mean – don't try to stop them. And see if you can recognise anyone else.'

'What do you mean – anyone else?'

'Well, you thought you were Helis, for a start. And then you got a funny feeling about Esther, and you said you thought Alain was the knight . . .'

Simone flexed her hands on the steering wheel.

'I didn't say anything of the sort. I said that when I came to I was still so far away that— ' She broke off, realising that Valerie had interpreted what had happened more accurately than she had herself. It was true. For a strange disorientated moment she *had* thought it was Philip Bertrand and not Alain who was standing in front of her.

'What I want to know is who *I* was!'

'I wondered how long it would be before you worked yourself into this,' Simone said drily. 'What makes you think you're in the dream at all?'

'Because souls generally reincarnate in family groups – it's a known fact.'

'Not known by me!' Simone objected.

'Well it is,' Valerie said passionately. 'I'll lend you some books on the subject, then perhaps you'll begin to understand. Groups of souls, enemies as well as friends, who have known one another in previous lives choose to reincarnate together so as to help one another work out whatever problems they encountered previously. They are not necessarily in the same relationships as before of course – a mother could be the child this time around, or a husband a brother – and not even always the same sex as before, but all bound together nevertheless. So if you and Alain and Esther are reincarnations of people involved with one another in the thirteenth century, then it's quite likely *I* was there too – and Maman, and Papa . . .'

Simone sighed. 'Look, I really don't want to talk about this any more, Valerie. I'm very tired.'

'All right, all right.' Half in, half out of the car, Valerie turned as a sudden thought struck her. 'This place – what did you call it? – Montaugure. Did it exist?'

'I've no idea. I've certainly never heard of it.'

'But if it did, wouldn't that prove something, at least? And the family who lived there – the Bertrands – if they were nobles there must be some record of them. Why don't you try to find out?'

Simone's skin prickled again.

'I have a book to finish, Valerie. I haven't got time to go scouting around Toulouse looking up old records.'

'But you wouldn't need to do it yourself. You've got lots of contacts – librarians, historians. They'd love to do it for you.' Valerie was wheedling now and Simone knew she would get no peace until she agreed.

'All right – if it will please you. But it still wouldn't prove a thing except that I'd read about it somewhere.'

'All the same . . .'

'Goodnight, Valerie,' Simone said. She let off the handbrake and executed a jerky three-point turn, wanting only to get away from her sister and the preposterous theories which not only went against everything she believed but also disturbed her in a way she could not begin to understand. But why should she be so disturbed by them? Could it be that in spite of her scepticism, in spite of her stubborn resistance, she was beginning to have her doubts? There was, after all, no rational explanation for what was happening to her. She had used the fact that she had felt ill as an excuse for her dreams – but she wasn't ill now. Apart from the lingering headache and a bad fit of the shakes her symptoms had disappeared. Yet tonight, in her mother's salon, the dream had come again, more real to her than anything that was happening around her.

And as if that were not enough . . .

Simone shivered violently as she thought again of the phrases that had inexplicably appeared on the screen of her word processor and which Valerie had echoed tonight.

It is beginning again. What happened before must happen again.

I am going mad! Simone thought. Quite, quite mad.

And the observation only added weight to the feeling of apprehension and impending danger which still hung over her, hovering in the air like the heaviness that precedes a thunderstorm.

'Time for bed, Henri.' Isobelle stubbed out her cigarette and transferred the ashtray from the arm of her chair to the rosewood table. 'Come along now, you've had a busy day.'

He stared at her blankly and she gave a small impatient shake of her head.

'Didn't you understand me, Henri? It's bedtime.' She levered him out of his chair with an ease born of long practice, then turned to Alain. 'Are you coming up now?'

'Not yet.'

'Oh.' Her lips tightened a shade. 'In that case, can I leave you to lock up?'

'Yes, of course.'

'Goodnight, then. Goodnight, Esther.'

She put an arm around her husband, urging him towards the door. It was, Esther realised, the first gesture of anything approaching affection she had ever seen Alain's mother make.

'Goodnight, Maman. Goodnight, Papa.' As the door closed after them, Alain laid a hand on Esther's knee. 'You don't want to go to bed yet, do you?'

She shook her head, smiling. All she wanted was the chance to be alone with Alain.

'We could go for a walk in the garden,' he suggested. 'It's lovely at this time of night.'

'Why not?'

The garden was bathed in soft moonlight, the air fragrant with the perfume of night-scented stocks and the sweetness of the shrubs distilled by the lingering heat of the day. In more affluent times it had been laid out in a formal pattern – borders of tall perennials, lawns edged with box and shaded with magnolia, a walled vegetable garden, a rose garden, and beyond, an orchard. Nowadays, with only one part-time gardener to look after it, nature had begun to take over, but Esther thought it was all the more charming for that. As they went through the trellised arch, thick with honeysuckle and a climbing rose which gleamed pure white in the moonlight, Alain slipped his arm around her waist and she rested her head against his shoulder.

'So – you've met both my sisters now,' he said.

'Yes.' She didn't want to talk about Alain's sisters. She wanted to talk about more intimate things, if talk they must.

'What did you think of Simone?'

'She's nice, but . . .'

'A bit strange at times? You mustn't take too much notice of that. She does tend to go off into a world of her own. It's her artistic nature.'

'I didn't know historians were artistic.' She smiled. 'But that wasn't what I was going to say, actually. It was the way she looked at me when we were introduced.'

'Because she thought she knew you, you mean? Odd, that. You must have a double.'

'Mm.' She was reluctant to admit how disconcerted she had been by Simone's penetrating gaze or the fact that for a moment she had felt an answering chord, although at the same time she had been quite sure she had never met Simone before.

'I find it very hard to believe, though.' Alain's voice was teasing, yet with vibrant undertones.

'What?'

'That you have a double. There couldn't possibly be two of you. The world could not be so lucky. If there is someone else a little like you, then she must be just a pale shadow.'

'Oh Alain!' She laughed, slightly embarrassed by his extravagant Gallic charm but pleased and flattered all the same.

'It's true. You are unique, chérie. From the moment I met you I have been your slave.'

'All right, slave – kiss me!' She twisted to face him, winding her arms around him and feeling the desire throb within her at the touch of their bodies. His lips were gentle at first, then as they became more demanding the longing twisted more strongly, dizzying in its intensity.

Oh, how she wanted him – body and soul! Every nerve ending,

magnetised and prickling with awareness, was responding to him, yet it went deeper even than the mere physical. There was a hunger within her to be closer to him than was humanly possible, not simply to join her body to his but to become a part of him so that they were not two people but one – merged into a single entity for all time.

His hands were caressing her, tender and urgent, his body, pressed close to hers, escalated the physical desire to fever pitch.

'Let's go to bed,' she whispered.

His lips skimmed her cheek; his tongue flicked into her ear.

'Why do we need a bed? It's nicer here under the stars.'

'Oh yes . . .'

Clinging together, intoxicated with desire, they stumbled through the rose garden towards the orchard. Beneath the trees, heavy with foliage and fruit, the grass grew ankle deep and the lush earthy fragrance of it was more sensuous even than the honeysuckle and roses. He pressed her against the gnarled bole of an ancient apple tree, undressing her deftly and kissing her throat, her shoulders, her small firm breasts. Together they sank into the cool deep grass, everything but their need of one another forgotten, and let the waves of passion sweep them to heights too dizzyingly ecstatic to be remembered beyond the glory of the shared moment.

Afterwards, Esther lay looking up at the moonlight splintering through the leafy branches. The glow of the recently experienced delights still surrounded her, making her languourous with fulfilled contentment, but there was also an edge of sweet sadness that it was over, and a sense of loss aching in her heart. In the valley the clock bell chimed, awakening the same nostalgia as it had done when she had first heard it, and with it some deep need for reassurance.

'Promise you won't leave me,' she whispered into Alain's shoulder.

'Sweetheart, I won't.'

But somehow his words failed to reassure her. He said he loved her, he was here with her now. Yet still she felt afraid. Because of Hélène? That must be it, she supposed. But inexplicably Esther felt that Hélène's all-too-obvious presence on the scene was not the whole reason for her fear. There was something else, some factor she couldn't put her finger on, which was at the heart of her insecurity. It was more instinct than substance, teasing and worrying away like a speck of grit, too small to find, too persistent to ignore. A shadow playing hide and seek with her emotions.

I love him, Esther thought, and he loves me. I have to hold on to that.

But the knowledge that Alain had deceived her once was still there, and this other, indefinable, sense of disaster looming.

Quite suddenly Esther found herself longing for home, where she belonged, knew exactly who she was. But home would mean leaving Alain.

It was a trap – a tender trap. She stared at the tracery of the trees, silver in the moonlight, and, in spite of the warm glow that had spread through her when they made love, Esther realised she was depressed and full of foreboding.

12

SIMONE'S KEY WAS in the lock when she heard the telephone ringing inside the house. She pushed the door open hurriedly and snatched it up.

'Simone, it's me.'

It was Hélène. Her voice sounded strained, panicky almost.

'Hélène! Are you all right?'

'No, not really. I'm . . . Oh, I'm really sorry to bother you but do you think you could come over?'

Simone's heart sank. She had thought Hélène was much better. Now she sounded in a terrible state.

'You mean now?' she said.

'Well . . . yes. I wouldn't ask, Simone, but— '

'What exactly is the matter?'

'It's these phone calls I've been getting . . .'

'What sort of phone calls?'

'Silent ones. The phone rings and when I answer it there's no one there. Except that I know there is. I can hear them breathing. Please, Simone, please come over. I'm really frightened. I daren't go to bed.'

'Perhaps you should ring the police.'

'What will they do? What can anyone do? But I'm here all on my own and I just don't know what to do . . .'

Her voice was rising with suppressed panic.

Simone sighed. The last thing she wanted was to go out again tonight, but she'd never get to sleep herself knowing Hélène was alone and frightened. Whoever it was who called on her for help she'd have them on her mind, but Hélène especially. For as long as she could remember, Simone had felt it her duty to look after her. Hélène was so vulnerable – always had been – and knowing what she did had added a layer of vicarious guilt to the burden of responsibility.

'Just give me time to feed Félix,' she said. 'I've only just come in the door.'

'I know. I've been trying to get you for ages.'

'Well now you've got me. Try to calm down, and I'll be there in half an hour.'

Hélène must have been watching from the window. As soon as Simone pulled on to the drive she opened the door, wearing only a negligée and a pair of fluffy mules.

'Simone! Oh, thank goodness!'

'So – tell me about these calls,' Simone said, following her into the house. 'How many have you had?'

Hélène retrieved a gin and tonic from a side table and swallowed some, cupping the glass between her hands.

'They started this afternoon. Three, more or less one after the other. Then this evening – two earlier, and another an hour or so ago. The last time I promised myself I wasn't going to answer it. But I just had to. It went on and on . . . ring, ring, ring . . . and I thought it might be something important. But of course it wasn't.'

Simone frowned.

'They don't say anything obscene or threatening?'

Hélène shook her head, reaching for her cigarettes.

'Oh no. Nothing. Absolutely nothing.'

'Perhaps it's a fault on the line,' Simone suggested.

'I don't think so.' Hélène laughed nervously and drew deeply on her cigarette. 'I know there's someone there. I can *feel* them. It's absolutely unnerving.'

'I'm sure it is. Why didn't you just take the phone off the hook?'

'Oh I couldn't do that. Suppose someone wanted me urgently? If something happened to Henri, for instance, and Alain . . .' She broke off, but not before Simone had heard the eager tone of her voice when she spoke his name.

'You didn't think of ringing him when you couldn't get me?' Simone asked, not adding that she had actually been with Alain.

'I thought of it, of course. But *she's* there, isn't she, that Esther? I didn't want to make a nuisance of myself.' Hélène stubbed out her cigarette and lit another.

'Well there are ways of dealing with this sort of thing,' Simone said. 'If it carries on we can get the calls intercepted.'

'Not tonight, surely?'

'No, not tonight.'

'If it rings again, Simone, I think I'll flip. I got ready for bed, but I just couldn't settle. I was so afraid I'd fall asleep and be woken up by that damned bell!'

She was working herself up into a state again, Simone could see.

'Have you had one of your tablets?' she asked.

'No, I've been drinking. I'm not supposed to mix it, am I?'

'True,' Simone said, and felt a stab of relief as she remembered that other time when Hélène had mixed antidepressants and alcohol. At least she seemed to have learned her lesson. But Simone had never been completely convinced that that had been an accident. If the circumstances warranted it she didn't think she would totally trust Hélène not to do something similar.

'Why the hell does this have to happen on top of everything else?' Hélène asked distractedly, reminding Simone that she certainly had had enough just lately to pull down a much stronger and more stable personality than hers.

'Troubles often seem to come all together,' she said soothingly. 'Now look, I think you should go to bed.'

'But— '

'It's all right, I'll be here. I'll sleep in the spare room and if the phone rings, I'll be the one to answer it.' And give the silent caller, whoever he is, a piece of my mind, she added silently.

'All right.' Hélène nodded. 'Simone – I don't know how to thank you.'

'By calming down and getting some rest,' Simone said. 'You go on up. I'll make you a hot drink and bring it up to you.' She saw Hélène glance longingly at the gin bottle and added sternly, 'You've had enough, Hélène. You really must stop drinking so heavily. And you smoke too much, too.'

'I know. It's the only thing that keeps me sane.'

'I'm not so sure about that. Go on, Hélène – bed.'

As she prepared the drink she was half expecting the phone to ring again but it did not. She took the drink upstairs. Hélène was already in bed.

'Thank you.' She took the drink from Simone with a wan smile.

'Feel better now?' Simone asked briskly.

'A bit. Simone – I know this sounds really stupid, but would you do something for me? Would you just sit and talk to me for a while, like you used to?'

Echoes of the past touched Simone with silken fingers. Hélène, as she had been when she had first come to live with them after her mother had died, sad, lost, alone but for her tearaway brother. Simone had felt so sorry for her – and the guilt because of what she knew had weighed heavily on her. Often she had sat with Hélène until she fell asleep, talking softly, telling her stories, and it had seemed to help a little. Now, with her hair falling loose around her face and the covers drawn up to her chin she looked just as childlike and vulnerable as she had then. There was a part of Hélène, Simone thought, that had never grown up.

'If you like.' She moved a heap of fluffy toys from the wicker peacock chair beside the bed and sat down.

When Hélène had finished her drink, Simone turned off the bedside lamp so that the room dimmed to soft twilight.

'What do you want me to talk about?'

'Oh, tell me about Languedoc in the old days. You know.'

'All right.' She began to talk, softly and soothingly, weaving the pleasanter stories of castles with minstrel galleries, of knights and their ladies, of feasts and celebrations and fairs. Her voice grew slower and more languorous, her eyes heavy. She could hear Hélène's breathing becoming deep and even. She probably wouldn't even notice now if Simone left her and went to bed. But Simone felt too weary to move. She slid down in the peacock chair, resting her cheek against its curved back and feeling the room going away from her, becoming indistinct. There was a whiff of what smelled like lavender and wild thyme in her nostrils. Did Hélène have a herb pillow? She had not noticed it. But the perfume was growing stronger and she seemed to be drifiting into it.

It was happening again! And so soon! For a moment Simone fought to resist, but the pictures were taking shape before her half-closed eyes, and she could do nothing but watch them.

Summer sunlight filtered through the high narrow windows of the bedchamber which had been Agnes's private apartment since the death of her mother, the old chatelaine, some fifteen years before. Within its splintered rays Jeanne stood twisting her fingers in the folds of her skirt and looking apprehensively at Agnes, who sat on the padded chest which contained her personal belongings.

In the three years since she had lived at Montaugure, Jeanne had spent many happy hours in this room with the older woman who had become a surrogate mother to her, but today Agnes's usually serene face was worried and Jeanne knew instinctively that when Agnes had summoned her it had been with a serious purpose in mind.

Jeanne's heart beat uncomfortably against her ribs as she wondered anxiously if something bad had happened. Bad things did happen all too often nowadays, she knew – so often that she had almost ceased to be shocked by them. What had begun as a crusade against the heretics had escalated to a full-scale war between Simon de Montfort's army on the one hand and the lords of the south on the other. As castle after castle and town after town fell to the man who fought with such brilliance and utter ruthlessness for his twin masters – the church and the French king – the southern nobles had rebelled against the atrocities that were being committed against their people and against the invasion of their lands. They knew now that this was no longer simply a holy war – Louis wanted to make Occitania a part of the Kingdom of France and they were very afraid he was going to succeed. Even Raymond, liege lord of the Bernards, had given up trying to convince the Pope that he was a zealous Catholic. He had been excommunicated by the church and Toulouse itself was threatened with a siege.

Jeanne had heard the talk in the castle, just as she heard the horrified murmurings of the terrible atrocities committed by the crusaders. She had heard how Simon de Montfort had mutilated his prisoners at Bram, sending them out blinded and with their noses cut off as an awful warning to anyone who defied him. She had heard of the mass burnings of heretics at Minerve, the execution of eighty knights at Lavaur and the cruel manner in which Geralda, lady of the castle, had met her end – thrown into her own well by the crusaders and stoned to death.

But never before had Agnes sent for her to tell her of these things. Indeed, she did her best to keep Jeanne in ignorance of them.

'My child, I must talk to you,' Agnes said now, and Jeanne

quaked inwardly. Whatever it was that had happened it must be serious indeed if Agnes intended to break her own rule.

'What has happened?' Jeanne was unable to keep the fear out of her voice. 'Has Toulouse fallen? Is Philip . . . ?' She could not bring herself to put into words the thing she feared most. Philip, as a knight of Toulouse, was now pitted against the very army with which he had once fought and Jeanne lived in constant fear for his safety.

'What do you know about Toulouse?' Agnes's eyes were sharp, and for once her tone matched them. But a rush of relief made Jeanne's legs weak. It wasn't that, then. Agnes would never respond in that way if she were about to break terrible news.

'Never mind.' Agnes smiled faintly. 'I suppose it is a vain hope that you should hear nothing of the dreadful things that are going on. No, that is not the reason I called you here. I want to talk to you about something quite different. Come and sit down, my dear.'

She moved to the edge of the chest, patting the space beside her, and Jeanne perched on the cushion, catching her lip between her teeth and turning her head expectantly.

Agnes took one of Jeanne's hands in her own. The child was still too thin, she thought; though she had put on some flesh since coming to the castle, most of the good food had served only to make her grow taller. Time and loving care would put that right; she only wished she would be here to see it, for she loved Jeanne dearly.

'Very soon, my pet, I shall be going away,' she began.

Jeanne frowned. 'You mean – on a visit?'

'No. I mean I shall not be living here for much longer. I may not be able to see you very often, perhaps not at all, until you are much older, at least. But I want you to know it doesn't mean I shall forget you or love you any the less. Just that . . . well, I won't be here.'

'I don't understand!' Jeanne whispered.

Agnes sighed. She had given a great deal of thought to what she would say to Jeanne by way of explanation. Now, faced with the small desolate face and wide frightened eyes, all the carefully prepared phrases deserted her.

'I am going south – to a place called Montsegur,' she said gently.

Although she had been born and raised in the faith, the significance of the name of Montsegur – a Cathar stronghold – was lost upon Jeanne.

'But why?' she asked.

'I am going to live with friends who have much to teach me.'

'Teach *you*!' Jeanne's voice was full of incredulity. 'But you know everything!'

Agnes laughed. 'That may be very flattering, Jeanne, but most certainly it is not true. There are a great many things I do not know. And some of them are the most important things of all.'

'But why can't you learn them here? Why can't your friends come to Montaugure?'

'Because I am afraid that my brothers Raymond and Benet do not approve of them. And having them here could bring danger to you all.'

'Oh!' Jeanne's mouth dropped open as understanding began to dawn.

She knew that Raymond and Benet were angry with Agnes because she no longer attended Mass, and once or twice men in the robes of Cathar Perfects had visited the castle. Jeanne had thought little of it. The men were travelling preachers, she knew, and it was usual to give shelter to those in need of it, no matter what their beliefs – an act of Christianity between neighbours even in these times of persecution. She had realised from the sometimes violent arguments which had followed these visits that it had been Agnes who had offered them hospitality and that Raymond and Benet were less than overjoyed at having them under their roof, but she had thought little of that either. There were always arguments about religion, sometimes private, sometimes public – arranged debates where both sides were given a platform to argue the merits of their case. She had, it was true, thought it a little strange that a household which had sent its son on the crusade against the Cathars should now offer them shelter, however rarely, but then, life was full of anomolies – had not Raymond of Toulouse also changed sides? But there had been one particularly fierce quarrel when she had heard Cecile telling Agnes that her stubborn waywardness would be the death of them all. Since then there had been no more travelling Good Men at the castle and though Jeanne had noticed that Agnes rode out alone a good deal more often than she used to, she had not made any connection or drawn any conclusion.

Now, however, her sharp brain made the link.

'You are going to become a Cathar!' she said with sudden certainty.

Agnes sighed. She should have known she would not be able to deceive Jeanne.

'Yes, I am,' she said quietly.

'But that's wonderful!' Jeanne's eyes were shining. 'Oh Agnes, can't you take me with you?'

Agens closed her eyes momentarily. This was exactly what she had feared would happen if Jeanne knew the truth of what she planned. Well as the child had settled at the castle, much as she adored Philip, Agnes knew she still yearned to be among her own people and longed to be reunited with the little brother she had lost.

'I'm sorry, my dear, but I cannot do that,' she said regretfully.

'Why not?'

'Because this is your home now. You are safe here. Bernard and Philip love you and want to protect you. But the world outside is a dangerous place. You know what happened at Béziers and Carcassonne – well, I am afraid the same sort of thing is still going on. All over Languedoc towns and villages are still being put to the torch and believers slaughtered and burned. Much as I would love to have you with me, I couldn't put your life at risk in that way.'

'But what about *your* life? If it is so dangerous, why are you going to join them?'

'Because there are some things one has to do, whatever the dangers. I hope and believe that I shall be safe at Montsegur. Raymond of Pereille has made it into a refuge for any Cathar, noble or peasant. He is a brave man and a good soldier, but it is not going to be easy or pleasant. There will be attacks, just like the one you experienced at Carcassonne. And – who knows? – even a fortress as secure as Montsegur can fall, given the circumstances.'

Jeanne was silent for a moment, remembering the terrors of the siege which still haunted her in nightmares. Then: 'I don't want you to go!' she cried, unable to control herself a moment longer. 'Oh Agnes, I shall miss you so much, and I don't want anything terrible to happen to you!'

Agnes squeezed her hand, upset by the child's distress, but determined not to be swayed by it. She had come too far now to allow anything to distract her from the path she knew she must take, and it had been Jeanne herself who had set her feet on the road. As she had nursed her back to health in this very chamber she had first begun to realise how disillusioned she had become with the religion which had once been so important to her, and she had railed silently against a church which could cause an innocent child so much suffering. Thank God Jeanne had recovered. But Agnes's love for her church had not, though her faith in God and Jesus Christ was as strong as it had ever been – stronger, if anything, for she now saw the Christ as a much more spiritual figure than the Church of Rome allowed, a son of God imprisoned in human form yet able to escape from it when the time was right. Gradually Agnes had come to realise she could no longer condone the actions of those wickedly misguided individuals who tried to enforce their narrow views on others by fire and the sword. Instead she must pursue her own way.

'Please, Jeanne, try to understand,' she begged. 'It may be when you are older you, too, will want to return to your faith, and if you do then I will be there for you. But for the present you must stay here.'

Jeanne bowed her head, trying to hide her tears.

'When will you go?' she asked in a whisper.

'Very soon. But at least you won't be lonely.' Agnes squeezed Jeanne's hand, glad to have some more cheerful news to impart to soften the blow.

Jeanne looked up, tears glistening on her lashes.

'What do you mean?' she asked, puzzled.

'I mean you will soon have a friend here at Montaugure. Her name is Alazais Rolland and she is ten years old. A little younger than you, I grant, but I am sure you will find games to play together.'

Jeanne's eyes narrowed with suspicion.

'I don't understand. Why is she coming here?'

Agnes smiled. 'Because she is betrothed to Philip.'

'Betrothed!'

'Yes, my dear. One day she will be Philip's wife. The marriage was arranged long ago. Her father's lands adjoin our own and a marriage between our two families will produce a useful alliance.

Alazais's mother has died recently and her father and Bernard have decided the time is right for her to come and live here so that she can begin to accustom herself to our ways.' She paused, realising from Jeanne's expression that the news had not come as the welcome revelation she had hoped. 'What's wrong, Jeanne? I thought you would be pleased. It can't be much fun for you here without friends of your own age.'

Jeanne stared at her, unable to speak. Tears of shock and disbelief were collecting in a knot in her throat, choking her.

'She will need you too,' Agnes continued. 'She will find it very daunting at first to be among strangers. You will be able to show her around and help her to feel at home.'

She looked up at Jeanne hopefully and smiled, the warm encouraging smile which made her undeniably plain face almost beautiful. But there was no answering smile in Jeanne's eyes. She had turned pale and her features were as hard and shut in as if they had been carved from alabaster.

'Jeanne?' Agnes said anxiously.

Jeanne made no reply. She tore her hand away from Agnes's, turned swiftly, and, picking up her skirts, ran from the chamber as if all the demons of hell were at her heels.

Her eyes were full of scalding tears. She raced down the spiral staircase as fast as her slippered feet would carry her, steadying herself with her hands against the rough stone walls, then skirted the great hall and ran across the courtyard to the stables. They were her refuge, her favourite place in the whole world. But soon even that would be spoiled. A girl called Alazais Rolland was coming to Montaugure to be Philip's bride and nothing could ever be the same again.

Jeanne pushed her way past a startled groom and ran to Braida's stall. The horse whickered a welcome and Jeanne buried her face in the coarse grey neck, shivering violently.

Philip betrothed! Oh no, it couldn't be! Why had no one ever told her of it? All this time while she had been loving him with her whole heart and dreaming that one day they would be together he had been promised to an unknown girl for the sake of a suitable alliance. How could she have been so stupid as to imagine for one moment that he might make her, a Cathar peasant, his wife – but she had, she had! Since that long-ago day in the Church of the Marguerite when she had looked at him and known without doubt that she loved him she had clung to the dream. And she had truly thought he loved her too. He was so good to her and they had such fun together. He had taught her to ride and to hawk and never once had he shown impatience that she was so often at his side. Oh, she was still a child yet, she knew, only eleven years old, but he would wait for her, she knew it. Except that he was not going to wait. He was going to marry a girl even younger than she . . . Oh, sweet Jesu, it was more than she could bear!

'You want to ride?' The groom's voice penetrated the haze of her pain, and she looked up, proudly blinking away the tears.

'Yes.'

She stood watching while he saddled Braida and led her into the courtyard.

'Wait while I saddle a horse for myself.' His voice was rough but kindly; he had seen her distress and he was fond of the child who spent so much time with his beloved horses.

'No! No – I am riding alone!'

'You can't do that! The Viscount would never allow it.'

She ignored him, climbing on to the mounting block and hitching her skirts into her kirtle. She should not be riding in her new gown, either, she knew, but she was past caring.

She urged Braida towards the gates, determined to make the guards open them for her. But for once the little mare's gait was halting and Jeanne realised to her dismay that she had lost a shoe. There would be no ride for her today. She slipped from the saddle, and biting back the tears led Braida back towards the stable. There, burying her face in the horse's neck, she sobbed as if her heart would break.

Simone stirred. The dream was fading but she could still hear the sobs, drawing her back through the dark void which separated the centuries. She stretched out her hand, half expecting to feel the rough hair of a horse's mane and encountering instead the soft fur fabric body of one of Hélène's teddy bears. For a moment she could not understand where she was. Then it dawned on her that it was Hélène who was crying. She leaned over the bed, taking Hélène's hand in hers.

'It's all right, chérie, I'm here.'

Hélène made no reply, but after a moment the sobs ceased and

Simone realised that Hélène had not been awake at all, but crying in her sleep.

She smoothed Hélène's hair away from her damp face, wondering if it was safe for her now to go to bed. Her whole body felt heavy and she longed to lie down and sleep. But she couldn't bring herself to move. The past was still holding her, an unwilling prisoner and she had no choice but to allow it to envelop her once more.

Alazais Rolland arrived at Montaugure a week later, bringing with her an old woman named Fabrisse who had once been her nurse, three haughty-looking ladies and a darkly sullen man who was her personal bodyguard.

Although a year younger than Jeanne, she was taller by an inch or more, and her body had begun to develop the curves which Jeanne still lacked. Her hair, when she removed the veil she had worn for travelling, was thick and lustrous, the colour of ripe corn; her eyes were china-blue and her face round and pretty. As for her gowns and mantles, there were two chests full of them – silks and velvets embroidered with gold and satin thread – and though Jeanne had never cared a fig for what she wore she could not help a sharp pang of envy.

'You like them?' Alazais asked eagerly.

Jeanne shrugged. 'They are all right, I suppose.'

'Oh, I've never had anything like them before,' Alazais admitted, a faint pink colour tinging her cheeks. 'My father said I would need fine clothes to please my husband.'

Her words twisted the knife deeper and Jeanne burned with jealousy. Oh, Alazais was so smug – such a goody-goody, always trying to say the right thing! Yet everyone seemed to fawn over her – especially Philip! He had presents for her – a brooch, a circlet for her hair and a small casket set with precious stones to keep them in – and Jeanne was sick with jealousy.

The only thing that cheered her somewhat was that Alazais seemed not to care for riding. Jeanne had noticed how awkwardly she sat on her horse when she had arrived, as if she were afraid of the gentle beast and even more afraid she might fall off, and she soon realised Alazais never went to the stables unless she had to. At least Jeanne still had Philip to herself when they rode together. But even this small compensation was to be short-lived, for Philip was soon urging Alazais to accompany them.

'I know you are nervous, but there is really no need,' he told her gently. 'Have you never enjoyed riding?'

She shook her head, colour rising in a blush on her cheeks.

'When I was little my sister fell from her pony and died. I was always frightened after that and Father didn't make me ride unless it was unavoidable.'

'There really is no need to be afraid,' Philip assured her. 'Trust me, and I will teach you – just as I taught Jeanne. You will soon be riding as well as she does, believe me.'

His words stung Jeanne to the quick. Philip *had* taught her well, of course, but she knew she had been an apt pupil and she was proud of her ability. Now he was belittling even that. And worse, if he intended giving Alazais lessons she would not only be accompanying them every day, she would actually be commanding most of Philip's attention! A wave of hatred and jealousy stronger than anything Jeanne had ever experienced before coursed through her veins and she clasped her hands into fists so tightly that her nails bit into the palms.

The horses were saddled and waiting in the courtyard – Braida, Philip's great black stallion Auguste, and Mistral, a pretty little roan mare which Philip had judged suitable for Alazais to ride. Jeanne mounted quickly, eager to show off her prowess, and waited impatiently while Philip settled Alazais in the saddle, then she led the way through the gates, urging Braida to a fast trot.

'Not so fast, Jeanne! We don't want Alazais to be frightened,' Philip called after her.

Much fun this is going to be! Jeanne thought resentfully.

'I'll wait for you by the wood!' she called back.

She touched Braida with her heels. In a moment the mare was cantering then at full gallop, and exhilaration made Jeanne forget all her jealousy and misery. But when she reached the wood and reined in, it returned all of a rush. Philip and Alazais were far behind, trotting sedately side by side, and as Jeanne imagined how he would be talking to her, encouraging her, the feeling of exclusion was more than she could bear.

I'll make sure she doesn't come riding with us again! she thought.

She reached down and tweaked a spiky seed head from one of

the thistles growing beside the path, concealing it in her glove and trembling a little at the daring of her plan.

'That wasn't so bad, was it?' Philip asked Alazais as they reached her. 'Shall we go on a little farther, or is that lesson enough for today?'

'We'll go a little farther if you like. It's nice riding with you. I don't mind at all.' Alazais's cheeks were flushed; Jeanne wondered if it was just the stiff breeze that had lent them colour, or the things Philip had been saying to her, and her desire for revenge grew.

They rode through the woods and into the open countryside beyond, and when they stopped to rest and water the horses Jeanne saw her chance. When neither of the others was looking she slipped the thistle beneath Mistral's saddle. Then she hung back slightly as Philip led Alazais to a fallen tree which would make a suitable mounting block for an inexperienced rider.

The moment she saw Alazais's foot go into the stirrup she regretted what she had done and opened her mouth to call out a warning. But even as she did so she realised that to say something now would be to give herself away, and in any case it was too late. As Alazais's weight crushed the thistle against Mistral's back the horse shied, then plunged forward.

'God's teeth!' Philip yelled.

He vaulted into the saddle and was off, giving chase. For a moment Jeanne stood transfixed with horror for what she had done. Then she mounted Braida and set off after them.

Braida was a fleet little horse, but Mistral, spurred on by pain, was equally fast. She covered the open countryside at full gallop and was into the woods before even Philip on Auguste could catch her. Screaming and sobbing, Alazais clung on as low branches scratched her face and tore at her hair and though she tugged at the reins it had no effect.

Deep in the woods the path forked; Alazais, beside herself with terror, thought mistakenly that the left fork led towards Montaugure, but Mistral knew better. As Alazais leaned to the left Mistral swung to the right, and before she could save herself Alazais was out of the saddle. The ground rushed up to meet her with a sickening thud and her screaming stopped abruptly as all the breath was forced out of her lungs.

Within moments Philip was beside her, reining in Auguste and leaping out of the saddle to kneel beside her.

'Sweet Jesu, Alazais – what happened?'

'I don't know,' she sobbed, and he bent to cradle her in his arms.

Fearfully, Jeanne watched as he gently tested Alazais's bones and helped her to stand. What on earth had possessed her to do such a terrible thing? She had never meant Alazais to have such a crashing fall – only to scare her a little. Supposing she was badly hurt? Jeanne knew she would never forgive herself.

But mercifully the deep leaf mould had gone some way to breaking Alazais's fall; though she was bruised and shocked it seemed no real damage had been done. And as she watched Philip lift Alazais on to the saddle of his own horse and ride homeward with her in his arms as he had once done with her, Jeanne's misery was ample punishment for her wickedness.

'What did you do to make my horse bolt?' Alazais asked.

Jeanne felt her cheeks grow hot. 'What do you mean?'

'You put something under the saddle, didn't you?'

The two girls were lying side by side in the huge canopied bed they shared. The smell of the linament Fabrisse had rubbed into Alazais's sore back had already been making Jeanne nauseous; now the feeling of sickness worsened.

'I don't know what you're talking about. But if you thought there was something wrong, why did you get on?'

'Because it was only afterwards I realised.'

'The grooms didn't find anything, did they?' Jeanne asked defensively.

'No, but I'm sure I'm right. Oh don't worry, I won't tell anyone.'

'Why not?' Jeanne asked, shocked into the tacit admission.

'I don't know really. Because I want us to be friends, I suppose. The trouble is, you don't like me very much, do you?' Her tone was regretful; Jeanne felt the impatience prickling within her veins once more.

What on earth was the matter with Alazais? Any normal person would be furious to think someone had deliberately schemed to have them thrown from their horse. Any normal person would have told of their suspicions. But not Alazais. Instead she lay here in the dark bearing the pain like a martyr and talking about being friends! It was beyond belief!

'Please give me a chance, Jeanne,' Alazais went on softly. 'I know you resent me, but it's not easy for me, either. I've had to leave everything and everyone I love to come here to marry a man I scarcely know . . .' Her voice wobbled a little, and Jeanne's disbelief grew. Alazais was actually complaining about having to marry Philip!

'I just wish I was more like you,' Alazais went on after a moment.

'Like *me*?'

'Yes. You don't know how much I admire you.'

'But I am only a peasant!' Jeanne burst out before she could stop herself. 'You are a lady!'

'Oh, you don't behave like a peasant at all,' Alazais whispered. 'No one would ever know you were not a lady. But you are bold and brave, not frightened of things as I am. If I had half your courage I would be proud of myself. Please, won't you share a little of it with me?'

Jeanne closed her eyes and counted to ten. She did not understand Alazais or anything about her. But somehow she had to live alongside her.

'All right, we'll try to be friends,' she conceded.

Simone came to with a start, jerking upright in the wicker chair so that the cushion at her head fell to the floor with a soft plop. The room was bathed in soft luminous moonlight and the aura of the past still surrounded her. But her skin was crawling with awareness that had no place in that other world.

Something had disturbed her – but what? Hélène was sleeping peacefully now and the silence of the night was broken only by the chirping of the crickets on the lawns beneath the window.

Simone stood up, feeling for her sandals with her toes and slipping her feet into them.

She tiptoed out of the room, intending to go to bed herself. It was darker on the landing, with only a patch of moonlight spilling out through the half-open door of the room which used to be Thierry's to provide illumination. Simone felt her way towards the spare room at the opposite end of the landing.

Her hand was on the doorknob when a sudden thud made

her almost jump out of her skin. What on earth was that? It had come from downstairs, she thought, and had sounded like someone bumping into a piece of furniture.

Simone's heart began to beat uncomfortably fast. Was there an intruder in the house? Burglars were almost unheard of in this part of the world but that didn't mean it was impossible.

She took a couple of steps towards the head of the staircase, waited, listening intently. Nothing. The noise must just have been a timber settling. This was, after all, a very old house. She was about to turn away when she heard a creak, followed by a sharp click, and she froze again. There *was* someone down there! What the hell should she do? Call the police? But heaven only knew how long it would take them to get here and in any case there was no telephone upstairs that she knew of. Her overwhelming instinct was to retreat to Hélène's room and jam the door shut with the back of the chair but she knew she could not do that. If there was someone burgling the house she couldn't let them get away with it.

Angry now as well as frightened, Simone felt for the light switch and snapped it on. The sudden brightness made her blink. She looked around for something to defend herself with and saw Hélène's tennis racket propped up in a corner of the landing alongside a net of balls. Not ideal as a weapon but better than nothing. Simone picked it up, gripping it by the shoulder.

Heart pounding, she crept down the stairs, then hesitated again. She wasn't sure where the sound had come from. But only the door to the kitchen was ajar and it seemed unlikely that an intruder would have shut himself in one of the other rooms. She crept along the hall, holding the tennis racket in front of her like a policeman's baton.

The kitchen was in darkness but for the light of the moon coming in at the unshuttered window. Simone lowered the tennis racket and peeped through the crack in the half-open door. Nothing. She raised the racket again, standing behind the door.

'Who's there?' Her voice came out as a croak.

Still silence.

On an impulse she flung the kitchen door wide open and snapped on the light.

The kitchen was empty. No sign of an intruder, and everything looked perfectly normal – no drawers pulled out or cupboards opened, her shoulder bag lying on the corner of the table where she had left it, quite untouched. Only one of the kitchen chairs appeared to be slightly out of place, a foot or so out from the table and set an at untidy angle. But Simone couldn't be sure exactly where it had been when she had taken Hélène to bed. She stood for a moment in the doorway, relieved yet puzzled. Then she crossed to the door and tried it. It was unlocked, but then, she couldn't remember having locked it and certainly Hélène had been in no fit state to do so.

Simone turned the key, shot the bolt for good measure, and with a last look round went back into the hall. Should she check the other downstairs rooms? Perhaps. But she was fairly sure now they would be as empty as the kitchen had been. On her way back along the hall she opened each of the doors, switching on the light and glancing quickly around, but as she had expected there was nothing out of place in any of them.

She went back upstairs, turning out the lights as she went. Imagination. It must have been her imagination. Just like the dream world of Montaugure. Except that she was beginning to wonder if the dream might not be imagination at all . . .

The spare room felt as muggy as a sauna. Presumably Hélène had not been in to open a window since she got back from Perpignan, and the room, south-facing, had taken the full force of the sun's heat all day. Simone crossed to the window, throwing it wide open. The sweet scent of the stocks in the garden below wafted up to her and she rested her head against the frame for a moment, breathing deeply. Tired as she was, she was reluctant to go to bed, afraid to close her eyes in case the dream began again, though she knew now that not even forcing herself to stay awake would necessarily save her from slipping into that other world.

That, she thought, was the worst part of it – the feeling of having no control over what was happening to her. She was usually so well disciplined; years of practice had taught her to close her mind to distractions and concentrate on whatever she chose. But this was different. Now she seemed incapable of switching off. The fantasy world seemed to be taking her over.

In the warm darkness Simone shivered. Something totally inexplicable was happening whether she cared to admit it or not. And Simone, practical, sensible, used to dealing with well-documented facts, did not like things she could not understand.

* * *

Esther was dreaming, and from the very moment it began she knew, deep in her subconscious mind, that it was not going to be a pleasant dream. With the first whiff of woodsmoke she recognised it, for, though it was years now since the dream had haunted her, this was how it had always begun. A feeling of dread enveloped her and she struggled to wake, knowing instinctively that was the only way to avoid what lay in store, though she could not, for the moment, remember what it was. But she couldn't wake. There was no escape. Knowing it filled her with terror.

The crackling sound came next, faint at first then deepening quickly to a roar which seemed to fill her ears, and then she saw the flames, creeping, licking and shooting. The thickening smoke was hot and acrid, burning her lungs, and the feeling of helpless dread mounted. She had to wake up! She had to wake up before it was too late . . .

But the flames – oh the flames! They were closer now and she was trapped! Esther twisted violently in her sleep, hilting out wildly with her bare hands, and then she was screaming, screaming . . .

'Esther! What on earth is the matter?'

Alain's voice – and her own screams – woke her. For a moment she lay rigid with terror as she had done as a child.

'Esther?' he said again, sleepy but concerned.

She was bathed in sweat, her hands felt stiff and her arm hurt. She must have been lying on it, she supposed.

'I had a bad dream,' she muttered, then tensed again, her eyes flying wide open in panic. She could still smell smoke! Not only smell it but see it – thickening the room like a heavy mist. It must have been the smell of real smoke that had caused the dream!

'There's a fire!' she gasped, pushing him away.

'What?'

'The house is on fire! Quick!'

She leaped out of bed and ran to the door, yanking it open. Behind her she could hear Alain's puzzled, still-sleepy voice: 'What are you talking about?'

'A fire!' she repeated, but less certainly. There was no smell of smoke on the landing, no crackle or flicker of flames. Only the moonlight slanting in through the half-shuttered window. 'But I thought— '

'For goodness' sake, Esther!' Alain was sitting up in bed now.

She went back into the bedroom. In the soft silvery light of the moon she could see him quite clearly. No smoke blurring her vision now. Not even a whiff of it.

'Oh . . . I'm sorry . . . I must have been still half asleep. I thought— '

'That the house was on fire – I know. What on earth gave you that idea?'

'It was the dream. I used to have them a lot when I was little but it hasn't happened for years now . . .'

'Come back to bed.' Alain said.

She did so, nestling against him while he murmured soft words of comfort and held her close. But the images of the dream and the echo of the terror still lingered. And as she lay awake, remembering it, she found herself wondering: why had it come again after all these years? And why now?

13

When Esther woke again the bedroom was flooded with bright sunshine and she was alone. Alain had told her he must work today and obviously he had got up to make an early start.

The memory of the dream she had had last night was still with her, imbuing her with a vague sense of unease. She couldn't understand why she should have had it – it was so long since something similar had happened. And the fact that she and Alain had still not really sorted things out was nagging at her too. On the surface everything had gone back to being the way it had been in England; certainly he was as passionate and loving as ever. But they were no nearer to sorting out their plans for the future; the word 'divorce' had not been mentioned and surely it should have been. Last night, for instance, would have been a good time to talk about it, but somehow they hadn't, and now Alain was going to be busy all day.

Did he think that by coming here she had accepted the status quo? He'd said that as a Catholic he was opposed to divorce; perhaps she had unintentionally given him the impression that she was prepared to simply go on being his mistress. The French were very blasé about that sort of thing, weren't they? But if he thought that, he was very much mistaken. She wasn't prepared to live like that – especially with Hélène so very much still part of the scene.

There were ten days of her holiday still left, but Esther was impatient suddenly to sort out exactly where she stood. She made up her mind to raise the subject at the very first real opportunity and not allow herself to be sidetracked by the passion that usually overtook them when they were alone.

She pushed aside the sheets and winced as her fingers rasped painfully on the crisp cotton. How very odd! She spread her hands and examined them but she could see no reason for it, not even the pattern of indentations which would have meant she'd been lying on them. The arm she had scalded in the bath was hurting too, she realised, and when she looked at that she saw that the half-healed scar looked angry again. She touched it gently, hoping it hadn't become infected. Perhaps in this hot climate she should have kept it covered.

She got up and went to the bathroom to shower and dress but the vague feelings of unease persisted and she found herself thinking again that it really was time she and Alain sorted things out properly.

The breakfast room was deserted though the table was still laid with croissants and jam and there was no sign of anyone in the drawing room either. Esther went back upstairs, tapped on the door of Alain's study and pushed it open.

'It's only me – coming to say good morning. I overslept!'

'That's what being on holiday is all about.' But his tone was preoccupied and distant.

'It looks like the *Marie Celeste* downstairs,' she said.

'I expect Maman and Papa are in the garden. Have you had breakfast?'

'Not yet.'

'Well, help yourself to whatever you can find. And make some fresh coffee.'

'Don't I get a kiss?' she asked ruefully.

He kissed her but it was obvious his mind was on other things. 'I'm sorry, Esther, but I really have to do some work.'

'Of course you do – I quite understand.' She said it, *meant* it even, yet at the same time felt unreasonably hurt and a little resentful. Ashamed of her own reaction when he so clearly needed to spend some time sorting out his business affairs, she went on quickly, 'I thought maybe I'd do a spot of sightseeing if the offer of the car is still open.'

'It is, of course. But you don't have to spend the day alone. You have a lunch invitation from some neighbours of ours.'

'*I* do?'

'Yes, they telephoned just now to ask us over. I explained that I would be busy today and they said they'd be very happy to entertain you anyway.'

'Oh I don't know about that.' Esther bit her lip, frowning.

'They're your friends, presumably. They don't know me from Adam and I don't know them.'

'You'd like them,' Alain encouraged her. 'They're English people. Actually I think the invitation was aimed at you anyway. Diana said she'd heard you were staying here – doesn't take long for word to get round does it? – and she thought you might like to meet some fellow countrymen. They have these expat lunch parties quite regularly, I think.'

'Well who are they?'

'Diana and Bob Slater. He used to be a police officer and they moved out here when he retired. It was actually Bob who suggested Bristol would make a good base for the English end of my business – it's his home town – so you'd find plenty to talk about.'

'I guess . . .' She was still hesitant.

'Look, I'd take you over and introduce you,' Alain said. 'It's just that I can't possibly spare the whole afternoon. I know what these lunch parties are like – half-three, four o'clock and the wine is still flowing free.'

'All right,' Esther said. 'It might be fun.'

'It will be, I'm sure. I'll pick you up about midday and drive you over.' He sounded relieved; there was no longer any need for him to worry about leaving her alone all day, she thought – and realised she liked being a burden even less than she liked feeling sidelined. What the hell was the matter with her today?

The telephone began to shrill.

'I'll leave you to it,' she said, trying to ignore this cocktail of doubts and forebodings that was worrying away at her.

He nodded without answering, reaching for the phone as she closed the door behind her.

'Alain – it's Simone.'

'Simone!' He was surprised but relieved. He had expected the caller to be another irate creditor. 'What can I do for you?'

'Not so much me. It's Hélène. She's been getting peculiar phone calls.'

'You mean *obscene*?' Alain asked sharply.

'No – silent. The phone rings and when she answers it there's no one there. It happened several times yesterday, apparently. She called me last night when I got home and begged me to go over. I had to stay the night – I'm still there now. She's very upset by it, Alain. I thought you should know.'

'Well yes – but what am I supposed to do about it?'

'I thought perhaps you could get the line monitored or something. It's still in your name, isn't it?'

'Yes, but . . .' He paused. 'Are you sure there's anything malicious in this, Simone? Isn't it more likely it's just someone getting the wrong number?'

'Hélène doesn't seem to think so. She's fairly sure there's someone the other end listening to her. It could be just that some crank picked the number at random, I suppose, and if they could hear that Hélène was reacting they got some perverse pleasure out of it and did it again. But then again it could be someone who knows exactly who she is. I can understand her being upset. Something like that must be pretty unnerving.'

'I suppose so, but unless they actually say something I don't see that it warrants all the fuss of getting the line monitored,' Alain said. 'I'm not even sure the telephone people would be interested in something so trivial unless it keeps happening over a much longer period. Yesterday was the first time, you say?'

'Yes, but . . . I'm worried about her, Alain. She's had an awful lot to cope with just recently and this could be the last straw.'

'She's certainly taken Thierry's death very hard – understandably.'

'Yes, and not only that. She's pretty cut up about you and Esther, I can tell. I know it's none of my business, but I think she was banking on you and she getting back together again, and— '

'Oh come on, Simone!' It was no more than the truth, he realised, and the realisation made his tone sharp.

'I know . . . I know. As I said, it's really none of my business. But that doesn't stop me worrying about her, Alain. After all these years it's not a habit one can break easily.'

'No.' That was true, too, he realised. As much for himself as for Simone. That they had separated didn't mean he had stopped feeling responsible for her, caring for her even.

Again he felt the twist of regret he had felt the night she had come over with her pitifully transparent excuse about her lights failing – regret for what they had shared before it had all begun to go wrong, and perhaps something more. Did he still love her? There were times when he could almost believe that he did. The old Hélène, the girl who could make him laugh and warm him through with her loving, still had a place in his heart. Even when she was tearing their marriage apart with her moods and her accusations, and her refusals to have his child, he had still loved her, still wanted only to make it work. Until finally he had come to the conclusion that he really did not have the will to try any more. Would he have given it one last shot, he wondered, if he hadn't met Esther? When the memory of the acrimony had become less clear than the memory of the good times? Very likely. Especially when Thierry's untimely death had brought him back to France. But he *had* met Esther. And fallen in love with her. The attraction he had immediately felt for her had become consuming passion – obsession, almost – so swiftly that it had startled him. He wanted Esther. But he still cared for Hélène, in spite of everything. And the confusion of emotion was beginning to get to him.

'Look, I'll try to look in on Hélène later,' he said now, a little curtly. 'If these phone calls continue, then we'll think again about what we should do. But for the moment, I simply must get on with some work.'

Simone stood for a moment, her hand still on the receiver, biting her lip. She had hoped that by telling Alain she would relieve herself of the responsibility, but it hadn't worked out like that.

She glanced over her shoulder at the stairs, listening for sounds of life. Hélène had still been asleep when she had looked in on her just now. When she woke, refreshed from a good night's sleep, she would have calmed down sufficiently to be less hysterical about the silent phone calls. But then again, she might not. And if it happened again . . . Anxious as she was to get home and get on with some work, Simone was seriously concerned about leaving Hélène alone.

Perhaps Valerie could help out, she thought. Her time was her own.

She reached for the telephone again and dialled. After a moment, Valerie's sleepy voice answered. Simone went through her story again.

'I'm worried about leaving her on her own,' she finished. 'It will really throw her if she gets another of these calls. I was wondering if you . . . ?'

'Poor Hélène!' Valerie said sympathetically. 'Silent phone calls are horrid! Yes, I'll go over and spend some time with her. I owe her a visit in any case.'

'Bless you!' But Simone smiled to herself. Valerie seemed to owe everyone a visit!

'Actually, I'm glad you phoned,' Valerie said, sounding more awake now. 'I wanted to talk to you. I spoke to Aurore after I left you last night.'

'Aurore!' Simone said, surprised. 'Whatever for?'

'I wanted to talk to her about what's been happening to you, of course! I wanted to know what she thought.'

'Oh.' Simone's initial irritation was tinged with curiosity. 'And what did she have to say?'

'Well, quite a lot, really. I need to talk to you about it, Simone, but it's not altogether easy to do over the phone.'

'You obviously managed it with Aurore.'

'Aurore and I are on the same wavelength, whereas you are determined to be sceptical.' She hesitated, fear of derision vying with the irresistible urge to tell Simone about the conversation she had had with her old friend. 'All right . . . just as long as you promise to listen and not go off the deep end.'

'I'll try.'

'Well, Aurore agreed with me that there's a connection with that third-eye experiment we did. She remembered it very clearly and she said you were definitely describing the life of a Cathar woman in the thirteenth century – a woman called Helis Marty. She thought then – and she thinks now – that Helis Marty was *you*, Simone, in a previous incarnation, and she thinks that doing that out-of-body experience opened the channels.'

'So why haven't I had some recurrence of this so-called out-of-body experience before now? That was years ago, Valerie.'

'Because you shut your mind to it – blocked it off.'

'And why can't I block it off now?'

'Because for the first time it's stronger than you are. There is some terribly important reason why you should learn the story of what happened. Perhaps subconsciously even you realise that, and you've let down the barriers.'

'What reason could there possibly be?' Simone demanded.

'Well, we don't know for certain, of course. But Aurore thinks it may be something to do with the laws of karma.'

'Karma,' Simone said flatly.

'Yes. You know about karma, Simone. Every one of our actions brings about its own reaction – good or bad. If we do a kindness it is rewarded, if we behave wickedly we have to put things right or be punished for it. I truly believe that, and so does Aurore. Sometimes it's worked out by "quick karma" within the present lifetime. But sometimes, if the mistake is too great or the action too wicked, or if we die before we can attone for it fully, it's carried over into the next life. Punishment for wrongdoing in a past life explains so many things that seem unjust – extreme poverty, dreadful disabilities, violent death . . . If you accept the laws of karma you can see that all these things are the sins of the fathers being visited on the children – except that that doesn't mean one's father literally: it means in the sense that the being we were in a former life is father to the person we are now.'

'Yes – we've been through all this before,' Simone said impatiently. 'But I don't see what it can possibly have to do with my dreams.'

'Because there is another aspect to karma. If we get something terribly wrong then we have to put it right before we can move on. We are caught on the Wheel, condemned to live through the same sequence of events again and again until we learn our lesson and do things differently. Aurore thinks, and so do I, that some sequence of events that happened long ago is happening again, and the story is being revealed to you in an effort to prevent a recurrence of some terrible wrongdoing.'

'Oh God.' That sentence again – 'What happened before must happen again.' Simone passed a hand across her gritty eyes, feeling the weight of the words like an albatross around her neck. 'But it doesn't make sense. Just supposing there is something in what you say – why should I be the one getting the revelations?'

'Because you are psychic, whether you like it or not, and because you were deeply involved before – emotionally, at any rate.'

'But I wasn't! I've already told you. If I was anyone, I was Helis – and she died.'

'I'm coming to that. Suppose Jeanne was the one who did some terrible wrong, and she is the one caught on the Wheel of Karma? Jeanne was Helis's daughter. Wouldn't it be only natural for Helis to care very deeply for Jeanne's immortal soul?

She might even have looked in on what followed after she died, earthbound because she was so concerned about the welfare of her orphaned children. And now . . . now that Jeanne's chance has come to do things differently in this life, it's given to Helis to help her avoid the same mistakes and the same fate – whatever that may be.'

Simone was silent. This was all too much to take in. And yet . . . somehow Valerie's explanations were touching a chord deep within her. For all her scepticism it somehow felt *right*. For didn't it somehow describe exactly the way she felt in her dreams – anxious, helpless, an onlooker with no control over what was happening?

'Simone?' Valerie said. 'Are you still there?'

'Yes, I'm here. Go on.'

'I told Aurore about Esther too – how all this started when she came to France and how you seemed to recognise her. And what we wondered was whether *Esther* might possibly once have been Jeanne.'

Another prickle, spreading like a sudden cold shiver over the whole of her body. Simone reached for a chair, hooking it into range and sitting down. She wasn't at all sure her legs would support her much longer.

'We can't be sure, of course,' Valerie was saying. 'If only Aurore wasn't so far away she might be able to help, but as it is the best suggestion she could make was that if we could send her something personal belonging to Esther she'd see if she got any vibes from it.'

'Something personal.'

'Yes, you know – a ring, a watch . . .'

'I can just see Esther handing over her watch so we can send it off for a psychic reading!' Simone said drily. 'She'd think we were crackers!'

'Well – a handkerchief, something like that . . .'

'A non-starter, I would think. Did she have any other suggestions?'

'Simone – you are actually listening to what I'm saying!' Valerie sounded incredulous. 'What's wrong with you?'

'Well – I have to tell you – it happened again last night.'

'The dream – again!'

'Yes, when I was sitting with Hélène.'

'Oh my goodness!' Valerie could hardly contain her excitement. 'They're coming thick and fast now, aren't they, these visions – as if it's urgent that you should find out what it's all about. But then, it would be, I suppose, if Esther is the linchpin. After all she's only here for a couple of weeks.'

Simone's skin crawled. Urgency. Yes. That described very well the way she was beginning to feel, though it was impossible to pin it down to any specific reason. Urgency – and impending danger. She could feel it in the air like the electric charges which precede a thunderstorm.

'Well?' she said.

'Aurore agreed it would be a good idea to try to trace the Bertrand family – see if there's anything in the records about what happened to them. And . . .'

'Yes?'

Valerie hesitated. 'The other thing she suggested was that you should read the tarot.'

'Read the tarot!'

'Yes. She gave you a tarot pack, didn't she, as a parting present when she left after that holiday. Because she was convinced you were psychic and you could develop your gift if you'd only give it a chance.'

'Well I didn't, I'm afraid,' Simone said with a short laugh. 'I haven't looked at them from that day to this. I'm not even sure where they are.'

'Then I suggest you find them,' Valerie said. 'She gave you a book as well – didn't she? – explaining how to read the cards?'

'Yes, but— '

'Do it, Simone, please! Just see what happens.'

'Oh I don't know . . .' Simone was beginning to feel stressed and disturbed again. She could hardly believe she had gone along so far with this; a few weeks ago – a few days even! – she would have dismissed it as utter twaddle. But she wasn't dismissing it any more. That was the measure of the effect it was having on her.

'Simone – you must! Don't you realise how privileged you are to be in this position? I wish it were me!'

'I wish it were you too, Valerie, believe me! I'd give anything to get back to normal.'

'And you will once this is over.'

But would she? After something like this, could anything ever be normal again?

'All right, I'll try it and see what happens,' she said. 'Though I doubt if anything will. And in the meantime, you'll look in on Hélène? She really does need someone around. She's right on the edge of her nerves.'

'You don't think *Hélène* has anything to do with this?' Valerie asked suddenly. 'It's always seemed to me that she was carrying a lot of baggage.'

'I think she probably is. After all, she had a very insecure childhood.'

'Yes, but supposing it's more than that?' Valerie sounded excited. 'Perhaps she's involved in whatever happened too! I mean – Esther is Alain's new woman, and Hélène is his wife.'

'Yes, Valerie, yes,' Simone said hastily, but she was shaking again. The last dream – the one from which she had woken to hear Hélène weeping – there had been two women in that too. Jeanne and Alazais. The parallel was suddenly too close to home for comfort. 'You will go and see her? I can safely leave her in your hands?'

'Yes. I told you.'

'In that case I'll take her a cup of coffee and get off home.'

It was, Simone thought, the most normal sentence she had spoken in the last five minutes.

'What was all that about?' Yves asked, emerging from the bedclothes. His handsome face was raddled and bleary, his long hair unkempt.

Valerie told him and he laughed shortly.

'So – Hélène has another admirer? Well, good for her.'

'What do you mean – *another* admirer?' She snuggled back under the sheet, curling her body close to his. 'You don't fancy her, do you?'

'Of course,' he said lazily. 'I've always fancied her. Hélène is a very fanciable lady.'

'Is she indeed! More fanciable than me?'

'Oh I wouldn't say that.'

He reached for her and she tangled her fingers in the hair which grew thickly between breastbone and navel.

'Yves Marssac, you are insatiable!' she teased, but she was enjoying every moment of it.

Valerie had loved her husband very much, but he had been so much older than she, responsible, serious-minded and a little pompous. He had treated her like a very special child, a porcelain doll to be spoiled and loved and looked after. He had never allowed her to be truly sexual and she had not wanted him to. To behave in that way with him would have been embarrassing – as bad, in a funny sort of way, as if she had flaunted herself in front of her father. But with Yves it was quite different. With him she could live out all her fantasies, behave like a whore if she liked, and it only made Yves want her more. She knew that none of her family or friends approved but she couldn't have cared less. It was none of their business.

He lay now enjoying her attentions for a while, then pulled her on top of him. She laughed softly, straddling him, her hair falling loose over his face, then sitting back on her heels so that she could watch his moment of climax as well as feeling it within her. Watching his enjoyment was her greatest pleasure – at this time of day, at any rate. Later there would be plenty of time for her own. As she had said, Yves was insatiable.

When it was over she rolled back on to the mattress, closing her eyes to bask lazily in the sunshine that streamed in through the unshuttered windows, her fingers loosely twined in his.

'I wonder who on earth it is who's ringing Hélène? It's really weird, isn't it?'

'You're not still worrying about that, are you?'

'Not worrying, no. Just curious.'

He laughed softly and she turned her head on the pillow to look at him.

'It's not you, playing wicked jokes, is it?'

'That's what I love about you, Valerie. You're so trusting.' He chuckled again. 'No, what I was thinking is that the most likely candidate is your brother.'

'Alain?' she said incredulously.

'Why not? Hélène's a bit neurotic, isn't she? She tried to top herself once, after all. Perhaps he thinks if he pushes her a bit she'll crack again and he'll be free to marry his new woman.'

'What a thing to say!' Valerie gave him a playful slap. 'You're wicked, Yves Marssac!'

'I know – and you love it. Come here, my sweet, it's your turn now.'

He reached for her again, gentling her with the touch that could make her senses swim.

Valerie sighed, all her good intentions melting away. Yves reminded her of a panther, she thought, sleek, strong and deceptively lazy. And dangerous. Very, very dangerous. The thought sent a shiver of excitement over her already sensitised skin and as it twisted sharply within her Valerie forgot all about Hélène.

The village clock was striking eleven as Simone let herself into her cottage. Félix heard the car and came streaking out of the bushes to rub himself around her legs as if to say that, independent soul though he was, he was glad she was home. Simone bent to fondle his ears and immediately he was off again, jumping up into a chair and curling into a comfortable ball.

She went around the house opening windows and tidying up the debris of yesterday, which had seemed perfectly acceptable when she had left it last night but now, a day later, made the house look slovenly – some correspondence lying on top of the ripped-open envelopes, a cup containing the dregs of her herbal tea, the cushions scattered untidily across the sofa where she had lain in the morning to try to get rid of her headache. Her desk looked as if a hurricane had hit it – Simone winced at the haphazard pile of books and rough printout sheets. She retrieved the plastic cover of her word processor from the wastepaper basket into which it had fallen and jammed it over the keyboard, feeling a stab of guilt as she did so. She should be switching her word processor on, not packing it up, but she knew that to try to work today would be as futile as it had been yesterday or the day before – more so, probably. There was even more on her mind now than there had been then – and none of it concerned Simon de Montfort.

When the house had been restored to some semblance of order Simone sat down on the sofa, drawing her legs up beneath her and thinking about the conversation with Valerie. The things her sister had said had shaken her badly – as if she had not already been shaken enough by the continuing story from which she seemed unable to escape. If one was prepared to suspend disbelief there was no doubt that Valerie's theory, far-fetched though it may seem under normal circumstances, actually went some way to explaining the inexplicable. The dreams, or 'visions', as Valerie preferred to call them, vivid and ordered – the fact that they had begun when Esther had come to France, the feeling of familiarity Simone had experienced on meeting her, the sense of urgency and apprehension which still hung over her . . . If she really was seeing a replay of something that had happened here in Languedoc eight hundred years ago, then Valerie's theory put all the pieces together as neatly as a completed jigsaw puzzle.

Was it possible that she had been wrong all her life to dismiss such ideas as superstitious mumbo-jumbo? Simone asked herself. Was it possible that she had lived before as a Cathar woman named Helis Marty? Could it be that her daughter in that other life had done something so terrible that her soul had been caught on the Wheel of Karma and forced to relive her actions until that wrong had been righted? And – the million-dollar question – was the story now being revealed to her so that she could help the soul in torment to do things differently this time around and be freed at last?

Simone buried her head in her hands, thinking furiously, and a sudden thought occurred to her.

When she had first had the 'dreams' she had put them down to a sort of delirium caused by a flu virus. But she was better now and yet the 'dreams' were continuing. Was it possible, then, that the feeling of malaise had come about because of the 'dream' rather than the other way round? She had felt perfectly well when she had gone to bed that night, she remembered. It was only after she had dreamed of being Helis that the symptoms had begun – the sore throat and aching limbs, the gritty eyes and the faraway feeling. Exactly the way someone would feel if they were sick with fever.

But Helis had died and she was alive. It didn't make sense, unless . . .

A sudden chill prickled on Simone's skin as she remembered the feeling of peace that had come over her at the moment of Helis's death. Could it be that she had somehow experienced it and the symptoms of fever had lingered into her everyday life?

As for the phrases that had appeared on her word processor, she couldn't understand them either. She no longer believed, she realised, that they had appeared through some fault in the software. As an explanation that was too convenient, and yet at the same time too much of a coincidence, considering Valerie had echoed them almost word for word.

Unless of course Valerie herself had put them there as some kind of joke.

Simone racked her brain, trying to remember the last time Valerie had been to visit her. Weeks ago – certainly before Thierry's death – and in any case she didn't think Valerie had been alone in the study. But even if she had, even if her computer had been left switched on – which it would have had to be if Valerie was responsible, for Simone was certain her sister would not be able to find her own way into the program – she couldn't believe Valerie would tamper with it. She had too much respect for Simone's work and she would be too afraid of messing it up.

So – where had the phrases come from? Had she unknowingly typed them in herself? But she didn't believe that either. They had simply appeared, like some dark prophesy. And then the visions had begun.

'I don't believe it,' Simone said aloud. 'I don't believe any of it!' But the words had the hollow ring, now, of a whistle in the dark. It was the old sceptical Simone who had poured scorn on what she had thought of as fantastic rubbish. Now, for the first time, she was beginning to believe – and not only because of all the inexplicable happenings, but because deep within her a knowledge she had suppressed all her life was beginning to stir.

'You have to go on with it,' Valerie had said, and in that at least Simone knew she was right. This was no longer something that could be ignored or dismissed. For her own peace of mind she must try to get to the bottom of it.

Well – first things first. Try to find out if Montaugure and the Bertrand family had really existed. As she had said to Valerie, it wouldn't prove anything, but at least it would be a start.

Simone levered herself up and almost fell as she put her weight on her foot. She must have been sitting on it – now it felt like an enormous pincushion, fat and fuzzy. She limped across the room to the telephone and flicked through her personal directory for the number she wanted.

Edith Lacroix was not only the local librarian but also an authority on the history of the Albigensian Crusade, and over the many years when she had helped Simone with her researches they had become friends.

A young assistant answered the telephone; Simone asked for Edith and after a few minutes she was on the line.

'Simone! What can I do for you?'

'Sorry to bother you, Edith, but could you check something for me? I'm trying to find out about a castle near Toulouse called Montaugure and a family named Bertrand who lived there in the thirteenth century. Have you ever heard of them?'

'Bertrand. The Bertrands of Montaugure. Yes, that rings a bell.'

Simone felt the hairs on the back of her neck rise.

'They did exist then?'

'Oh yes, I'm sure they did. The castle is gone now – it was razed to the ground in a terrible fire in fourteen-something, and the name of the village was changed when the whole area became part of the Kingdom of France, but certainly it was once called Montaugure.'

Simone swallowed at the lump of excitement which had risen in her throat.

'What do you know about the Bertrands?' she asked.

'Offhand, not a great deal, I'm afraid. They were vassals of the Count of Toulouse, as far as I can remember.'

'And you don't know anything of what happened to them during the crusade?'

'Sorry, no. Do you want me to look them up for you?'

'Oh, would you? It's the early part of the thirteenth century I'm interested in.'

'I'll see what I can find. It might not be much. There were so many minor nobles in those days, as you know. But I've a feeling there is some story attached to them – it's nagging away at the back of my mind. I have heard something – a story, a legend – I'm sure.'

'Edith, you are an angel.'

'Well, I don't know how long it will be before I can get around to it, that's the only thing,' Edith said regretfully. 'It's the holiday season, I'm short-staffed, and it's organised chaos here.'

'Well – when you can.'

'I'll get back to you in a day or two.'

Simone replaced the receiver with mixed feelings. Though of

course it proved nothing, it was incredibly exciting to discover that the Bertrands of Montaugure had really existed – and that there was some kind of story attached to them. But Simone couldn't help feeling that she needed to know what it was *now*, not in a day or two, or maybe even longer. An awful lot could happen in a day or two, considering what had happened in the last forty-eight hours or so. Years passed in the blinking of an eye where the story was concerned, and Esther was here for only a short time. More than a day or two and it may be too late . . .

I'm even getting to *think* like Valerie now! Simone thought. But there was no denying the sense of urgency which prickled in her veins.

Well, she'd tried the commonsense, logical way of finding out what all this was about and drawn a blank. Perhaps she should try the extraordinary – follow Aurore's suggestion and do a tarot reading.

Again Simone's skin prickled, this time with a sense of unreality. How could she even consider it – she who had always regarded such dabbling as silly futile fantasy which might just possibly be dangerous? She had never allowed Aurore to read the cards for her, let alone tried it for herself, and she didn't know where to start. She would be struggling even with the help of the instruction book, for it was probably written for people who had at least some idea of what they were doing. She wasn't even sure where the tarot pack was . . . No, not quite true. She *did* know where it was – or at least she thought she did: pushed away in the drawer where she kept most of her junk.

Simone crossed to the heavy old sideboard, yanked open the drawer and rifled through it. As she had thought, the tarot pack was right at the back, wrapped in a silk handkerchief, just as Aurore had given it to her.

Simply handling it made her nervous. It was, she thought, as if the tarot pack was the forbidden fruit of the Tree of Knowledge, and just one bite would change her for ever. But that was being stupid. Whatever happened – or did not happen – she would still be the same person.

She found the book – *The Tarot Explained* – on a shelf, sandwiched between her history books, and leafed through it. There were diagrams of the different spreads and clear illustrations of each one of the cards accompanied by notes on how to interpret it. Simone propped it open on the table. Then she removed the cards from the silk square. As she touched them she felt a tingle run from her fingers into her wrists like a mild electric current, and shivered. But there was no going back now. In spite of her reservations Simone somehow felt compelled to continue with what she had begun.

She held the cards between her hands for a moment, concentrating on the questions to which she required answers as the book had told her to. Then, carefully following the instructions, she laid out her chosen spread and turned them over one by one.

According to the book the Emperor, the first card, signified a need to seek advice. Well, that seemed apt enough. But there was more to it than that: apparently the Emperor also represented excessive emotion, swift infatuations and enthusiasms leading to total disillusion, and a need to rebuild following disasters. It wasn't a wholly bad card, though, but also indicated the ability to tackle problems and the courage to overcome.

Beneath the Emperor were two Queens – Simone identified them as the Queen of Cups and the Queen of Pentacles – and between them the Five of Cups, a card which the book said was associated with loss: a love affair, perhaps, which refused to die. But the Five of Cups was not totally bad either, it seemed. 'Let go the past and all will be well,' was a message that seemed to offer hope in a sad situation.

Simone checked the meaning of the next card and felt her heart sink. The Five of Swords – a card which the book described as 'nothing but disaster'. Dishonour and treachery, conflict, jealousy and deceit – the Five of Swords signified all of these. Simone stared at it, and though she had never read the cards before she could feel the dark cloud it cast over the whole spread.

She shivered, forcing herself to look at the next card. The High Priest, the card concerned with the future and one which conveyed spiritual awareness. Was there some mystical significance here? Could it be telling her that she did indeed have some role to play in what was happening? Simone was suddenly quite sure that it was. But what . . . what?

She looked again at the two queens and felt her skin prickle. She could feel a rivalry between them so clear it seemed to crack and spark in the air. Yet somehow she knew it was more than simply rivalry. Much, much more than that . . .

The sudden sense of impending danger was so strong it made her head swim. She gripped the edge of the table, closing her eyes momentarily, and when she opened them again the faces of the two queens seemed to be swirling, changing.

Esther and Hélène.

Simone sobbed aloud, pressing her hand over her mouth. Her head had begun to ache, a sharp hot pain knifing through her temple and her throat had gone dry.

She closed her eyes again, breathing deeply. Two cards printed with the pictures of two queens. That was all they were. They hadn't changed. It wasn't possible. She had seen it only with the eyes of her mind. It was all in her imagination. She looked back at the cards, willing them to be the garish etchings they had been before.

The faces *had* changed. They were no longer Esther and Hélène, but they weren't the Queens of Cups and Pentacles either. As the tiny dots swirled and regrouped before her eyes Simone gasped again, for now she was seeing the faces which haunted her dreams – two faces which spanned the centuries.

Simone looked at the cards and saw Jeanne and Alazais.

14

THEY STOOD TOGETHER on the battlements as the contingent of men-at-arms with Philip at their head rode out beneath the great portcullis which had been raised to let them pass. The wind, whipping across the plain, had brought a flush to Alazais's fair skin, but Jeanne was deathly pale and she gripped the rough stone coping to keep her hands from trembling with fear for his safety, though at the same time her heart was full of pride.

Oh sweet Jesu, how she loved him! It was eight years now since the day she had looked at him through her fingers as she knelt beside him in the Church of St Marguerite and felt that first overwhelming surge of adoration, five years since Alazais had come to live at Montaugure and Jeanne had been confronted with the devastating news that he was betrothed to another, and still the flame burned as brightly as ever.

Throughout all the separations she had been forced to endure as Philip fought with the lords of the south against Simon de Montfort and the French armies, her devotion had been unwavering. Night after night she had fallen to her knees, begging God to keep him safe, and her prayers had been answered. Somehow he had escaped death at the Battle of Muret, though King Peter of Aragon and many knights, his own brothers Martin and Raymond among them, had been killed and the infantry had been driven into the River Garonne and drowned, and the same held true for all the other skirmishes he had been involved in. Though God seemed to be on the side of de Montfort and the battles all went his way, Philip had escaped unscathed.

Eventually things had gone so badly for the south that the Raymonds of Toulouse had been forced to flee to England to escape de Montfort's revenge and Philip had had no option but to show his allegiance to the Church of Rome by joining a new crusade to the Holy Lands or forfeit Montaugure to the French.

Once again Jeanne had lived in constant fear for his safety, and though the dangers he faced were less familiar to her, they were no less daunting. Rough seas that could devour the ships taking them to Constantinople, dark-skinned men on horseback, their faces swathed against the searing heat, their deadly scimitars raised – she had only to think of the frieze which decorated Agnes's chamber to be able to picture them and quail inwardly. But once again her prayers had been answered.

The Raymonds of Toulouse had returned to France to raise an army and Philip and his men had raced home to join the battle for their homeland. Already they had retaken the city of Beaucaire and now they were riding out in the hope of being able to do the same for Toulouse.

As she watched them go, Jeanne knew hope as well as fear. Perhaps this time the tide would turn in their favour. Beaucaire had proved that de Montfort was not invincible after all; if only they could evict the French garrison and restore the Raymonds once more to their rightful place as liege lords, some semblance of normality might return to their troubled lives. And when – if – it did . . .

Jeanne pressed her hands against the rough stones as excitement bubbled up in her, tinting the hope, the fear and the pride with a rosy glow. Impossible as it seemed when she stood here beside the girl who was betrothed to Philip, Jeanne could not help feeling that the time was very near when Philip would be hers at last.

In the first bleak months after Alazais had come to Montaugure, Jeanne had feared she had lost Philip for ever and as time passed she had tried to accustom herself to accepting the inevitable. But, these last days, all that had changed and Jeanne was quite certain now that Philip felt as she did, and reciprocated her deep unswerving love. If she was right, then surely he would find some way to extricate himself from the promise made on his behalf so long ago when he was no more than a child and Alazais a baby.

Jeanne's heart beat wildly against her ribs and longing tightened the muscles of her stomach.

Though not a single improper word had passed between them, she was quite certain Philip loved her.

* * *

The joyous awakening had begun when he had returned from the Holy Lands.

As he had ridden into the courtyard with his men, Jeanne had run out to greet him, caring for nothing but that he was home safely once more, but Cecile had grasped her arm, holding her back.

'Wait, Jeanne.'

She had known what Cecile meant. Alazais was Philip's betrothed bride; it was her right to be the first to greet him. Jealousy had seared her. She cared far more for Philip than Alazais ever could, and it was so hurtful to have to watch as he embraced her tenderly. Then, as she fought to control her emotions, Philip had looked up, and as his eyes fell on her a strange expression that might almost have been wonder came over his face.

When it was her turn, Jeanne ran to him, unable to contain herself a moment longer. Oh, it was so good to feel his body pressed against hers, however briefly, the metal of his hauberk biting into her flesh through the thin material of her bodice, his strong arms around her! A thrill ran through her body, her heart lifted and her pulses raced. After a moment he held her away, looking down at her, and that expression was there again in his eyes.

'Jeanne – how you've changed!'

High spots of colour rose in her cheeks. It was true, of course. In the long months while he had been away she *had* changed, growing up suddenly so that she was no longer the scrawny child she had once been. At long last the curves which she had thought would never come had developed, her breasts firm and high above a still-slender waist, her narrow hips rounding a little for womanhood. Her face had grown fuller and softer, too, a bloom of health replacing the pinched look which years of undernourishment had stamped upon it, her skin taking on a fresh radiance. Now, for the first time, Philip was looking at her not as the orphan child he had rescued but as a woman. Jeanne had returned his gaze and smiled, her joy at his homecoming heightened with heady delight.

'You noticed, Philip!' she teased, her dimples playing with unintentional coquetry.

In the days that followed, while Philip made his preparations and waited for the call to rejoin Raymond of Toulouse, Jeanne often caught him looking at her with that same deep and pensive look, and each time she did excitement darted within her. She knew what that look meant and the knowledge filled her with fierce joy. Philip wanted her, just as she wanted him. There was no mistaking it.

At times Jeanne wondered if Alazais too was aware of Philip's feelings for her. She said nothing but there was a shadow sometimes in her eyes and a bright defensiveness about her that might have been hiding hurt. But Jeanne was too obsessed with her own emotions to give it much thought and she refused to let anxiety about the future spoil her elation either.

The call to arms, when it came, was an unwelcome return to reality.

Unbelievably, Simon de Montfort had left the City of Toulouse with only a small garrison to defend it while he rode to Provence with the bulk of his army to punish the lords there who had opposed him. Now the burgesses of Toulouse had offered to surrender the city to their old liege lord provided he could muster enough support to hold it against de Montfort's men.

The realisation that Philip was once again leaving the safety of Montaugure to ride into danger brought Jeanne back to earth with a bump. She had known, of course, that the time would come when he must; she had simply not wanted to think about it.

Now a new urgency filled her. She longed to tell him of her love and hear him tell her he loved her too, longed to kiss him and hold him in her arms as a talisman against the long weeks and months of separation she knew must lie ahead. But there had been no opportunity for that.

Now she could only stand on the battlements and watch him leave, praying that he would come safely home to her once more.

Cecile, Philip's mother, had certainly noticed the way he looked at Jeanne, if Alazais had not, and she began to fear for her carefully laid plans.

Philip had already delayed too long in making his marriage vows, she thought. Alazais was no longer a child and besides, since Bernard had died the previous year after a fall from his horse, Philip was now Viscount of Montaugure and it was important to ensure the succession by providing it with heirs.

Worried by Philip's obvious feelings for the young Cathar girl he had brought home so long ago, Cecile made up her mind. There must be no further delay. She would take matters into her own hands and begin making preparations for the marriage. This time when Philip came home he would find everything arranged. This time she would allow no excuses. The marriage would take place without delay.

The months dragged by on leaden feet.

At first the plan of the burgesses of Toulouse had worked well: Raymond's army had easily overcome the small garrison de Montfort had left behind to defend the city and every able-bodied soul had joined them to help rebuild the shattered walls – nobles and peasants, men, women and children singing as they worked side by side. But de Montfort was not to be so easily defeated. The moment he learned what had happened he raced back from Provence in a fury and laid siege to the newly restored walls.

When she heard of it, Jeanne was horrified. She knew only too well what a siege could be like. But Toulouse was not Carcassonne – it was too big to be surrounded so completely and the River Garonne provided a source of fresh water and a route by which supplies could be smuggled inside. And at first even the weather was on the side of the armies of the south, for the winter rains made it impossible for a new crusade to march to de Montfort's aid.

With the coming of spring the expected reinforcements arrived, but there were reinforcements for the defenders too. They slipped into the city by way of the river, and still the siege dragged on.

As spring became summer Jeanne began to despair. Would Philip never come home? she wondered as she lay tossing and turning in her bed. And was it partly her fault if he did not? When she had prayed for his safety in the past it had been with a pure heart. Now the thoughts she had of him were anything but pure. Might it be her punishment that this time her prayers would go unanswered?

Beads of sweat rose in a fine sheen on her face and she tumbled out of bed, falling to her knees and clasping her hands together.

'Oh please, dear God, bring him safely home!' she prayed. 'If I've been wicked, I'm truly sorry. If only he comes back safely, Alazais can have him and I swear I won't mind!'

But even as she said it, silently so as not to wake the sleeping Alazais, Jeanne knew in her heart it was a promise she would be unable to keep.

The news came a week later, brought to the castle by a jubilant messenger on a lathered horse, and at first they could scarcely take in what he had to say, let alone believe it.

Simon de Montfort dead? Impossible! He was immortal, wasn't he?

But it was true, the messenger assured them. De Montfort had been struck by a stone from one of the giant catapults which defended Toulouse, and fired, so it was said, by a team of women.

Disbelief gave way to wild rejoicing. De Montfort's death must mean the end of the siege, if not their troubles – surely. Without their leader the crusaders would give up their battle for the city and run away, their tails between their legs. Once more Toulouse would be free. And, best of all, Philip and others who had defended it so bravely would be coming home!

At once Cecile put into the action the plans she had been laying throughout the long months. Messages were sent to Alazais's family that the marriage was imminent, the linen for the bridal gown, purchased from a merchant in readiness, was brought out from the chest where it had been stored, and a seamstress was hired, since Fabrisse, Alazais's old nurse, could no longer see well enough to work on the fine stitching.

One afternoon, when a June sun beat down on the castle walls so that the stones were almost too hot to touch, Alazais sent one of her ladies, Serena, to ask Jeanne to come to her solar. As she climbed the staircase Jeanne's throat felt tight with misery; she had a good idea why Alazais wanted her. Alazais had been very secretive these past days, spending a lot of time closeted with her ladies, and Jeanne thought she knew the reason.

The moment she entered the solar she knew she had been right. Alazias, radiant with happiness, stood in a shaft of sunlight wearing her newly finished wedding gown.

Jealousy flooded through Jeanne's veins in a scalding tide and pain twisted in her chest, fierce as if a giant's hand had closed around her heart and was squeezing it tightly.

'Well – what do you think?' Alazais twirled excitedly, showing off the fine white linen, embroidered with gold thread at the neck and hem and the long points of the sleeves, and the cornflower-blue veil, held in place by a gold fillet, which reflected the colour of her eyes.

Jeanne pinched her lips together, biting them hard, quite unable to speak. Seeing Alazais decked out in the gown she would wear to become Philip's wife was almost more than she could bear.

Alazais stopped twirling, a shadow flickering across the brightness of her face.

'What's the matter? Don't you like it?'

Jeanne found her voice, though it sounded flat to her own ears.

'It's very nice.'

'And you think Philip will like it too?'

Another wash of jealousy; another twist of pain.

'I expect so,' she muttered through clenched teeth.

'Oh, I do hope so!' Alazais said earnestly. 'I do so much want to please him! Sometimes, you see, I am so afraid . . .'

'Afraid? Why?'

Alazais's hands fell to her sides, nervously bunching the fine linen skirt between her fingers, and her face, alight with happiness a moment ago, was troubled.

'That he doesn't really want me for his wife,' she whispered. 'After all, he didn't choose me, did he? And he has been in no hurry for the marriage to take place. When I first came here I thought I would be a bride before the year was out. But that was five years ago! Why has he waited so long? Oh, I know he said it was because I was too young and he wanted to wait until I was grown. But Eleanor de Puisse was only twelve when she was wed, and Fabrisse says that men like girls when they are young and fresh— ' She broke off, hot colour flooding her cheeks.

Jeanne's heart had begun to beat very fast; she thought she knew the reason.

'The thing is, I love him so much!' Alazais rushed on. 'When I came here I was so afraid I wouldn't even like him! So many girls whose marriages are arranged for them have to put up with repulsive old husbands, but Philip is— ' She broke off again, blushing. 'All I want is to be a good wife to him. But he doesn't even know, does he, that everything has been arranged for the wedding to take place on his return? What is he going to say, Jeanne?'

'I don't know.' Jeanne had begun to feel sick with an elation she hardly dared put into words, even to herself.

Philip loved *her* – she knew it! And if he did, how could he allow himself to be forced into a loveless marriage with Alazais? He would refuse, surely!

She folded her hands together to keep them from trembling and prayed with all her heart that it would be so.

A week later the siege was over and, with Count Raymond once more installed at Toulouse, Philip was at last free to come home.

As Jeanne greeted him she was shocked by the air of weariness which made him look somehow much older than when he had left – as if the siege had lasted far longer than eleven months, she thought – but as his eyes crinkled at her while at the same time seeming to look deep inside her she was also aware of the magnetic attraction sparking between them once again.

'God's teeth, and it's good to be home!' he exclaimed, and she felt sure it was not only the comfort and safety of the castle to which he was referring.

'We are certainly glad to see you, my son,' Cecile said, cutting swiftly across the exchange. 'Especially Alazais. She has a surprise for you.'

'A surprise?' He smiled fondly at Alazais. 'What might that be, little one?'

Alazais blushed scarlet, lowering her eyes, and Cecile went on, 'We have made all the arrangements for the wedding. I am sure after the long months you spent incarcerated in Toulouse you will be glad of the comforts a wife can bring.'

Philip looked from one to the other of them, his smile fading. 'You have made the arrangements in my absence?'

'Indeed we have.' Cecile drew herself up, the look in her eyes defying him to argue. 'The marriage will take place next week.'

Philip laughed shortly.

'Well, mother, this certainly is a surprise! But you will forgive me if I do not begin to celebrate just yet. For the moment, the things I want most in the world are a bath and a meal!'

* * *

In the days which followed Jeanne found not one single opportunity to be alone with Philip, and despair and a sense of urgency began to overcome her.

Why did he not raise some objection to the plans? How could he let this happen? And what could she do to stop it? In her heart she was as certain as ever that her love for him was reciprocated – there were still the times when she looked up to see his gaze fixed on her, still the spark when their eyes met which turned her blood to fire. But now, when she came close to him, she could feel him draw away as if he could not bear her touch. His demeanour was silent and brooding; because of his experiences at Toulouse, Cecile said, but Jeanne thought she knew different.

As the day of the wedding loomed ever nearer her feeling of urgency grew. Somehow she must persuade Philip that their happiness mattered far more than some convenient promise made long ago. But how?

That evening a troubadour visited Montaugure. Already his repertoire had been brought up to the minute by including songs about the death of Simon de Montfort and the defeat of the French at Toulouse, and when the meal was over, Cecile requested that he should entertain them for a little longer.

Jeanne bit her lip, staring into space. The haunting quality of the music was making her feel sadder than ever, as if it were plucking at the strings of her heart, and the sight of Alazais's face, radiant as she listened, was yet another barb. She couldn't bear it – she couldn't! Tears glistened suddenly on her lashes.

'What's the matter, Jeanne?' Philip was leaning forward; his voice was low in her ears.

She shrugged, blinking hard and hoping he had not noticed her tears. Even now she was too proud to allow him – or anyone – to see her cry.

'Nothing.'

'Aren't you enjoying the music?'

She shrugged again, striving to hide her misery.

'It's all right. But I'd rather be with the horses any day!'

He laughed aloud.

'You don't change, do you Jeanne?'

'Hmm!' She tossed her head. 'I think I have changed a good deal! But I still love to ride better than anything in the whole world. I couldn't bear to be cooped up, as you were, for a whole year and not be able to go for a good gallop. But then, I suppose you had other things on your mind.'

He sipped his wine. The talk of horses seemed to have made him relax with her.

'Not really. Mostly there was nothing to think about and nothing to do but wait for de Montfort to attack. There were plenty of times, I assure you, when I wanted nothing so much as to take Auguste out for, as you say, a good gallop – and I think he has missed it too.'

Whether it was the effect of the wine she had been drinking or the heady delight of talking properly with Philip for the first time since his return Jeanne could never afterwards be sure. All she knew was that her pulses were racing suddenly and a reckless boldness took her over.

'Well, there is nothing stopping you now. Let's do it! Let's go for a ride!'

'Now? Tonight?' He sounded startled.

'Why not?'

He laughed again, shaking his head.

'I was right, Jeanne, whatever you might say, you haven't changed. You are still as wild as ever you were.'

'What are you two whispering about?' Alazais asked.

'Oh, we were just talking horses, sweetheart. We didn't mean to leave you out.' Philip's tone was contrite, but it was the endearment which hurt Jeanne more.

'We are going to race,' she said defiantly. 'It is so long since we raced! You will spare him to me for an hour won't you, Alazais?'

She saw the shadow of doubt flicker in Alazais's eyes and felt a stab of triumph, quickly followed by the fear that Alazais might try to stop them. But it was Cecile who intervened. Jeanne's last words had come just as the troubadour ended his song, and in the hush before the applause began they had carried clearly to her sharp ears.

'Race – tonight? Are you mad, Philip? The Viscount of Montaugure does not race at any time – certainly not in the middle of an evening's entertainment!'

She glared at Philip and for a moment the clash of wills was there for all to see. Then he pushed back his chair and stood up.

'The Viscount of Montaugure does as he pleases.' He bent and took Alazais's hand, kissing it. 'We shall be back within the hour.'

'Oh Philip!' Her lip trembled. 'You will be careful, won't you?'

'No harm will come to us. Enjoy the rest of the entertainment and we will be back before you even know we are gone.'

Jeanne rose too. She was trembling with excitement and the look of fury on Cecile's face and Alazais's obvious anxiety only added spice. To ride with Philip – alone – was almost more than she had dared hope for.

Darkness had already fallen, the sun slipping behind the mountains so swiftly that the minutes of soft dusk were but fleeting, but the night was still warm and the moon so huge and bright that it was almost as light as day. Outside the stables the grooms and ostlers were crouched on their haunches around a flat flagstone enjoying a game of dice. They looked up in surprise as Philip and Jeanne approached, but at Philip's bidding they saddled Auguste and Braida without comment – it was not their place to question what the Viscount did. The guards at the gate were equally surprised: they were not used to anyone going in and out between the hours of sunset and sunrise, but again, if they thought their master was behaving recklessly by riding alone with only a slip of a girl for company, they were not going to risk his wrath by saying so.

Beyond the castle gates the *garrigue* gleamed silvery in the moonlight. Jeanne touched Braida's sides with her heels and at once the little mare was off, fleet and sure of foot as ever, delighted at the chance to exercise so late in the day. Behind her Jeanne heard the thunder of hooves as Philip kicked Auguste to a gallop and neck and neck they raced across the open ground. As they neared the woods Philip drew ahead and as the trees thickened he drew up, laughing back at her.

'So – you concede defeat?'

'I suppose I must.' She was breathless with the exhilaration of the ride. 'The hillside beyond the wood will be a different story, though. Braida's sure-footedness will tell there.'

'We'll see about that! But take care in the woods, Jeanne. The wind was high yesterday: it will have brought down some branches and it is not easy to see them in the dark.'

'I know. Perhaps . . . should we rest the horses awhile? There's a fallen tree just here. We could sit and talk. It's so long since we talked . . .' She saw his look of surprise and bit her lip apprehensively. Perhaps it had been only a ride he had wanted after all . . . 'Soon you will be married and we won't be able to talk at all!' she rushed on with a tiny nervous laugh.

'Jeanne – you know I will always have time for you.'

Hope soared, died, rose again. She did not know what to think.

'Are we going to rest then?' With a quick decisive movement she dismounted, leading Braida towards the fallen tree and hooking the reins around a convenient stake. After a moment Philip followed.

'This is even more crazy than racing by moonlight! Did you know that?'

She shrugged, sitting down on the fallen tree.

'I don't see why. It's lovely here. Nicer than in the heat of the day. And . . .' Her heart jumped nervously. 'I so much wanted to be alone with you, Philip. We haven't had a single chance since you came home.'

She felt him stiffen though their bodies were not touching.

'Jeanne . . . what is this?'

'Oh Philip, you must know!' Suddenly she could hedge and manoeuvre no longer. 'You can't go through with this marriage to Alazais! You simply can't! You don't love her, I know you don't . . .'

'Jeanne – I am betrothed to her . . .'

'But it's me you love, isn't it? Oh Philip, please . . .'

'Jeanne!' His tone was sharp. 'You must not say such things.'

'Why not? I must say them – before it's too late!'

'It is already too late. It has been too late from the moment my mother and Alazais's father agreed upon the marriage.'

The bright moonlight illuminated the bleakness in his face and Jeanne grasped his hand in hers. In spite of the warmth of the night it felt cold beneath her fingers.

'But you don't love her, do you?' she persisted.

'Love has nothing to do with it, Jeanne. It is all a matter of duty and honour.'

Duty and honour! What ridiculous words! And yet – what wonderful words, telling her everything she had longed to hear and been afraid she never would . . .

'Oh Philip . . .' She inched towards him and he did not move away. Amazed at her own daring, she wound her arms around his neck, pressing her body against his and touching his lips with her own. For a moment he remained stiff and unyielding, but as she tipped back her head a fraction she saw the anguish and desire mingling in his face and knew that she had won. She slipped down to kneel between his knees, twining her fingers in the hair which grew thickly at the nape of his neck and pressing herself close to him. No hauberk to come between them now, only the thin fabric of her bodice and his tunic. She kissed him with all the love, all the desire which had been too long suppressed, and after a moment, with a low groan, he was kissing her back, no longer trying to put her away but holding her as if he would never let her go.

'I love you so!' she whispered.

His only reply was to push her back on to the scratchy dry grass, kneeling astride her, feeling for her breasts at the low neck of her gown, fumbling with her skirts. She felt the strength of his passion as clearly as her own and lay back in the dark shadow of the fallen tree, all hopes and fears forgotten. There was no past and no future, only the here and now, and the here and now was Philip, thrusting his body into hers, making her his own. She wound her arms around him, closing her eyes against the searing pain between her legs, glorying in it, even as her teeth drew blood from her lower lip. She must not cry out, must not do anything to spoil the wonder of this shared moment.

Philip's body spasmed and a shout escaped his lips and she knew it was over. She lay clutching him to her, trying to hold him within her. His face was still buried in her neck and she could hear the beating of his heart at one with her own. Then suddenly another sound impinged on her consciousness – the sharp cracking of a twig! She froze, afraid, even as she tried to tell herself it was only one of the horses, and she felt Philip stiffen too. For long seconds they lay motionless, listening, then, just as Jeanne tried to pull Philip close once more, another sound startled her – the unmistakable chinkle of stirrups and saddle leathers as a horse was spurred into action.

Philip was on his feet in a flash, the sword which he had unbuckled and laid on the grass beside him already in his hand. Jeanne lay too shocked to move. Then she pulled herself up to look over the rim of the fallen trunk. A figure on horseback was galloping away across the open ground. Philip stood watching him go, the moonlight glinting on the blade of his sword and illuminating the expression of horror on his face.

'Christ's blood!'

Jeanne pulled her bodice together across her breasts.

'Who . . . ?'

'Oliver.' Philip's voice was low and terrible. 'I'd know his horse, Fabian, anywhere, even if I didn't recognise my own brother from a hundred feet away in the dark. He must have followed us. God's teeth, what have I done?'

Jeanne grabbed at Philip's arm, frightened by his tone.

'It's not important, is it? It doesn't matter that he saw. You love me, Philip. We belong together now!'

'For God's sake, Jeanne! I have to catch him!' Shaking himself free, he vaulted the fallen tree and unhooked Auguste's reins.

'Wait – please!' Jeanne sobbed.

But Philip only kicked Auguste into a gallop and was off across the *garrigue* without so much as a backward glance.

Next day Philip found her in the stables.

'I have talked with Oliver,' he said, glancing over his shoulder to make sure none of the grooms was within earshot. 'He has given me his word that he will say nothing of what he saw.'

Jeanne raised her head from Braida's neck. Her eyes were haunted.

'I'm sorry,' he said harshly. 'I should not have done . . . what I did.'

'But Philip – it was so right! We love one another! You can't marry Alazais now – you can't!'

'I have to.' Philip's voice was low, angry. 'It is a matter of honour.'

'And what about my honour? I suppose that doesn't matter. After all, I am only a peasant!'

'Don't say such a thing!' he said fiercely. 'You know it's not true.'

'I know you are going to deny me and marry her!'

'I have no choice.'

'You do have a choice!' She hated herself for begging but

couldn't stop. 'Let Oliver wed Alazais. Then you and I could be together! It's what we both want isn't it?'

'Jeanne, it cannot be. I do love you – yes, there, you made me say it. But I also love Alazais and she is the woman who is to be my wife. Nothing can change that. You must try to forget what has happened – for all our sakes.'

He turned and left the stable.

Tears of heartache and humilation ran down Jeanne's cheeks. Oh Sancta Maria, how could he do this to her? She couldn't bear it! And to make it even worse she had made a fool of herself and not only Philip knew it, but Oliver also. She would die inside each time they looked at her. And as for having to watch Philip kneel at the altar beside Alazais – see the door of their bedchamber close after them at night – watch her belly grow large with his children . . . oh, it was insupportable.

The pain was a fierce fiery furnace, a red mist before her eyes, and Jeanne knew there was only one thing now that she could do. Tomorrow she would leave Montaugure. And she would never come back.

The vision was fading. Simone was still sitting at the table, her eyes fixed on the cards, but the Queens of Cups and Pentacles looked now exactly as the artist had intended. Jeanne and Alazais had gone, back to the shadowlands.

Simone passed a hand across her eyes, feeling sick and shaky.

What was happening? What did it all mean? A few short days ago she would never have believed she could experience such incredible fantasies, much less believe in them. Now the past seemed to be taking her over – possessing her. But why – why?

What happened before must happen again. Until the Wheel is broken it must go on.

The voice in her head was so clear that Simone spun round, startled, half expecting to see someone behind her. But there was no one. Even Félix had left his comfortable chair and disappeared.

Simone glanced back at the cards. The High Priest – the card concerned with the future, and with spiritual awareness – seemed to leap out at her. There was a purpose in all this, there had to be. The story was being revealed to her because there was something she was required to do. The trouble was she still had no idea what.

Jeanne and Alazais. Esther and Hélène. Two pairs of women separated by the centuries yet linked by a common theme – their love for the same man. Could it really be that their story was being played out again in the present day? But what was this Wheel they were treading? And how was she supposed to help?

15

THE VILLAGE CLOCK was striking noon as Andrew Slater parked his hire car on the steeply sloping lane behind his father's house and kicked a large stone under the rear wheel. At the moment a spreading chestnut provided some shade, but it wouldn't last. Another hour or so and the sun would be shining directly on to the windscreen, turning the car into an oven. Well, it couldn't be helped. Garaging was at a premium here.

Andrew vaulted the low stone wall and made his way through a small orchard to the rear entrance of his father's house. As he climbed the flight of uneven stone steps at the corner of the house he could hear the sound of voices coming from the patio. The guests must have already arrived!

A man and a woman were leaning against the balcony rail, drinks in their hands. But both were indisputably middle-aged and Andrew realised this couldn't be Alain Lavaur and his English girlfriend.

'Andrew!' Bob appeared in the kitchen doorway, a bottle in one hand and a dish of nuts in the other. 'You're back then. Meet Ray and Janice Gibbs – Ray, Janice, my son.'

'Hi.' Ray put down his glass and extended his hand. He was an athletically built man whose relaxed lifestyle was beginning to show in the slight bulge beneath the shirt worn loose over khaki shorts.

'Yes – hello.' Janice pushed her sunglasses up on to neatly cropped silver-blonde hair. She was also wearing shorts – olive-green linen Bermudas – but unlike her husband she had retained her slender figure. 'We've heard a lot about you.'

'That sounds ominous!' Andrew grinned at Bob, who was busily refilling glasses. 'Whew – it's hot here! If you'll excuse me for a minute, I think I'll go up and change.'

He crossed the patio, noticing the table, already set for six, in the shade thrown by the upstairs balcony.

Diana was in the kitchen basting something at the range. Andrew sniffed appreciatively.

'That smells good!'

'Barbecued pork.' Diana scooped a last spoonful of sauce over the chops and returned the tin to the oven. 'How did you get on?' She turned to Andrew, still wearing the ovenglove on one hand and reaching for her glass with the other.

'Not too well really. Nothing to report.'

He had spent the morning visiting the bistro where Thierry had been on the evening before his death in the hope that the bar owner might be able to tell him something. But Andrew's conversational French was patchy and the barman's English non-existent, and even with the help of a customer who was more or less bilingual he had been unable to learn anything new. Yes, Thierry had been in the bistro on the night of his death; yes, he had been with another man and there had been an argument; no, the bar owner didn't know the other man. He hadn't even been able to describe him. When Andrew's interpreter asked the question he had waved his arms impatiently and burst into a stream of rapid French which Andrew guessed roughly translated into: How the hell am I supposed to remember all my customers on a busy night? Andrew would have thought the argument might have been enough to make him take notice but the barman couldn't, or wouldn't, say anything beyond that Thierry's companion had been in his middle thirties, perhaps, and a stranger to him.

'Let's hope you have better luck with Alain Lavaur.' Diana sipped her drink and reached for the olive oil to make a salad dressing.

'He's coming then?' Andrew had already left the house before Diana had phoned her invitations.

'Yes, but only briefly, I'm afraid. He can't spare the time for lunch but he's bringing his girlfriend over and he'll have a drink with us.'

'I'd hoped for longer than that.'

'Yes, but you can always work on the girlfriend. She may know something.'

Andrew glanced at his watch. 'If I'm going to change I'd better do it now, or I might miss Alain Lavaur altogether.'

'Off you go then. They could be here any minute.'

Andrew stole a piece of celery from the salad bowl, avoiding

Diana's playful slap, and ran upstairs crunching it. He was stripped to his underpants, hunting for the least creased of his clean shirts, when Diana called up to him, 'That sounds like them now. I think they're here.'

Andrew grabbed a yellow polo shirt and a pair of shorts. Judging by what his father and Ray were wearing, these lunch parties were informal affairs. He dressed hastily, ran a comb through his hair and ran downstairs.

The new arrivals were already on the patio where Bob was introducing them to Ray and Janice. Andrew cursed silently that there would be no chance to talk to Alain alone.

He looked at Alain, summing him up. Very handsome, very Gallic, very casually smart. Altogether too smooth for his liking. But the girl was definitely worth a second glance. Slim, pretty, with unfussy hair and wearing a brightly patterned sundress. Unlike the others she was only lightly tanned, except for her shoulders, which were red-stained where they had caught the sun. Alain Lavaur could certainly pick his women, even if his choice of business partner was suspect!

Bob introduced him. 'My son – over here on holiday.'

'Ah – you are from Bristol?'

'Not any more. I work in London.'

'We were very sorry about your brother-in-law,' Bob said, steering the conversation away from what might prove to be awkward questions. 'A terrible thing.'

'Yes. It was a great shock to us all.' Alain's sunglasses concealed any emotion he might be feeling.

'What happened?' Andrew asked, pretending ignorance.

Bob played along.

'Alain's brother-in-law was killed a few weeks ago.'

'Oh, I'm sorry. An accident?'

'Yes, an accident.' Alain's tone was short but emphatic. As if he thought I was querying it rather than simply curious, Andrew thought.

'These mountain roads can be treacherous,' Ray said, reaching for a nut. 'I know they have crash barriers on the worst bends but all the same, in the dark . . . I've come pretty close to it myself once or twice.'

'The way you drive it's hardly surprising,' Janice said. 'Let this be a lesson to you. If a local can misjudge things . . .'

'Familiarity breeds contempt, that's the trouble. Thierry was so used to haring about he ignored the dangers.' Again there was an edge to Alain's voice and Andrew thought: He certainly wants to impress on us that this was an accident. Why, I wonder?

Aloud he asked, 'Was he on his own at the time?'

'Yes, thank God.' Alain glanced at his watch. 'I really think I should be going. You know everyone now, don't you, Esther?' He turned to Bob. 'Sorry to leave you in such a rush, but business calls.'

'How is business?' Bob asked, and Andrew blessed his father. He was doing his best under difficult circumstances. But Alain was annoyingly vague.

'Oh fine. Though Thierry's death has caused me one or two problems.'

'Yes – sure . . .'

'But nothing I can't handle. Now, I really must go.' He touched Esther's arm. 'I'll pick you up around three.'

'There's no need for you to bother if you're busy,' Bob said. 'Our lunch parties always drag on. We'll get Esther home for you.'

'I couldn't trouble you . . .'

'No trouble. We've got nothing better to do.'

Andrew was pleased. A chance to talk to Esther on her own might give him the break he had been looking for. He could certainly do with one. Bartenders who conveniently forgot what Thierry's companion on that fatal night had looked like, relatives who accepted a little too readily that his death had been an accident – either he was barking up the wrong tree completely or this was a mystery death which everyone involved was determined should go down in the records as misadventure. Unless he could find a witness or someone willing to talk this was one investigation he was going to have to write off almost before it had begun.

But it did have its compensations! Andrew glanced at Esther. What a pity she was spoken for! If she hadn't been she was certainly one line of enquiry he would have enjoyed pursuing!

Bob was seeing Alain out and Andrew reached for the tray of nuts, offering it to Esther.

'So – are you on holiday too? Or do you live here?'

She smiled. 'I'm on holiday. Actually I think we came over on the same flight. I'm sure I saw you at the airport when I was waiting for my bags.'

'Really?' He couldn't believe he hadn't noticed her. Good lord, Slater – you're slipping! 'The flight from Bristol, last Tuesday?'

'Yes.'

'Well I'll be blowed – what a coincidence! Do you live in the Bristol area, then?'

'Yes.' She reached for another nut; he noticed she was not wearing a ring. So there was nothing official between her and Lavaur – but then there wouldn't be. After all, he was still married.

'And what do you do in Bristol?'

'For a living, you mean? I'm a journalist for my sins. I work on the local daily there – *West Today*.'

Andrew experienced a sense of shock, followed almost immediately by a jolt of recognition. Esther Morris – of course! That had been the byline on the piece on Lavaur Wines he'd uncovered in the archives. He should have clocked it when they were introduced but he hadn't. He certainly was slipping! But at least she didn't seem to have recognised his name either – she must have been out of the office when he'd called last week.

'What do you do?' she was asking.

He thought quickly; he couldn't admit the truth.

'I'm in the investigation line,' he said ambiguously.

'You mean you are a policeman, like your father?'

'My father's not a policeman now. He's retired.'

'But he was, wasn't he?'

'Right – I think we're all ready to eat.' Diana, emerging from the kitchen with a bowl of salad, saved him from replying. He touched her elbow.

'Come and sit down. If the smell from the kitchen is anything to go by we are in for a treat!'

The lunch party was coming to an end. Gastronomically and socially it had been a great success; professionally Andrew was no nearer to learning any more about Thierry Rousseau's untimely death and the events leading up to it. But there was still the drive home. When they were alone he'd pump Esther remorselessly for any last little morsel of information.

'Time we were going, I'm afraid.' Ray Gibbs pushed back

his chair and stood up, patting the stomach which was now even more in evidence than it had been before. 'We have some bookings to attend to, don't we my love?'

''Fraid so.' Janice drained her glass and followed suit reluctantly. 'We manage the letting of some properties to English tourists,' she explained, seeing Esther's quizzical look. 'Even former income tax inspectors need to earn a crust.'

'By the time the international banks take their cut, even government pensions look a bit sick,' Ray added.

'A small price to pay for a life in the sun,' Diana beamed.

'It's all right for some – those folk not a million miles from here with independent incomes!' Ray returned tartly and Andrew glanced at his stepmother in surprise. So, Diana was well off in her own right. He'd often wondered how his father managed to live so well on a police pension. Well, good luck to him!

'I should be going too.' Esther, too, sounded reluctant. She had enjoyed herself, Andrew thought. He had been watching her during the leisurely meal and the last lingered-over drinks, and noticed how the slightly strained air she had had when she had arrived had gradually disappeared.

'I'll do the honours then,' he said, getting up.

'Are you sure I'm not being the most dreadful nuisance?'

'Quite. Always provided I can find my keys . . .'

'They're on the kitchen table.' Diana was faintly flushed; Andrew noticed how she reached over and squeezed his father's hand.

'Great lunch – as usual. You must come to us next time,' Ray said, retrieving his sunglasses and swinging them between finger and thumb.

'Yes – thank you. I've really enjoyed it,' Esther said.

They all went through the house to the front door and walked up the road together. Though the back garden provided the quickest route to his car, he could hardly ask Esther to climb over the wall wearing a dress and strappy sandals, Andrew decided.

The hire car was like an oven. Andrew opened all the windows and pulled out so that Esther could get into the passenger seat.

'You'll have to direct me,' he said. 'I'm a stranger in these parts, remember.'

'I only hope I can remember the way!' Esther said, laughing.

'Shame your fiancé couldn't join us.' Andrew glanced at her slyly as he reversed the car and started down the hill.

'Oh, he's not my fiancé.' She had coloured slightly. 'It is a shame, though. But he's tied up just now.'

'I can imagine. Losing a partner must cause all kinds of problems.'

'Yes. Though from what I can make out, Thierry was behind a lot of them.' Her flush deepened. 'I shouldn't say that, I suppose. But I get the impression he had got things in rather a mess and Alain is having to sort it out.'

'Really?' He decided against pressing her too much, hoping that all the wine she had consumed would do the job for him. His hunch was rewarded.

'I never met him, but I gather he was a bit of a disaster area,' Esther went on. 'No one seems to have a good word for him – except his sister. She was Alain's wife.'

'Ah – a family business.'

'I don't know about that. It's Alain's business really and he's passionate about it. I think he gave Thierry the job of running this end of it for Hélène's sake. But it's all gone wrong. I only hope Alain can sort it out. I honestly don't know what he'll do if he can't.'

'So was this Thierry the sort to make enemies?' Andrew ventured.

'I wouldn't know. But his friends weren't exactly what you'd call fine upstanding citizens. Oh – turn left here. Le Château Gris is about a mile further on.'

Andrew negotiated the junction but his mind was busy. A falling out of thieves – was that what was behind all this? But if Thierry was the goose who was laying the golden egg by way of some kind of fraud, why should one of his friends turn on him and murder him?

Well, perhaps it hadn't been murder. Perhaps it had been suicide. Thierry the embezzler had come to the end of the road. Nowhere to go that didn't lead to exposure and ruin. The man in the bar had threatened him and Thierry had decided to end it all. Or simply driven over the edge because he'd had too much to drink and wasn't concentrating on what he was doing, just as the records showed. Either way there was no real story in it.

But still Andrew's instincts were telling him there was something which didn't fit. His father had felt it and he felt it too.

'Here we are – this is the drive,' Esther said and Andrew cursed silently in frustration. Investigative reporting was never easy, but this was just one brick wall after another.

'If Alain is busy why don't we do some sightseeing together?' he suggested. 'I'm at a loose end too.'

She hesitated. 'Oh, I don't know. It's very kind of you but— '

'Alain might not approve,' he finished for her. 'It's OK – I understand. But look, let me give you my number anyway in case you change your mind.'

He scribbled it on a card and gave it to her, deliberately nonchalant.

But as he watched her walk away up the drive, swinging her bag by its handles, his overwhelming feeling was one of regret and he found himself wondering whether it was the story getting away from him or the girl that was making him feel so rueful.

The story, of course. Work was far and away the most important thing in his life. But he was honest enough to admit to himself that Esther Morris had something to do with this feeling, too.

Esther was humming the Marseillaise and marching in time to it. She felt cheerful and ever so slightly tiddly and she was looking forward to spending the evening with Alain. Then, as she saw the Renault drawn up on the turnaround alongside Alain's silver Rover, her happy mood dissipated. Hélène's car. Oh, not again!

She walked around the side of the house and into the kitchen. The aroma of roasting meat and garlic met her, but, though a pile of half-prepared vegetables lay on the worktop, the kitchen was empty.

'Hello – it's me!' she called.

'Ah – you're back then.' Isobelle appeared in the doorway behind her, a basket of apricots which she had obviously just picked over her arm. 'Did you enjoy your lunch party?'

'Yes – they're really nice people, aren't they?'

'I wouldn't know. I've never met them.' Isobelle's tone was faintly disdainful; expats were not, and never would be, part of her social circle, it seemed to say.

'They made me very welcome,' Esther said, annoyed.

'I'm sure . . .' Isobelle put the basket down on the table and turned to look directly at Esther. 'Esther, Hélène is here – you may have noticed her car on the way in. She has had a most distressing experience today and she is very upset. Naturally, I have asked her to stay. I just thought you should know that.'

Esther was determined not to give Isobelle the satisfaction of an adverse reaction, though inwardly she was seething.

'Why shouldn't you? It is your house,' she said, trying to sound unfussed.

'Yes, Esther, it is.' Her tone, and her gaze were challenging. 'And whether you like it or not, it is also Hélène's home. It has been ever since she was a child. But even if that were not so, the fact that she is Alain's wife gives her the right to be here. She is, after all, still his wife.'

Her meaning was so clear Esther could no longer pretend to ignore it. It was time, she thought, to get this out into the open.

'Isobelle, I realise you don't approve of me being here, and of course I'll move out if you would prefer it. But I think I should point out that I came at Alain's invitation. And then only after he had assured me that his marriage was over.'

'Really?' Isobelle's thin lips curled in what was almost a sneer. 'He said that, did he? Well of course – a lonely man will say all kinds of things. And he must have been lonely so far away from all his family and friends. But he's at home now. That means the situation is quite different.'

'Different how?' Esther challenged, holding on to her temper with difficulty. 'Perhaps you could explain what you mean by that, Isobelle.'

'With pleasure. I'm glad we've had this opportunity for a chat. It gives me the opportunity to tell you a few things Alain may not have told you. He and Hélène have been together since they were children. She was his first sweetheart and he hers. They belong together. I have no doubt that they still love one another. They've had their difficulties, I grant you, but then – who doesn't? They'd been through a bad patch just before Alain went to England. But now he's home again it's perfectly obvious that he and Hélène would like to sort things out.'

'Perhaps you'd like to think so, Isobelle,' Esther said, her voice steady though she had begun to tremble with the shock of the unexpected onslaught. 'I can only repeat – I came here because Alain asked me to and for no other reason.'

Isobelle shook her head in a deprecatory manner.

'But surely you must see what an impossible position you are placing him in? He asked you here, yes, but he shouldn't have done. I am quite sure he regrets it now, but he's too much of a gentleman to ask you to leave. That is why I feel I must speak out. He is my son and Hélène is my daughter-in-law, and my first and only concern is for their happiness.'

'I'm sure it is,' Esther said. 'But if Alain is regretting anything then I think it is up to him to tell me so himself. Of course, as regards me being *here*, that's another matter. It's your house, and I wouldn't wish to stay where I'm not welcome. I'll get my things together and leave at once. I'm sure I can find a hotel that will give me a room.'

'I don't think you'll find one at this time of day.' Isobelle said quickly. 'And in any case there's little point going to a *hotel* when what you should be doing is going home.'

'I expect Alain will be able to find me one. Where is he?'

'He's with Hélène. As I said, she's very upset. Please don't go causing a scene and making things worse.'

There was a sharp note in Isobelle's voice that might almost be anxiety. She's gone too far and she knows it, Esther thought. Well, if she thinks I'm going to let her get away with it, she's got another think coming!

'Are they in the salon?'

'Yes, but—'

'Thank you.'

The salon door was ajar. On the point of pushing it open, Esther stopped short. Alain and Hélène were seated together on the sofa; his arm was around her and their heads were close together.

It wasn't so much the physical contact that shocked her. If Hélène was as upset as Isobelle had said she was then it was only natural that Alain should comfort her. No, it was the aura of togetherness that made her heart sink with dismay, the feeling that they were totally at one, and oblivious to anyone else. There was a rightness about them; they looked like a couple and Esther felt like an outsider suddenly.

What was it Isobelle had said? 'They belong together.' Yes, looking at them now, she could almost feel it. The first shock became a sharp pain and she almost backed away, reluctant to intrude. But why should she? This whole thing had to be sorted out, and now. She pushed open the door.

Alain looked up. 'Esther! I didn't hear you come home— ' He broke off, seeing the expression on her face. 'What's the matter?'

'Alain, we must talk.'

'Well yes, but . . .' he gestured towards Hélène. 'Not right now, Esther. It's not a good time.'

'Don't mind me,' Hélène said. Her voice was unsteady but determinedly bright. 'I'm better now, honestly.'

'You're not,' Alain said. 'Esther, Hélène has had a horrible experience and she's very shaken. Whatever it is, can't it wait?'

Hélène certainly looked genuinely upset. But Esther didn't see she had any choice but to get things settled once and for all.

'No, it can't,' she said shortly. 'Your mother has just made it abundantly clear that she doesn't want me here. I'll be in my room, Alain. Packing.'

'What?' Alain looked shocked, bewildered. She turned and left the room. There was no way she was going to have this conversation in front of Hélène.

She made her way up the stairs. Her hand was unsteady, fumbling on the handle of her bedroom door. Then she stopped short. Someone was in her room. Who the hell would be in her room?

She pushed the door wide, stopped again. The room was empty. What on earth had made her think someone was there? Yet even now it *felt* as if she was not alone. As if there was a presence behind her . . . no, not behind her – *around* her . . .

A shadow flickered across the periphery of her vision and she was aware suddenly that the room was full of the haunting scent of rosemary and thyme. She turned her head sharply. Nothing. No one.

Esther gave herself a small shake. The shadow was just the creeper outside the window, blowing about in the stiff breeze. And the perfume must have wafted in from the garden and been trapped in the hot afternoon air. She was overwrought, imagining things.

She yanked her holdall up on to the bed and unzipped it, gathered armfuls of clothes from the wardrobe and tossed them on top of it. But the feverish activity did nothing to dispell the feeling of unease which now lay across all her other churning emotions like the skimming of cream on a jug of warm milk. There was something here she didn't understand. And she didn't like it one little bit.

16

FOR A LONG while after the pictures had faded Simone sat staring at the tarot spread. She could scarcely credit what was happening, yet at the same time she knew she could no longer deny it, though it struck at the roots of everything she had ever believed.

Something beyond her control – and beyond her understanding – was taking place. No – something that had taken place in the past was happening again, and somehow she had been drawn into it.

Simone shivered, filled suddenly with a feeling of awe. This, she thought, was the way one felt looking into the velvety blackness of the night sky, knowing that it stretched out endlessly into the eternity of the universe because science has told us it is so, yet unable to grasp the concept because the sheer vastness of it is beyond comprehension. Sometimes, gazing at the myriad stars, she tried to imagine the distant galaxies to which they belonged, only to realise that many of those self-same stars no longer existed – had not existed for centuries. Yet because they were so many thousands of light years away, for her and for other observers in this world of ours, they lived on.

And it was the same with this. Somehow she was seeing the imprint of events that had taken place hundreds of years ago and were normally hidden by the mists of time. She didn't understand it any more than she understood the awesome mystery of the universe, yet she was suddenly quite certain that it was so, and the certainty was somehow deeper and more total than her scepticism had ever been. Scepticism was negative; denial, however heartfelt, left a vacuum. And into that vacuum had come a knowledge that was so instinctive, so profound, that she found herself accepting it without question. She had glimpsed, she realised, a deep unwritten truth, an uncharted law of nature, and for a moment the realisation elated her. Then, with a rush, the frustration and anxiety were back. Believing wasn't enough. She also needed to understand.

Restless now, and overcome by a feeling of helplessness, Simone wandered out into the garden, wandered in again, trying to make sense of it all.

Long ago, Jeanne and Alazais had loved the same man, and their emotions and the actions arising from them had been so potent they had survived the passage of the centuries. Now Esther and Hélène were smiliarly locked into what was described, with more accuracy than she had ever credited it, as an 'eternal triangle'. Perhaps the story of Jeanne and Alazais had ended in tragedy; perhaps Esther and Hélène were inexorably headed in the same direction. Unless she could unlock the secret of what it was she was meant to do to prevent it.

I need help, Simone thought. I can't do this alone.

She picked up the telephone and dialled Valerie's number. It rang and rang and Simone felt the beginnings of despair. Then, just as she was on the point of giving up, her sister's voice was on the line.

'Valerie!' Simone wanted to weep with relief. 'It's happened again.'

Two hours later Valerie was at Simone's door. She was flushed and eager – she was enjoying this whole thing, Simone thought. But then that was Valerie all over.

'I've managed to get hold of Aurore,' she said, dumping a tapestry holdall on Simone's kitchen table. 'I was very lucky to catch her – she's off to some psychic convention.'

'She's in demand these days, isn't she?' Simone said.

'She's a very respected authority in her field.'

Once upon a time, Simone thought, she would have allowed herself a wry smile at the notion that anyone, let alone the girl who had been Valerie's friend, could be an authority on something as unlikely as the supernatural, or that there should be enough gullible individuals to allow her to be described as such. It was a measure of how Simone's own experience had changed her that she was now prepared to accept it without question.

'What did she say?' she asked.

'Well, she's more than ever convinced that our theory of what is happening is the right one. The very fact that you are still having these visions without even trying means that there is some very strong paranormal influence at work here – a spirit guide making contact with you in an effort to break the chain of karma.'

'A spirit guide,' Simone repeated. Again it struck her that just a short time ago she would have considered the suggestion ludicrous. She laughed a little nervously. 'Aren't they usually supposed to be Indians or Chinamen? I certainly haven't been visited by anyone like that!'

'Oh Simone, you pay too much attention to what you hear about fake mediums! Indians and Chinamen go hand in hand with floating trumpets and clouds of manufactured ectoplasm. Real spirit guides are much more subtle than that. They might be what the church calls guardian angels, or even the voice of conscience – you know, that still small voice that seems to speak inside your head . . .'

'Oh God.' A voice in her head. Unexplained words appearing on the screen of her word processor . . .

'You mean it's happened to you? You know what I'm talking about?' Valerie sounded excited.

Simone nodded. 'Yes, I think it has. Oh Valerie, I don't like this . . .'

'But you can't avoid it,' Valerie said reasonably. 'You've already proved that. So all you can do is go on with it and try to do whatever it is you are supposed to do.'

'But I don't know what that is! I don't even know if it was Hélène or Esther who was Jeanne.'

'I thought we decided it was Esther. The way you seemed to recognise her . . .'

'That's true. But I've always been very fond of Hélène and felt responsible for her. Did you look in on her, by the way?'

'Shit! I forgot all about it!'

'Oh well, never mind. I expect she'd have been in touch if she'd had any more silent phone calls. But about me feeling responsible for her . . . I thought it was because of what happened when she was a child – you know, when her mother died. But now I'm beginning to wonder if it's more than that. That I had a reason even then for feeling I wanted to look after her. I wonder if I feel responsible for her because— '

'Because you were her mother in another life.'

'Well . . . yes.' She was silent for a moment, thinking about it. Then she sighed, shaking her head. 'If I knew what it was Jeanne did that was so terrible maybe I'd begin to understand. But I don't. I mean – she seduced Philip when he was betrothed to Alazais, but that hardly seems bad enough to warrant a punishment lasting hundreds of years and several lifetimes. If it were, there'd be heaven knows how many millions caught on your Wheel of Karma!'

'*Several* lifetimes,' Valerie repeated, and the barely suppressed excitement was back in her voice. 'You don't think this is the first time they've replayed whatever it was they did?'

Simone shook her head. 'I don't know.' She didn't even know why she'd said it. The words had simply sprung to her lips.

'Well, whatever, Aurore thinks it might be becoming very urgent,' Valerie went on. 'She did a meditation about it after I spoke to her last. She didn't get anything concrete – as I said before, she really needs some personal item belonging to Esther or Hélène to get anything really clear – which is why she didn't call me back about it. But she had the definite feeling that time might be short.'

Simone shivered. Wasn't that the feeling she had experienced herself?

'And she thinks you should try to hurry things along a bit.'

'How?'

'By not simply waiting for the next part of the story to come to you, but inviting it.'

'And how do I do that?'

'By putting yourself into a trance.'

Simone gesticulated helplessly. 'I wouldn't know how to begin!'

'That's where I can help.' Valerie went to the bag she had deposited on the table, opening it and rummaging inside. 'I've got everything we need here – joss sticks, candles . . .'

'Oh Valerie, I don't know . . .'

'Look – do you want to have to spend the rest of your life blaming yourself if something terrible happens and you could have prevented it? Come on, Simone, let's try. I'll be here with you and afterwards we can discuss whatever you see and try to make sense of it.'

Simone sighed. She didn't like it, but she didn't feel she had a choice any more. Once, long ago, Valerie and Aurore had put her into a trance and she had become Helis Marty. They had begun something then which needed to be seen through to its conclusion.

'Very well,' she said resignedly.

An hour later they were ready to begin. Valerie had insisted Simone should take a salt bath – 'to purify the body', she had said – and wear something loose so as to be totally comfortable and not impede the vibrations. Simone, who rarely wore anything that was less than comfortable, thought this was rather unneccessary, but she did as Valerie said anyway, looking out an Indian cotton kaftan she had brought back with her from a visit to Morocco. Valerie had drawn the curtains to shut out the late-afternoon sunshine, jammed a joss stick into a small pot of cacti, and lit it. Then she instructed Simone to lie down and close her eyes.

'Float, Simone – float like a leaf on water.' Her voice was soft, encouraging. 'Just empty your mind and float free.'

Simone couldn't. In spite of the bath, in spite of the cool loose kaftan, her brain was whirling and the sounds of the outside world were too intrusive. She could hear the village clock chiming, the buzz of a fly caught in the curtains and the clank and chink as workmen emptied the bottle bank just down the road. But the scent of the joss stick was pungent and evocative and gradually Simone's racing thoughts slowed down to a soothing rhythm like gentle waves washing a sun-kissed beach.

She was beginning to drift, the here and now receding as she slipped into a state of altered consciousness. She could still hear the sounds of the everyday world but they no longer seemed so real to her. They belonged to another time, another place. Even the frenzied buzzing of the fly had become muted, no longer a prisoner trying to escape but bees humming in sun-drenched grass.

Simone breathed deeply, sliding into the stillness and the peace.

And then she saw Jeanne.

The track, narrow and dusty, led steeply upward around bend after hairpin bend. Braida was tired. She dragged her feet, her head held low, and Jeanne glanced thoughtfully at a small copse which spilled down the mountainside to meet the track a few hundred feet ahead. Should they stop and rest awhile? With the sun beating down mercilessly from a cloudless sky and the heat rising in waves from the parched ground it was a tempting prospect. But it would be a temporary respite only. Jeanne raised her eyes, looking towards the castle which topped the mountain spur, and sighed. For three days now she had been in the saddle, two nights she had slept under the stars, surviving only on water from the streams and fruit and berries which were ripening fast under the August sun. Now at last her destination was in sight. If it killed both her and Braida she was not going to stop again until she reached it.

She leaned forward on the horse's neck, rubbing her nose gently.

'Not far now, my darling.'

As if encouraged by her words Braida plodded forward a little more eagerly, flicking her ears against the flies which buzzed ceaselessly around them, and Jeanne's heart filled with love. Dear Braida, upon whose loyalty she could rely; Braida, who had never let her down. Would Philip be angry when he discovered she had taken her? Well, she did not care much if he was. Philip and Montaugure were in the past now. She had left them for ever.

Her lips tightened with determination, yet still the yearning refused to go away. Perhaps, far from being angry, Philip would be sorry when he realised she had gone. Surely he must at least have been anxious when she did not return from her morning ride, for she had told no one what she planned and taken nothing but a few scraps which she had saved from the table, some sweetmeats for Braida and her best mantle, folded now in a tight roll behind her. All that first day Jeanne had found herself glancing over her shoulder in the hope that he might come after her. But he had not, and she had seen no one but a small contingent of men-at-arms. When she had first caught sight of them, a dark knot in the shimmering heat haze on the horizon, Jeanne had been very frightened in case they might be crusaders. She had dismounted and led Braida down into a tree-lined gully which fell away from the track, hiding both herself and the horse in the bushes. When the riders had come close enough she had seen that they were not crusaders but men wearing the livery of the Count of Comminges, but she had remained hidden until they had passed anyway. In her present state of mind she trusted no man – at best they might escort her back to Montaugure, at worst they might sport with her or even rape her. Jeanne did not want to take the chance of any of these things befalling her.

Braida's step was faltering again and Jeanne realised it was too much to expect her to carry a rider up this steep path at the end of such an arduous journey. Slight though she was, she was still an encumbrance Braida could do without.

'Whoa, Braida!'

Gathering the remnants of her own fading strength she rose in the stirrups and slipped from the saddle. Her legs felt weak and every muscle in her body screamed a protest. For just a moment she leaned heavily against the horse, looking back down the valley from which they had climbed and seeing it through a haze of perspiration – the tree-speckled expanse of green stretching away towards the bluish rising ground, the cluster of houses which made up the nearest village. So many villages Jeanne had passed through on her journey had been reduced to nothing but charred rubble and she had guessed they were Cathar villages which had been sacked by de Montfort's armies. This one, at least, survived intact. Perhaps now that de Montfort was dead it would remain so.

Jeanne wiped the sweat from her forehead with a trembling hand, unknowing and uncaring that she added yet another streak to her already dirty face. Then she tugged on Braida's reins and started once again towards the castle.

Montsegur. Never had any name been more synonymous with a haven of peace and rest. Jeanne dragged herself up the hillside towards it, drawing on her last reserves of strength as fatigue, hunger and thirst took their toll. One step. Another – and another. Endless – endless. Then, just when she thought she was condemned to climb for ever, the ground flattened out, then narrowed for the last steep rise to the castle gates, and her first rush of relief was followed by sudden panic. This place was a refuge for Cathars, a fortress against the crusading armies. Its defences would be impregnable – more so even than the defences at Montaugure. There would be sentries at the gates, men-at-arms ready to ward off any threat. Supposing their orders were that the gates were to be opened to no one? Supposing they refused to let her in? She and Braida could not survive much longer without water or shelter from the fierce sun.

Hardly had the thought crossed her mind when a door in the thick wall to one side of the portcullis swung open and a guard's rough voice called to her.

'Who goes there?'

They had seen her coming, she realised and – thank God – had realised she posed them no threat.

'My name is Jeanne Marty,' she called back, her voice hoarse with dust. 'I have come to see Agnes Bertrand of Montaugure. Please – oh please – let me in!'

'Oh my dear, dear Jeanne! Is it always to be my fate to nurse you back to health after you arrive in my life half dead and on horseback?'

Agnes was smiling, the serene smile which Jeanne loved so much and which she had first seen when she had opened her eyes on recovering from the fever at Montaugure. Only now Agnes was wearing not a beautiful rose-pink gown such as she had worn then but a simple black habit, hooded and caught at the waist with a girdle. The moment Jeanne had seen it she had known what it meant. Agnes had not only turned to the Cathar faith, she had also become a Perfect, and these last years had been spent in preaching and ministering, living a life which was pure, holy and unmarred by any of the sins of the flesh.

'I am not ill,' Jeanne said. 'I simply needed food and rest, that's all.'

'And now you have had both and still you look pale,' Agnes said seriously. 'You still have to explain to me, my dear, what you are doing here.'

'Well, I've come to see you, of course! I always said I would, didn't I?'

Agnes shook her head. 'There is more to it than that, I think. No one rides so far alone simply to see an old woman.'

'Don't say that!' Jeanne protested fiercely. 'You are not old – and I have longed to see you! Scarcely a day has gone by but I have thought of you.'

'And I have thought of you, my dear! I still find it hard to believe you left the comfort and safety of Montaugure and went through all this simply to be with me.'

Jeanne's lip trembled. She bit at it fiercely.

'There was nothing for me at Montaugure any more. I don't want to talk about it.'

'I see.' Agnes nodded sagely.

'So I have come to you. But you are quite right: I do have other reasons too. For one thing, I want to search for Pons.'

Agnes sighed, folding her hands in the sleeves of her habit.

'I fear that could prove an impossible task. Have you any idea the destruction these terrible crusades have wreaked on every community here in the south? So many towns and villages destroyed, so many people dead . . .'

'Pons isn't dead – I'm sure he's not. If he was I'd know.'

'You may be right, but I think you have little chance of finding him. The people have scattered and begun new lives – those who were spared.'

'He was with Guillemette,' Jeanne said stubbornly. 'She was a Catholic. She may have raised Pons as a Catholic too. I have to try to find him – surely you understand that?'

'Oh yes, *ma petite*, I understand. But I am counselling you not to set too much store by it when your chances of success are so remote.' Agnes smiled gently. 'What is your other reason?'

Jeanne hesitated, shy suddenly of putting into words what was in her heart – the one thing she really wanted to do now that Philip was lost to her. The pleasures of the flesh no longer beckoned – without Philip they were as dust and ashes. Only one thing had meaning now: the faith of her childhood.

'I want to train to become a Perfect,' she murmured.

For long moments Agnes looked at her. Something had happened to Jeanne which she did not understand. She had grown up, of course – and grown up at a time of hardship and unrest, of treachery and change. She had suffered so much and though she and Bernard had done their best to help her they had been unable to heal the deepest of the scars. She was suffering now, Agnes was certain of it. There was no mistaking the pain in her eyes, the hurt she was trying so hard to hide. But it was more than that. There was some physical change in Jeanne – a roundness to her features which had not been there before in spite of the fact that she was still painfully thin . . .

Agnes sighed, wondering how best to tell her that this aspiration of hers was as impossible as the other.

'You are far too young to become a Perfect,' she said gently.

'How old are you? Sixteen – seventeen? You need to live first, marry, have children. It is because the Church of Rome imposes chastity on its priests at too young an age that they find so much difficulty in keeping their vows, for it is against the laws of nature. I will help you to be a good Cathar again, but do not talk of renouncing the world and the flesh yet. Not for another twenty years at least – if then.'

Jeanne's lip was trembling. Why was it that tears always seemed to be so close these days?

'I can't wait so long!'

Agnes took her in her arms.

'My dear, I am afraid you must.'

Jeanne was very frightened. It was almost three months since she had come to Montsegur, and in all that time she had not once had her monthly courses. At first she had thought their absence was due to the long and arduous ride from Montaugure – everyone knew that undue stress could interfere with the workings of nature. But there was no getting away from the fact that she was usually so regular that the calender could have been set by her, and besides . . .

Jeanne took her breasts in her hands, examining them. Here in her chamber she was quite alone, stripped to the waist to wash at the small tub of water she had fetched for herself, but as she looked at the areolae, noting how large and dark they had grown, a faint colour rose in her pale cheeks. Her breasts *shouldn't* look like that – they never had done before. And they were swollen, too, and tender to the touch.

She was with child. She had known it in her heart for weeks now and tried not to think about it. The problems which would be heaped on her, the shame she would bring to Agnes, the final nail in the coffin of her hopes of becoming a Perfect – it had all been more than she could face. Somehow she had blotted it out of her mind, but the echo had remained, a constant shadow from which she could not escape. Now the shadow was taking on substance and she could ignore it no longer.

She pressed her hands to her stomach, imagining the new life beginning there, and suddenly in spite of all her fears and misgivings she felt a jolt of pure joy.

Philip's child! Why had she not thought of it that way before?

She might have lost Philip, who would, by now, be Alazais's husband, but she was carrying his child!

For a moment Jeanne stood stock still, lost in the wonder of it. And knew that whatever pain she had to endure, however great the difficulties which would beset her, she could not regret this one small miracle which would change her life for ever.

Simone stirred, a sense of confusion returning her to the edge of consciousness.

So, Jeanne had had a child – Philip's child. Not so surprising, really. But where did a child fit into all this? Hélène had positively refused to start a family – it had been one of the bones of contention between her and Alain, Simone knew. And as far as she was aware, Esther had no child either.

She twisted her head on the cushion, muttering in confusion and quite unaware of Valerie bending closer to try to make out what she was saying, though she could see the thin stream of smoke from the joss stick, swirling in a thick frothy mist like low cloud over the mountains before her half-closed eyes.

Then the swirling mists cleared a little and Simone saw Jeanne once more – no longer the slender girl she had been, but big with child. Some months had passed, Simone knew – Jeanne's time was near. Simone moistened her dry lips, folded her hands once more across her breasts and let the past envelop her.

The Marin wind, cold for December, drove a thick misting of sleet into the hillside so that both the valley below and the castle clinging to the peak above were hidden from view.

Jeanne shivered, drawing her mantle more closely around her swollen body and bending her head against the sleet. This was no weather to be out in the woods searching for kindling, but she had had little choice. She had fallen down on her job of keeping the stocks in the woodshed high – if she did not replenish them before the snow settled the fire would go out and, pregnant or not, her husband would probably beat her for her stupidity.

Her husband. At the very thought of him something seemed to close up in Jeanne's chest as though a giant hand was squeezing her heart.

She should be grateful to him, she supposed. He had given her a home and he would provide for both her and the baby. But she could not feel grateful. She was too numb with weariness and cold to feel anything but fear of him and resentment against both him and Agnes, who had arranged the match.

Helpless tears sprang to Jeanne's eyes and she found herself wondering again, as she had wondered so many times these last weeks, how Agnes could have done this to her and forced her into a marriage with a man she despised. It would not have been easy, of course, raising a child without the support of a husband, but she felt sure that with Agnes's help and support she could have done it. But that Agnes had refused to give. When Jeanne had no longer been able to conceal her condition and she had confessed to Agnes, the older woman's response had been stern and unyielding.

'I knew there was something different about you,' she had said, unsmiling. 'Tell me, Jeanne, who is the man who has taken advantage of your innocence?'

Jeanne had gulped, ashamed suddenly. What had happened was not Philip's fault, it was her own. She had seduced him and she had no one but herself to blame for her plight.

'Who was it?' Agnes had persisted. 'I must know so that he can be made to take responsibility for you and his bastard.'

Jeanne bit her lip. She could not bring herself to tell Agnes that Philip was responsible and in any case there was nothing he could do to help her – he was married to Alazais now. Jeanne knew to her shame that if it had not been so she would have confessed and hoped that Agnes would insist that he should marry her instead. But it was too late for that. The truth would do nothing but harm now.

She brought up her chin with a jerk, her eyes meeting Agnes's defiantly.

'It was no one.'

'Come, child, I was not born yesterday!'

'It was no one who matters. I don't want to see him again – ever. I just want to stay here with you.'

'Oh Jeanne, surely you must realise that is impossible now? Montsegur is no place to raise a child. What sort of a life would it have here, confined in this bleak little castle with no playmates and the constant threat of siege? A child needs a home and a family, brothers and sisters. And besides, I am a guest of Raymond of Pereille. He has allowed me to have you here these last months, but I cannot foist a bastard child on him. No, if you will not tell me who the father is, then I am afraid you will have to leave it to me to find a husband for you.'

Jeanne had begun to tremble then. The last thing she wanted was to be married – that would be the final betrayal of her love for Philip, and she could not bear the thought that her child would grow up thinking some other man was his father.

'Oh Agnes, you can't mean it!' she begged, but in vain. With her mind made up Agnes could be as unmoving as she could be gentle. A husband must be found for Jeanne and quickly, before her condition was obvious to all and sundry. And she thought she knew the very man.

Pierre Vital was a farmer who owned half a dozen small plots of land and a flock of sheep for which he employed a team of shepherds. His animals and the land, which was ploughed and used to grow oats, wheat and turnips when it was not lying fallow, made him well off compared with many of the villagers. As a Cathar sympathiser who often attended the meetings where Agnes and the other Perfects spoke and gave instruction, he was well known to her and he had confessed to her that he had been lonely since the death of his wife giving birth to their first child a year before. Agnes had approached him and Pierre had agreed to the marriage without delay.

Numb with misery, Jeanne had moved into his *ostal* in the village, which lay on the slopes below the castle of Montsegur. She was uncomfortable with the big rough man whose uncultured ways made him the very opposite of Philip, and though he was not unkind to her, he was often angered by her inability to carry out the wifely duties for which she had never been trained. At Montaugure she had lived the life of a lady; now suddenly she was expected to do the cooking and fetch the water, tend the fire and the garden, wash the pots at the well and mend the farm equipment.

She hated the *ostal*, which, though not so different from the one she had lived in as a child, seemed cramped and mean after the huge rooms at Montaugure, hated the fact that the livestock shared the house in winter. The constant snorting and snuffling of the pigs played on her nerves and the stench they made pervaded the air and made her feel constantly nauseous. As for the ox who drew the swing plough, he had a habit of lowing loudly and unexpectedly and making her jump out of her skin.

Worst of all was the fact that she had to share a bed with Pierre. So far she had managed to persuade him that it would be dangerous to her condition if he insisted on his conjugal rights and with the memory of his first wife's untimely death as a warning he had refrained from bothering her. But she shrank from lying beside him, disgusted by the ugly smell of sweat and dirt and animal excrement which lingered on his clothes and in his matted hair. It would not be long, she knew, before he insisted on knowing her carnally, and the very thought made her sick to the stomach.

Just now, however, it was her fear of his anger when he discovered she had allowed the fire to go out which was uppermost in her mind. Trying to forget that her fingers were numb with the cold, Jeanne rooted about at the edge of the path, scrabbling up the thickest twigs and fallen branches she could find and putting them into the handcart she had brought with her. The sticks were sodden and she wondered anxiously whether she would be able to get them to burn. But if she could only keep the fire going she would be able to dry the rest out before they were needed.

At last the little cart was full and Jeanne started back down the steep path. The sleet was thicker and whiter now, settling in places on the frosty ground beneath, and Jeanne quickened her step. She did not want to be caught too far from home if it turned into a blizzard.

Afterwards she was never quite certain how she came to fall – it all happened so fast. One minute she was hurrying down the path, the next she was fighting to keep her balance and crashing to the frozen ground. As the shock reverberated through her body she lay motionless for a moment, her only thought for her baby. There was a sharp pain in her leg; looking down she saw that the sharp corner of the cart had ripped through her skirt and made a jagged gash in the flesh just above her knee. Already blood was gushing out and staining the gathering whiteness of the snow.

Sick and shaky, she scrambled to her feet, grabbing the handle of the cart and starting off once more down the path. Snow swirled into her face and she sobbed aloud, pain and wretchedness plunging her into a dark abyss of despair.

The snow was already beginning to build into soft drifts on the rough ground by the time Jeanne reached the *ostal*. She pushed aside the slat which covered the entrance and let herself in, almost gagging as the overpowering smell of the animals assailed her nostrils. She dragged her cart into the kitchen so that the kindling would not get wetter than it already was and lit a taper from the embers of the fire. By its light she examined her leg again. It was still bleeding, running a sticky scarlet river from knee to ankle, and the first sharp pain had become a steady throb. Jeanne fetched a bowl of water and sat down on a stool beside the fire to bathe it, wincing as the water washed away the glutinous mess to reveal the wound beneath.

She was still tending it, pinching the gaping edges together with her fingers, when she heard the creak of the slat being pushed aside and she glanced up to see Pierre coming into the kitchen. His coat was white with snow and he stood for a moment stamping it off his boots and blowing on his fingers.

'The weather has turned for the worst,' he said, stating the obvious. 'If this keeps up we'll be cut off by morning.'

She made no reply and he glanced at her, his beady eyes narrowing to slits so that they all but disappeared in the weather-beaten folds of his face.

'What are you doing?'

'I fell in the snow and cut my leg.' She did not want to tell him what she had been doing, did not want to draw attention to the fact that she had let the kindling run low again, though the cart, now dripping melting snow on to the floor, announced it for any who cared to notice.

He crossed to the fire, stretching out his hands to the meagre warmth, and she moved defensively, letting her skirt fall over her legs. But he reached out, tweaking it up again.

'That's a nasty cut.'

'It's not so bad.' Her breath was coming fast; she had noticed the look on his face as his eye fell on her bare leg, long and slender among her bunched-up skirts.

''Twill leave a scar.' His work-hardened fingers rasped cold against her flesh and she flinched.

'It's hurting you.' There was something close to tenderness in his voice but Jeanne was too frightened to notice it. This man might be her husband but he was still like a stranger to her. She did not like him seeing her legs, liked his closeness and the touch of his hand even less.

'Leave it!' she said sharply. 'I'm all right.'

Pierre drew back startled by her tone, but he did not remove his hand from her thigh. Since he had married her he had felt pity and irritation in equal measures for the beautiful child with the huge frightened eyes and though she stirred him in a way he had not been stirred since the death of his first wife he had made up his mind to have patience with her in this regard at least. Her warnings that it would be wrong for him to make love to her in her present condition had reawakened the pangs of guilt he still felt at Esperte's death. Had he caused it by lying with her when she was already with child? he had wondered. But Esperte had never complained, even when she was eight months gone and he had had to take her from behind, and Na Maurs, the old woman who had attended her at her confinement, had said it was the *size* of the child that had been the death of both of them. Now, the long-suppressed desire stirred in his loins, turning his concern to anger.

He had given Jeanne a home and promised to take care of her and her bastard child. He had treated her with as much kindness and consideration as any man treated his woman. How dare she deny him what she had plainly put on offer to some other man and attempt to make him guilty for desiring even the most harmless physical contact?

'I am your husband,' he said harshly. 'You would do well to remember that.'

'How can I forget?' Again she tried to push him away and he took her by the arm, his fingers biting into the flesh through the thin wool of her gown. His face was close to hers; she could smell his fetid breath and she jerked her head back, sobbing aloud as pain jarred her from neck to shoulder. Her obvious repulsion inflamed him further; her refusal to have him near her had nothing to do with fear for her unborn child. It went much deeper than that. Unless he showed her who was master, and soon, she would continue to take advantage of his good nature and he would become less and less of a man.

With a grunt he reached for her, scooping her up from the stool with one hand beneath her knees and the other pinioning her arms. Jeanne screamed and struggled – in vain. Pierre was not a tall man but he was stockily built and strong from years of working on the land, and he carried her almost effortlessly across the kitchen and down the stairs to the cellar which served as a bedroom. There he threw her bodily on to the bed, holding her down while he rucked her skirt up to the waist.

'My baby!' Jeanne beat helplessly against his chest with her fists.

'You have used that excuse long enough, girl,' he growled. 'It is time you became my wife in more than name.'

Her leg had begun to bleed again, dribbling a scarlet stream on to the rough mattress, but neither of them noticed it. The weight of him was forcing the breath from her lungs and for a moment she could think of nothing but drawing breath. Then he was forcing her legs apart with a thick muscled knee and entering her roughly. A fresh wave of pain knifed through her, sharper than all the other pains which were setting her body on fire, and it seemed to Jeanne that the world had suddenly gone dark and she was falling, falling, into the blackness, into the pain . . .

When he had finished with her he pushed himself away, standing up to straighten his clothing and looking down at her. She was still gasping and sobbing softly and with the release of suppressed desire he felt the beginnings of shame.

'Cover yourself and see to the fire,' he growled.

Jeanne made no move. There was a dull ache deep in the core of her and she was terrified suddenly that there might be some substance to the warnings she had used to keep Pierre at arm's length. If she had submitted willingly perhaps it would have been all right. But her own resistance had given him no option but to take her by force. If she lost Philip's baby now she would never forgive herself. Worse, her last reason to live would have been taken from her.

Jeanne wound her arms protectively around her swollen belly, sobbing soundlessly but with such passion that she thought her heart would break.

The trance was lifting so that only the aura of it remained, dark and pervasive. Simone opened her eyes and the familiar room took shape around her.

'Well?' Valerie asked eagerly. 'What happened?'

Simone was silent for a moment, too distressed to speak. Then she wiped away the tears that had sprung to her eyes, and her hand was trembling.

'Oh Valerie – it was awful! Poor Jeanne!'

'You mean you know now?'

Simone shook her head.

'No, I don't think so. It was just that she was having Philip's baby and Agnes forced her to marry a peasant man. He took her by force . . .' She closed her eyes momentarily. 'I don't want to talk about it. It was too horrible. And I can't see what it could possibly have to do with Hélène or Esther.'

'You don't think . . .' Valerie's eyes had gone round. 'You don't think perhaps *Esther* is pregnant, do you – by Alain? And he's going to refuse to marry her because of Hélène, and she'll have to marry someone she doesn't love instead?'

'I should hardly think so! Well – she may be pregnant for all I know, but she certainly wouldn't be forced into marriage with someone she despised because of it. This is the late twentieth century, not the early thirteenth. Times have changed, Valerie. You of all people should know that!'

'Yes, I suppose so . . .' Valerie sighed. 'We're no nearer to finding out what happened then?'

'Not really, no.' Simone sat up. Her kaftan was moist with perspiration and she felt dirty and used. She wished she could go and run another bath to wash away the lingering feeling of violation, but she knew she had used up all the hot water already. And in any case, it hadn't been she who had been raped in that mean little cottage in the shadow of Montsegur, she reminded herself. It hadn't even been her alter ego. But if they were correct in their theories, perhaps it had been her daughter . . .

'I did ring Edith at the library to ask her about the Bernards of Montaugure,' she said, trying to steer Valerie away from asking any more about her vision. 'She's fairly certain they existed and she's going to try and find out something about them for me. But I can't really see that it's going to help much. Jeanne is no longer at Montaugure, and she's the central character.'

'Couldn't you ask Edith to check on Jeanne too?' Valerie suggested.

'I don't think she'd be mentioned anywhere. It wasn't until the Inquisition began that they started detailed records of ordinary people – for the purpose of winkling out anyone with Cathar connections and exterminating them.' She shivered as a sudden horrible thought occurred to her.

'Oh God!' Valerie looked shaken too as she picked up on the possibility that had crossed Simone's mind. 'You don't think – '

'I don't know, Valerie, I honestly don't know,' Simone said wretchedly.

For a long while the sisters sat in silence, brought closer than they had been for years by the shadow which stretched down the centuries and was drawing them both in.

17

'WHAT'S ALL THIS about?' Alain asked, coming into the bedroom where Esther was packing. He sounded stressed, as well he might, Esther thought. But he was not the only one.

'I can't stay here, Alain,' she said, straightening up. 'Not now. Not after what your mother said.'

'What did she say?'

'Enough to make it perfectly clear I'm not welcome. And also that you regret asking me here. She said that you want to get back together with Hélène and that I'm making things difficult for you. And I can't help thinking that's not far from the truth.'

'What do you mean by that?'

'Well – it's obvious you still care for her. Just now . . .' She broke off. She didn't want to put into words the closenes she had sensed between them.

'Esther – Hélène is terribly upset.'

'So your mother said.'

'Did she tell you why?'

'No. Because of Thierry, I suppose. And also because . . . she doesn't want me here either.'

He sighed, not denying it.

'It's not just that. Hélène has been receiving silent phone calls. She was already upset by that – Simone had to stay with her last night, apparently. Then, this afternoon, she was out in her car and she got the impression someone was following her.'

'Following her? Why should anyone do that?'

'I don't know, Esther. That's what makes it so worrying. It's possible she's attracted some unwelcome attention.'

'A stalker, you mean?'

'Well – yes. It's all pretty odd. Anyway, she was really frightened this afternoon. She put her foot down and managed to shake him off, then she drove straight here.'

'And your mother asked her to stay.'

'Well yes. I don't think she's going to but Maman felt she should offer. Look, Esther, I'm really sorry if she said something to upset you. I'm sure she didn't mean it.'

'Oh, I think she did.'

'Maman isn't always the most tactful of people. I expect she was concerned that it might be awkward, you and Hélène under the same roof. I'm sure she didn't intend you to feel you had to leave.'

'There we shall have to differ,' Esther said. 'I'm sorry, but I really wouldn't feel right imposing on her any longer, Hélène or no Hélène. I'd prefer to stay in a hotel tonight.'

He ran a hand through his hair, looking more harassed than ever.

'I doubt we'd get you into one now. Look, I'll have a word with Maman— '

'It's not just that though, Alain,' Esther said. 'It's this whole business of Hélène being around all the time. You told me your marriage was over – I'd never have come otherwise. But it's not, is it? Not in any real sense of the word.'

Alan gestured helplessly.

'It is . . . it was. But since all this has happened . . . Hélène is very vulnerable. We're all she's got now. We can't just pretend she doesn't exist.'

'No, but there are limits. I suppose I can understand that you still feel a certain responsibility towards her. But it's not just you. Your whole family seem obsessed with her.'

'They're worried about her – as I am. Perhaps I should explain. Hélène's mother died when she was very young under . . . well, rather suspicious circumstances. She had worked for my family and they took Hélène and Thierry in. It was all very tragic and I think it was the root of Hélène's problems.'

He broke off, not wanting to talk in any detail about the things that had never been openly discussed. His was a secretive family, but even as a young man he had wondered about the truth of what had happened to Odette, realised there was more to it than met the eye. A healthy young woman, dying suddenly like that – it didn't make sense. He had remembered the whispered discussions between Isobelle and Henri, from which he and his sisters were excluded, wondered that someone as apparently ruthless as Isobelle should be prepared to offer a home to two potentially troublesome youngsters. The mere fact that Odette had worked for them didn't seem enough to explain it. Much later Hélène had told him something of what had happened the night her mother died and it had made him wonder again. But Hélène had been too young to really understand much of what was going on and again Alain had swept it all to the back of his mind and forgotten about it. Only when Hélène's black moods came did it come uncomfortably to the forefront again and he had wondered just what had been her legacy.

'Having cared for Hélène for so long, it's only natural they are very concerned for her welfare,' he said now, 'but it's not just that. Hélène once tried to take her own life. It was passed off as a mistake – a cry for help that went too far – but the fact remains. She could very easily have died. I think we are all very afraid something of the sort might happen again.'

'I see.' Esther bit her lip. 'So you're saying that's why you won't ask her for a divorce? You're afraid she might try to commit suicide? It doesn't bode very well for the future, does it?'

'I have asked her for a divorce,' Alain said. 'I phoned her about it after I met you. And I will ask her again, when the time is right.'

'Will you? I'm not so sure . . .'

'I told you, I already did.'

'So why are you still married to her?'

'She wasn't agreeable.'

'Well there you are. I rest my case.'

'It wasn't something we could talk about over the telephone,' Alain said irritably. 'It needed to be sorted out face to face.'

'But you haven't sorted it out.'

'For heaven's sake, what chance have I had?'

'I don't know, Alain. What I do know is that I'm in an impossible position. I know this has been a difficult time for you but I honestly think the time has come for you to make up your mind. Do you want me – or do you want Hélène? You can't have us both.'

'Oh Christ, Esther . . .' He turned away, running a hand through his hair again as the dilemma he'd been trying to avoid was suddenly there, confronting him.

The truth was, he didn't know. He honestly didn't know. Crazy as it seemed, impossible as the situation was, he loved them both. Differently, yes, but each in their own way as much as the other. Hélène aroused his protective instincts, Esther excited his passion. From the moment he had met her he had been drawn to her so strongly he had been powerless to resist. He had been able to think of nothing but her. And he had thought that he and Hélène were finished. But it wasn't that simple. Hélène still needed him; hurting her hurt him.

What a bloody mess!

But when it came to the point, Esther was quite right. He couldn't have them both. He had to choose.

'Well!' Esther's voice, hard with hurt and humiliation, cut across his tangled thoughts. 'I suppose you've just told me what I need to know. I think the best thing is for me to go home, don't you? Leave you to get on with your life.'

He turned back, saw her standing there, proud and defiant and strong, though her eyes were suspiciously bright, and knew suddenly that he couldn't bear to lose her. It was that morning in Bristol all over again; he remembered how bereft he had felt when she had thrown him out, how overjoyed he had been when she had telephoned. He might not want to hurt Hélène, but the thought of never seeing Esther again was just too much.

'Don't go,' he said before he could stop himself. His voice was rough.

'Give me one good reason why I should stay.'

'Because I love you – and you love me. You do love me, don't you, Esther?'

'That has nothing to do with it.'

'It has everything to do with it. I will sort things out, I promise. Just as soon as the dust settles. Only please . . . don't go.'

He saw the indecision flicker across her face and knew that her feelings were as powerful as his, subjugating reason. She wasn't quite ready to give in yet, though.

'I don't want to go,' she said. 'But we can't go on like this. I have to know where I stand, Alain. I have to know that you really are going to make it clear to Hélène that you want a divorce.'

'I will, I promise.'

'And you'll find a hotel for me for the rest of my stay?'

'If that's what you want. It's too late to do anything about it today, but we'll find somewhere for you tomorrow. And I'll book in with you.'

She nodded, making up her mind.

'All right.'

'Oh Esther!'

He reached for her, pulling her into his arms, his need for her made urgent by his fear of losing her.

She buried her head in his chest, hating herself for weakening. Nothing had really changed. Nothing was resolved. But at least she had given him the chance to end it if that was what he wanted and made her own feelings clear at the same time. And he was here with her. Hélène was downstairs, but he was here with her.

For the moment she felt it really was the only thing that mattered.

After Valerie had left, Simone decided to make a quick call to check on Hélène. Trust Valerie to have forgotten all about her promise to visit! Simone dialled Hélène's number, but there was no reply. Either she was not answering the phone or she was out. But Simone thought that if she had been there Hélène would not have been able to resist answering and she certainly wasn't going to drive over to find out. She didn't want to risk being talked into staying another night, and in any case, she was ravenously hungry. She hadn't eaten all day, she realised, but as usual her fridge was almost empty.

Simone changed into trousers and a loose shirt and drove the eight kilometres to the nearest mini-market where she bought ready-cooked chicken, fresh crusty bread and salad and several bottles of lime-flavoured mineral water. But delicious as the food was, she hardly tasted a mouthful. She was still too preoccupied with worrying about what was happening to her and what it might mean.

She sat for a long while on the patio while the swifts wheeled and swooped in great circles over her head and the sky deepened through shades of blue to soft grey twilight. Then she carried the dirty dishes into the house, fed Félix, and went upstairs. The bed looked welcoming and she almost collapsed into it as she was, but she forced herself to go to the bathroom to wash her face and brush her teeth.

Her face looked back at her from the mirror over the basin,

the muscles of her jaw sagging a little, eyes puffy and red-rimmed from lack of sleep. Oh Simone, you're growing old! she thought. But then, you never were any beauty!

That indisputable fact made the ageing easier to bear. One didn't miss what one had never had. Pity the Helens of Troy of this world when their looks began to disintegrate.

She wiped the towel across her face and frowned. The mirror had misted up, as if she had just taken a hot bath or shower. Yet the water in the sink was only tepid and a moment ago she had been able to look at her reflection with perfect clarity. Simone felt her stomach fall away, knowing somehow what was about to happen.

Oh no, not now! she thought. She'd had enough for one day!

She tried to move away but the misted mirror drew her eyes like a magnet. It was crazing now, like a windscreen cracked by a pebble, and becoming opaque. She could see what looked like a stone wall and heavy drapes and particles like dust motes in a ray of sunshine swimming and swirling against them to form shadowy images. The scent in her nostrils was no longer the soft sweet smell of her soap but the more pungent smell of dried herbs and the faint wafting aroma of woodsmoke and roasting meat and the images were growing stronger, taking shape. The towel slipped from her fingers and she frowned, a little bewildered. It was happening again, without a doubt. But this time the figure materialising in the misted mirror was not Jeanne, but Alazais.

'Milady, I must speak with you.'

Alazais looked up, surprised, from the Book of Psalms she had been reading, as Robert Giraud, steward of the castle of Montaugure, entered the small solar, his red-veined face flushed from his hasty ascent of the steep stairs. It was unusual for the steward to seek her out at this time of the afternoon when she retired for an hour's quiet contemplation.

'What is it, Monsieur Giraud?'

He hesitated for a moment, fighting to catch his breath and looking pointedly at her three ladies, Amicia and Blanche, who sat spinning, and Grazide, the youngest and prettiest, who had been playing softly on her lute to entertain them.

Alazais's heart missed a beat, her thoughts flying, as they invariably did, to Philip. Three days ago he had left Montaugure on a visit to Roger Bernard of Foix and as always Alazais was deeply concerned for his safety. The civil war might be over now, ended, a few months ago in the spring of 1229 by an ignominious treaty, but Alazais knew her husband too well to suppose he would submit quietly to French rule. There had been peace before, after the death of Simon de Montfort, but it had been broken, and Alazais lived in fear that it would be broken again. All very well to be proud of Philip for plotting with the other southern lords to protect his heritage but it was a dangerous business. The French had the might of the the monarchy and the wealth of the Church of Rome on their side; the mountain barons, wearied and impoverished by years of warfare, had nothing but their own indomitable spirit.

When Philip had left to visit Roger Bernard he had told her nothing of his purpose and this had disturbed her. She had tried to tell herself it did not necessarily mean that something was afoot; while his mother had been chatelaine at Montaugure he had fallen into the habit of secrecy since in recent years Cecile had disapproved openly of rebellion against the French. But Cecile was no longer here. During the first peace, three years ago now, she had struck up a friendship with one of the officials of the King, in Languedoc to administer the new regime, and when he had gone north once again to his own lands she had gone with him as his wife, taking her two younger sons with her to train as knights. Now Philip had no need of secrecy, for he knew, surely, that he could count on Alazais to support him in any course of action he might decide upon and she could only suppose his silence might be because he did not want to worry her with plans that might be at best foolhardy and at worst perilous.

She took a deep breath now, closing her Book of Psalms and laying it down in her lap.

'You may speak freely in front of my ladies, monsieur. I have no secrets from them.'

'Very well – if that is your wish.' Giraud's tone indicated that he doubted the wisdom of her instruction. 'You have a visitor, milady. A Dominican friar.'

'Oh!' Alazais's eyes widened in alarm. In these unhappy times the advent of a Dominican friar was not something to be welcomed. The order which had been formed to instruct and preach now had a new and frightening role to play in the troubles that afflicted Languedoc.

With the coming of peace between north and south the Church of Rome was more determined than ever to put an end to heresy. An inquisition had been set up to seek out Cathars and bring them to justice and the inquisitors were drawn mainly from the Dominican order. Already they had made a name for themselves as conscientious zealots, and the sentences handed out to those found guilty were severe enough to strike terror to the bravest heart. Lands could be confiscated, life sentences imposed, and for those who refused to recant there was only one punishment: death by burning.

Alazais trembled now as she wondered what had brought the Dominican to Montaugure. Had Philip aroused suspicion by his continued support for Raymond of Toulouse and his refusal to accept French rule? Or could it be that his aunt Agnes, now a Cathar Perfect, had been arrested? It was many years since she had been part of the household but memories were long and the slightest connection might be investigated. Oh, if only Philip were here! He would know what to do. But Philip was not here, and neither was Oliver, who now spent most of his time in Toulouse. In their absence it was she who must deal with the Dominican.

'Very well, Monsieur Giraud. You had better send him to me,' she said, setting her book down on the small table beside her.

'Here?' The steward sounded faintly surprised.

Alazais nodded.

The steward backed out of the chamber and Alazais turned to her ladies. Blanche's face was pinched with anxiety and Amicia so white with fear that Alazais wondered for a fleeting moment whether she might be the one who was guilty of heresy. Only Grazide looked as though she might be enjoying the drama. Her pretty round features had been composed into an expression of suitable solemnity but the full, puckered lips only made her dimples play, and Alazais thought there was an edge of excitement in her sharp green eyes.

'Leave me, all of you,' she commanded.

'But milady . . .' Blanche protested. Frightened as she was, she did not like to think of her mistress alone with an inquisitor.

'It is best I see him alone,' Alazais said firmly.

As the ladies left the chamber she crossed to the narrow window and stood looking out at the clear blue sky. Oh what torture and torments that sky had seen! What cruel injustices! Would it never end? In that moment Alazais found herself glad that she had as yet brought no child into this harsh world. That she had failed to conceive had been a source of sadness to her and she mourned the fact that she had failed to give Philip the son he longed for. But a baby would have been one more soul to worry over. Bad enough to be continually concerned for Philip's safety; to offer a vulnerable child such an uncertain future would be a thousand times worse.

'The priest, milady.'

The steward announced him and withdrew, and Alazais turned, lifting her chin and tucking her hands into the sleeves of her gown so that he should not see them trembling.

'Good day, Father.' Her voice was calm and level. 'To what do we owe this visit?'

The monk smiled faintly and she knew from the expression in his sharp grey eyes that in spite of her efforts he had recognised her fear. He moved towards her, his sandalled feet making a soft swishing sound in the rushes which covered the floor. He was a young man, she saw, much younger than she had expected, and tall and lean. But there was the hint of muscular grace in the way he moved and she guessed that his body beneath his loose flowing habit was strong and powerful.

'Don't be alarmed.' His voice was deep, with a trace of a southern accent. 'You are a good Catholic, I see.'

Her hand flew from the folds of her sleeve to the crucifix she wore around her neck.

'I try to be.'

'And I am certain you succeed. Be assured, milady, I am not here to question you on your faith or the faith of those around you. Mine is a personal errand. For long years I have searched for my sister and recently I came by some information which leads me to believe you may know her whereabouts.'

Alazais stared at him, puzzled and alarmed. A Dominican monk coming by information of any sort spoke of inquisitorial questioning, whatever his reassurances.

'Your sister?' she repeated.

'We were separated many years ago.' He raised a hand, pushing back his cowl and revealing a tonsure of flaming red hair. 'Her name is Jeanne. And mine is Pons. Pons Marty.'

For a moment suprise rendered Alazais speechless and she stared in disbelief at the young monk. This man – Jeanne's brother? She had heard the story, of course, of how Philip had found her hiding in the woods after the fall of Carcassonne and she knew too that Jeanne had lost a brother in the confusion. But like everyone else she had assumed that he must be long since dead, yet another nameless victim of the holocaust. Now she looked into the face of the Dominican monk, searching for some sign of family likeness – anything to make his startling claim seem feasible – and could see none. Except perhaps those eyes. Alazais pictured Jeanne's eyes and began to believe.

'Sancta Maria!'

'So – do you know my sister?'

Alazais clutched at her crucifix. 'I know a Jeanne Marty. She used to live here but she left these ten years since.'

'Where is she now?'

'I don't know.' Alazais shook her head. It was so long since she had thought about Jeanne, so long since she had ceased to wonder about her sudden disappearance from Montaugure. 'She took a horse and rode away. We never heard of her afterwards.'

'Was no one concerned to discover her whereabouts?'

'Philip thought— ' Alazais broke off, her hand flying to her mouth. She could not tell him what Philip had said – that Jeanne would almost certainly have gone to Montsegur to be with Agnes. Montsegur was a stronghold of heretics and, while this man might be Jeanne's brother, he was also, first and foremost, a Dominican and an inquisitor. She must not say anything to bring suspicion on the family.

'Yes?' Pons had noticed her confusion.

Alazais collected herself. 'I am sorry. If Philip had any idea where Jeanne had gone he never told me. As for myself, I could never understand why she left without a word. We were friends, she and I, but she never confided her thoughts to me. Believe me, Father, I would help you if I could, for Jeanne's sake. I know she longed to find you again. But I have never seen her from that day to this.'

'I see.' His fingers rasped thoughtfully over the reddish stubble on his chin, and Alazais felt a bolt of pity which momentarily overcame her fear.

'It must have been terrible for you too, Father,' she said.

He shrugged a little impatiently. 'I don't remember much about the siege. I was only four years old. All I know is what I was told by Guillemette, the woman who raised me. My mother died of the fever and Guillemette was her friend. Jeanne was older than me by four years, a wilful child. She ran away then too – she resented Guillemette and what she was trying to do for us. If I thought about Jeanne at all I supposed she must be dead. But recently, while compiling registers in the course of my work, I chanced to hear the story of a child rescued by Philip Bertrand and I thought it might be she.'

A nerve jumped in Alazais's throat. She had been right, then. It was a part of this man's job to investigate anyone who might have connections with heretics, and somehow she could believe it of him – there was something about him she did not like. Who had told him of the child Philip had befriended? she wondered. And why? Was it possible the Bertrands were under investigation and in danger? Yet this man had once been a Cathar himself!

'Why did you enter the church, Father?' she asked before she could stop herself.

'Because I was called by God. Why else?' He saw her perplexed expression and smiled briefly. 'Why a Dominican is what you meant, I think. Well, I have my reasons. The heresy must be wiped out, milady. It is an abomination. And I, perhaps more than most, have reason to hate it. It was the stubborn refusal of the Cathars to renounce evil which brought about the destruction of my family – that and the misguided generosity of spirit of their Catholic neighbours in protecting them. Thousands of God-fearing folk suffered because of them. Now we must see that they burn on this earth for if they do not, make no mistake they will burn in hell for all eternity.'

As he spoke his voice resonated with passion and a curious light made his eyes steely. Alazais shivered. This was the fervour which sent men and women to the stake. But she did not think it was the fervour of a convert. From what he said Alazais felt sure he had no idea he had ever been a Cathar. Rather it was that he took some sadistic pleasure in what he did.

'I am sorry I cannot help you, Father,' she said, anxious suddenly to be rid of him.

The monk's face darkened with suspicion. 'And you are certain there is no one in the household who might be able to enlighten me as to my sister's whereabouts?'

'No one. Cecile, the Dowager Viscountess, is now the wife of Amaury de Brantome and lives with him there, and my husband's uncle Benet, who was a priest, died three winters ago, but I don't think either of them knew what became of Jeanne.'

'And your husband, the Viscount?'

'Is away – as in his brother Oliver.' The nerve jumped again in her throat. She did not want to have to admit to this man that Philip was with the Count of Foix, whose allegiance to the Church of Rome was often questioned.

'I have travelled far, milady, and I had high hopes of learning of my sister's fate from the Bertrands. Would it be a great imposition if I asked if I might remain at Montaugure until his return?' His words were polite enough but she knew they constituted less of a request than a command and her heart sank. She did not want him here, but to refuse him hospitality would be most unwise.

'It is no imposition at all, Father,' she said smoothly. 'Of course you would be most welcome to stay at Montaugure as long as you wish.'

Grazide, the youngest and prettiest of Alazais's ladies, sipped her wine and looked over the rim of her goblet at the young priest who shared their table.

He was, she thought, the most handsome man she had ever seen and his sombre all-concealing habit gave him an air of mystery which only added to his attraction. If only he had not taken a vow of celibacy! But then, that too added a certain spice. Oh, it might not be of any use to look on him as a possible future husband, but it might be fun to try to make him fall in love with her! Grazide was very good at making men fall in love with her. Troubadours wrote her songs of unrequited love, knights fell over themselves to carry her colours to the joust, pages gazed at her in adolescent adoration. But a monk . . . Now that would be interesting! Difficult, but all the more rewarding for that. And surely, when it came down to it, a monk was a man like any other . . .

Grazide lowered her goblet, watching him speculatively and awaiting the chance to catch his eye. When it came she dimpled at him prettily, knowing that the flame from the flaring sconces on the walls were making lights dance in her auburn hair and throwing interesting shadows in the cleavage revealed by the low neck of her gown. She saw a faint flush colour his fair-skinned face and he looked away quickly, but a few moments later his eyes were on her again and she felt a thrill of triumph. So – he was not immune to her charms! She had known he would not be. She dimpled again, lowering her lashes flirtatiously.

Throughout the meal the game continued. Though he conversed with Alazais, who sat at his side, Grazide could tell he was intensely aware of her and her excitement grew. He would much prefer to be talking to her, she knew. Alazais, sweet natured as she was, could be very boring, and compared with her own slender curves, Alazais was plump and matronly. Grazide nibbled at her food seductively, licking her lips with a moist pink tongue and rewarding him now and then with a flash of her long curling lashes.

When the meal was over Alazais suggested, as Grazide had hoped she would, that she should should entertain them on her lute. It was, she knew, a very fetching accomplishment, and it gave her the opportunity to show off her sweet soprano voice. Glancing yet again at the monk, she saw that a faint sheen of perspiration had broken out on his face and she smiled to herself. Who knew how much she was stirring his body, hidden as it was by that all-concealing habit? Grazide's pulses beat faster as she imagined those deep grey eyes mentally undressing her and small shivers of excitement ran over her skin like trickles of water from a clear mountain stream. What would it be like to be kissed by a priest? she wondered. She had made him *want* to kiss her, but how to give him the opportunity? As her fingers plucked the strings of her lute and her clear voice rang out the songs of love she had learned from the troubadours her mind was busy searching for a plan.

There was only one way she could be alone with him – and that was to go to his chamber. It was, she guessed, the small upper room which was always allocated to guests, next to the one in which Alazais would be sleeping. Would she be able to slip out of the chamber she shared with the other ladies without their knowing she had gone? It was a risk, but the danger only added excitement to the adventure, and Grazide found she was trembling with anticipation.

At last Alazais rose, indicating that only one of her ladies need accompany her tonight to help her prepare for bed. It was a far better opportunity than Grazide had dared hope for and she grasped it greedily.

'I will attend you, milady!'

Blanche and Amicia exchanged surprised glances. Grazide was usually the last one to volunteer to carry out a duty.

In the big chamber which Alazais shared with Philip when he was at home Grazide unbraided her mistress's hair, brushing it with the customary hundred strokes, and helped her into her bedgown. Tonight Alazais was quiet and thoughtful. She did not engage Grazide in conversation and soon the girl was able to leave her.

In the narrow passage which separated Alazais's chamber from the one which had been allocated to the priest, Grazide hesitated, suddenly overcome by nervousness. Then, her heart beating very fast, she slipped into the guest chamber.

The monk was on his knees, a rosary in his hands. When he realised he was no longer alone he looked up, startled, and once again Grazide's courage almost failed her. She took a step into the room, letting the heavy curtain at the door fall into place behind her.

'Father, I have sinned.' The words she had planned slipped out effortlessly, and her eyes sought his, not teasing now but meek and penitent.

He rose from his knees and crossed the chamber to her.

'My child, it is not for me to hear your confession.' There was an edge to his voice and she saw how tightly his fingers gripped the rosary beads. 'You must make that to your own priest.'

Grazide lowered her lashes. 'I cannot. I am ashamed.'

'Surely it is easier to confess to a man who should be as a father to you than to a stranger?'

Grazide shook her head. 'It is because he is like a father to me that I cannot confess to him. But I think you would understand.' She raised her eyes to his once more and this time she allowed a little of the coquetry with which she had been tempting him all evening to creep into her glance. 'There is a man I desire with all my heart . . . and, God help me, my body too.'

She saw the narrowing of his eyes and there was a faint tremor in his voice which she had never before heard in the voice of a priest.

'That is a natural thing, my child, and in itself is not sinful. Perhaps you may marry this man and then you will be able to assuage your desire.'

'No, Father, that is not possible.'

'He is married already?'

'No.' She moistened her lips with her tongue. 'No, that is not the reason. He is a priest, Father. I met him only today and tomorrow he will be far away . . .' She glanced up at him from beneath her lashes.

He was sweating now, his eyes trying to avoid her and being drawn back again and again by her pouting mouth, her lustrous flowing hair, the tempting glimpse of her breasts at the neck of her gown. Grazide trembled with excitement and elation. Then he turned away abruptly.

'You should not have come here.'

'Who is to know?' She caught at his sleeve. 'Father, kiss me I beg you, and take away my sin . . .'

Pons Marty was a young man with normal appetites which had been too long suppressed. For long moments he fought against the temptation offered by this beautiful daughter of Eve, then with a groan he turned towards her, his body aching with desire. And she was there, looking at him still with an expression that was somehow both innocent and knowing. He reached for her and as their lips touched in that forbidden ecstasy the last remnants of resistance deserted him. Had not almost every village priest had at least one concubine in disobedience of his vows? Tomorrow he would wear the hair shirt he carried in his baggage for penance, tomorrow and every day for a month he would scourge himself until his sin was expiated. But tonight belonged to Satan and the pleasures of the flesh.

As the desire rose in hot waves he tore roughly at her bodice, burying his face in her creamy breasts and biting at them with a hunger born of months – years – of denial. She gasped in pain, and, frightened now, tried to push him away, but he was too strong for her. Greedily he ripped at her gown, shredding it from neck to hem, and fumbling with his own clothing.

'What is going on here?' Alazais's horrified voice cut through his inflamed passions.

She was in the doorway, a robe over her bedgown, and in the flaring candlelight her face was pale and her eyes round with horror. Pons released the frightened Grazide, who scrambled to her feet, sobbing.

'Milady! I came to him to make a confession, milady, and he . . . oh, Sancta Maria, he . . .'

Pons found his voice. 'It is not what you think, milady.'

'Really? You take me for a fool, Father? How dare you abuse my hospitality so! You, a man in holy orders – attempting to rape a child in my care!' Alazais, usually so mild and gentle, was beside herself with outrage. 'Get your things together and leave my home at once! And you, Grazide – go to your chamber.'

Grazide fled, whimpering. She had never for one moment intended things to go so far.

As she ran down the stairs, her tattered gown trailing behind her, Alazais's voice followed her.

'You disgust me, Father. Your abbot will hear of this, never fear. You are not fit to wear the cloth and you will not wear it much longer if I have anything to do with it!'

'Milady, I am mortified. I shall do penance for as long as it takes. But I promise you, this was no rape. She offered herself to me.'

'I do not wish to hear, Father.' Alazais was too angry to be afraid any more. 'Shall I send for my men-at-arms to help you on your way?'

He shook his head, his anger, fuelled by his shame, matching hers.

'I will save you that trouble, madame. But do not think I shall easily forget your accusations and your treatment of me.'

'Nor I your treachery!'

With a swish of her skirts, Alazais left the chamber.

'Alazais, think, I beg you, of the harm you could do. Don't make further trouble. Let this thing lie.' Oliver, who had been summoned by the worried steward and had come rushing home to find the castle in uproar, faced Alazais across her solar. 'There is no harm done from what I can discover.'

'No harm! How can you say that?' Alazais was still beside herself with fury. She had slept little and her eyes were huge and dark in her pale face, but Oliver thought he had never seen her looking more beautiful. Why, by all that was holy, could it not have been he whom their mothers had chosen when they had decided on a marriage to cement the alliance between their two families? He had loved Alazais for as long as he could remember. But she was Philip's wife. Oliver only hoped his brother had learned to appreciate her instead of hankering after the peasant girl who had been brought up as their sister.

He sighed. Philip should be here now, sorting out his own domestic problems, not cooking up more trouble with Roger Bernard of Foix.

'From what your other ladies say Grazide asked for everything she got,' he said now. 'What was she doing in the monk's bedchamber anyway?'

She tells me she went to ask him to hear her confession. Oh, don't look like that! She is an innocent child, Oliver. She does not know the power of her own charms.'

'Really?' Oliver could not help thinking it was Alazais who was the innocent.

'That is what she has told me and I believe her. And in any case, a man of holy orders should be trustworthy and chaste. He can't be allowed to get away with such scandalous behaviour.'

'Alazais.' Oliver ran a hand through his hair. 'Don't you realise how unwise it would be to pursue this? Surely you must see the position such a move would place us in. We cannot afford to make an enemy of a Dominican. They have too much power at their disposal.'

But Alazais's face was set firm.

'He must be denounced, Oliver. If he is not, who is to say he will not try to deflower some other innocent virgin? I am responsible for Grazide. Her father entrusted her to my care. No, I am sorry, but my mind is made up. I intend to send word to his abbot today.'

Oliver sighed, shaking his head. Perhaps Philip would have

been able to control his wife, but he could not. He had done his best to dissuade her and failed. He could only hope now that her determination to have justice would not turn out to have consequences they would all live to regret.

18

ESTHER WAS IN her room, trying to decide what to do today and what she should wear to do it. She was also, she admitted to herself, keeping out of the way of Alain's family, but she wasn't going to have to do that for much longer, and she was feeling cheery and optimistic.

Alain had had words with his mother the previous evening, she thought, and as a result Isobelle had done something of an about-face.

Alain had suggested they should go out to eat at a restaurant, and while Esther was getting ready, Isobelle had come to her room.

'I believe I owe you an apology.' Her tone was stiff. She didn't sound sorry, but Esther realised what it was costing her and bit back the tempting but ungracious retort which was hovering on her lips.

'You were just speaking your mind, Isobelle.'

'I shouldn't have done. You are, after all, Alain's guest.'

'But this is your house and I'm sorry if my being here has upset you. Alain is going to find a hotel for me tomorrow, so the situation should resolve itself.'

'There's no need for that,' Isobelle said shortly.

'Oh, I think there is. I don't want to impose on you a moment longer than I have to.'

'You won't be imposing. Henri and I have decided to go away for a few days to stay with friends. We shall leave the day after tomorrow. And Hélène will be going home today. You and Alain will have the house to yourselves.'

'I didn't know you had any plans,' Esther said before she could stop herself, then broke off, embarrassed. There was, of course, no reason why she should have known. But all the same, she couldn't help thinking this visit had been arranged somewhat hastily.

She had asked Alain about it later, over a delicious meal in a country *auberge*.

'I didn't know your mother and father were going away.'

He smiled faintly.

'I think Maman might have decided it as a result of a conversation we had.'

'Alain!' Esther was horrified. 'You can't mean you've driven them out of their own home because of me!'

'Of course not. But I did tell Maman she had behaved in an unforgivable way and this is her olive branch. She's sorry for what she said and she wants to make amends.'

'Your mother – sorry? Oh, I don't think so.'

'She apologised to you, didn't she?'

'In a sort of a way. Well yes she did apologise, but . . .' She broke off, remembering the tight lips, the grudging tone.

'There you are then,' Alain said, looking pleased with himself, and Esther had let it go. She didn't think Isobelle had really retracted a single word she'd said, but if she was now prepared to go off and leave them alone for a few days at least that was something. Exactly what her motives were Esther didn't know, but this didn't seem the time to question them.

'So you see there's no need for us to go to a hotel at all,' Alain said. 'And I must say I'm glad. It would have been a bit of a nuisance really, particularly since I'm still trying to sort out my business problems.'

'I'd still rather— '

'Esther, it would be making trouble to throw it back in her face.'

And so she had reluctantly agreed; if Isobelle and Henri really were going away and Hélène was going home, she would stay on for the time being at Le Château Gris.

But that didn't mean she wanted to spend any more time in Isobelle's company than was absolutely necessary. Which was why she had beaten a hasty retreat from the breakfast table when Alain had gone to get ready to go to the office.

She could hear the telephone ringing somewhere in the house and hoped it didn't mean some hitch with Isobelle's arrangements. If they didn't go away, she was going to insist on booking into a hotel whether Alain liked it or not.

'Esther.' It was Alain in the doorway. 'It's Simone on the phone. She wants to speak to you.'

'To me?'

'Yes. She's offering to take you sightseeing. I think it would be a good idea – you know I have a lot of work to do. But of course, it's up to you.'

'Yes – it sounds nice.' Esther liked Simone. She would rather be with Alain, of course, but that was not an option.

'Will you come and talk to her then?' Alain said. 'I really do have to get on.'

'Yes, sure,' Esther said. And went downstairs to take her unexpected call.

Simone had slept badly.

When the vision in the mirror had faded she had gone to bed where she had lain staring into the darkness and wondering what the seduction of a priest by a young lady-in-waiting could possibly have to do with her mission to help 'Alazais' and 'Jeanne' to work out their karma. Pons seemed to have disappeared from the story when he and Jeanne were separated at Carcassonne, and Grazide was a new character entirely. Why, then, should she have witnessed such a totally gratuitous scene? Was she beginning to gain vicarious pleasure from the unfolding of the story? She didn't think so – she felt as disgusted by the near-rape as she had with the ravaging of Jeanne by her own husband. But how could she be sure it wasn't some dark side of her own nature taking over?

And yet . . . if she had been Helis in another life then she had not only been the mother of Jeanne, but also of Pons. She now knew what had become of the little boy and if it was not what she might have hoped for that was neither here nor there. Perhaps Pons, too, figured in the story. Perhaps Pons had an alter ego, here and now, in Languedoc. But if so, who?

Don't start worrying about Pons, Simone told herself. Not yet, at any rate. Worry about Jeanne and Alazais. If you knew which of them is now Hélène and which Esther then you might be getting somewhere.

But where? She still did not know, yet the feeling that conclusive events were gathering pace towards some terrible inevitable was stronger than ever. Something was happening. Something was going to happen. But as yet she was powerless to know what to do to prevent it.

Simone lay staring into the darkness, marvelling at the way her perception of this whole thing had changed. Somewhere along the line her scepticism had disappeared. She no longer doubted that something beyond her comprehension was happening – unlikely as it had seemed such a short time ago, the evidence was too overwhelming to be dismissed. But she still didn't understand. If anything she was more confused than ever.

At last Simone drifted into a fitful sleep, but with the dawn she was fully awake once more, tired still to the point of exhaustion but pricking with the need to do something – and do it urgently.

The solution lay with Esther, she was certain. She had known Hélène all her life and nothing like this had ever happened before. Somehow she must get to know Esther better, find out what made her tick.

Soaking in a long hot bath, Simone found herself thinking of stories she had heard of people who had experienced inexplicable déjàvu on visiting a place where they had never been before – sometimes even described the layout of a building they had yet to enter or one which had long since gone. Valerie had always maintained that such instances were proof of reincarnation and Simone had scoffed, as she always scoffed. But now she found herself wondering. Supposing Esther had once been Jeanne or Alazais – was it possible she might recognise places she had known in that other life, dredge up memories from the depth of her subconscious?

Simone felt her skin prickle with sudden excitement. If she were to take Esther to one of the places in the dream, might she show some sign of recognition? If she did, it would be interesting if not conclusive. Pointless, of course, to try the same exercise with Hélène. She had lived here all her life and was totally familiar with her surroundings. But Esther . . .

Simone got out of the bath and slipped into a towelling robe without bothering to dry herself. Almost nine o'clock. Was it too early to ring Esther? But the family were early risers and Simone did not want to risk Esther's making other plans.

She dialled her old home number. Alain answered and she thought he sounded tired.

'I wondered if Esther might like to go sightseeing,' she said, somewhat tentatively.

And Alain almost answered for her.

'I'll get her to the phone, Simone, so you can ask her yourself. But I'm sure she'd like that very much.'

Although it was still barely mid-morning the sun was already hot, promising another scorching day. To the right of the motorway the Mediterranean sparkled blue and silver, to the left mountain peaks towered above plains and foothills.

Simone headed her Citroën north towards Montsegur. She had given a great deal of thought as to where she should take Esther in the hope of unlocking some memory and evoking a reaction. Montaugure would have been the best choice, of course, since both Jeanne and Alazais had known it, but it was too far away and she wasn't even sure of its exact location; and Carcassonne, with its milling tourists, seemed a little too obvious. In any case, Jeanne had been very young when she had been inside Carcassonne, and under siege conditions it might have been very different. Besides, if something did happen, if Esther *had* been Jeanne, and the place unlocked memories they would be those of a terrified child, too traumatic, perhaps, to be borne. Simone did not want to risk starting something she was in no way qualified to handle. No, better to take Esther somewhere Jeanne had known in adulthood. There any memories, though they might be unpleasant, would at least be viewed from the standpoint of a mature woman.

'Do you know anything about Montsegur?' she asked now, pulling into the overtaking lane to skim past a big refrigerated lorry which, judging by the smell which was quickly drawn in by the Citroën's fan, was carrying fish.

'Only that it was a Cathar fortress,' Esther admitted. 'Their last stronghold, wasn't it?'

'Not quite. Queribus has that honour. But it was one of the last. It held out almost alone against king and church until 1244, and when it fell it really was the beginning of the end for the Cathar faith.'

'Quite a history.'

'Yes. It's well worth a visit, I think.'

The road was busier now and she lapsed into silence, concentrating on her driving and looking for the junction where she needed to leave the motorway.

It came just outside Perpignan and soon they were on a winding road which led past vineyards and woods, dry river beds and sunbaked expanses of open ground stretching out beyond the London plane and cypress trees which lined the verges.

After a while Simone drew in to a gravelled pull-in at the roadside.

'There's a wonderful view from here. And it would be nice to get a breath of fresh air, wouldn't it?'

'It certainly is hot,' Esther agreed, unhooking her seat belt and fluffing the skirt of her sundress away from her legs. 'My clothes are sticking to me! I wish I could wear shorts, but I can't – or at least, I don't usually. I've got an enormous birthmark just above my knee. I don't suppose anyone else would take the slightest bit of notice, but I'm self-conscious about it.'

Simone smiled.

'I'm sure you've no need to be. But if you were wearing shorts you'd stick to the seat instead of your dress sticking to you. Believe me, I speak from experience, though I don't often wear shorts either.'

They walked together along the dry grass verge, dotted with prickly shrubs and clumps of pink thrift and bright yellow gorse, to lean against a wooden fence which hemmed the road at this point. They were already quite high up, Esther realised. Beneath the road the hillside fell steeply away – arid meadowland with more clumps of gorse and thrift and a dusting of scarlet poppies, neatly laid out vineyard plots and the occasional rocky outcrop jutting jaggedly from the greenery. The hot air was full of the smell of wild thyme, and a dragonfly, big as a small bird, drifted past Esther's face.

It was heaven, pure heaven, scarred only by a network of pylons and telegraph poles which ran an ugly line across the unbroken blue of the sky. What a pity it had to be there, Esther thought. People were as much entitled to the comforts of modern living here as anywhere else, but it was sad that the otherwise unspoiled countryside should be marred in such a way.

'Ready to go on then?' Simone asked after a few minutes.

They started off again, climbing now all the while, and each twist and turn in the road opened up new vistas. Sometimes they passed through a village, deserted but for the old women who sat in the shade outside their houses. The villages, too, had a timeless feel about them, as if virtually unchanged by the passage of the ages – cottages with shuttered windows and doors which appeared bare of paint, archways of stone, carved wooden porticos. The occasional public telephone looked as out of place as the pylons had done, sitting in the shade of gnarled old trees. But for a few motor cars and a rumbling old lorry or truck the road was virtually free of traffic, and they too looked out of place. This was the country of ruined castles and châteaux, clinging to the peaks, of vineyards and cottages drowsing in the heat of the noonday sun.

Then, as they rounded a bend in the road, they saw it.

'Montsegur,' Simone said.

The village nestled among green wooded hillsides, dreaming and peaceful, yet Esther felt there was something oppressive about it. Above it, a great rocky pinnacle loomed, surmounted by the ruined fortress which loomed stark grey and jagged against the deep blue of the sky. Looking at it, she was assailed by an emotion not unlike the one she had experienced on her first night here in Languedoc, but stronger, sweeter and tinged with haunting sadness.

'Shall we go up?' Simone was asking.

'Yes . . . sure . . .' But she wasn't sure. She didn't care for the way this place was making her feel. She would rather go back to one of the wine cooperative 'caves' they had passed on the road, taste some wine, perhaps buy a bottle or two . . . But she didn't like to offend Simone by saying so.

'It's not an easy climb, I'm afraid, and it's even more difficult coming down,' Simone looked doubtfully at Esther's sandals. 'I've got a spare pair of trainers in the boot, but I should think my feet are quite a bit bigger than yours . . .'

'I'll manage.' Esther reached for her straw hat, which she had dumped on the rear seat.

'I wouldn't wear that, either, if I were you,' Simone advised. 'It'll probably be windy up there.'

They parked the car and started across the grass. At the foot of the hill was a simple stone monument carved with the sign of the cross.

'This is the spot where two hundred Cathar Perfects were burned rather than renounce their faith when Montsegur fell,' Simone said. 'It's still known by the locals as "*prat dels crematz*" – the field of the burned.'

Esther shuddered, remembering she had seen a picture of this monument in one of the guide books.

'What a barbarous lot our ancestors were!' she said, but she couldn't bring herself to look at the monument any more than she had been able to look at the picture. The images it conjured up were too horrific.

As Simone had warned, the climb was steep and difficult – dangerous almost – and they had no breath left for talking. But Esther's feeling of sadness had lifted a little; pausing on the mountain path and looking back, it seemed to her that the cloud hung over the village itself. She was getting fanciful in her old age, she told herself, and that would have to stop. Journalists couldn't afford to be fanciful!

At last they reached the top of the rocky spur. From here the view was breathtaking; they paused for a few moments to admire it before starting up the steep little track to the ruined castle itself. But Simone had been right about the wind. It buffeted them relentlessly as they emerged from the first flight of stone steps into what had once been one of the castle chambers, but was now open to the elements.

'You see – it must have been pretty bleak up here, mustn't it?' Simone said.

'Yes, but very safe.' The feeling of oppression had almost gone now, replaced by a childlike eagerness. 'Let's look out of the solar window – the one which faces the sunrise during the summer solstice.'

She turned to run up the flaking stone steps.

The window, deep and broad on the inside, narrowed to a slit in the masonry. Esther leaned her head against the stones, cold in spite of the sun's heat, and peered through, enjoying the slightly distorted yet panoramic view of the countryside and the wooded slopes beneath the castle, unchanged for hundreds of years. No pylons here to desecrate and shout twentieth century. No cars. No refrigerated fish lorries. No intrusive telephone kiosks. Simply a timeless vista, over which had settled the peace of the ages. Quite suddenly the ache of nostalgia was back, and with it a feeling of dreaming. Esther half closed her eyes, breathing in the soft scented air, feeling almost that she might be floating in time and space, no longer herself, no longer anyone, just a part of the universe, a speck of matter, a molecule of energy in the long reaches of time, insignificant yet at the same time not insignificant at all, because she was at one with the whole . . . It was an incredible feeling, as if, for a brief fleeting moment, she was glimpsing a concept so enormous it was beyond human comprehension but also stunningly, unbelievably simple . . .

'Well, what do you think?' Simone's voice, slightly breathless, drew her back to the real world.

'Beautiful.' She turned away reluctantly from the view and the feelings it had evoked.

'And familiar too? As if you'd been here before?' There was a slight edge to Simone's voice which might have been excitement.

Esther laughed.

'Yes – a bit.'

'Perhaps you have been.' The edge was more pronounced. Esther looked at her in surprise.

'What on earth do you mean? You know this is my first time in this part of France.'

'I didn't mean in this life. I meant in another. Perhaps you were once a Cathar, Esther – here at Montsegur.'

A prickle, like the shivering of a sudden breeze, ran over Esther's sunwarmed skin. For a moment the intensity of Simone's tone had quite unnerved her. What a peculiar thing to say! Then she laughed, albeit a little uncertainly.

'Oh come on! You don't really believe in that sort of nonsense, do you?'

'You seemed to know all about the solar window.'

'Because I've been looking at guide books, I expect.' She didn't actually remember having seen anything about the solar window, but that had to be the explanation, since she had known exactly where to find it. 'Reincarnation – honestly, Simone!'

But as she turned, picking her way back across the crumbling stones, Esther wondered why, in spite of the heat of the sun, she was still shivering.

Midway through the morning Bob Slater swung over the wall at the back of his house with the agility of a man half his age and strode up to the patio where Andrew was glancing through yesterday's English papers. He was looking very pleased with himself.

'You won't find out much about your story lazing around here,' he said as he greeted Andrew.

'I'm not finding out much, however hard I try, so I thought I'd have a morning off.'

'Well, no matter. I've been doing your job for you.' Bob dropped into the chair beside Andrew, fishing in his wallet and extracting a black-and-white photograph, which he dropped on to the table in front of him.

Andrew reached for it. The photograph showed three young men, arms round one another's shoulders, glasses raised in what appeared to be a toast to a good time. 'What's this then?' he asked.

Bob jabbed the central figure with his finger.

'The late lamented Thierry Rousseau with his two closest friends. The Three Musketeers, they used to call themselves, by all accounts. Three toe-rags, more like.'

'Yes, they certainly look a bit wild.'

'Not only wild. They were gamblers, certainly, but they were villains too. It's only a miracle all three of them didn't end up in prison from what I can make out.'

Andrew glanced up at his father. 'How did you find all this out?'

'I had a chat with a mate of mine. He's a retired policeman like me and this used to be his patch. I thought he might know something about Thierry Rousseau – and he did. He had plenty of run-ins with him and his pals when they were in their heyday. He even came up with this old photograph for me. God knows why he'd kept it – as a memento of days gone by, I suppose. Anyway, I thought it might be useful to you.'

'Yes.' Andrew was looking at it thoughtfully. 'So who are the other two?'

'That one is a chap by the name of Jean-Luc Lorrain. He left the area years ago and hasn't been seen since. But the other one might interest you.' Bob grinned slyly.

'Why? Who is it?'

'Yves Marssac.'

'Yves Marssac. Alain Lavaur's sister's boyfriend.'

'Exactly.'

'Well, well. Perhaps I should pay them a visit.'

'I think you should. Valerie paints. You could always pretend to be interested in buying one of her pictures.'

'Dad, you're a genius.'

Bob grinned modestly.

'Let's just say there's life in the old dog yet!'

* * *

Shortly after midday Andrew rang the doorbell of Valerie's cottage. It was not at all the sort of place one associated with violent and mysterious death, he thought, but then that was the very factor that would make this whole story more potent – if a story there turned out to be. Readers expected crime and murder in seedy surroundings; here the sun, the sea and the aura of leisured, affluent living lent a whole new dimension.

Someone was coming. Andrew waited expectantly.

'Hello.' The young woman who had opened the door looked at him questioningly. She was slim and pretty, wearing a black bikini top and a brightly patterned square tied sarong-style around her waist.

'You must be Valerie,' he said in English.

'Yes.' But she looked more puzzled than ever.

He held out his hand. 'Andrew Slater. You won't know me but my father, Bob, lives locally and I'm staying with him. I realise this might seem a bit of a nerve, but my father tells me you paint. I'm looking for an unusual present to take home for my girlfriend and I wondered whether you sell any of your work privately.'

'Oh!' A faint flush coloured her cheeks. 'You mean you want to buy one of my pictures?'

'Well . . . possibly. I'm fed up with touring souvenir shops and finding nothing but tack.'

'Oh, right! You'd better come in . . .'

She led the way into the house and he followed her, thinking that that part, at least, had been easy.

A man was lounging on a rattan sofa, a newspaper spread out over his bare knees. He glanced up, truculent and suspicious.

'Someone wants to look at my paintings with a view to buying one.' There was a hint of barely concealed excitement in Valerie's voice, but the man merely raised an eyebrow and went back to his newspaper.

Yves Marssac, Andrew thought, pleased. He hadn't been sure whether he'd find him here or not. As he ran through his concocted explanation again for Yves's benefit Andrew was busy summing him up. A CRO if ever he saw one! No wonder the ex-policeman had remembered him. This was certainly the most promising lead yet.

'My studio is upstairs,' Valerie said, shooting a black look at Yves as he sniggered at the word 'studio'. 'Would you like to come up? It would be easier than me bringing everything down here.'

Andrew followed her up the narrow staircase to a small sloping room under the eaves. An easel and paints stood near the window; the walls were covered with pictures and more were stacked in piles against them.

'You're very prolific,' he remarked.

'Not really – I just keep most of what I paint,' she admitted artlessly. 'It's not often I sell anything.'

'They're very good.' It was no more than the truth, though the paintings were not really to his taste, and she coloured again with pleasure.

'You're not a dealer by any chance, are you? I could do with being discovered.'

'Sorry, no.' He looked at the pictures, pretending interest.

'How much?'

'Oh, I don't really know. A hundred and fifty francs, say?' She sounded embarrassed.

He selected one, apple blossom against a clear blue sky. He hoped Diana would like it.

'I'll take that one.'

'You don't take long to make up your mind,' she said with a small rueful smile.

'No, I'm a man of decision.' He got out his wallet, counted out a wad of notes, and took the painting.

'I'll wrap it for you,' she said.

He was about to tell her not to bother, then changed his mind. A genuine buyer would want to ensure the safety of his purchase and besides, waiting while she wrapped the painting would give him the chance to talk to Yves. Not that he thought he would get much out of him. He looked a surly bastard.

He raised the subject of Thierry Rousseau with Yves while Valerie wrestled with brown paper and string.

'You were a friend of his, weren't you?'

Yves shrugged. 'We go back a long way.'

'Yes, I'd heard. You and Thierry and Jean-Luc Lorrain. The Three Musketeers.'

A startled expression crossed Yves's face briefly. 'That was a long time ago. We went our seperate ways. Jean-Luc left the district.'

To go to prison, I shouldn't wonder, Andrew thought. Or to avoid it. Aloud he said, 'You don't see him now?'

'No – haven't seen him for years.' Yves's eyes narrowed. 'What's your interest in all this?'

Andrew shrugged. 'Just curious. Everyone seems to be talking about the accident.'

'Oh, for a moment there I wondered if you might be a policeman, like your father.'

'No. Whatever gave you that idea?'

Yves grinned. 'I've got a nose for that sort of thing. Anyway, I heard you tell Valerie who you are, and for a minute it occurred to me you might be trying to find out who murdered the bastard.'

Andrew felt the hairs on the back of his neck prickle.

'You think he was murdered?'

Yves's eyes held his for a moment, sly and taunting.

'If you were a policeman it would be for you to find out, wouldn't it? Since you're not . . .' He looked down at his newspaper, reaching for a glass which stood at his elbow with a gesture of finality, and Andrew knew he would get no more from him.

Valerie had finished packing up the painting. He took it from her and left. But the prickling at the back of his neck had spread so that the whole of his body felt electric.

So – his father wasn't the only one who thought Thierry's death was no accident. Yves Marssac knew something, he was sure of it. Finding out what it was, however, would be another matter.

'Why did you say that about Thierry being murdered?' Valerie asked when she had seen Andrew out. The flush of pleasure that had come from selling a painting had been replaced by a look of consternation.

Yves shrugged. 'He probably was. If anyone ever asked to be murdered, it was Thierry.'

'How can you say such a thing? You were his friend!'

'Which is why I know more about him than most. The people Thierry mixed with would murder if it suited them and never give it a second thought. Fringes of the underworld, chérie. And

Thierry was always a double-dealer and a cheat. He's crossed a good many people in his time and got away with it. This time he didn't.'

Valerie had turned pale. 'Yves . . . you didn't . . . you don't know anything about the accident, do you?'

Yves laughed. 'What makes you think that?'

'Oh, I don't know . . . You seem to know a great deal more than you're saying, that's all. I know Thierry has a pretty chequered past, but I still can't see why anyone should want to murder him!'

'Well, Alain, for a start.'

'*Alain*! Oh, don't be so stupid!'

'Not so stupid. He has a very good motive, if you ask me.'

'Such as what?'

'Well, the business is in one hell of a mess, isn't it? Alain left him in charge and God only knows what he was doing, but a great deal of money seems to have gone missing. Suppose Alain wanted to get rid of him? Could prove awkward, with him being Hélène's brother. With Thierry out of the way Alain is in control again.'

'Alain would never do such a thing! Besides, he was in England when Thierry died.'

Yves grinned lazily. 'Haven't you ever heard of contract killings?'

She stared at him in horror. 'You're crazy!'

'Am I? Perhaps I'm just a little more in touch with the real world than you are. You're so sweet and trusting, my love.' He grabbed her wrist, pulling her down into his lap. 'I'll tell you something else, too. That man is no tourist. And he didn't come here to buy your pictures.'

'What do you mean?' she demanded indignantly. 'He bought one, didn't he?'

'Yes, but what does that prove?'

She frowned. 'Yves Marssac, you really are a bastard!'

'I know,' he quipped. 'I'm mad, bad and very, very dangerous. Wonderful, isn't it?'

When he left Valerie's house, Andrew turned his car towards the main road. He drove slowly, thinking. Yves Marssac had certainly been startled when he had mentioned Jean-Luc Lorrain, and then, almost in the same breath, had come the suggestion that Thierry Rousseau had been murdered. Now what had brought that on? Had he simply been trying to create a sensation, or did it mean he knew, or at least suspected, something?

More than ever, all Andrew's instincts were telling him that there was a story here, and for the first time he was beginning to scent a trail.

He glanced at his watch, wondering whether to go home for a spot of lunch or continue with his investigations, and deciding on the latter. With any luck the bistro where Thierry had spent his last evening would be open but not too busy. This would be as good a chance as any to have another crack at the owner who had witnessed the quarrel and been one of the last people to see Thierry alive. And this time, of course, he was armed with the photograph . . .

He pulled into a lay-by, reaching for the local road map which lay open on the back seat in order to refresh his memory as to the best way to get to the bistro. Down to the turnpike, on to the main road, being careful not to end up on the motorway, straight on for about twenty miles – *kilometres*, he reminded himself – off the main road again heading west, and he should hit the village. He was just about to lay the map down on the passenger seat beside him when a thought occurred to him and he pored over it again, tracing the road with his forefinger.

That was the best and most direct route by far – at least according to the map. So why had Thierry ended up at the spot where his car had gone over the edge? Unless there was a short cut he didn't know about, and a local would, Thierry had gone miles out of his way.

Andrew's pulses began to race. Why hadn't he thought of it before? Why hadn't *anyone* thought of it? No wonder his father didn't think much of the efficiency of the local police. Give them what appeared to be an accident, add an influential local family, and the files were closed in the blinking of an eye. Well, he wasn't going to be put off so easily!

The village, when he reached it, appeared to be taking a siesta. Most of the shops, which faced each other across the narrow street, appeared to be closed, and even the Portakabin-style loos in the shady square where he parked his car bore an 'out of commission' sign. But the doors of the bistro/bar were open and a blackboard listing the day's specials was still propped up on the pavement outside.

Andrew locked up his car and crossed the square. He wondered how he would fare making himself understood this time if there was no one who spoke English to help him out. He should have brought his father along to act as interpreter, he realised. But this was his investigation, not Bob's, and in any case, this time he had the photograph. With any luck that would speak for itself.

But for a couple of locals, sprawled on bar stools, and a gangly lad playing the pool table, the bistro was empty. They were hardly making a killing on their lunches! Andrew thought wryly. He approached the bar and the tender appeared as if by magic, a large man with a striped apron tied twice around his ample waist, a bald head and a moustache so Gallic that Andrew found it amusing. But to his surprise the man recognised him instantly.

'You – Eengleesh,' he said, looking pleased with himself. 'You ask questions, yes?'

'Yes.' Andrew nodded. 'But I'll have a drink first.'

The bartender looked puzzled and Andrew pointed at the bottles of lager lined up in the cooler.

'*S'il vous plaît.*'

When he had refreshed himself with a long pull of lager, Andrew got out the photograph his father had given him.

'Monsieur Rousseau, who died,' he said in careful French, pointing to Thierry.

'Ah – *oui*.'

'And this man – was he the one who was with him that last evening?'

'*Je ne sais pas*.'

'Look carefully, please.' It was a long shot, he knew, but he held his breath all the same as the bartender took the photograph, scrutinising it.

'*Je ne sais pas*. It could be . . .'

Andrew cursed himself for his lack of French. It is a very old photograph, he wanted to say. He'd look older now. But even that might not help. Perhaps it was time to change tactics – come out into the open. He pulled a wad of notes out of his wallet and showed them to the bartender. In his experience, money usually talked.

'*Un moment.*' The bartender's eyes had narrowed at the sight of the notes; now he called to one of the men lounging at the counter, speaking in rapid French. The man came over, taking the photograph and looking at it by the light of a table lamp in the shape of a wine bottle. Andrew waited, and after a moment the man nodded.

'*Oui. C'est lui.*'

Andrew's breath came out on a low whistle. 'You're sure?'

The man shrugged. 'I think so. Who is he?'

Andrew could hardly believe his luck. After all the frustration he'd scored a hit at last.

'His name is Jean-Luc Lorrain,' he said. 'Do you know him?'

The men looked at each other, shrugged. '*Non.*'

'Never mind.' Andrew took one of his cards from his wallet, scribbled his father's telephone number on the back, and handed it to the bar owner. 'If you think of anything else, this is where you can find me.'

Back in his car he took another look at the photograph. Did you murder Thierry Rousseau, Jean-Luc Lorrain? he asked it silently. You look the sort who could have. But if so, why? And where are you now? Well, perhaps now his luck had changed; he might be on the point of finding out.

Esther and Simone were sitting on the dry grass in the shadow of Montsegur. The car, when they had returned to it, was uncomfortably hot, and Simone had suggested they open the doors and windows and wait awhile before attempting to begin the drive home. They had shared a bottle of lemonade and a packet of biscuits which Simone had brought with her, and now Simone appeared to be dozing. Esther leaned back on her elbows, half closing her eyes and looking up at the ruined fortress, silhouetted against the clear blue of the sky.

Just a ruin now. Just a pile of ancient stones perched on an impossible mountain peak. Yet once it had been a refuge for a persecuted people, a small haven of safety in the midst of a sea of ruthless enemies. And, ultimately, the graveyard of a faith. Esther thought of the monument to those who had died in the flames of the pyre rather than renounce their beliefs. The '*prat del cramatz'* – the field of the burned. She shivered, her imagination conjuring up the leaping flames and the thick black smoke, the crackle of burning faggots, the screams of the dying. The vision had the flavour of her childhood nightmares, claustrophobic and terrifying.

She jerked her eyes wide open, sitting upright for a moment and remembering the feeling of oppression which had overcome her earlier. She didn't believe a word of Simone's theory of reincarnation, of course. That was total rubbish. But perhaps it was possible that some echo of the horrific things which had once happened here remained, trapped in the ether. These very stones, this same earth, had been here then. Could it be that some shadow of the tragic events had remained, like a footprint in time, and she had picked up on it?

For goodness' sake, Esther, get real! she admonished herself.

Simone was still sleeping and though she was beginning to be anxious to get back – Alain might finish work early and be at home waiting for her – Esther was reluctant to disturb her. She shifted slightly, resting her back against a boulder and looking up at the fortress again.

The wind had dropped now and the air shimmered, both from the heat and from a swarm of midges. Esther's own eyes were growing heavy and there was a buzzing in her ears. At first she thought it was the midges, but when had midges ever made a noise, especially like this one? It wasn't a buzzing, exactly, more of a murmuring, like a host of voices, rising, falling, indistinct, all blurring into one. The heat haze was swirling, as if millions of tiny particles were moving together, altering the very density of the air, making shadows in the light. They were coming together now, forming patterns. No – not patterns. Pictures. Three-dimensional pictures. She could still see the wooded hillside, but against it figures were materialising. Dark figures in long black robes, clearly visible yet transparent so that they were superimposed on that green backdrop without in any way obstructing it. And all the while the murmuring was growing louder, so loud it filled her head . . . Esther pressed her hands to her ears, yet still she could hear it, and she couldn't move, couldn't look away . . .

'Excuse me, ma'am, is the castle still open, do you know?'

The voice, male and broad transatlantic, cut across the murmuring in her head. Startled, Esther jerked around. A man waring a garish shirt loose over vast Bermuda shorts was looking down at her, a bemused expression on his sunburned face. A straw trilby was jammed on his head, a camera slung over his shoulder.

'Hey, I'm sorry, I didn't mean to . . . I didn't know you were asleep.'

'It's all right, I wasn't.' Esther felt very strange, very far away. Her voice sounded strange too, to her ears at least.

'I was just asking if the castle is still open,' the man repeated apologetically. 'We don't want to climb all the way up there and find it closed.'

'I don't think it's the sort of place that closes,' Esther said.

'Sure. We'll get up there then. Thanks, ma'am.'

He and the woman with him walked off across the parking area. Esther watched them go, rubbing her eyes. She had told the American she wasn't asleep but she must have been . . . mustn't she? Either that, or the sun had got to her. Perhaps that was it – heatstroke. Wind or no wind, she should have worn her hat.

Simone was stirring now. The American had woken her too. She sat up.

'Sorry, Esther, I must have dropped off.' She looked at her watch. 'Good lord – is that the time? We'd better be going. We've got a long drive back.'

Esther looked up at the fortress. No figures now, yet in her mind's eye she could still see them. No voices murmuring in her head, yet she could still remember with startling clarity the way they had sounded.

Giving herself a small impatient shake she walked around to the passenger door of the Citroën.

As she pulled herself up Simone noticed something glittering in the grass. She reached out and picked up a silver hoop earring. Esther's. Simone had noticed them earlier. The earring must have come off when Esther was lying there dozing. Lucky Simone had noticed it!

'Esther . . .' she called, then stopped, suddenly remembering what Aurore had said to Valerie. If she had something personal belonging to either Esther or Hélène she might be able to throw some more light on what was happening.

'Yes?' Esther was looking round at her, on the point of sliding into the passenger seat.

Simone made up her mind.

'Nothing. I'm just coming,' she said.

And slipped the earring into her pocket.

19

VALERIE HAD SET her easel up in the garden and was trying to paint, but for once she was quite unable to concentrate. She knew that Simone had taken Esther to Montsegur and she could not stop wondering how she was getting on. And what Yves had said earlier about Thierry being murdered was nagging at her too. In all probability he was simply winding her up, of course. That would be Yves all over. But she couldn't rid herself of the suspicion there might be something in what he had said. Thierry had been a very dubious customer, even more dubious than Yves himself, because he was less obvious. Yves loved nothing more than to shock, whereas Thierry had been driven by undercurrents of misguided ambition.

The sound of a car coming down the lane carried clearly on the still evening air and Valerie looked up, listening. It sounded like Yves's car! He had gone out earlier and she hadn't expected him back for hours yet – he had told her he was going to visit friends, and that usually meant cards and cans of beer and making a night of it. But at least he did always come back – eventually. When he had first moved in, she had been very afraid he might not.

The engine cut and Valerie frowned. It was Yves, she was certain of it. A moment later she heard the front door slam and then Yves came out into the garden.

'Still painting? It'll be dark soon! Selling a picture has gone to your head, Madame Monet.'

She ignored his sarcasm.

'What are you doing home so early?'

Yves removed his sunglasses, swung them tantalisingly for a moment, then put them back on, though the brightness had long since gone out of the day. He wore them for effect, Valerie had long since decided – or because his eyes weren't meant for daylight at all. Smoky bar-rooms and casinos – that was Yves.

'Well there's a warm welcome for you!' he quipped. 'Nice to have you home, Yves.'

'Don't be silly. You know what I mean.'

'Well, supposing I was to tell you I came back to tell you something I thought would interest you.'

'Such as what?'

'Your mysterious visitor this morning. I was right when I said he couldn't care less about your pictures. That was just his excuse.'

'Don't be so mean, Yves.' She began to pack her brushes together. 'Don't spoil my one moment of commercial success.'

'Oh well, if you don't want to know . . .'

She looked up at him, curious in spite of herself.

'Why did he come then?'

'To snoop around. Your friend Andrew Slater is an investigative journalist with a special interest in crime.'

Valerie stared, horrified. 'Are you sure?'

'Sure as can be.'

'How did you find out?'

'He's been a touch more up front with certain people than he was with us. It's Thierry's death he's interested in, all right. And Thierry's friends . . .'

'Yves!' she said sharply. 'Are you sure you don't know more about this than you're telling?'

'Me?' He held her gaze mockingly. 'You have a very low opinion of me, don't you, chérie? No, he's barking up the wrong tree if you ask me. Like I said, it's Alain he should be looking at, and the mess his business is in.'

'Yves – tell me . . .'

He grinned at her tantalisingly. 'I'm going to get myself a drink. Want one?'

'No. Oh yes – all right, I think I do.'

He disappeared into the house and she went on packing up her painting things. She didn't for one moment believe that Alain had had anything to do with Thierry's death, but she was sure Yves was keeping something back. And he was enjoying the whole horrible business so much, too – just as he had enjoyed disillusioning her about the sale of the painting.

Sometimes I don't like you at all, Yves Marssac, she thought. And wondered if the time was coming when she should cut him out of her life.

Simone was getting ready for bed.

In one respect, she thought, the day had yielded nothing new. Apart from the fact that she had seemed to know her way about the castle of Montsegur, Esther had given not the slightest indication that she might have recognised her surroundings, and she had been clearly sceptical when Simone had raised the subject of reincarnation.

But at least she had the earring! If Aurore really did have psychic powers it might help in getting to the bottom of this whole thing. First thing tomorrow she would get Aurore's address from Valerie and send it to her.

She retrieved the earring from her pocket, looking at it curiously and wondering what on earth Aurore – or anyone – could pick up from something so ordinary. Nothing, probably. But at least it was worth a try.

A sudden sharp pain like an electric current prickled Simone's palm. She jumped in shock, dropping the earring as if it were red hot. What on earth . . . ? She pressed her hand to her mouth blowing on to the tingling spot. She was trembling – and not only from the physical sensation.

Danger – for Esther. She had seen it, felt it. And the certainty that events were gathering pace towards some awful inevitable conclusion was stronger than ever.

What happened before must happen again . . . and again. History repeating itself relentlessly over the centuries – a love triangle which ended in . . . what? The scene was set, the players once more on the stage, but still she did not understand what she was supposed to do.

Should she try to persuade Esther to go home before something terrible happened? Much use that would be – she could just imagine what Esther's reaction would be. She would assume that Simone wanted her to leave the field clear for Hélène and the rapport which had built up between them would be destroyed. And besides, if this really was a replay on the wheel of karma then it couldn't be avoided so easily. Until the debts had been paid, the wrongs righted, this same situation would occur again and again.

No, there was only one way – and that was to learn what it was that had happened in the past, try to tie it in with the present, and work out what must be done in order to absolve the souls caught up by recurring fate.

Simone bent down and picked up the earring. Just a hoop of silver now – no strange electric currents burning her hand. She placed it beneath her pillow, undressed and got into bed. Then she lay staring into the soft twilight.

At this time of year her room was never completely dark; even the smallest sliver of moon produced a soft grey opalescence. In it Simone could see the shapes of pieces of furniture, the jut of the door. But now, even as she looked, they were becoming indistinct, blurring, not into darkness but into swimming silvery light. The walls had disappeared entirely and it seemed to Simone that a panorama similar to the one she had looked down on today from the slopes of Montsegur was opening up. Weeded hillsides and open ground, small irregular plots of land. Colour was fading into them, softly brushing the silver hue of moonlight to turn it green and brown. Simone's head began to ache as if from the effort of staring, too hard, to catch a glimpse of something hidden. Except that she was making no effort at all. Rather, the scene was coming closer to her, enveloping her.

Simone closed her eyes, caught a strange flickering like a magic lantern. And then she saw them, there in the field. The young woman she had come to know as Jeanne, older now than when she had last seen her, and a boy. Thin, brown as a nut, tall for his age . . . How did she know what age he was?

And for the first time she heard his voice.

'How much longer, Mother? I'm hungry!'

The boy turned, his hand still resting on the harness of the ox which was pulling the swing plough across the rough plot of ground.

Jeanne, following the plough, tossed another handful of seed into the furrow from the basket which she wore strapped around her waist.

'Not much longer, my son. Twice more across the field and we'll be finished.'

He sighed in resignation, then shrugged and tugged once more at the harness, and Jeanne smiled, pride and tenderness making her forget for a moment how weary she was.

It had been a hard life, these ten years, and since Pierre had died it had been even harder. At least while he had been strong and healthy she had had to contend with only the woman's work around the farm and the *ostal*, and, although she had continued to be repelled by his insatiable demands for her to perform her wifely duties, at least she had grown used to them. Then, almost without warning, Pierre had succumbed to the lung disease which took the lives of so many of the villagers. His hacking cough had kept her awake at nights and soon he was spitting blood, his once sturdy body wasting away until he was little more than skin and bone. It was two years now since she had buried him and she had stood dry-eyed at his graveside.

The realisation that somehow she must carry on the work of the farm in order to provide for herself and her son had not daunted her then. But it had not been long before her difficulties had begun. Ploughing, sowing and harvesting made for backbreaking work. The team of shepherds, when they realised they must answer to a woman, became truculent and uncooperative, and often she fell asleep over the accounts, which she kept meticulously. There had been times when she had been tempted to give up and find a more suitable way of making a living – by selling wine, perhaps, as her mother had. But the farm was all she had in the world, all she would be able to pass on to Bernard – always provided it was not destroyed by the French armies, as so many farms had been. Jeanne had gritted her teeth against her screaming muscles and aching head and carried on. And it had been worth it. Whatever she had to do, for Bernard's sake it was worth it.

She looked at him now, at his tall young frame, lithe yet strong, at his bare legs and arms, tanned by the sun to a rich nut-brown, and felt the love sustain her. Bernard, whom she had named for the knight who had taken her in and given her a home. Her son. Philip's son . . .

How like him he had grown! she thought. Bernard was now just a year or two younger than Philip had been when she had first set eyes on him, and the image of him as he had been then. His hair was darker and his eyes more grey than blue, but his features were just the same. Bernard was her pride and joy. But he was also a constant reminder of the man she had loved.

At the edge of the field Bernard turned the ox and she followed. The plot sloped downward now and she could see the village laid out in tiers beneath them, row upon row of *ostals* clinging to the hillside, with their pocket handkerchiefs of garden and the bell tower rising above them like a pointing finger. The sun, low in the sky, caught the rooftops, making them blaze scarlet as if, she thought, the whole village was on fire. The illusion stirred a distant memory and she shivered suddenly.

There was a horseman on the path leading from the village. Jeanne frowned slightly, wondering who it might be. Horses were not common in these parts. The farmers owned sheep, pigs, oxen if they were lucky, but rarely horses, and it was a sadness to Jeanne that since her beloved Braida had died she had never again had the opportunity to ride.

The horseman was closer now. He seemed to be making directly for them. He was wearing a scarlet surcoat, Jeanne saw, and the sun was gleaming on hair like burnished gold.

Her heart came into her mouth with a thud. She was imagining things – she must be! Had she not just been thinking about Philip? But then, did so much as a single day ever pass when she did not think of him? She drew a hand across her tired eyes, half expecting the horseman to disappear like a wraith. But he did not. He had reached the end of the track now, pulling his mount up at the edge of the ploughed field and looking towards her.

Jeanne's knees began to tremble. It couldn't be Philip – not here at Montsegur! But her leaping heart and racing pulses were telling her differently.

'Bernard – stop for a moment!' she called.

He looked round at her, puzzled, but she scarcely noticed. She had eyes only for the horseman. Moving as if in a dream, she slowly crossed the corner of the field towards him.

He looked older, much older than she remembered him, and for a moment the shock of it made her doubt again. But there was no mistaking the way he sat on his horse, the reins draped loosely between his hands, back straight, head erect.

'Philip?' she said in a small breathless voice. 'Is it really you?'

'Jeanne.' He dismounted with a quick fluid movement.

For a moment they stood looking at each other, then he opened his arms and with a small sob she went into them.

* * *

It was almost a month now since Philip had returned from his tactical talks with Roger Bernard of Foix and learned of what had taken place at Montaugure in his absence.

At first his only concern had been the dangers into which Alazais had plunged them by the complaint she had made to the Dominican abbot concerning the behaviour of his monk, for like Oliver he realised that Pons Marty could be a dangerous enemy. It was typical of Alazais to have done such a thing – timid though she was in many ways, if her passion for right was offended she would not rest until she had seen justice done, and he could not help being proud of her. But it was of concern to him that she had drawn attention once again to the Bertrands. Good Catholics they might be but if the Inquisition set out to prove otherwise then it would not save them any more than it had saved the Catholics of Béziers and Carcassonne. Things were done differently now; the days of wholesale slaughter were over and the burnings were ordered not by a rampaging army but by the courts. But that did not mean the danger of injustice was any less likely. Most families had a skeleton or two in their chapel vaults and under torture most of them could be resurrected. No one who had supported the Cathars – or even failed to persecute them – could ever feel completely safe, and that meant most of the God-fearing south. The Church of Rome and the King of France were still hand in glove and their reign of terror continued. By her actions, Alazais had placed them in danger, not a doubt of it.

But the incident had also brought Jeanne to the forefront of Philip's mind once more.

For Alazais's sake he had tried very hard to forget the girl who had once meant so much to him. He had a duty to his wife and his heritage, he had reminded himself, and never again must he betray them by his weakness and selfish desires. But although his memories of Jeanne had faded from an agony of guilt and longing to a sweet haunting dream, he had never forgotten her and now he found himself thinking of her constantly and wondering what had become of her. When she had left Montaugure she had gone to Agnes at Montsegur, he knew, for Agnes had sent them word when Jeanne had arrived there in order to ease their minds. But it was many years now since any communication had passed between them. Aware that her defection to the heresy could imperil her family, Agnes had cut all ties. Philip did not even know whether she was alive or dead, for many Cathar Perfects had perished in the flames. But Montsegur was, he knew, still a Cathar stronghold, and although it had been attacked not once but many times, its impregnable position had so far saved it from capture.

Was Jeanne still at Montsegur with Agnes? he wondered and the curiosity soon deepened to obsession, sharpened – and excused – by the duty he felt to let Jeanne know that the brother she had believed lost had survived the turbulent years.

No doubt it would be a dreadful shock to her to learn that Pons was not only a Catholic monk but also one of the dreaded Dominican inquisitors. Besides this, a man who could behave as he had done at Montaugure was hardly the sort of brother Jeanne would wish for. But Pons was still her brother for all that and in any case, Philip could not find it in his heart to condemn the priest for his attempted rape of Grazide with the same ferocity Alazais had done. He did not believe Grazide was as innocent as Alazais maintained she was; he had noticed the way she enjoyed flaunting her wiles and was not entirely surprised that she had at last got more than she had bargained for. And besides, who was he to cast the first stone? Philip was overcome with shame as he remembered all too clearly how he himself had succumbed to temptation.

No, Jeanne should be told that her brother was alive and searching for her. As long as Philip had known her she had tormented herself with wondering about his fate and blaming herself for losing him. Whether or not she chose to contact him when she knew the truth, at least she must be given the opportunity to make her own decision.

When he had told her what he planned Alazais had done her best to persuade him against it, but his mind was made up.

'I shall not be gone long, and you have nothing to fear. Oliver will be here to look after you,' he had said to comfort her.

'It's you I'm thinking of.'

'I shall come to no harm. The days of open warfare and attack are over – for the time being at least.'

'But Montsegur! If it is known you are going there everyone will think you are a Cathar sympathiser.'

'I shall be careful,' he assured her.

At last Alazais had given up the argument. Philip was her husband. He knew best and his decisions must be obeyed.

As he rode south, Philip had been shocked by the destruction he saw all around him. In many ways the second crusade had been more bitter and vengeful than the first, for the northern barons had taken their revenge on the stubborn southerners by destroying the livelihoods of any who dared oppose them. As he passed through ravaged farm lands, where crops had been trampled underfoot or burned, Philip realised how lucky they had been at Montaugure to escape unscathed. Here the people looked cowed and hungry, and as he rode through the villages ragged children came running after him begging for coins or something to eat. The thought that Jeanne might be suffering conditions such as these was unbearable and Philip had spurred his horse on impatiently.

When at last he had arrived at Montsegur he was surprised at how small the castle was, but impressed by its defences. No wonder the Cathars had been safe here for so long! Somewhat apprehensively Philip enquired for his aunt and the response proved to be the one he had hoped for – Agnes was indeed still here and she would see him.

Though he had known she was now a Perfect the sight of her in her sombre black robes was still quite a shock. But her smile was as serene as it had always been, although she was soon expressing her anxiety for his safety.

'These are dangerous times, Philip. You should not have come.'

'I had to.' He explained the reasons behind his visit and saw her face grow grave.

'How strange are the twists of fate! Jeanne's brother is a Dominican while she is deeply committed to our faith. She wanted to train for a Perfect, you know.'

'God's teeth!' Philip exclaimed, imagining Jeanne in the same black robes Agnes was wearing, and she smiled, as if reading his thoughts.

'It's all right, I dissuaded her – though I think that one day she may yet wish to be prepared for the *Consolamentum*. No, Jeanne married a farmer, a village man. They had a son.' She paused, watching Philip's reaction.

'A son!' He shook his head. 'Would that Alazais had been able to do the same for me. Is she happy, do you know?'

'I think so. She works hard in the fields, I hear – her husband has died and she struggles on alone.'

Philip thought of the devastated farms he had seen on his ride south. 'Her land has been spared then? It hasn't been destroyed?'

'So far she has escaped the notice of the oppressers but none of us knows what tomorrow will bring,' Agnes told him. 'We walk a fine line between survival and disaster. That is why I would counsel you against telling Jeanne of her brother. He is after all her only living relative and she may rush to seek him out without thought for the consequences. She is, as I say, a committed Cathar. If her brother is as committed to the dictates of his faith, then I would fear for her safety.'

'Surely he would never betray his own sister!' Philip exclaimed, then stopped, his voice tailing away into uncertainty. Who knew what a man possessed of religious fervour might do, especially since this one would very likely be trying to redeem himself in the eyes of the church.

'Go and see Jeanne if you like,' Agnes continued. 'I am sure she would be more than glad. But don't tell her about her brother, not just now, with things as they are, I beg you.'

Philip had agreed, but as he rode his horse down the steep track to the village it occurred to him that the excuse he had used to himself for seeking out Jeanne no longer existed. But he was going to see her anyway. And the only possible reason now was that he wanted to do so.

'I still can't believe it, Philip! I thought I would never see you again as long as I lived.'

Philip had returned with Jeanne and Bernard to the *ostal* and shared their evening meal – a stew which had been simmering all day on the fire while they had worked in the fields. He had been shocked by her poverty and the conditions under which she lived. Yet it struck him that in some ways it was as if the wheel had come full circle. This Jeanne was simply a grown version of the child he had brought home from the crusade on the neck of his horse – too thin, with skin burned almost black by constant exposure to the summer suns, and dressed in the meanest of rags, yet still radiating an almost incandescent beauty. With an effort Philip had concealed what he was feeling, for it was not for him to pass judgement on this life which Jeanne had chosen.

He looked at her over the cup of wine with which he was washing down his meal.

'You are the one who ran away, Jeanne.'

'Yes.' She knotted her hands together on the table top, looking down at them, and he was suddenly painfully aware of how cracked and calloused they were.

'Why did you go?' he asked.

Still she refused to meet his eyes, instead casting a sidelong glance at Bernard. 'You know why,' she said softly.

Bernard, who was becoming bored with this conversation which he did not understand, got up, scraping his stool noisily on the flagstoned floor.

'Mother, can I go out?'

Jeanne nodded, smiling at him indulgently.

'Yes, off you go.'

As he left the *ostal* Philip's eyes followed him thoughtfully.

'He's a fine boy.'

'I think so – but then I am his mother.'

'No, you should be proud.'

'I am.'

There was a small awkward silence. After a moment Philip asked, 'Does he take after his father?'

Jeanne stared at him in disbelief. How could he have failed to realise the truth when Bernard was so like him that looking at the boy should have been like looking into a mirror?

'Yes, he does,' she said pointedly. 'I named Bernard for your father, you know.'

'A nice gesture. He would have been pleased.'

'More than a gesture. It was the one thing I could give him which was part of his heritage.' Her eyes flashed suddenly with the pride he remembered so well. 'Oh Philip, must I spell it out for you? Or have you already realised what it is I am trying to tell you and just don't want to acknowledge it? Yes, that's it, I suppose. You turned your back on me once before and I suppose you will do so again.'

Philip frowned. 'What is all this about, Jeanne?'

She shook her head in disbelief. 'You mean you really don't know? All right, I'll tell you. I was already with child when I wed Pierre. When I said Bernard favours his father it was not him I spoke of but you. Bernard is your son, Philip.'

He froze. Yes, he thought he had known from the moment he had set eyes on the boy, but he had been afraid to believe it. Now, as the first surprise faded, fierce joy came rushing in. When Alazais had failed to conceive he had secretly feared it was he who was to blame and he had given up hope of ever fathering a son. Now, without warning, he found himself presented with one who was almost fully grown. But – a peasant boy! His son was a bastard peasant boy working in the fields! God's teeth!

'Don't look so surprised.' Jeanne laughed shortly. 'Did it never occur to you that I might have been with child? I thought it had – and that was the reason you never came to look for me.'

He shook his head. 'I never thought. Why should I? It was but once— '

'Once can be enough!'

'Does Bernard . . . ?' Philip glanced towards the door.

'No. He believes Pierre to have been his father. As he should. Pierre was good to him.'

'And to you?'

She shrugged. 'I was his wife.'

For a moment he sat in silence staring at the bare boards of the table. Then he brought his fist down with a resounding thud which made the pots rattle.

'You must come home, Jeanne.'

A small frown wrinkled her forehead. 'Come home?'

'To Montaugure.' He realised now that this was what had been in his mind from the moment Agnes had told him Jeanne's husband was dead, and certainly ever since he had seen the conditions under which she laboured. But now there was another reason, and that reason was Bernard.

'What would I do there?' She laughed shortly, as if the prospect was not only amusing but ridiculous, and he reached across the table to catch her calloused hand in his.

'You would be a companion to Alazais, just as you were before. Oh, she has her ladies, it's true, but they are not her friends as you were. Don't look like that, Jeanne. It would be better, surely, than the life you have here.'

She was silent, and he went on: 'For the sake of your child, Jeanne, if not for your own! Alazais and I have never been fortunate enough to be blessed with children. Bastard or not, Bernard is my son, and I would like him to enjoy the benefits of what is, after all, his inheritance.'

Her lips tightened. In ten years he had never once bothered to seek her out – for ten years she had been left to fend as well as she could for the child he had fathered. For him she had worked and slaved, sacrificed her hopes and dreams, prostituted herself to a man she loathed. Philip had spent those same years trying to beget an heir with Alazais . . . and had failed. Now he had the gall to think he could take her son and fill the gap in his life.

'This farm is Bernard's inheritance!' she blazed angrily. 'His by right of the man he called his father.'

'A few meagre plots of land to sweat over? What kind of a life is that, Jeanne? And for how long will he be able to call them his? Only as long as the French allow him to. Have you not seen what they are doing? They intend to starve into submission those they cannot conquer by fire and the sword. Think, for God's sake, what the future holds for him here – and what it could hold if only you would do as I suggest.'

She was silent, her anger dying as swiftly as it had risen. He was right of course. Here Bernard's future was uncertain on all but one count – the harshness of the life of a peasant. Montaugure could offer him so much that she could not. And besides . . .

Jeanne glanced at Philip and loved him as she had always loved him. Oh, it would be hard to be part of his household once more and know that she could never be more than companion to his wife. But would it be more intolerable than sending him away and knowing without doubt that she would never see him again as long as she lived? And if the worst happened – if the land over which she slaved to give Bernard a livelihood should be snatched from them – would she ever be able to forgive herself for denying him this opportunity?

The motives were muddied in her mind by emotions beyond her control but Jeanne knew she could no longer afford the luxury of indulging her pride.

She lifted her chin, meeting his eyes with a clear and direct gaze.

'Very well,' she said simply. 'I will accept your offer.'

20

ALAIN WAS ALREADY at work in his office when Esther got up next morning. His door was ajar and he was sitting at his desk behind a sheaf of files looking strained and worried.

'I'm terribly sorry, sweetheart, but I have to go to Perpignan today,' he greeted her. 'My accountant thinks we should have a meeting and I'm afraid it can't wait.'

She crossed to him, massaging the taut muscles of his shoulders with her fingers. 'I could always come with you.'

'Oh no, you don't want to do that. It might be a long meeting – I should think it will be. It wouldn't be much fun for you. Why don't you take the old runaround and go off to do some sightseeing?'

The 'runaround' as he called it was a Saab 96 which he had bought at one time as a second car for Hélène and kept when she acquired a new model because it was solid, reliable and, despite its age, still in good condition.

On the point of arguing, Esther changed her mind. The meeting was obviously important and it could be that Alain wanted to prepare himself on the drive to Perpignan without her there to distract him.

'There's a map in the salon,' he went on, gathering his files into a neat pile and getting up. 'It shows all the places of interest.'

'Are you coming down for breakfast?' she asked.

'I've already had mine. I'm leaving now.'

'Right.' Another reason he didn't want to take her with him, she realised. He didn't want to have to wait for her to get ready.

'You'll be all right, won't you, chérie? And when I come home tonight it will be just you and me. Maman and Papa are off to their friends today.'

She nodded.

'I know, and I must say I'm looking forward to it.'

'Me too.' He kissed her, then turned away, businesslike once more. 'Have a good day.'

'Yes. And Alain – I hope everything works out for you.'

A muscle tightened at the corner of his mouth.

'It had better is all I can say.'

Isobelle and Henri's bags were already packed and piled up in a heap at the foot of the stairs. Obviously they too intended to make an early start. As Esther went towards the kitchen she could hear Isobelle talking to Henri.

'Now you must make a good breakfast. We have a long journey ahead of us.'

She speaks to him as if he were a child! Esther thought – but then, of course, that was it in a nutshell. Henri *had* returned to a sort of second childhood.

He looked up as she entered the kitchen, a crumb of croissant rolling down his chin, a smile of pleasure lighting up his face.

'Oh my dear, how lovely it is to see you again! It's been so long!'

'For heaven's sake, Henri, it's only been one night!' Isobelle snapped.

'Has it?' He looked puzzled, his eyes opaque. 'Oh no, I don't think so. It's been years – years! And it was all *your* fault she went away in the first place, Cecile. You've got a lot to answer for, I'm afraid.'

'Cecile?' Isobelle snorted impatiently. 'Who's Cecile?'

'Well you, of course! Dear, dear me. And you tell me *I'm* the one who forgets things! I don't know, sometimes I think I'm the only one here who remembers anything.'

Isobelle raised her eyebrows, shrugging an extravagent gesture of resignation. But Esther felt only an unexpected warmth towards the old man.

He was a sweetie, she thought, and she wished she had known him before the degenerative illness had taken its toll, and that Isobelle could find it in her to treat him more kindly.

When she had finished breakfast Esther spread the tourist map out on the table, trying to decide where she should go. Another Cathar fortress, perhaps. The small castle-shaped symbols that showed where they were situated seemed to be drawing her like a magnet and she selected one at random – Peirepetreuse.

She set out, a little anxious at first about her ability to manage the unfamiliar car with its left-hand drive and column gear change, but after a few near misses with low stone walls and sandy grass verges – because she was driving too close to her nearside – she began to gain confidence and actually enjoy herself.

There was something rather nice about being a totally free agent with wheels to take her wherever she fancied going. She meandered along, stopping to buy lemonade and biscuits at a mini-market she passed, and calling in at a wine cave to take a look around and purchase a bottle or two as she would have liked to do yesterday.

At Peirepetreuse she wandered and explored, loving the sense of history that clung to the ancient stones but not experiencing any of the haunting sadness or feeling of claustrophobic oppression which had descended on her at Montsegur. There were no murmuring voices either, no inexplicable movements in the shimmering sunshine, even when she lay with the sun warm on her face after eating her picnic.

The only shadows today were the very real problems of the present, such as when would Alain actually do something about divorcing Hélène? In spite of his assurances she couldn't forget his momentary hesitation when she had told him he must choose between her and Hélène, and the suspicion that he still cared for her nagged uncomfortably at Esther. But for the moment there was nothing she could do about that. To all intents and purposes, he had chosen her, and she must accept that and trust him. The only alternative was to give up and go home, and she was not ready to do that.

Then of course there were these ongoing problems with his business. He was very worried, she knew. But hopefully his meeting today would help him come up with a solution. Wasn't that what accountants were for?

She levered herself up, gathering up the remains of her picnic and glancing at her watch. Almost four – time to head for home. Perhaps, if she took her time, Alain would be back by the time she got there. She set out at a leisurely pace and slowed down even more when she left the main road and found herself in the meandering lanes that led to Le Château Gris.

A flash in the driving mirror attracted her attention and she glanced up, startled, to see the reflection of a black car close behind her. Had it flashed its lights at her? Surely not! It must have been the sun. But something about the car was bothering her. It really was awfully close – and she rather thought it was the same car as had been behind her on the main road. She had noticed it a couple of times – black cars were fairly uncommon round here, or anywhere, come to that, these days.

The car was edging out towards the centre of the road now, as if it wanted to overtake. Esther pulled well in to give it plenty of room, realised she was too close to the verge, and swerved quickly out again. She heard the squeal of brakes and the shaft of reflected light hit her eyes again. She hadn't imagined it – he was flashing her! But why? Was there some French rule of the road she was unwittingly contravening? Well, she was almost at the crossroads now, a few kilometres outside the village. It wasn't likely he'd still be going her way after that. The other roads led to much larger villages and a small town, a mini-market, and a hospital, while hers led only to the Lavaur house and a handful of others, similarly isolated. She put on her indicator, checked her mirror. To her annoyance, the indicator on the car behind her came on too, and as she swung right he followed her.

Esther put her foot down on the accelerator. The following car matched its speed to hers and the lights flashed in her mirror again. What the hell was going on? The idiot was pulling out, trying to pass. She stepped on the accelerator again, glanced in her mirror. He was still there, still on her tail, still flashing those damned lights!

Her eyes on the mirror rather than on the road ahead, she felt, rather than saw, that she was too close to the verge. She yanked on the steering wheel, but already the wheels were skidding in the soft gravel and the hedge was rushing up at her, crablike. Directly ahead of her was a tree; she pulled on the wheel again, skimmed past the tree, hitting it with her wing mirror, and then the car was over the verge and into the ditch beyond, tilting at a crazy angle, wheels spinning, engine still racing.

It had all happened so fast that for a moment she sat rigid with shock. Then she realised that the car which had been following her had stopped too. It was directly alongside her, the driver staring down at her with a surprised expression on his face before accelerating away.

'You bastard!' she yelled. 'What do you think you were doing?'

The ignition light was still on; she switched it off and tried to open the driver's door. It was jammed. She wriggled across and tried the passenger door. To her immense relief it opened and she scrambled out.

Surprisingly the car – old and solid – showed little sign of damage apart from a dented wing and the torn-off mirror. But it was firmly anchored in the ditch and Esther knew she had no chance of getting it out without help.

She clambered up the bank, annoyed to find her legs felt like jelly, and sat down for a moment, wondering what to do. If this were England, she would have her mobile phone with her. But it wasn't, and she didn't. Was there a public telephone anywhere nearby? She couldn't remember seeing one, but then, she hadn't been looking. Certainly there were no houses for miles and this road was so quiet it could be hours before another car came along. Well, there was nothing for it: she'd just have to start walking.

What the hell had that driver been playing at – running her into a ditch and then speeding off? Was he a road hog or a lunatic? Both, probably . . . Esther stopped walking as a sudden thought struck her.

Two days ago someone had followed Hélène and frightened her half to death. Was it possible it was the same man? Today Esther was using Hélène's old car – had he thought she *was* Hélène? It seemed awfully far-fetched, but then so was the alternative – that Languedoc was full of crazy motorists trailing lone women drivers. And the expression on his face when he'd stopped beside her . . . He had actually looked surprised, as if he had been expecting to see someone else in the driver's seat.

Esther gave her head a little shake. Someone following Hélène. But who? Why?

She started to walk along the road again. The air was still and stiflingly hot, although it was now late afternoon, and Esther realised she felt a little shaky – delayed reaction, she supposed.

When she saw the glint of sun on perspex up ahead she thought at first it must be a mirage. But it wasn't. It was a telephone kiosk. She found some money and dialled the number of Le Château Gris, then waited, sweating because it was stiflingly hot in the kiosk, which had attracted all the heat of the day. There no reply. Alain wasn't home yet, she supposed, and today wasn't one of Beatrice's days to work. Not that she could have made the old woman understand her anyway. She was half deaf and spoke no English.

Esther hesitated for a moment, wondering what to do. There was no directory in the kiosk to tell her the number of a garage and in any case she doubted she could have made them understand either. The police then? What did one have to dial here to get them? She thought it might be 999 as in England, but she wasn't sure.

The Slaters. Of course. Why hadn't she thought of them before? They would help, she was sure.

She searched in her bag for the number Andrew had given her and dialled, hoping desperately that they weren't out too. But a few moments later Diana Slater answered.

'Good lord! Are you hurt?' Diana asked, concerned, when Esther explained what had happened.

'No, I'm fine.' She didn't feel fine. She felt shaky and hot and harassed, but it wasn't in her nature to whinge. 'Look, I'm really sorry to bother you, but I really am a bit stuck . . .'

'Think nothing of it. I'm only glad you thought of us,' Diana assured her. 'We'll ring the recovery people. You stay where you are and either Bob or Andrew will come out to you.'

'Oh, there's no need for that. Just as long as I get a tow-truck or something.'

'Nonsense!' Diana said briskly. 'I'd like to know you're all right and don't have any more problems. I'd come myself, but I think one of the men might be more use if the car's well and truly stuck.'

'I'll go back to it and wait then,' Esther said gratefully. 'I'm a bit worried about it.'

'Well, I'm sure Alain won't be. The main thing is that you are all right. That man could have killed you!'

'Well he didn't. But I'd certainly like to kill him!'

She walked back to the Saab and sat down on the grass verge to wait. She really was beginning to feel very strange – shaky and a bit sick – and when she heard the sound of an approaching car and got up a little too quickly her legs felt like jelly.

It was Andrew in his Spanish hire car and she thought she had never been more pleased to see anyone in her life. He pulled up beside her and got out, looking anxious.

'Are you all right?'

'Yes. Oh, I'm really sorry. I feel a complete fool.'

'Don't be silly! Diana said some idiot tried to run you off the road.'

'Yes. It was unbelievable really.'

'There are some awful swine about. But you're in one piece, and that's the most important thing.'

'But the car . . .'

'It doesn't look too bad. Once it's back on the road we'll be able to tell better. The garage people should be here soon. Ah, that sounds like them now.'

A smartly painted, surprisingly new recovery vehicle manned by two swarthy Frenchmen was drawing up alongside them. The men tutted, scratching their heads, then set about the operation with deceptively casual efficiency. Before long the Saab was back on the road but Esther realised with a sinking heart that it was going to be undrivable. A buckled front nearside wheel would see to that.

'Don't worry, I'll drive you home,' Andrew said as the men loaded the damaged car on to the truck.

'Are you sure?'

'I can't leave you here, can I? Come on, get in.'

'It really was very odd,' she said as they headed in the direction of Le Château Gris.

'Him running you off the road like that?'

'Yes. I just don't understand it.'

'A local yob, I expect, getting a kick out of frightening you.'

'Maybe, but . . . something similar happened to Hélène the day before yesterday. She didn't have an accident or anything, but she thought she was being followed.'

'A nutter preying on women drivers, you mean?'

'Well, no actually. I know it sounds crazy but I was driving Hélène's old car and it occurred to me to wonder if he thought I was her. He stopped for a minute after I crashed, you see, and I thoght he looked sort of surprised, almost as if he was expecting it to be someone else.'

Andrew was silent for a moment.

'I know – I expect I imagined it,' she said.

'What did he look like?' Andrew asked suddenly.

'Oh, thirtyish, dark – it's really hard to describe someone, isn't it?' A thought occurred to her. 'Do you think I should tell the police?'

'I think what you need is a stiff drink.' There was an edge to Andrew's voice which Esther failed to identify as suppressed excitement. He was rummaging in his pocket for his wallet, laying it on his knee and extracting a photograph with one hand while steering the car with the other.

'That wouldn't be him, would it?'

He passed her the photograph of the Three Musketeers. She took it, puzzled, looking at the laughing faces of the young men.

'Which one?'

'The one in the middle.'

'Oh, I don't know. I don't think so. It was more like that one, except that he had a beard . . .'

Andrew slowed the car and leaned over to look, hoping that he had been wrong about Jean-Luc Lorrain's position in the group. But it was at Thierry Rousseau that Esther was pointing.

'It couldn't have been him,' he said, disappointed. 'He's dead.'

'Dead?'

'Yes. That's Hélène Lavaur's brother, Thierry. Didn't you know him?'

'No.' She stared at the photograph. So that was Thierry! Well, clearly he couldn't have been the man in the car. She didn't really know why she'd said it might have been – perhaps she had seen a photograph of Thierry somewhere in the Lavaurs' house and that was why he had looked familiar to her.

But why should Andrew Slater have a photograph of Thierry anyway? If he was a policeman like his father, could it be there was some kind of investigation going on into his death that Alain didn't know about – or had failed to mention?

Andrew was turning into the drive of Le Château Gris.

'Can I offer you a coffee or something?' she asked. 'I'm on my own today. Alain's in Perpignan on business and his parents are away, visiting friends.'

'Yes, you can offer me a coffee.'

Andrew grinned at her, his eyes crinkling, and looked away, embarrassed. She had only meant to be friendly; she hoped he hadn't misunderstood her.

She led the way around to the back of the house, retrieving the key from its hiding place under a pot of geraniums and unlocking the door. The house felt very empty and she was very conscious suddenly that she was a visitor here and had no right inviting anyone in for coffee when Alain and his parents were not at home. Still, it was too late now.

She was just filling the percolater when the telephone began to ring. Before she could reach it the answering machine came on and Alain's voice filled the kitchen.

'Esther? It's me. Where are you? I thought you'd be back by now.'

She fiddled with the unfamiliar buttons, hoping she wouldn't manage to cut him off.

'Alain! I'm here!'

'Oh good. Look, chérie, I'm going to be later getting back than I thought.'

Her heart sank. 'You're going to be late?'

'Yes. It's all taken a lot longer than I expected. You're all right, aren't you?'

'Well . . . yes, but I did have a bit of a problem. With the car.'

'Nothing serious?'

'Well . . . no, but— '

'Look,' Alain interrupted her. 'Tell me about it when I get home. I should be back by – eleven, say.'

'Eleven!'

'I can't stop to talk now. I'm with someone. I'll see you later, all right?'

'Yes, all right.' But it wasn't all right. It wasn't all right at all. She'd been run off the road by a maniac who could have killed her and he couldn't even be bothered to listen. Some difference from the way he treated Hélène! If it had been her he'd have come rushing home to comfort her, business or no business!

Steaming, she went back to the kitchen.

'That was Alain. He's going to be late. Tonight, of all nights. Just when I could have done with . . . Oh, sometimes he makes me so furious!'

'You told him about the accident?'

'He didn't give me the chance. He was in too much of a rush. So now I'm stuck. God knows what I'll do about eating tonight with no car to go and get anything. Some day this is turning out to be!'

'I have a car,' Andrew said innocently.

She looked at him quickly. 'Oh – I didn't mean— '

'I could always take you out for a bite to eat,' he went on as if he had not heard her. 'And a drink, too. You look to me as if you could do with a drink.'

On the point of refusing she thought: What the hell? Why shouldn't I spend the evening with Andrew? Alain's not here and doesn't seem the least bit worried about me.

'All right,' she said. 'Why not?'

'Good. Forget the coffee and we'll go and find somewhere where they serve something much stronger. If I could just use the phone – let Diana know I won't be home for dinner . . .'

'Help yourself,' she said. 'It's not my phone anyway. 'I'll go and change. I feel a bit sticky to go out as I am.'

He waited until he heard the bathroom door click shut after her and then he picked up the phone and dialled his father's number.

'Dad? I don't know what time I'll be home. I've had a bit of luck.'

'Oh, on what score?' Bob sounded amused.

'Every score. I'm taking Esther out for supper.'

'Ah!' Bob said. 'Mixing business with pleasure now, are we?'

'You could say that,' Andrew replied.

Hélène was on her third gin and tonic when the telephone began to ring. She froze, gripping the glass so tightly that her knuckles showed white, and wondering what to do. It had rung several times today already and she had refused to answer it. She couldn't face the thought of hearing that horrid silence again, followed by nothing but a hollow click. But perhaps it wasn't the mystery caller, whoever that might be. Perhaps it was someone who genuinely wanted to speak to her. Simone, maybe – or even Alain. Perhaps he had opened the box file at last and found the insurance policy . . . She banged her glass down on the table and half ran across the room, suddenly as afraid it would stop before she reached it as she was that once again there would be no one there.

She snatched it up. 'Hello?'

For a moment there was nothing but the echoing silence.

'Who is it?' Hélène sobbed. 'Who's there? Will you stop doing this to me!'

At last someone spoke. Hélène blanched as she heard the voice, trembling now from head to foot.

'It's not true!' she whispered. 'I don't believe it!'

There was a chair beside the telephone table. She sank into it. And the voice at the other end of the line went on, like a ghostly whisper in her ear.

It was almost midnight when Esther heard Alain's car on the drive. She went to the window, drawing aside the curtains to check. Yes, it was him – at last!

It was an hour and a half now since Andrew had brought her home. They had enjoyed a delicious meal at a country *auberge* – cassoulet, a speciality of the region, washed down by good local red wine – and his pleasant and undemanding company had helped her to unwind. She couldn't remember when she had felt so much at ease with any man, she had thought – Alain and her father excepted, of course, and then tagged on the rather disconcerting rider that she never felt actually at ease with Alain any more. She loved him – too much probably – but these days there always seemed to be tensions hovering between them. Andrew, on the other hand, felt like an old friend, someone she had known all her life and as she had relaxed the traumas of the day had somehow ceased to matter.

Waiting for Alain to come home she had found herself tensing up again, however. Surely he need not have been as late as this? Didn't he care that she was here on her own? Or had there been an accident? Where on earth was he?

But now he was here. She hurried out to meet him, her resentment and doubts forgotten in a rush of relief.

'Oh Alain, thank goodness you're home!'

He kissed her briefly.

'Hang on – let me put my briefcase down.'

She held on to his free hand as they went into the kitchen.

'I've had an awful day.'

'That makes two of us.' By the light of the lamps his face looked tired and strained. 'What was this trouble you had with the car?'

'I'm afraid I had an accident. It wasn't my fault, honestly. This idiot ran me off the road.'

'Where?'

She told him. He ran a hand wearily through his hair.

'And where's the car now? Still there?'

'No – the garage men from the village recovered it.'

'Is it badly damaged?'

'Not too badly.'

'Thank heavens for small mercies! I can do without repair bills just now.' He ran a hand through his hair. 'Of course, the important thing is that you are all right. I suppose that puts everything else into perspective.'

'What do you mean?' she asked, sensing that something other than her accident was on his mind.

'I haven't had a very good day either I'm afraid,' he said heavily. 'Financially things are even worse than I feared. It's beginning to look as though I might lose the business.'

'Oh no!' She was horrified.

''Fraid so. My accountant thinks I can hold out for another couple of weeks at most, then that's it. The bank will call in the loan I took out to get started and what assets I have will be sold off to pay the creditors. End of Lavaur Wines. Christ, I need a drink!'

'I'll get you one.' She found a bottle of cognac, poured a measure and handed it to him. She was feeling guilty now for having judged him so harshly. Obviously he had a great deal on his mind.

Alain drained the glass. She reached out and ran her fingers over the back of his hand, loving the way the hairs grew thickly around his wrist.

'I'm sure it won't come to that.'

'Are you? I'm not. Things have gone too far. Even if I can find the money to settle the debts, confidence has been damaged and if people don't have confidence in me then that's it. Who's going to trust their business to a company that can get into this sort of mess?'

She didn't know what to say. She could see he had a point. For a few minutes they were silent, then Alain got up to pour himself another drink.

'Hélène hasn't been here today has she?' he asked, coming back to sit down.

'Hélène? No. Why should she have been?'

'No reason. I just wondered . . .' He hesitated, aware that he was stepping into a minefield. 'I'm a bit concerned about her, that's all. She's not at home.'

Remembering her suspicion that the man who had run her off the road might have mistaken her for Hélène, she felt a frisson of alarm.

'Alain, I don't know if I'm way off beam, but . . .' she began, but he was not listening to her.

'She may have gone out to friends, of course, but . . . The house wasn't locked. It was all in darkness and her car was gone, but she hadn't locked up. It's very unlike her . . .'

Instantly Esther's hackles rose and she forgot all about what she had been on the point of saying.

'How do you know?'

'What?'

'That the house was unlocked and all the rest of it.'

'I called round on my way home to make sure she was all right.'

'You called round?' Esther said, furious. He'd known she was here alone, waiting for him, but he'd still called on Hélène before coming home.

For a moment he stared at her blankly, then reacted with aggression to match hers.

'Yes – I did. Is that a problem?'

'I think so, yes.'

'Oh for God's sake, Esther – not that again!'

'Yes – that! I just wish you were half as concerned about me as you are about bloody Hélène!'

'I am. But you're not likely to do something stupid if things get on top of you.'

'And that means I'm not worthy of consideration, does it? I was involved in an accident today, and when I tried to tell you about it on the telephone you didn't even want to bother to listen. Yet you continually find time to worry about Hélène. I'm sorry Alain, but I've just about had enough of it.'

'Oh chérie . . .' Suddenly he was contrite. 'I'm sorry, honestly. I know how it must look to you. But it's hard to break the habits of a lifetime, and if something happened to Hélène I would never forgive myself. You must understand that.'

'I understand that she seems to be your first concern.'

'But I am here with you.' The Gallic charm was being turned on full blast, Esther thought, trying to harden her heart to it and failing miserably. 'You said I must choose and I chose. Doesn't that tell you that it is *you* who are my first concern?'

'I don't know, Alain. I honestly don't know.'

'Then I must show you. Come to bed, chérie.'

'You think that's the answer to everything, don't you.'

'Isn't it?'

'No, it's not. I don't want you making love to me with half your mind on Hélène.'

'It won't be. When I am with you I think of nothing else. Forget about Hélène, please. I have.'

He reached for her, pulling her close, and she thought at least there was some truth in what he said. He *was* here with her, it was her he had chosen. But the disconcerting shadow of Hélène was still there, hovering in the background, and Esther found herself wondering just how much more of it she could take. Resentment and jealousy would eventually sour any relationship they had without any conscious decision on her part. In the end it would wither and die and Hélène would get what she wanted.

But that stage hadn't quite been reached yet. The feel of his body against hers was still exciting enough to make everything else seem unimportant and she still wanted him enough to allow the optimist in her nature to overcome the doubts.

Andrew sat on his father's patio, feet propped up on the balcony rail, and looked up at the stars. It was late, the others had gone to bed, and he should have gone to bed too. But he didn't feel sleepy. He felt restless.

'Did you have a good evening?' Bob had asked when he had come home.

'Yes.'

'Find anything out?'

'Not really.'

'Oh! I can see you're in one of your *communicative* moods,' Bob said sarcastically.

'That's right. Can I have a brandy?'

'Help yourself.'

And so he'd brought the bottle out on to the patio intending to try to organise the titbits he'd gleaned so far and plan the next step towards establishing whether or not there was a story. But he hadn't got any further. In fact he had scarcely thought of Thierry Rousseau at all. Instead he had kept thinking of a girl with a swinging wedge of light-brown hair and grey-green eyes, a girl who was somehow vulnerable in spite of being fiercely independent, a girl he might have met a long time ago if he had stayed on *West Today* instead of chasing the big time in London.

If I'd got to her first, Alain Lavaur wouldn't have stood a chance! he thought ruefully. But there it was. His timing might be excellent where work was concerned; in his private life it was definitely lousy.

Andrew reached for the bottle and refilled his glass. It would take quite a lot of his father's good brandy to put Esther Morris out of his mind, he suspected.

21

SIMONE HAD JUST eaten breakfast on the patio and was lingering over a cup of coffee when she heard the telephone begin to ring. She stacked her cup and saucer on to the empty, crumb-strewn plate and carried them into the house on her way to answer it. She was half expecting it to be Andre Ladurie chasing her again for the manuscript of her biography, and wondering how she could explain to him that it was no nearer completion, but when she lifted the receiver it was a woman's voice on the other end of the line.

'Simone? This is Aurore.'

'Aurore!' Simone was taken totally by surprise; she had not expected to hear from Valerie's friend so soon – Aurore was a very busy person, she knew.

'The earring you sent me arrived safely and I thought it best to speak to you direct. Valerie gave me your number.'

'This is very kind of you, Aurore.'

'Not at all. I'm absolutely fascinated. From what Valerie tells me this appears to be a most interesting case. And my own feelings bear that out.'

'You mean you've been able to pick something up from the earring?' Simone was prickling with eager anticipation now.

'Not as much as I'd have expected.' Aurore hesitated. 'I did get some distinctly disturbing vibes though. 'I don't quite know how to explain this: what I was getting was mostly – *dark*.'

'Dark?' Simone echoed.

'Yes. I had the distinct impression of danger – danger for the owner of the earring. But – and this is odd – I couldn't seem to get any further. It was almost as if the channel was blocked in some way. The more I tried to open my mind and clarify what I was feeling, the more I felt I was coming up against a brick wall.'

Simone's skin crawled suddenly as she remembered the electric shock which had made her drop the earring. She'd had a frightening premonition of danger, too.

'I can't really understand it,' Aurore went on. 'I've never felt quite so shut out before. But then it occurred to me to wonder if the reason I couldn't get anywhere is because all the cosmic energy is being channelled in your direction.'

Simone's heart sank. She had been banking on Aurore's being able to help. But now the suggestion that whatever was happening was meant for her and her alone made her feel not only desperately disappointed but also suddenly sceptical again. It was ridiculous beyond belief! And yet . . . for all that she couldn't deny it was happening.

'Didn't you get anything else at all?' she pressed Aurore.

'Nothing Valerie hadn't already told me. I did feel very strongly that this earring belongs to a very old soul – one who has lived not just once, but many times before. The Cathars were there in my mind, but, considering your home area is such a shrine to them, that is hardly surprising. And as I say, I felt danger, which seemed to be directed at the person to whom the earring belongs – danger, I think, which may be connected with fire. More than that I really can't say.'

Simone ran a hand through her hair absently. She had not yet tied it into the bunch in which she usually wore it and it felt knotty and heavy between her fingers.

'All I can suggest is that you continue to open yourself up to the story and hope that things begin to come clear,' Aurore went on. 'I really think this is meant for you and you alone.'

'But why me?'

'Didn't you say you felt an affinity with the character of Helis – Jeanne's mother?' Aurore asked gently. 'If that is the connection – if you were once Helis – then you would still care very deeply what happens to the soul who was your daughter in that incarnation. Who better than you to try to save her from whatever awful fate it is that she is forced to suffer over and over again?'

'And you think that Esther – the owner of the earring – might once have been Jeanne?'

'I didn't say that. As I see it there are two candidates for that role.'

'And the other one is Hélène.'

'Yes. Look, Simone, I'm going to send the earring back to you so that you can use it to help you get to the bottom of all this. But you must try to relax. The more uptight you are the more difficult it will be. Just open yourself up so that whatever it is can come through. I'll be thinking of you.'

'Thanks. And thank you for trying.'

'Not at all. I only wish I could be of more help.'

Simone replaced the receiver and sank to the floor, drawing her knees up to her chin and wondering again about the present-day identities of the souls who had once been Jeanne and Alazais. Surely if one of them had once been her daughter she would recognise her? But she didn't – she didn't!

Of course, looking at it logically – if logic had any place in all this! – Helis Marty had never known Alazais, so the feeling of familiarity she had experienced on meeting Esther would indicate that it was she who had been Jeanne. Yet it was Alazais who had stolen the love of Jeanne's life, and if this was a modern replay of the same scenario, then it would point to Esther as the more likely candidate for Alazais. As for the fact that both she and Aurore had sensed danger for Esther, she couldn't make head or tail of that either. What possible danger could Esther be in? It was Hélène who seemed under threat in all kinds of ways. Unless of course there was danger for both of them. But what – what?

Simone raised her head, rubbing her eyes. She felt confused and helpless, and the dreadful certainty that events were gathering pace towards some tragic and inevitable conclusion was stronger than ever. The only thing she could do was to try to look in on the past again and hope for enlightenment, but she didn't want to do it. The story, when she was seeing it, was so real – and somehow she knew instinctively that there had been no happy ending for any of them. Simone shivered, dreading the thought of witnessing some horrific scene, but knowing she had no choice. If the relentless turn of the Wheel of Karma was to be halted she must steel herself to face the past and learn the lessons it was so desperate to teach.

But Simone wished with all her heart that it was not so.

Esther had had a long lazy bath. She was feeling pleasantly relaxed, both from the warm scented water and the aftermath of lovemaking, not only last night but this morning too, and she thought that she was ready to face whatever the day might throw at her. But as she came downstairs she could hear Alain on the telephone, and instantly her hackles were up again. He was talking about Hélène – she was sure of it.

'No, there's still no reply,' Alain was saying. 'No – I don't know if she's with Simone. I've tried to ring her but her line is engaged. To be honest, I really don't know what to do for the best.'

Esther glared at Alain's back, hurt and angry. So he was still worrying about Hélène. She went into the kitchen, found some orange juice in the fridge, and poured a glass for herself. She didn't feel like pouring one for Alain. Let him fend for himself!

'Who were you on the phone to?' she asked aggressively when he joined her a few minutes later.

'Valerie. I wanted to see if she knew where Hélène is.'

'Oh! I see!'

'Don't start that again, please, Esther!' Alain sounded exasperated. 'I'm very concerned about her. In her present state there's no knowing what she might do.'

Esther turned away, biting her tongue to stop herself saying something she would later regret. And in any case, what was the point of going over it all again?

'Valerie did tell me something else, though,' he said, reaching for the orange juice. 'That son of Bob Slater's – the one who's staying with him . . .'

'Andrew, you mean?' She felt a stab of guilt as she realised she hadn't told Alain that she had spent yesterday evening with him.

'It seems he's an investigative journalist – prying into Thierry's death. God knows what he thinks there is to pry into, but apparently he went to see Valerie on the pretext of buying one of her paintings, and he's been asking questions right, left and centre. It was probably his idea Bob and Diana asked us to lunch.'

'Andrew Slater – an investigative journalist?' Esther repeated, shocked.

'Yes, and you can just see the juicy story it would make, can't you?' Alain went on bitterly. 'Dishing the dirt on a man who can no longer defend himself and writing the obituary of Lavaur Wines at the same time. What a way to earn a living!'

'I can't believe it,' Esther said. She had really liked Andrew Slater, been grateful to him for his apparent kindness, and all the time . . .

Alain sighed.

'Anyway, let's forget about that for the moment. We'll have breakfast and then I'll ring Simone.'

'About Hélène.' Her voice was dangerously hard.

'I'm sorry, Esther, really I am. But if she's gone missing we have to find her. You must see that.'

He reached for her hand across the table and she jerked it away, making a pretence of reaching for a croissant.

All she could see was that everything she'd hoped for was falling apart around her and the time was fast approaching when it would be too late to ever put it back together again.

Simone lit one of the joss sticks Valerie had left and stuck it into the pot plant. No use putting off the moment any longer: she would have no peace of mind until she got to the bottom of whatever it was that was happening to her.

She lay down on the sofa, pulling a cushion under her head. Think. Drift. Esther and Hélène. Jeanne and Alazais. Once again they are in love with the same man. Whatever happened then must happen again . . . and again . . .

She stared at the thin spiral of smoke from the joss stick curling up into the shaft of sunlight. Smoke. Fire. Somehow fire came into this. But how? No, don't try to force it. Let it come of its own accord. Drift . . . drift . . .

Something was moving in the shaft of sunlight, small and dark. A dust mote? No – it was growing larger, taking shape. A bird. Small, graceful, deadly. Simone jerked convulsively. A bird – in the house? She must try to get it out. But she could not move. Her limbs felt like lead, her head lay heavy against the cushions. The bird wasn't here at all. It was outside, flying free against a clear blue sky. But it wasn't real. It wasn't alive. It hadn't been alive for nearly eight hundred years. The bird was a hawk and it belonged in the past.

The story had begun again. Simone breathed deeply, fixing her eyes upon it, and let the scene unfold.

The hawk hovered, dark and graceful, against the blue September sky, then swooped with deadly precision, and the young man who had flown her let out a cry of triumph.

'A kill!' He urged his horse forward, swinging the weighted

lure with easy grace. The sun, high in the sky but not yet overhead for noon, caught the gold thread with which his tunic was embroidered and highlighted the reddish tints in his hair.

Watching him, Jeanne felt her heart swell with pride and she thought that now, more than ever, she enjoyed hawking. As a young girl she had thrilled to the feel of the powerful talons gripping her wrist through the heavy leather gauntlet and she had thought there was nothing to match the satisfaction of flying a bird as wild and free as her magnificent little merlin. Now, though she knew she could still match any of the party kill for kill when she chose, her chief pleasure came from quite another direction. Instead of being in the forefront, eager to be close to the quarry when the beaters made it fly, she restrained her pony, watching proudly as Bernard displayed the skills Philip had taught him.

It was three years now since they had returned to Montaugure and in that time Bernard had not only grown from a child to a young man but changed from a peasant to something resembling a prince, and Jeanne, marvelling at the ease with which the transformation had taken place, could only suppose that it was the noble blood that ran in his veins that had made it possible. Not that he had been easily persuaded to leave the farm. He had fought fiercely for the right to remain on the land he regarded not only as his home but also his inheritance, and it had taken all her powers of persuasion to talk him into giving Philip – and Montaugure – a chance. But it had not been long before sulks and truculence were replaced by enthusiasm for the new way of life.

Bernard had learned to ride with the same ease as Jeanne had done, and disappeared to the stables with the same regularity. Philip had arranged for a tutor to teach him to read and write, and though he was always bursting with impatience to leave his books and be back in the saddle, Bernard had proved a quick and able pupil. Philip rewarded his diligence in the classroom with lessons of his own which Bernard found much more to his taste: lessons in swordplay, jousting – and falconry. Soon he had trained his own bird – a long-winged peregrine falcon taken from the wild before she had learned to fly. He could sport now with the best of them, and Jeanne was content to keep the hood on her own bird and leave her son to take the glory.

'He's quick, that one!' she said proudly. She turned to Alazais, at whose side she rode, and noticed with a slight twist of irritation how pale she looked.

Why did she insist on riding with the hunt? Jeanne wondered. Alazais was no horsewoman and it was obvious she liked hawking even less now than she had done as a girl. The sight of the hawks taking defenceless smaller birds never failed to upset her, and though she was doing her best to hide it, Jeanne knew that today was no exception. As the feathered corpse of Bernard's latest kill was trussed with the others Alazais turned her head away, closing her eyes briefly.

Perhaps she comes along because she does not trust me alone with Philip, Jeanne thought. Not that they would be alone, of course, since Bernard and at least a dozen grooms and austringers rode with them, not to mention the men on foot who went ahead to beat the bushes. But at least Alazais's presence ensured there could be no private conversation between them.

As quickly as the thought occurred to her, however, she dismissed it. Jealousy and suspicion had no place in Alazais's nature. When Philip had brought Jeanne and Bernard home with him Alazais had given no sign of anything other than delight at seeing Jeanne again, and she appeared not to have noticed Bernard's resemblance to Philip, which Jeanne thought so strikingly obvious. Perhaps he did not look as much like his father as she liked to think, Jeanne thought grudgingly, since no one else appeared to have noticed it. But then again, Alazais was too good-natured to think ill of anyone, much least her husband and the girl she called her oldest friend, too naive still to see what Jeanne felt sure was written all over her face whenever she looked at Philip.

But at least Alazais need not worry about Philip's faithfulness to her now. Since bringing Jeanne home he had never once put a foot out of line. He still cared for her, she felt sure; sometimes when their eyes met it was all there just as it had always been – the love and the longing, unspoken messages from the heart. But these exchanges were fleeting. In that very instant of awareness Philip's defences would rise, impregnable as the portcullis which guarded the entrance to the castle. To Philip, chivalry and honour were more important than the dictates of the heart. He had betrayed Alazais once. He would not do so again.

His stubborn denial of her hurt Jeanne but she had made up

her mind that this was the price she must pay in order to secure Bernard's future. And besides, did she not love Philip for what he was? If he had been an unprincipled philanderer he would not have been the man she had adored for as long as she could remember. But she longed, all the same, to have a little time alone with him and Bernard so that she could pretend that all her dreams had come true and make-believe they were a proper family.

She glanced again at Alazais's set pale face.

'I don't know why you come hawking,' she said, a little impatiently. 'You know you hate it.'

A faint colour rose in Alazais's cheeks and, surprised, Jeanne realised she was blushing.

'I have a special reason for accompanying the hunt today,' she confessed. 'This may be the last time for some while. I have something to tell you, Jeanne. Some very surprising news.' She hesitated briefly, then suddenly her face was wreathed in smiles. 'Something has occurred which I had begun to think never would. I am with child.'

'Sancta Maria!'

Jeanne could not have been more shocked if Alazais had struck her. Sensing her agitation, the merlin stirred uneasily on her wrist and she raised a hand to soothe her though her mind was racing and the muscles of her stomach tying themselves into knots.

'The baby will be born at Eastertide,' Alazais was saying. 'I have not told Philip yet but I know he will be as excited as I am. Just think, Jeanne, all these years and we thought I was barren! Now . . . oh, isn't it wonderful? I can scarcely believe it, and I know Philip will feel the same. To have a child of his own at last!'

Oh dear God, the pain of it! Bad enough to have to watch the door of the bedchamber close after Philip and Alazais and know they were lying together as man and wife, but this . . . !

A child of his own. A legitimate child who would usurp Bernard as his heir. Jeanne wanted to scream at the injustice of it. She had given up the farm, dragged Bernard north, endured the humiliation of living at Montaugure as Alazais's companion and the heartache of watching her exercise her privileges as Philip's wife, and all for the sake of Bernard's future. Now, with those few words, the whole carefully constructed edifice had crumbled about her like a house built of sand.

'Tell me you are happy for me, Jeanne!' Alazais murmured eagerly. 'I shall need you more than ever now – after all, you have experience in these matters while I . . . I am a little afraid, I must confess. I am no longer young to bear a child for the first time. But the physician says I have good wide hips and I should have no trouble.'

'I am sure you will not,' Jeanne said, scarcely able to keep the bitterness out of her tone. Alazais was one of the healthiest women she had ever met. Her ancestors had not left her the legacy of weakness through too much intermarriage as was the case in many high-bred families, but neither had she suffered the deprivations of poverty and hunger. No, Alazais would carry her baby to full term and produce a fine bonny child if Jeanne knew anything about it. If it was a boy it would mean the end of her hopes that Bernard would be Philip's heir; and even if it were not, who was to say that having fallen pregnant once Alazais would not fall pregnant again? With the spell broken she could produce a child a year for the next decade and beyond . . .

Oh, I can't let it happen! Jeanne thought desperately. Somehow I'll find a way to make sure Bernard inherits what is rightfully his! But for the moment she had no idea how she would manage it.

From the bushes away to her right a small bird suddenly rose with a frightened flutter and quick as a flash Jeanne pulled the hood from her merlin's head and released the jesses. As the merlin swooped mercilessly on her pitiful prey she heard Alazais's involuntary gasp and gritted her teeth in satisfaction. For the moment the vicarious violence was the only release for her pent-up rage and frustration.

Something was calling her back, sending the figures of Jeanne and Alazais away into the shadows. The joss stick was still burning, sending its thin spiral of smoke upwards to fan out in the slight breeze coming from the open window.

For a moment Simone stared at it, bemused, then she twisted her head sharply against the cushions. The telephone. That was what had disturbed her. She had forgotten to take it off the hook before attempting to enter her trance; now it was shrilling imperiously.

Simone swung her legs down from the sofa and stood up, too quickly, so that the room went away from her once more, and she grabbed the back of a nearby chair to steady herself. Then she hurried across the room, disorientated still, yet desperate to reach the telephone before it stopped ringing. She hated it when that happened, hated being left wondering who it was who had tried to get in touch and given up. A bit like what was happening to her with the story, really. She didn't know who was trying to get in touch with her through that, either.

She grabbed the receiver, holding it to her ear with a hand that felt clumsy.

'Hello?'

'Simone.' It was Alain. 'Is Hélène with you?'

'Hélène? No. Why?' Simone felt the first stirrings of alarm.

'She's not at home. She wasn't there last evening either and I don't think she's been back all night. I was hoping you might know where she was.'

'Sorry, I don't.'

'Well, if she turns up there, will you let me know?'

'Of course.'

She put down the telephone, very frightened now. Had it begun, whatever it was that was going to happen? The sense of urgency pounded in her temples and she wondered briefly if she should go out and look for Hélène. But there were others who could do that. She was the only one who could unlock the secret of the past – and with it, the future.

Simone took the telephone off the hook and returned to the sofa, lying down again. She must try to recreate the trance. If Alain had not chosen that moment to ring perhaps she would have learned the ending of the story; unwittingly his anxiety for Hélène had hindered the one thing that might save her.

Simone stared at the spiral of smoke from the joss stick, willing it to induce the pictures to begin again. But try as she might, they refused to come.

Esther stood at the window looking out at the bright sunshine and feeling utterly fed up. It was almost an hour since Alain had gone out to search for Hélène.

'I've got to find her and make sure she's all right,' he had said. 'I'm seriously worried. Do you want to come with me?'

Esther had looked at him, his eyes hooded with anxiety and deep lines etching themselves into his tanned skin between nose and mouth, and thought with a sinking heart that whatever he might say to the contrary, Alain cared a good deal more for Hélène than he cared to admit, perhaps even to himself.

'No,' she said shortly. 'I'll stay here.'

'All right. I'll be back as soon as I can.'

He kissed her briefly but it was obvious his mind was elsewhere and as she watched his car go away down the drive she was overcome with anger and despair. She'd come to France as he'd asked – and as she'd wanted – but she had achieved nothing. He was no nearer to asking Hélène for a divorce than he had ever been. In fact, if he was so concerned about Hélène's mental stability, he probably never would. He'd procrastinate for ever, afraid of pushing her over the edge. But if he thought Esther was going to put up with such a state of affairs then he was very much mistaken. She wasn't going to go on playing second fiddle to a neurotic wife for the rest of her life. She wasn't sure she was going to put up with it any longer at all.

I'm going home, Esther thought with sudden resolve. I'll ring the airport now, while he's out, and find out about flights. If he comes home and finds me gone perhaps he'll realise I'm not prepared to be messed about any more. And do something about it.

She picked up the phone; put it down again, racked once more with indecision. If she went without even saying goodbye there was always the chance she would never see him again and even now, when she was so angry that she felt she almost hated him, that prospect was unbearable. Besides, by going away she could be playing right into Hélène's hands. Perhaps it was worth staying to give him one last ultimatum. She might end up hurt and humiliated again, but at least she would have given it her best shot. If she didn't, she might end up regretting it for the rest of her life.

She was still wandering about the house, trying to make up her mind whether to go or stay, when she heard a car on the drive. She hurried out, hoping it was Alain, but it was only the man from the garage in the village returning the Saab.

Esther was surprised to see it back so soon – the pace of life here in Languedoc was so leisurely she had thought it would be days if not weeks before the little garage got round to sorting it out. But the man was alone and even without his elaborate pantomime language it was obvious that he expected to be driven back to the village.

Esther took the keys from him and he piled comfortably into the passenger seat beside her, chattering a stream of colloquial French that she found totally unintelligible. It was only as she was dropping him off that it occurred to her that she had left the house unlocked and not even thought about it. Obviously some of the casual attitude of this part of the world was rubbing off on her too. No one seemed to bother with locking doors during the day. So why had Alain been so concerned about Hélène's house being open? Because it must mean she had left it during the hours of daylight, presumably, intending to be back before dark. Or because something had happened to make her go out in too much of a hurry to think about it later on.

Esther turned the car on the garage forecourt and started back on the road to Le Château Gris, still thinking about it. She simply didn't understand the situation with Hélène, didn't understand where she was coming from – apart from her obvious desire to get back with Alain – didn't understand why all the Lavaurs seemed so obsessed with her. Their anxiety for her wellbeing bordered on the unreasonable, as if there was some hidden agenda no one ever actually mentioned.

Esther sighed, her determination to fight Hélène for Alain threatened again by a feeling of hopelessness. She simply couldn't see how she could ever win when Hélène had this kind of psychological hold over him. She might as well be beating her head against a brick wall.

Once again the inner turmoil began. Go home, Esther. Call it a day. No – I can't! Why should I? He asked me here – he *must* care. If only he would see he doesn't have to feel so responsible for Hélène we could still make it work . . .

She turned into the drive and gasped, hardly able to believe her eyes. Surely that was Hélène's car drawn up on the turnaround? No sign, though, of Alain's. He was obviously still out looking for her.

Esther parked and headed for the house, spoiling for a confrontation. The kitchen door, which she had left unlocked, was ajar, but there was no sign of Hélène. Neither was she in the salon.

'Hélène – where are you?' she called.

A sound from upstairs. Alarm flared as she remembered Alain's concern that Hélène might 'do something stupid'. That wasn't what all this was about, was it? She hadn't come here with the intention of—

Esther ran up the stairs.

'Hélène! Are you there?'

'Yes, I'm just coming . . .' Hélène's voice, a little breathless, but also somehow reassuringly normal, seemed to be coming from the room Alain used as a study. Esther made for it and met Hélène in the doorway coming out. Her face was pale, her long hair untidy and windswept. She was carrying a sheaf of papers, envelopes and files thrust into an untidy pile.

'What on earth are you doing?' Esther asked.

'Nothing. Just getting some things I need . . .' Her expression was a mixture of guilt and defiance.

'Alain is out looking for you. Where have you been?'

'Nowhere . . . you can tell Alain I'm perfectly all right.'

'And what's all that stuff you've got there?'

But even as she said it a thought occurred to her. Had Hélène accepted that a divorce was inevitable? Was she taking away financial documents with a view to briefing her solicitor as to what she could expect in the way of settlement?

'You can't just go off with papers that belong to Alain,' she said. 'He's not going to like that.'

'They're not Alain's.' A faint pink colour had risen in Hélène's pale cheeks. 'They're Thierry's. Excuse me please . . .'

A little flustered, she went to push past Esther and some of the sheaf of papers slid off the pile and fell to the floor. 'Now look what you've made me do!' she said sharply.

She dropped to her knees, scrabbling them up, and Esther noticed what looked like a passport among them.

'Hélène, I don't know what you think you're doing . . .'

'I told you! I'm just getting some things that belong to Thierry. Now will you please let me go? I'm in a hurry.'

She gathered up the papers, holding them firmly now, squeezed past Esther and headed for the stairs.

'Hélène!' Esther called after her, but she took no notice.

Esther went into the study, looking for signs of disturbance, and saw a box file she recognised as the one Hélène had brought for Alain lying open on the desk. Perhaps all she had taken were papers belonging to her brother, then, but it was an odd thing to do all the same. It would have made much more sense for her to ask Alain for anything she needed.

But then there was something decidedly odd about Hélène's behaviour altogether. Where had she been last night? Why had she gone off leaving the house unlocked? And more to the point, where was she going now in such a hurry? Suddenly Esther was determined to find out. The last thing she wanted was for Hélène to disappear again. If she did, Alain would probably still be worried enough to go on looking for her, and though Esther wished heartily that Hélène would disappear permanently she knew it would not solve anything.

She ran downstairs. Hélène had already left the house, and by the time Esther reached the back door she heard the engine of Hélène's car spark into life.

With the intention of following her, Esther hurried back inside, searching in vain for the keys of the Saab, before remembering: she had probably left them in the ignition in her haste to find out what Hélène was doing at the house.

She ran outside. Hélène was already disappearing down the drive. Esther yanked open the door of the Saab; as she had thought, the keys were in the ignition panel between the front seats. She turned it and the engine fired at once, but by the time she had executed a three-point turn – not easy since the car was old and heavy and had no power steering – Hélène was out of sight.

Esther swore, jamming the gear stick into first and shooting forward down the drive. If she didn't manage to catch Hélène before she reached the lane she wouldn't know which way she had gone.

Luck was with her. Hélène must have had to give way to passing traffic, for as Esther rounded the bend in the drive she saw her pulling away and turning right.

When she reached the junction herself the way was clear and she pulled out, thrusting her foot flat to the floor as she followed the red car along the lane. Then, as she saw Hélène follow the curving crash barriers down on to the main road, she eased up, matching her speed to the Renault and allowing overtaking traffic to slot in between them. She didn't want to get close enough for Hélène to realise she was being followed in case she panicked her into driving recklessly. But where on earth was she going?

Not to her own home, certainly. That was in quite the opposite direction!

The road had been cut through a relatively flat band of the valley floor; it stretched into the distance straight as a flattened silver ribbon, and it was easy to keep Hélène's car in view. Then, when they had covered what Esther judged to be four or five miles, it turned left across the full width of the carriageway, heading towards the mountains, and was quickly lost to view. Esther put her foot down once more and screamed across the junction, narrowly missing a lorry laden with farm produce which was coming in the opposite direction.

This road, narrower, and lined with the now familiar London planes, their trunks marked with white reflector paint, ran straight for a while past open pasture land and vineyards, then wound through a village and past a country *auberge* before beginning a winding ascent to higher ground. On several occasions the red Renault disappeared from sight but each time, just as she thought she had lost it, she would catch a glimpse of it ahead of her.

The countryside was wild now, with hardly a sign of civilisation but for the occasional isolated farm or cottage and the inevitable Cathar ruins, some distant, one so close that she seemed to pass directly beneath it. For a moment she took her eyes off the road, looking up at the battered grey-stone tower surrounded by bushes of bright yellow gorse, and felt overwhelmed by a deep feeling of sadness. Then she was concentrating on the road once more and wondering where she was exactly and how far they had come. She should have checked the milometer before starting out – it would have helped to give her some indication of her whereabouts – but in her haste it had not crossed her mind. The one thing she was sure of was that it was a long way.

She glanced anxiously at the petrol gauge. It was showing almost on the red and she had no idea of the capacity of the reserve tank. Well, useless to worry about that now. After coming this far she had no intention of giving up unless she had to.

She was a good deal closer to the red car now – it had slowed down considerably, she realised. She slowed too. The car turned left into a narrow track and Esther crawled up to the junction in order to read the name on the rickety white signpost. Marteilleuse. She'd never heard of it but she tried to memorise it anyway as she swung her own car left into the track.

The hedges were high and thick here, obscuring most of the view except the lower slopes of the mountains, which rose green and verdant above them. As she rounded a bend she saw another track, even narrower than the one she was on, leading away to the right. Had Hélène turned into it? She couldn't be sure. She slowed, hesitated, and took a chance, bumping over the rather uneven surface.

The track led on for about half a mile and Esther cursed, beginning to think she must have made the wrong choice. But the track wasn't wide enough to turn around in. She'd just have to go on. And then, quite suddenly, through a gap in the hedge she saw it – a low ramshackle old farmhouse and Hélène's car, pulled up outside.

Esther braked to a stop, puzzled as to what on earth Hélène could be doing in such a God-forsaken place. It appeared to be totally deserted – no other cars drawn up outside, no tractor or produce lorry, no sign of farm animals or machinery. She sat for a moment, looking through the gap in the hedge and wondering what to do. Then, making up her mind, she eased the Saab into gear again and crawled into the farmyard.

As she came to a stop Hélène appeared in the doorway of the farmhouse. Something in her manner suggested eagerness as well as her earlier tight-strung nervous tension, but when she realised it was Esther she stopped short, her face falling.

'Oh – it's you. What are you doing here? Did you follow me?'

'Yes,' Esther said flatly. 'Alain's wasted enough time already looking for you.'

'Well he shouldn't!' Hélène said fiercely. 'What I do and where I go is my own business.'

'I couldn't agree more,' Esther said, hope springing. Perhaps Hélène was beginning to accept after all that their marriage was over. 'But the fact is he was worried. He thought something might have happened to you when you didn't go home last night . . .' She broke off, realising she no longer had Hélène's attention.

She was staring in the direction of the lane, her head cocked to one side as if she were listening, her expression the same mixture of eagerness and anxiety as it had been when she had come rushing out of the farmhouse a few minutes earlier. From somewhere in the distance came the hum of a motor engine, but it was growing fainter, not coming closer, and Esther saw Hélène's face fall again.

It was obvious she was expecting someone, and again Esther felt a flicker of hope. Could it be a man? To choose such an out-of-the-way place for a meeting implied a need for secrecy. Perhaps Hélène had someone else, a secret lover she didn't want Alain – or anyone – to know about. But what was the point in that? She had as much right to a new relationship as Alain. The only possible explanation was that she didn't want him to know so that she could retain her hold over him for some reason – emotional, or financial, or both.

Well, the time had come to put a stop to her games, sort things out once and for all. And this was as good an opportunity as any.

'Hélène, I really think you and I should have a talk,' she said firmly.

'Perhaps, but not now.' Hélène turned towards the farmhouse and Esther followed her, determined not to let this chance slip away.

'Yes, now. There's no point putting it off any longer.'

The expression on Hélène's face was a mixture of indecision and something that might almost have been panic. Then she shrugged helplessly and turned back towards the farmhouse.

'All right. I suppose you had better come in.'

22

SIMONE HAD ALMOST given up hope of re-creating the trance which Alain's telephone call had interrupted when she became aware of a faint musty smell quite unlike the scent of the joss stick or the perfumes of the garden wafting in through the open windows. She wrinkled her nose, sniffing and trying to identify it. Damp. It smelled like damp. She shivered, and realised suddenly that she was cold, her skin clammy, her whole body aching with a chill that seemed to have crept right into her bones.

She tried to move, with some idea of closing the window, though she could not understand why the weather should have changed in this way, but her limbs refused to obey her and her eyes remained fixed on the thin spiral of smoke from the joss stick. Beyond her focus the walls of the room seemed to be changing, so that they were no longer the familiar rose-patterned design which she had meant for so long to replace with something lighter and more modern, disappearing into swirling darkness and reforming into bare rough stone which dripped with water. Under cover of the darkness something scuttled noisily – a mouse? A rat? Simone was aware only that after the hours of trying unsuccessfully to conjure it up, the past was opening up for her once more.

A feeling of dread crept through her along with the cold, and for a moment she found herself wanting to resist being drawn into the scene which she had tried so hard to recreate. Useless. She should have known it would be. The horrific climax of the story from the past was fast approaching and Simone knew that now she had no choice but to be a witness to it.

Jeanne awoke from a fitful sleep with a start, unable for the moment to think where she was or why she felt so cramped and cold. Then, as she looked around the small dark cell in which she found herself, at the walls, bare and running with water, she remembered, all of a rush.

Carcassonne. After all these years she was back in La Cité – not in an *ostal*, as she had been as a child, but in the dungeons of Le Mur – the prison. Someone had betrayed her. Someone had given her name to the inquisitors as one who had been born a Cathar and was still a believer. Two days ago the inquisitors had come and demanded she go with them for questioning. In spite of their threats and silky efforts at persuasion she had resisted them, denying all knowledge of any other heretics, denying her faith – and despising herself for doing so. But they had not been satisfied. They had brought her here to Carcassonne and locked her in this hell-hole to await further questioning.

At the very thought, Jeanne quailed inwardly. She would never satisfy them – never – and the longer she held out, the more severe her punishment would be. At the very least she could face years of incarceration in a prison such as this one, or be forced to wear the yellow cross to mark her out as a Cathar and as such an outcast for the rest of her days; at worst . . . Jeanne shivered. Everyone knew the fate of heretics who refused to confess and recant. They were burned at the stake.

Who had given her name to the inquisition? she wondered wretchedly. Could it be that Agnes had been captured and tortured? But she could not believe that Agnes would ever betray her no matter what they did to her. Her faith was too strong. No, it was more likely to have been a servant, or someone who had known her long ago. The inquisitors were well known for investigating the most tenuous of links with the heresy stretching back generations.

This thought, too, chilled her. Supposing the shadow should fall on Bernard? He was still a child, but religious zeal took no heed of that. If anything should happen to Bernard . . .

No, Philip would not let it! she thought fiercely. Bernard was Philip's own flesh and blood, and he would fight for him, trading the indulgences he had received for his part in the ill-fated Italian crusade for Bernard's safety. But even this gave her scant comfort. The Bertrands had once fought with the Count of Toulouse against Simon de Montfort and, though the Count was once more allied with the Church of Rome, memories were long. And in any case, Philip was not even at Montaugure at present. He was away in France, visiting his mother, and as yet knew nothing of what had happened.

Slowly, painfully, she eased herself up from the rough ledge which had formed her bed. She had slept clad only in her thin shift and covered with her cloak for she had been determined not to appear for her questioning today in a crumpled gown. As she put her weight on her cramped legs a sharp pain shot through her knee and she winced, catching her breath. The wound she had sustained so long ago when she had fallen on to the handcart had never healed properly and it still caused her trouble from time to time. But that was the least of her worries just now. Even the fact that Alazais carried a child who could usurp Bernard as Philip's heir had paled into insignificance against the enormity of her predicament.

Somewhere within the prison a barred door clanged hollowly and Jeanne reached hastily for her gown. Perhaps the inquisitors were coming for her; she did not want them to find her here in nothing but her shift! She pulled it over her head, shrinking from the cold damp feel of the fabric, and heard the key rasp in the lock of her cell.

The door swung open, and by the flaring light of the wall sconces in the passageway outside she saw the short squat figure of her gaoler. He was grinning, and Jeanne felt herself blush from head to foot as she wondered whether he had been watching through some peephole as she dressed herself. But she raised her head proudly, determined not to give him the satisfaction of seeing her embarrassment – or her fear.

'Am I to be allowed water to wash myself?' she demanded. 'And what of breakfast? Do you intend me to die of hunger and thirst?'

The man shrugged, jangling his bunch of keys.

'My orders are to take you for questioning. No doubt my masters will decide whether or not you have earned such luxuries.'

He led the way along the dungeon passage and up a flight of uneven stone steps to a small chamber which was bare but for a scrubbed-wood table, two chairs and a three-legged stool. Outside the narrow window, set with bars, the sky was grey and lowering, the dawn light a curious ochre as if the rain which lashed the countryside might turn to snow before the day was out.

Jeanne stood erect, trying not to shiver, and a few moments later two Dominican friars entered the chamber. The face of one was hidden by the folds of his cowl, but she recognised the other as the monk who had interrogated her the previous day, a middle-aged man with thin patrician features, pale skin and huge cavernous eyes. He looked like a death's head, she thought. His vows might prevent him from carrying out the sentence of death – that was left to the secular arm of the Inquisition, the soldiers – but she felt sure that he gained pleasure from its pronouncement, and her heart turned over with a fresh wave of dread.

He moved now to the carved chair, seeming almost to glide as his habit brushed the bare floor, and indicated that she should approach the desk.

'So.' His lips were tight, sneering. 'Did you sleep well, madame?'

'What do you think?' She tried to speak boldly but her throat was dry and her voice came out a mere whisper.

'I am the one who asks the questions, and if you are wise and give me some answers, you may yet save yourself.'

She moistened her parched lips with her tongue but still her voice cracked. 'I know nothing of interest to you.'

'Oh come!' He spoke impatiently now. 'It is known to this court that you lived until a few years ago in the village of Montsegur. That is a hotbed of heretics, surely you would agree?'

'I was the widow of a poor farmer, Father. I worked the land to provide for myself and my son. I had no time for consorting with my neighbours and certainly no time for gossip and speculation.'

'No time, either, for the sacraments. No time to attend Mass.' She was silent. 'Very well. Let us turn our attention to more recent times. You have been living these past four years with the Bertrand family at Montaugure.'

Her heart thudded painfully. She had been right. It was the Bertrands the Inquisition was interested in. A noble heretic would be worth a good deal more to them, both in prestige and in the value of lands to confiscate, than a few poor peasants.

'I have lived with them, yes, as I lived with them as a child. But the Bertrands are good Catholics. Father Benet, Sir Bernard's brother, was a priest.'

'Perhaps not all of the family follow his example.'

Agnes! she thought. Was that what he was getting at? But Agnes was a Perfect, who did nothing to hide her faith. If Agnes had been arrested, Jeanne's testimony would not be needed in order to convict her.

'You were a Cathar – we know it. The name of Marty has appeared not once but many times in the testimonies of those who have helped us with our enquiries. If a blind eye was turned to your heretical origins it is safe to assume the Bertrands were similarly sympathetic to others of the same persuasion.'

'No!' Jeanne said fiercely.

'Ah!' He smiled triumphantly. 'And you would take an oath to that effect?'

Jeanne lowered her eyes. This was a trap; the interrogators were well aware that it was against the creed of a Cathar to swear an oath.

The friar leaned towards her across the table, his hollow eyes boring into hers.

'You are a Cathar and those who sheltered you are Cathar sympathisers. There is no point denying it. Give me a full confession – and you will be spared. Defy me – and I swear you will be purged of your sin in the way the church has prescribed. You will go to the stake, madame.'

Fear turned her blood to ice.

'No – please!' she whispered. 'I was born a Cathar, I confess it. If you wish me to I will recant . . .'

His lips twisted in a thin smile.

'I am glad to hear it. But I am afraid your penitence is no longer enough. I must have the names of those who protected you – and your sworn testimony so that they may be dealt with accordingly.'

Jeanne stared at him, horrified. Was he asking her to betray Philip? Was that to be the price of her life? Well, she wouldn't do it – no matter what they did to her!

'The Bertrands are innocent, I swear it!' she said urgently. 'You must believe me! They have done nothing – nothing!'

'Give me a few minutes alone with her, Brother.'

It was the other friar who spoke. In her terror Jeanne had almost forgotten he was there, standing quietly behind her; now he came forward, joining her interrogator on the far side of the table. The interrogator glanced up at him, neatening with bony fingers the parchment which he had laid out ready for her confession.

'Alone?'

The second friar nodded and the two men's eyes locked for a moment in silent communication. Then the interrogator rose, straightening his habit.

'I hope my brother can make you see the error of your ways where I cannot.'

As the door closed behind him, the second monk slipped into the chair he had vacated and Jeanne glanced at him fearfully through lowered lashes. What now? Why did this man want to speak to her alone? What new torture had he in store for her?

'Sit down,' he instructed her.

A stool stood in a corner. Jeanne dragged it to the desk and sank on to it. She did not think her legs would have supported her much longer.

'I have waited a long while for this moment. I must say I never envisaged that it would come under circumstances such as these.'

She looked up at him, puzzled.

The face which looked back at her was young and handsome, the eyebrows thick and reddish over eyes of a curiously piercing grey. There was something familiar about that face, though she could not place it, nor explain the nerve which jarred somewhere deep inside her.

The monk thrust back his cowl and she saw a tonsure of red hair.

'Well?' He smiled faintly and the nerve jarred again, making her catch her breath. She could not believe the thought which was beginning to take shape in her mind. She was going mad – fear had unhinged her!

'Who are you?' she whispered.

'Don't you recognise me?' he asked. 'No, I don't suppose you do. It is too long since you last saw me and I have changed a good deal since then. I am your brother. I am Pons.'

The room swam around her. Pons – it couldn't be! Yet she knew without doubt that it was.

'You need water.' He poured some into a goblet from a pitcher which stood on the table beside him and passed it to her. She gulped at it, her hands trembling so much that droplets ran down her chin and drizzled on to her chest at the deep neck of her gown. Then she set down the goblet and reached across the table for his hands, tears of happiness streaming down her cheeks.

'Pons – oh Pons! I don't believe it! I thought you were dead!'

He withdrew his hands, tucking them into the folds of his sleeves to prevent her from touching them.

'Did the Bertrands not tell you I came looking for you?' His voice was curiously cold, reflecting none of her own tumultuous emotions.

'You came looking for me? When?'

'Four years ago I went to Montaugure. I spoke with the Lady Alazais. She told me you had left and she did not know where you were.'

'Oh!' Jeanne was faintly puzzled. She could guess why Alazais had denied any knowledge of her whereabouts; to have said Jeanne was at Montsegur could have incriminated them both. But why had Alazais not told her of Pons's visit? Still, it hardly mattered now. 'Oh Pons, I thought this was the worst day of my life and it has turned out to be the best! You don't know how I've blamed myself for leaving you that day, how I've tortured myself all these years wondering what had happened. And now you are here! It's a miracle! But all the same . . .' She gazed at him in wonder. 'I can't believe you are a Dominican! What happened to make you change your faith?'

He laughed shortly. 'I have not changed my faith – at least, not knowingly. I have always been a Catholic.'

'But . . .' she broke off, realising what must have happened. 'Guillemette raised you, I suppose.'

'Yes. Dear Guillemette.' The hard lines of his face softened briefly. 'Without her I don't know what would have become of me. She was as a mother to me.'

'I'm sure she was.' Jeanne could not help remembering how Guillemette, with no children of her own, had always tried to wean Pons away from his family, even when Helis had been alive. 'But did she never tell you the truth about yourself?'

'Never. I am sure she thought it was best for me not to know. I grew up believing that like her we were innocent victims of the siege. I can't tell you, Jeanne, what a shock it was for me to learn otherwise. You – my whole family – Cathars!' He shook his head in horrified disbelief. 'Still, I suppose it explains why you all abandoned me.'

'But we didn't abandon you, Pons!' Jeanne said urgently. 'Our mother died of the fever – surely Guillemette must have told you that? And you and I were separated when the city fell. I had left you with Guillemette while I went out to search for food and when I got back you were gone.' She shivered as the horror of it reached out to her across the years, sharp as if it had been just yesterday. 'It was terrible! I searched everywhere for you but I couldn't find you. And then Philip Bertrand came upon me, hiding in the woods, and took me with him to Montaugure.'

'Hmm!' Pons was silent; his expression told Jeanne he was still in two minds as to whether or not to believe her.

'It's the truth, Pons, I swear it!' she said. 'I was only a child myself, remember, only eight years old. There was nothing I could do. Guillemette should have known that. She should have told you – we never abandoned you!'

'She wanted to spare me the truth, I expect. And who can blame her?' His face hardened again. 'Cathars!' He almost spat the word. 'It is a heresy, Jeanne. It must be crushed. I became a Dominican in order to help restore our homeland to the Church of Rome, and I must pursue that end with every means at my disposal. Do you not see the untold harm it has done?'

'No!' she said before she could stop herself. 'The harm was done by the Church of Rome, for refusing to allow people to follow their own path. Cathars mean no harm to anyone – they would live peaceably alongside Catholics if only they were allowed.'

'Enough!' She shrank back in shock at his sudden roar. 'Languedoc and Roussillon must be restored to the church. I may have been born a Cathar, God help me, but I swear to you I shall not rest until the last stronghold has been destroyed and the last heretic gone to the stake!'

The fervour in his voice sent a chill through her and she remembered with a sense of shock the predicament she was in. Joy at being reunited with her brother had obliterated her fear; now it returned with a rush, making her stomach fall away and her limbs turn to jelly.

'Pons . . . you wouldn't let them burn *me*, would you?' she whispered.

'That depends.' His eyes, cold and hard, held hers. 'Your fate is not in my hands, but your own. You must show your repentance in order to be saved.'

'But I said I would recant! He . . .' She gestured towards the door. 'He said it wasn't enough.'

'That is true. We need the names of sympathisers from you in order to prove your repentance.'

'But I don't know any . . .'

'The Bertrands, I suggest.'

Jeanne was horrified. 'They are devout Catholics!' She protested. 'I know nothing against them – nothing!'

'Then I advise you to think carefully and remember something. Unless, of course, you wish to be burned at the stake.'

Jeanne folded her arms around herself, speechless with horror. She couldn't believe her own brother could be issuing her with an ultimatum such as this. The sweet small boy she had remembered with such love and longing had become a cold and ruthless man who had not only allied himself with the oppressors of his family's faith but become one of them.

'I couldn't do it!' she whispered. 'I couldn't lie about something like that. Why, Philip's Uncle Benet was a priest . . .'

'That, I am afraid, means nothing.'

'. . . and they took care of me just as Guillemette took care of you. Would you lie about her to save yourself? Would you, Pons?'

He was silent for a moment, fingering the crucifix that hung about his neck. Then his eyes narrowed, giving a sly look to his handsome face.

'Very well, I will make a bargain with you. There is one of the Bertrands I am more concerned with than all the others. The Viscountess Alazais.'

'Alazais!' Jeanne repeated, startled.

'Yes. Now, surely you do not regard her as one of your surrogate family? After all, she denied you, pretending to me that she did not know where you were and omitting to tell you that I was searching for you.'

'I am sure she had her reasons . . .'

His lips tightened. 'I am sure she did. A wilful woman, and an untruthful one. Can you not remember occasions when she has given you cause for suspicion – talk she has turned a deaf ear to, perhaps, heretics she has sheltered under her roof?'

'Alazais!' Jeanne was so shocked that Pons had singled out Philip's wife that clear thought was beyond her. 'But she's as timid as a kitten! She wouldn't . . . she couldn't . . .'

'I advise you to think carefully, Jeanne. There may be a great deal more to Alazais than you think.' His eyes were burning with what looked like an old hatred. 'I said I would make a bargain with you and I will. Give me evidence against her and I will see to it that the others are left in peace. What is more, I will arrange for you to be set free.'

'And if I do not?'

'Then I will find the necessary evidence that they are traitors. It won't be difficult. Philip Bertrand fought with Raymond of Toulouse, I believe. And you, Jeanne – much as it pains me to condemn my own sister, I fear that for your own good I would have no option but to have you relaxed to the secular arm.'

Jeanne felt her stomach knot again with terror. She knew what was meant by 'relaxing to the secular arm'. It was the way the church dealt out the death penalty to those who refused to recant. It would be the military who built the fire and put a torch to the stake. But the sentence was that handed out by the officials of the Inquisition – the Dominicans – of which Pons was now one.

He rose. 'I will have some breakfast sent to you and leave you to think about what I have said. Remember – your life, and the lives of the other Bertrands, depend upon you.'

Left alone, Jeanne buried her face in her hands, her thoughts racing. Pons hadn't even seemed pleased to see her! And why did he want Alazais so badly? Not just because she had lied to him, surely? But Jeanne was certain her brother had meant every word of his unspeakable threats.

As always in times of stress her fingers fumbled for the locket which her mother had entrusted to her so many years ago, and sudden hope sparked. The Star of the Domus – the spirit of the family – which was passed from father to son! If she now gave it to Pons as Helis had intended perhaps he would be touched by its magic!

The guard brought her food and a flagon of rough wine but

though she had not eaten for more than a day Jeanne could not bring herself to touch it.

After a while Pons returned. 'Well?' he demanded.

'Pons, I want you to have this. It is the Star of our Domus.' She slipped the leather thong over her head and held the locket out to him. 'Mother asked me to give it to you when you were grown. Perhaps it will remind you of other times and other loyalties.'

He took it, staring at it for a moment, and hope flared in her heart. Then, with an oath, Pons strode across the chamber to the log fire which spat and flared.

'Sorcery! May God forgive you, Jeanne!'

'What are you doing?' she cried, horrified.

'This confirms my worst suspicions. I should have you burned for the sake of your immortal soul, whether you testify against Alazais or not!'

'But Pons . . . !' Her eyes were round with terror. 'You promised.'

'I made a bargain. You have yet to keep your side. Will you do it?'

'I don't know . . . I can't . . .'

His hand shot out, imprisoning her chin and lifting it so that she was forced to look directly into his eyes, and the metal of the locket he still held bit into her flesh.

'You are very stubborn, sister. I would have thought you would be only too ready to help me bring about the downfall of the Lady Alazais.'

'What do you mean?'

'My sources tell me that you have a son whom Bertrand has made his heir. They also tell me that the Lady Alazais is with child. Suppose it is a boy, Jeanne? What will happen to your son's inheritance then?'

She couldn't answer; could barely think. In her terror she had quite forgotten that Alazais was carrying Philip's child.

'Give me the Lady Alazais and your son's position will be secured.' His voice was low and tantalising, the voice of the devil whispering in her ear. He had found her weak spot and he knew it.

'Well?' He laughed shortly. 'Don't tell me you hadn't thought of that. I think I shall return you to your cell to give you time to reconsider. As for this . . .'

He released her, stared for a moment with distaste at the Star of the Domus which lay in the palm of his hand, then turned and tossed it into the flames.

A low groan of despair escaped Jeanne, but it was not only for the destruction of the talisman but for herself, because she knew in that instant what she was going to do. She could not have betrayed Alazais in order to save herself. She was not even sure she could have done it for Philip. But to secure a safe and prosperous future for her beloved son . . . that was a different matter entirely.

'Bring me paper,' she said. Her voice was trembling but hard; it no longer sounded like her own.

Pons smiled.

'The indictment is already prepared. All you have to do is sign.'

He slid a parchment to the table's edge, dipped a quill into the inkpot and passed it to her.

In the flames of the log fire the Star of the Domus flared briefly and died.

The farmhouse was dim and musty-smelling. The front door led directly into a room overcrowded with battered and stained furniture, some of which was covered with grimy dustsheets. The shuttered windows were thick with dirt, cobwebs draped the corners. But there were used coffee cups and an ashtray overflowing with cigarette butts on the bare wood table, and a collection of half-empty bottles on an ancient, rickety chiffonier.

'So – what is it you want to talk to me about?' Hélène asked, reaching for a cigarette.

'Well, the situation we're in, of course,' Esther said. 'I would have thought that was obvious.'

'The situation?' Hélène sounded alarmed almost. 'You mean— '

'You, me and Alain,' Esther said, puzzled by Hélène's response.

'Oh – that!' Hélène laughed shortly. 'I thought you were talking about something else.'

She crossed to the chiffonier, pouring a generous measure of gin into a used glass and gulping from it.

'What else would I be talking about?' Esther asked.

For reply, Hélène waved the gin bottle in Esther's direction.

'Do you want one?'

'No thank you. Look – I really do think it's time we sorted things out, don't you?'

'I'm sorry . . . ?' Her tone was vague, bemused, as if her mind was still elsewhere.

Esther glanced at her sharply.

'Our situation. I know it's not always easy to let go, but dragging things out only makes it worse. In the long run a clean break is far less painful. It's a long time now since you and Alain split up, and he and I want to be together. So why won't you accept that and give him a divorce so that we can all get on with our lives?'

Hélène's hands tightened round her glass. For a moment she looked totally shocked and on the point of tears. Then her expression hardened and she turned to the chiffonier, pouring herself another drink.

'Well I must say you have a nerve!'

'I'm sorry if you see it that way, but it's about time somebody around here did some straight talking. It's a ludicrous state of affairs.'

'But between me and Alain, don't you think?'

'Not entirely. I'm involved too, whether you like it or not.'

'For the moment.'

'Not just for the moment. Surely you must realise he'd never have asked me here unless we were serious about one another?'

Hélène shrugged.

'He's already asked you for a divorce, hasn't he?' Esther persisted.

'No.'

'I think he has. He phoned you from England.'

'Oh – that. That's a long time ago,' Hélène said dismissively. She finished her drink and replenished it yet again. 'I've forgotten all about that.'

'I find that pretty hard to believe,' Esther said. 'The truth is, Hélène, that you're determined to cling on to the bitter end.'

'Well if he meant it why hasn't he mentioned it again?' Hélène asked. There was a challenge now in her eyes and her voice. The alcohol was giving her a confidence that had been lacking before; standing there with a glass in one hand and a cigarette in the other she was suddenly the one with all the trump cards.

'Because of what's happened,' Esther said, disconcerted at

feeling on the defensive suddenly. 'Alain has a very soft heart. You've just lost your brother and he's reluctant to cause you any more upset.'

'You think so,' Hélène said.

'I know so.'

'It hasn't occurred to you that it might be because he still loves me?'

A jar of discomfort. Esther tried to ignore it.

'You see? You're still avoiding the truth. Your marriage is over, Hélène. Alain is with me now.'

'You're wrong!' Hélène said fiercely. 'You may think you know Alain, but you don't. You don't know anything about him – or any of us. Alain will never divorce me – never! You might have had a fling with him, but that's all it is. We belong together, Alain and I. We always have.'

Esther held on to her temper with difficulty.

'I know he feels a responsibility towards you, Hélène. That's only natural. But it's not enough to hold a marriage together.'

'And how would you know?'

'Because he's told me. You and he couldn't live together. You were making one another miserable.'

'We went through a bad patch, yes. Doesn't everyone?'

'It was a great deal more than that and you know it. You were tearing one another apart. You couldn't agree about a single thing. Christ – you wouldn't even have his child . . .' She broke off, realising she had gone too far.

'He told you that?' Hélène's voice was full of the horror of betrayal.

'I'm sorry, but yes. Yes, he did.'

'How could he?' Hélène whispered. 'How could he tell you something like that?'

Esther hardened her heart.

'We are planning a future together, Hélène. Of course we talk about these things.'

'And what else has he told you? No – no, don't tell me, I don't want to know. I can't stand it!'

Hélène's mood had changed abruptly again. She had begun to tremble and there was an almost wild expression in her eyes.

'Hélène, get a grip for goodness' sake!' Esther said, alarmed.

Hélène banged down her glass on the table.

'Why don't you just go away and leave me alone? I've got enough on my plate at the moment without you coming here and making things worse.' She ran to the window, looking out. 'Where *is* he?' she muttered. 'Where the hell is he?'

'Who?' Esther asked.

'Thierry, of course! He should be here and he's not.' She rammed her thumbnail into her mouth, chewing on it in agitation.

'Thierry,' Esther said flatly.

'Yes. He was here when I went out. Now he's not. I don't understand!'

So Alain was right to be concerned about her, Esther thought. She was totally unbalanced. Not only was she refusing to face the truth about her marriage, now she was deluding herself that her brother was still alive too.

'Hélène – Thierry is dead,' she said gently.

Hélène spun round. Her eyes were wild.

'No he's not! Don't you understand? I was here with him last night. He's not dead at all. Thierry is still alive!'

Alazais sat at the table in the interrogation room where Jeanne had sat before her. Her face was pale and moist with cold perspiration and her fingers moved ceaselessly on the beads of her rosary.

When they had come to summon her to the court of inquisition she had been shocked and frightened, but her fear had been more for Jeanne than for herself. She was being called to give evidence against her friend, she had thought, and she had spent the journey wondering how best to speak in her defence and wishing with all her heart that Philip was there to advise her. It was only when she had been shown into the small upper chamber at the Mur and found herself face to face with the Dominican she had denounced to his prior for his scandalous attempt to rape Grazide that she had felt the first real qualm of alarm.

'So – we meet again.' His lip curled slightly. 'Little did I think, milady, when I accepted your hospitality that I was among heretics.'

'And neither were you!' Alazais returned. 'I was the one who was mistaken. I believed you to be an honourable man of God.'

The cold grey eyes snapped with fury.

'I am not the one on trial here. You would do well to remember that.'

Alazais folded her hands together to keep them from trembling.

'Are you saying *I* am on trial? How can that be? I have never been anything but a good Catholic.'

'And I have evidence to the contrary. You are a friend to heretics, milady.'

'Evidence? What evidence?' Alazais demanded. 'Who says such things?'

The Dominican eased himself back in the carved chair, tapping with one finger on a parchment document which lay on the table before him.

'I have here the sworn testimony of Jeanne Marty. It would be well for you to confess at once and have done with it. If you do not, it will be the worse for you.'

Alazais scarcely heard his last words. Her eyes had gone round with horror. 'Jeanne would never say such a thing of me!'

'She has done so.'

'Then you must have tortured it out of her! Sancta Maria – how could you do it? How could you torture your own sister?'

'She is a heretic and no sister of mine.'

'She is not a heretic!' Alazais blazed, fear for her friend lending her courage. 'She is no more a heretic than you are. Oh, she was born to the faith, I admit – as you were. But in all the time I have known her she has never practised it – never! You must believe me and release her!'

'My sister is not the subject under discussion here,' Pons said smoothly. 'It is your heresy we are dealing with now. A confession, milady, is what I require – and your assurance that from henceforth you will renounce the works of the devil.'

Within her, the baby moved. Alazais pressed her hands momentarily to her belly. She must remain calm. As long as she told the truth, all would be well.

'I have done nothing wrong. I have nothing to confess.'

He sighed, making a bridge of his fingers and resting his chin upon them.

'I feared you would prove stubborn. You are indeed a very

stubborn woman. Well, we shall see how long it takes before you change your mind.'

And so it had begun, hour after hour of relentless questioning until Alazais was scarcely aware any more of what she was asked, much less of her replies. Only two things burned bright as beacons in her mind; one that she must not say anything to incriminate Jeanne, the other that she could not – would not – confess to what she knew she was innocent of.

At long last the friar rose, his patience exhausted. As he leaned across the table, towering over her, Alazais smelled the rank sweat impregnating his habit and gagged with both revulsion and terror, but she no longer possessed the strength even to turn her head away.

'I have wasted long enough on this interview, milady. It seems to me that you are incapable of penitence.'

Alazais remained silent. Nothing she could say, it seemed, could convince him of her loyalty to the church, and she was beginning to realise with growing despair that he had no intention of believing her. She looked up at him, quailing inwardly, yet summoning the last reserves of her strength.

'I cannot renounce what I have never embraced,' she whispered. 'I have nothing to confess.'

'Very well.' He reached for a bell which stood beside the inkwell on the table and ringing it impatiently for the gaoler. 'In that case you leave me no option but to relax you to the secular arm. They will deal with you, milady, as you deserve.'

The colour drained from her face. She half rose, felt her knees give way beneath her and slumped once more to the stool, her rosary slipping from her fingers.

'You mean . . . ?'

'I mean, of course, that your soul will be purified by the fire, milady. You will burn, as all heretics must. At the stake.'

Esther looked anxiously at Hélène. Standing there at the window, smoking yet another cigarette and gulping gin as if her life depended on it, she looked totally deranged. Or, perhaps, just drunk . . .

'Thierry was killed, Hélène,' Esther said quietly. 'Don't you remember?'

Hélène shook her head, and gin slopped out of the glass and

over her fingers. 'No, he wasn't! That's the whole point! It wasn't him!' She turned abruptly, stubbing out her cigarette. 'Oh I shouldn't be telling you this . . .'

Esther was seriously concerned now, beginning to regret the impulse that had made her follow Hélène, yet reluctant to leave her here alone in this state. Alain had been right to be worried about her, she thought. There was no telling what she would do next.

'Look – why don't I take you back to Le Château Gris?' she suggested.

'I can't. I'm meeting Thierry here, I tell you!'

'Well, I don't know . . .' Esther thought furiously. She was fairly sure there would be no telephone in this derelict farmhouse and in any case Alain was probably still out looking for Hélène. Perhaps the best thing would be to try to sober her up.

'What you need is some black coffee, Hélène. Is there any in the kitchen?'

She pushed open the door. The kitchen was muggy and smelled stale and she opened a window, pushing aside the grimy curtain nets to let in some fresh air. Flies were buzzing around some half-eaten packs of food on the table and a pile of unwashed dishes were stacked untidily in the sink. Esther frowned. Someone had obviously been living here, and not for just one night. She shivered, uncomfortable suddenly. There was something here she did not understand. The sooner she could get in touch with Alain and let him know what was going on the happier she would be. But for the moment she was stuck in a derelict farmhouse in the middle of nowhere with a woman who had clearly lost all touch with reality. The responsibility was hers and hers alone.

There was a kettle on the draining board and she filled it from the single cold tap, looking around for a way of heating the water. The big old range was totally cold – had not been lit for years, by the look of it – but there was a camping gas stove on a stained, linoleum-covered cupboard and a box of matches beside it. Esther shook one out and lit the stove, propping the kettle precariously over the flaring blue flame. Then she swilled out one of the dirty cups under the tap and looked around for coffee.

She found it in one of the cupboards, a jar which looked almost startlingly fresh among the faded labels and mouldy bottles. But it was half empty – someone had made a good few cups of coffee from it. The feeling of discomfort washed over her again. Who used this place? Just Hélène – as a retreat where she could play out her fantasies? Or was there someone else – another man – as she had first suspected? It really was all very strange.

Esther spooned coffee into the mug and glanced at the kettle. It would take forever to boil on that little flame. She went back into the living room.

'Why don't you— ' She broke off. The room was empty, the front door wide open. What the hell was Hélène doing now?

Anxious, irritated, Esther went outside.

'Hélène!' she called. 'Where are you?'

No answer. She looked around. There was a barn on the opposite side of the yard and the door was open. Esther was fairly sure it had been shut before. She crossed the cobbles and peered inside.

'Hélène – are you in there?'

After the brightness of the midday sunshine the barn was gloomy and dark, empty but for unevenly stacked bales of hay along one wall. Hélène was standing in the middle of the vast straw-strewn floor, one hand pressed to her mouth, the other holding a cigarette.

'I'm making you coffee, Hélène,' Esther said.

'Umm?' Hélène whirled round.

'I'm making you coffee. Come back inside.'

'His car's gone,' Hélène said. 'He's taken his car.'

Esther groaned.

'What are you talking about?'

'Thierry's car has gone. This is where he kept it. Out of sight.'

'Hélène – Thierry's car was destroyed in the accident. It couldn't possibly be here.'

'No – not *that* one,' Hélène said crossly. 'The one he's been using *since*.'

Esther hesitated, wondering how on earth to deal with Hélène. She seemed to have completely lost her grip on reality.

'Look, you must try to accept the fact – Thierry is dead,' she said.

'He's not!' Hélène's voice was shrill. 'Do you think I'm crazy or something? Is that it? Oh, that would suit you, wouldn't it? You'd love that! But I'm not. Thierry has been here ever since . . . His things are all here. Look.'

She ran towards the stacked hay, transferring her cigarette to her mouth and tugging at one of the bales with both hands.

'Oh for goodness' sake!' Esther exploded. This had gone far enough. Hélène needed help. 'Look – you're coming with me whether you like it or not.'

She grabbed Hélène's wrist.

'No!' Hélène began to struggle. 'I have to wait here for Thierry! You don't understand!'

Esther yanked at Hélène's arm, and as she did so Hélène's free hand swung round, hitting her full in the face. Esther gasped, releasing Hélène with such suddenness that Hélène lost her balance and staggered backwards. Her heel caught against a single low bale of hay and she toppled back on to a taller mound.

'You bitch!' Esther gasped. Her face was stinging from the force of the blow, tears of shock springing to her eyes. 'Well stay here if that's what you want. I couldn't care less!'

She marched out of the barn, back to the Saab. She was shaking, and as she wrenched open the door and got in the heat that had collected from the sun beating on the windscreen hit her, making her feel slightly sick.

What a nightmare! What a bloody nightmare! She'd have to find Alain, tell him Hélène had finally flipped her lid. He'd have to cope. There was nothing more she could do. She felt for the ignition keys in the most familiar place – the dashboard – then remembered that in the Saab they were between the front seats. But as she fumbled for them the nausea twisted in her stomach again and with it a flash of apprehension so sharp it was almost terror.

Something was wrong. Something was dreadfully wrong, and she didn't know what it was. Only that her face was hurting and the heat of the car was suffocating and she'd had enough of this place! But it wasn't just that. It was more – far more. Something terrible had happened – or was going to happen – or both. And it had to do with Hélène. With her and Hélène . . .

She couldn't go. She couldn't leave her. Goodness only knew what she'd do next. Esther got out of the car again and started back across the farmyard. Then she stopped short, the nebulous feeling of fear sharpening, escalating, materialising into reality.

There was smoke coming from the barn, a thin dark cloud,

blowing on the strong breeze and dispersing into the sunshine. For a moment she thought she was imagining it, the stuff of her nightmares. It was only a cloud of midges or the light and shadows playing tricks. Then the breeze gusted and she smelled it too, sharp and acrid. And heard the faint yet unmistakable crackle of flame creeping, flaring, consuming.

There was a fire in the barn. But how – why? In a sudden illuminating flash Esther relived the moment when Hélène had tripped. She had had a cigarette. She must have dropped it with the shock of falling, and it had set light to the straw.

Esther froze, eyes wide with horror. The hay in the barn was old, tinder-dry. The whole lot would go up in no time. And Hélène was still inside. Why? Why hadn't she come running out the moment the fire started? Had she hurt herself in some way? Or was she too drunk to stand?

I have to do something! Esther thought wildly. But her feet seemed to be rooted to the spot and the clammy cold waves of terror washing over her were stifling any coherent thought. The phobia which had haunted her for as long as she could remember had always had this effect on her. But never before had it been of any importance to anyone but herself. This time it was different. Hélène's life might depend on her overcoming her terror. And Esther honestly did not know if she could do it.

At dawn the guard came to fetch Jeanne from her cell.

'What's happening?' she asked.

'You'll see.' He grinned unpleasantly as he tied her hands behind her back.

After the darkness of her cell even the grey morning light seemed bright. The guard hurried her along the cobbled streets and out through the city gates.

The stake had been prepared on a mound of faggots just outside the city walls. When she saw it, Jeanne's knees went weak. Was she to be burned as a heretic after all? Was that the reason they had kept her here? She had thought when she signed the indictment that she would be released but it hadn't happened and she had seen no one to ask the reason why, no one but the guards who came to bring her food and water, and who would never say anything. For a moment her step faltered, then, as the guard gave her a push, her fierce pride made her brace herself.

She wouldn't let them see she was afraid. She wouldn't give them that pleasure.

The open ground around the stake thronged with French soldiers. They were responsible for carrying out the executions decreed by the church. Jeanne saw a group of Dominicans and felt a rush of anger and hatred. What hypocrites they were, handing out their death sentences and then leaving it to others to do their evil work so that there would be no stain on their immortal souls!

Some of the crowd who had gathered drew back as she passed, crossing themselves. Jeanne stared at them defiantly and tossed her head to throw back her hair which the gusting wind was blowing across her face – there had been no time to put on her veil and fillet.

The guard jerked on her arm, motioning her to stop, and a murmur ran through the waiting crowd. Another small party had come out through the city gates – a Dominican priest, reading aloud from a prayer book as he led the procession down the hillside, and two guards half carrying a woman whose head sagged on to her chest and whose bare feet dragged painfully on the rough ground.

With a chill of horror Jeanne recognised the priest as Pons and the woman as Alazais. Her face was bruised and battered, her gown torn and bloodstained. As the procession reached Jeanne, Pons halted and turned to Alazais.

'Your friend has come to watch you meet your maker.' There was a ring of satisfaction and false piety in his voice.

With an effort Alazais raised her head. Her eyes were full of terror and mute pleading.

'What have they done to you?' Jeanne whispered. 'What have *I* done?'

'Not you, Jeanne.' Alazais words were scarcely audible and she swallowed painfully. 'I brought this on myself.'

Frantically Jeanne struggled with the cord which bound her wrists and threw herself on her knees in front of her brother.

'You cannot have her burned! For the love of God . . .'

Pons smirked. 'It is for the love of God that she must be burned.' He pulled Jeanne to her feet. 'Loose her hands,' he ordered the guard. 'And when she has seen what happens to heretics, give her a horse and set her free.'

'Pons, I beg you!' Jeanne was beside herself. 'Alazais has done nothing! I am the one who should be burned! Take me – but let her go!'

For a moment Pons's eyes met hers, cold and callous, then he turned away, reading once more from the prayer book. The little procession set off once more, the guards dragging the half-fainting Alazais between them.

Jeanne's guard unsheathed his sword, slicing through the cord which bound her wrists. They were numb and raw, and the heavy dew had soaked her thin slippers so that her feet were like blocks of ice, but she noticed neither. She was aware only of Alazais being lifted on to the pyre and tied to the stake, and the men arranging the faggots around her feet.

Another man approached with a flaming brand and thrust it into the brush.

'No!' Jeanne screamed as the flames leaped. 'No! No!'

Before the guard could stop her she darted forward and ran towards the stake. Already the fire was so fierce she could feel the heat of it on her face and the gusting wind blew the thick black smoke into her open mouth. Tears were streaming down her cheeks, horror overwhelming reason. She couldn't save Alazais but at least she could die with her . . .

A piece of burning brush blown by the wind landed on her arm. She flicked it away and felt no sharp burning pain as the brand seared her flesh. Then the guard reached her, hauling her away, and holding her fast.

Past struggling, past weeping, past praying, Jeanne was forced to watch as the flames rose higher and fiercer and the last of Alazais's agonised screams was carried away on the gusting wind.

Simone came out of her trance with a jolt. Her whole body was bathed in sweat and she was shaking from head to foot.

So – the story had a terrible ending, just as she had known it must. And now the scenario was being played out again. With a feeling of sick certainty Simone knew it was true.

Once more the souls that had once been Jeanne and Alazais were fighting for the man they both loved – and unless the pattern could be broken the story would reach the same terrible conclusion. Esther and Hélène. Jeanne and Alazais. They were one and the same, they had to be, just as Alain must have once been Philip. But which of them was fated to cause the other to die a terrible death? Which of them was which?

Simone drew her hand across her eyes, desperately trying to force herself to think straight. There must be a clue somewhere – there must be!

It came to her in a flash, so clear she could not think why it had not occurred to her before. The birthmark on Esther's leg! It corresponded exactly with the scar Jeanne had sustained as a result of the accident when she had been a farmer's wife. So – Esther had once been Jeanne. A sense of urgency swept over Simone. Somehow she must make her realise how close she was to condemning her immortal soul to more aeons of darkness.

Simone grabbed up the telephone, pressing her finger down on the connect button to re-establish a line, then slamming it down again. If she tried to explain all this over the telephone Esther would simply think she had taken leave of her senses. This was something which had to be said face to face – and even then the chances were she would not believe it.

But at least she could try. At least then, when the modern parallel to the past arose, Esther might recognise it and be deterred from whatever she might otherwise do.

Simone grabbed her car keys and ran out of the house.

23

THE FIRE WAS gathering strength. Esther could hear the pop and crackle as it took hold in the ancient bales of tinder-dry hay and the smoke billowing out of the open barn door was thicker now.

She stood transfixed with terror, all the use drained from her shaking limbs, her whole body bathed in cold sweat. Her mind, her emotions, were chasing the same wild circles of panic they always did when she was confronted by fire, but now there was an added dimension. In the past the fear had been irrational. This time, layered on the overwhelming phobic reaction was the realisation of danger that was not imagined but all too real. Hélène was in the barn. For some reason she had not escaped when the fire began. And if she didn't get out soon there was every chance that she would die.

I can't let that happen! Esther thought wildly. I have to do something – but I can't! I can't!

You can. The still small voice spoke within the depths of her panic.

I can't!

Yes, you can. You must.

She took a step forward on legs that threatened to give way beneath her.

Don't think about the fire. Just think about Hélène.

Somehow she forced herself towards the barn door. The smoke was thick inside and behind it the bright orange flames leaped. She gritted her teeth. If Hélène was still where she had fallen, there was no way she could reach her.

And then she saw her. A dark huddled shape in the centre of the floor, not moving.

Esther's heart thudded into her throat, and again she felt the weakness flood through her in a cold debilitating tide. But just seeing Hélène lying there, helpless, gave her something to focus on.

She dropped to her hands and knees. The smoke was less thick at ground level and before she could lose her slender hold on the courage that was somehow keeping the panic under control she began to inch forward. She could feel the heat of the flames now, on her face and on her bare arms, but she had reached Hélène.

Concentrate on that. Just concentrate on getting her out.

There was no way she could lift her, she knew. She grabbed Hélène by the ankles and began to drag her towards the door. The smoke was making her eyes burn and stream, filling her throat, making her want to cough. She resisted the urge, hawking against her tight closed mouth.

Not far. It wasn't far. Just keep going . . .

Her butt connected with something solid – the door frame. She altered course and suddenly she was breathing fresh air – tainted, acrid still, but no longer choking – and the heat on her arms was the heat of the sun.

She yanked Hélène out, too, let her go while she took deep gasping breaths. Then she twisted Hélène's arm around her own neck and heaved her up. To Esther's enormous relief Hélène cried out in pain as the weight went on to her ankle. But it wasn't over yet. Hélène had taken in an awful lot of smoke and fumes. She needed treatment urgently. Esther somehow managed to drag her to the Saab. Only then did she realise she was sobbing.

She propped Hélène against the car, wrenched open the door and bundled her inside. Then she half fell into the car herself, her legs barely able to support her any longer, her hands shaking so much she could hardly grip the keys. The engine spluttered to life, she slammed the gear stick into reverse and let out the clutch. The car lurched backwards. She pulled on the heavy steering wheel and crunched into first gear. Then she was jolting down the lane, bouncing off the banks, jarring in the potholes. She had no clear idea where she was going, only that she had to get help.

When she saw the *auberge*, set back from the road, she began sobbing again with relief and release of tension. She swung into the track leading to it, careered across a patch of grass and lurched to a stop beside picnic-style tables and benches set out beneath huge blue and white umbrellas.

The people at the tables looked startled, a waiter wearing a white wraparound apron came running in alarm. Esther jumped out of the car, tears streaming down her cheeks.

'Please! You've got to help me!'

Then, once again, her legs buckled beneath her and this time she felt the ground come up to meet her in a rush.

Simone had been at Le Château Gris for about half an hour. She had raced over, impatient to talk to Esther, but although the door was open no one was at home and Simone had decided the best plan was to wait. She had no idea where to look for Esther, but if she'd left the house unlocked, it wasn't likely that she'd be gone for long.

While she waited Simone tried to use the time to work out what she was going to say to her, but she was feeling more dubious by the minute. How could she possibly make Esther understand when she still scarcely understood herself? The whole thing was so incredible that even now she could scarcely credit it herself, and she felt sure a sceptic like Esther would think she had taken leave of her senses. But she had to try – had to touch some chord with Esther, stir some forgotten memory that would convince her, or at least make her wonder. Something – anything – so that when the time came for the final, tragic act she would recognise it for what it was and behave differently. But it wouldn't be easy . . . oh, it wouldn't be easy!

When she heard the sound of a car on the drive, Simone ran outside eagerly. But it wasn't Esther. It was Alain – and he was alone.

'Simone! What are you doing here?' he said. His voice was taut and anxious and his face was haggard with strain.

'I came to see Esther, but she's not here.'

'Not here?' He looked puzzled. 'What do you mean, she's not here?'

Simone laughed shortly.

'What do you think I mean? The house is empty.'

He looked around helplessly, running his fingers through his hair, and the bright sunshine picked up a streak of grey in the jet-black which Simone had never noticed before. Then he shrugged.

'I called at the garage on the way back and they said they'd returned the Saab. It's not here now, so presumably she's taken it and gone out somewhere.'

'Where would she go?'

'I haven't got a clue! And I've got other things on my mind just now. Hélène is missing.'

Simone experienced a twist of alarm.

'Missing? You mean—'

The telephone had begun to ring inside the house.

'Hang on. I'll talk to you in a minute.' Alain was hurrying to answer it.

Simone followed more slowly. The deep sense of misgiving was weighing heavily on her and the shrill of the telephone jarred on her ragged nerves. Hélène – missing. Did that mean the revelation had come too late – that the Wheel of Karma had already turned full circle again?

In the doorway she almost collided with Alain. He pushed past her without stopping, making for his car. His face was grey.

'What is it?' Simone asked, running after him.

'That was the hospital. Hélène and Esther – they're both there . . .'

'Why? What's happened?'

'I'm not sure. They said something about a fire.' He was opening the door of his car, getting in. 'Do you want to come with me?'

'Yes. All right.' But she was shaking, all the tiny hairs on the back of her neck prickling as ice-cold waves shivered over her skin.

Fire. Oh dear God, fire!

Not again! Simone prayed. Oh please, not again!

She fastened her seat belt and sat with her hands tightly knotted together in her lap as Alain started the engine and reversed at high speed down the drive.

Esther was sitting, head in hands, on a hard upright chair in the reception area of the hospital. As Alain burst in, followed closely by Simone, she leaped up, wanting to run to him but finding herself quite unable to take so much as a step.

'Esther!' He reached her, gripping her by the arms. 'What's happened? Where's Hélène? Is she all right?'

'I don't know. I think so.' Her voice was shaking. 'She came to Le Château Gris and took away some things from that box file she brought you. I thought she was behaving oddly, so I followed her . . . to an old farmhouse . . .'

'Farmhouse? What farmhouse?'

'I don't know. It was at a place called . . .' She struggled to recall the name she had memorised. 'Marteilleuse. She was in such a state – drinking like a fish and hallucinating about Thierry. And then . . .'

She broke off again, unable to bring herself to talk about what had happened. It was too overwhelmingly horrendous, too real still, and besides, Esther felt sick with the guilt that had begun as soon as the urgent priority of getting help for Hélène had been achieved. The fire had been her fault. If she hadn't followed Hélène to the farm, if she hadn't struggled with her in the barn, none of this would have happened.

'Monsieur Lavaur?' A nurse had emerged from a doorway and was hovering.

'Yes.' He had stiffened with urgent apprehension.

'I'm glad you're here. The doctor would like to speak to you.'

'My wife is going to be all right, isn't she? If something should happen to her . . .' He was speaking in rapid French and though she did not understand exactly what was being said his manner left Esther in no doubt as to the gist of it. And in no doubt as to the depth of his concern, either.

'If you'd like to come with me . . .'

'Yes, of course.' Without so much as a backward glance he followed the nurse along the corridor.

Esther stared after his retreating back, numbed for a moment by the abruptness of his departure. Then a feeling of desolation began to creep in, barely identifiable at first, then growing stronger as it struck her that he hadn't seemed to give her a second thought, hadn't shown the slightest concern for her beyond what she could tell him about Hélène. When the chips were down he had thought only of her.

The realisation was a sickness in the pit of her stomach, a hurt so sharp it was a physical pain. Alain was still in love with Hélène. It was a truth she could no longer avoid.

She felt a light touch on her bare arm and turned to see Simone looking at her. There was a wealth of understanding in that look and the irregular features were softened by sympathy.

'Shall we go outside – get some fresh air?' Simone suggested.

Esther's stomach clenched. She liked Simone but she didn't want her pity. It only highlighted the humiliating realisation that she had made a complete fool of herself. What she wanted, more than anything, was to run away and hide, live through these excruciating waves of shame and pain with no one to see. But she didn't see how she could possibly escape without drawing yet more attention to herself, and make Alain's rejection of her a *fait accompli*.

She nodded. 'If you like.'

A walkway bordered with flower beds led along the side of the hospital building until, interrupted by a jutting wing, it branched away across a patch of lawn to a wooden bench, set in the shade of a gnarled old tree.

'Let's sit down,' Simone said. 'You look as if you're all in.'

'Oh, I'm all right.' But she didn't sound all right. She sounded stressed and close to tears.

'Why don't you tell me what happened?' Simone said.

Esther was silent, looking down at her hands, clasped tightly in her lap. 'Bottling things up isn't really a very good idea,' she added. 'It would help if you could talk about it, you know.'

'Would it?' Esther smiled bleakly. 'I'm not so sure. But I suppose there's no way I can avoid it really. The police are bound to be asking me questions soon, aren't they?'

'Well yes . . .' Simone said uneasily, wondering suddenly just what Esther's part in all this had been.

'The thing is, there's not a lot to tell really. As I said, Hélène had too much to drink, and she ran out to the barn while I was making black coffee to sober her up. She was smoking. I suppose she must have dropped the end in the hay, and it caught fire. Perhaps she was too drunk to realise what she'd done, I don't know, and I think she'd twisted her ankle or something, but anyway, she was overcome by smoke. I found her just lying there.'

'And you managed to get her out,' Simone said, relieved.

'Yes. I don't know how I did it really.'

'At times like that we find an almost inhuman strength.'

'Yes – but it's not just that. I'm terrified of fire, you see.'

Simone nodded. It all followed, the last pieces of the jigsaw slotting into place.

'Then you were very brave.'

'Brave?' Esther laughed shortly. 'I wasn't brave! I was scared to death.'

'Isn't that what bravery is? Being absolutely terrified and still managing to do what has to be done?'

Esther was silent, staring into space. Then she drew a long shuddering breath.

'The thing is . . . what I haven't told you . . . it was my fault, the fire . . .'

Simone felt the skin on the back of her neck crawl.

'What do you mean?'

'It was me who made Hélène drop her cigarette – and twist her ankle, come to that.'

'But you said— '

'I know. I was being economical with the truth. The thing is, I followed Hélène out to the barn. She was being . . . impossible. I lost my temper with her and we struggled. That's how she came to fall over. I stormed out, leaving her there. And the next thing I knew . . .' She broke off, trembling violently again as she relived the terrible moment when she had realised the barn was on fire.

'That's all?' Simone asked.

'Isn't it enough?'

'Oh Esther!' Simone took her hand. In spite of the heat of the sun it felt icy cold. 'My dear, that's not so terrible, is it?'

'It nearly cost Hélène her life. Don't you realise, Simone, she could easily have died today and it would have been my fault.'

'But she didn't,' Simone comforted. 'What's more, it was you who saved her. That's all that matters.'

'I wish I could believe that.'

'You must. You hear me? You must!' Simone said forcefully. 'It was all meant to be. And this time— '

She broke off as she saw Esther's incredulous expression. There was no point explaining. She'd tried once before, and Esther had obviously thought her quite mad. In any case, it hardly mattered now. The Wheel of Karma had turned full circle. Once again Esther had been in a position whereby her actions could have brought about Hélène's death by fire. But this time it hadn't happened. The soul that had once been Jeanne Marty had been redeemed by somehow finding the courage to prevent history repeating itself yet again. The chain had been broken and she was free.

Simone wished with all her heart that she could share with Esther her enormous relief that at long last it was over and no more harm had been done to cast its long shadow down the centuries, and also her guilt that she had not been able to do more to help. If only she hadn't been so sceptical in the beginning perhaps it would have been easier. And then again, perhaps it wouldn't. There are some things we can do only for ourselves . . .

'You have nothing to reproach yourself with,' she said, and realised Esther was no longer listening to her.

She turned, following the direction of Esther's gaze, and saw Alain coming towards them along the path. Her heart came into her mouth. Supposing . . .

But there was a spring in Alain's step now. He looked like a man who has had a burden lifted from his shoulders.

'How is she?' Simone asked.

'Resting. She's inhaled a lot of smoke but the doctor thinks she's going to be fine.' He turned to Esther. 'Look – I'm really sorry, but I think I need to stay here. Hélène needs me . . .'

'That's all right,' Esther's voice was bright, tight. 'I quite understand.'

'Esther . . .'

'You really don't need to say any more, Alain. Honestly.'

'Then if perhaps you could run Simone home . . .'

'Yes. Sure. Anything to help.'

He hesitated, as if on the point of saying something more, then nodded.

'Would you mind? I don't know how long I shall be.'

'No, I've already said. It's quite all right.'

'OK. Then I'd better go and see Hélène.'

'Esther . . .' Simone laid a hand on Esther's arm.

'Simone, please don't say anything,' Esther warned. 'Come on, I'll drive you home.'

Andrew Slater parked his hire car in the usual spot, climbed over the wall and made his way through the orchard to the rear of his father's house.

Bob was on the patio, shelling peas into a collander, and Andrew grinned in amusement. How domesticated and mellow the old fox had become! Andrew thought that if his mother could see him now she would never believe it.

'Diana's got you hard at it, I see,' he teased.

'Oh, she's a slave-driver, that woman.'

'Nonsense!' Diana emerged from the kitchen with a long cold drink which she placed at Bob's elbow. 'Sitting in the sun and shelling a few peas is hardly chain-gang stuff, especially when you're fortified with fresh lemonade every half-hour.' She glanced at Andrew. 'Has your father told you? There was a phone call for you while you were out.'

'Give me a chance, he's only just this minute got back!' Bob grumbled. 'There was a phone call for you, Andrew. There – I've told him now.'

'Who was it?' Andrew asked, hoping that the answer might be that it had been Esther. Unlikely, of course, since she was spoken for, but one never knew.

'Oh, some chap by the name of Yves Marssac,' Bob said, deliberately casual, and Andrew's initial disappointment melted so fast he forgot his lingering hope that Esther might have changed her mind about seeing him again.

'What did he want?' he asked, trying to match his father's casual tone and failing.

'He wouldn't say. Wanted to talk to you.'

Andrew whistled softly.

'Did he indeed! Are you thinking what I'm thinking?'

'That he's "remembered" something about Thierry Rousseau that might be of interest to you? Yes, the thought did cross my mind.'

'Well, well. Just when I was on the point of giving this one up as a bad job! If Yves Marssac wants to talk to me, maybe I'm going to get a break at last.'

'You two are like little boys playing detectives,' Diana remarked. 'Why don't you just ring him and find out what it is he wants?'

'Because there are some moments in this life that have to be savoured,' Andrew quipped back. 'I'll phone him now, though, and put us all out of our misery.'

But there was no reply from the number Yves Marssac had left with Bob. Whatever it was he wanted to say would have to keep for the moment, Andrew realised. And if the smell of the lamb cutlets which the peas were intended to accompany was anything to go by, the waiting time was going to be employed most pleasurably!

* * *

'Now, are you sure you are going to be all right, Esther?' Simone asked.

She had ridden back to Le Château Gris with Esther in order to collect her own car, leaving Alain at the hospital, and now she was preparing to leave.

'Yes, I'll be fine.' Esther smiled at her wanly.

'I'll stay with you a while longer if you like.'

'No, really. I think I need to be on my own for a bit.'

'Alain might be a long time.'

'I'm sure he will be,' Esther said wryly.

'Well, if you're quite certain . . .' Simone was still reluctant to leave her alone.

'Quite. I shall be busy packing, anyway. I think I'm going home.'

'Ah.'

'There's really no point in staying, is there? It's obvious Hélène means far more to Alain than I do. Oh – I don't mean that to sound petty. She needs him just now, I know. But the way he was behaving . . . well, it's pretty clear how much he cares for her whether he realises it or not. I think it's time for me to cut my losses. I think I've known that for a long time. I just wasn't ready to give up. But now, well, there comes a point when you realise you're flogging a dead horse.'

Her voice still had the same bright controlled tone she had used to Alain but Simone could see the depth of hurt it was concealing and felt her heart bleed for Esther.

'He and Hélène have been together for a very long time,' she said. 'It's not so easy to put all that aside.'

'I'm sure.'

'She's a lovely person really beneath all that insecurity . . . No, that's a rotten thing to say. It's no help to you at all. I'm just trying to point out that where Alain and Hélène are concerned, you really are up against it. They've had their problems, of course, probably still will have, but . . .'

'There's no explaining the strange ways of the heart.'

'That's right.'

'What I really don't understand,' Esther said, 'is why they split up in the first place if they are so close.'

'I know.' Simone was silent. Because it had to be, she wanted to say. Because if he hadn't met you, fallen in love with you, the chance for putting right old wrongs would have been lost for more centuries. But she couldn't say it.

'The other thing I don't understand is why everyone feels so responsible for Hélène,' Esther was going on. 'OK – Alain – I can accept that. I don't have to like it, but I can accept it. But you . . . your mother . . . I've felt as though I've been fighting you all.'

'Oh Esther, I'm sorry you've felt like that! It's nothing personal, honestly. It's just that . . . well, I suppose we feel to blame for Hélène's insecurities.'

'Why should you feel to blame?'

Simone sighed. 'I don't know if I should tell you this. It's something that's never discussed, even among the family. But perhaps I owe it to you. You know Hélène and Thierry grew up at Le Château Gris, I imagine?'

'Yes. Isobelle gave them a home when they were orphaned, Alain told me.'

'That's right. But did he tell you why?'

'Because their mother worked for you.'

'That's true, but not the whole story. There's a lot more to it than that, I'm afraid. She and my father were lovers.'

'Henri . . . and Hélène's mother?'

'Yes. She was very young, very pretty and a widow. Her husband had been a good-for-nothing – Thierry took after his father unfortunately. Anyway, she and Henri . . . had an affair. Nothing so unusual in that. The trouble arose when Odette became pregnant. When she got to hear of it, Maman was absolutely furious. She couldn't bear the thought of all her friends knowing Papa had a child with a servant. It wasn't the affair that upset her – it was who it was with. That and the fact that his bastard child would be growing up right under her nose. Maman told Odette she would have to get an abortion or she'd see to it she was out of a job and never worked in the area again. Papa argued, I'm sure, that he would be willing to support the child – the whole family if need be, but Papa has always been a gentle man. Weak, really, I suppose. Maman always got her way in the end. So Odette had her abortion – done, I expect, by some old woman in the village with a knitting needle. And it all went horribly wrong, as these things so often did.

'It was Hélène who found her mother bleeding to death that night. She was completely traumatised by it, poor child. To my knowledge, she's never spoken of it since. But it's the reason, I'm sure, why she always refused to even consider having a baby herself. She associates— '

She broke off suddenly as a thought struck her. Perhaps there was another, deeper, reason for Hélène's reluctance to have a child. Hadn't Alazais been pregnant when she had gone to the stake? Wasn't it the fact that she had been about to give Philip a child that had been the indirect cause of her death?

'Does Alain know about this?' Esther asked.

Simone dragged her mind back to the present.

'I don't know. As I told you, it's something we never discuss. I only know because I heard Maman and Papa talking about it, but I was older than Alain and Valerie, more aware of what was going on. Hélène may have told him, of course, but somehow I doubt it. It's as if she's shut it off in a compartment of her mind, refusing to think about it even. But it's affected her very deeply, not a doubt of it. Just losing her mother at such an impressionable age would have been bad enough, but given all the circumstances it's hardly surprising she suffers from all kinds of neuroses. Maman and Papa are to blame for that. They gave Hélène a home, tried to make it up to her, but they still bear the burden of responsibility for her insecurity. And I . . . well, I suppose I share it with them in a way. As does Alain.'

'But if he doesn't know . . .'

'He's seen the way she has been ever since that day. And besides . . .'

'He loves her.'

'Yes,' Simone said gently, 'I honestly think he does. I'm sorry, Esther, but in spite of all their problems, I really believe he does. I don't know what happened between you and him – it's none of my business – but I promise you I am not being biased when I say I think you are doing the right thing in cutting your losses and going home.'

'I should never have come,' Esther said flatly.

'I don't think you had any choice,' Simone said, then realised she was being enigmatic again. 'No – you were right to give it your best shot if it meant that much to you, but now I think that if you stay you'll only end up being even more hurt.'

'I think so too.' Esther smiled wanly. 'I'll say goodbye, Simone, in case we don't meet again. And thanks for being a good friend.'

Simone squeezed her hand.

'I just wish it could have been under different circumstances. And I'm sure we *will* meet again.'

But even as she said it she knew it was unlikely. If things had turned out differently perhaps there would have been other times, in some future life if not in this one. As it was, Esther had paid her karmic debts. There would be no need now for their paths to cross again.

A feeling of terrible sadness washed over Simone and she felt she was saying goodbye to someone who had once been very close to her. But she told herself this was no time to be sad. She must concentrate on giving thanks that at last Esther's better nature had triumphed and the pattern of tragedy had been broken.

She started her car, swung a wide arc and turned to smile at her one last time. Poor Esther, she was so unhappy now. But in all likelihood her path would be smoother from now on, blessed even. The past was behind her and there would be the reward of new beginnings. Jeanne could rest in peace. It was over.

It is not over.

The voice in her head was so clear, so totally unexpected, that Simone froze, her hands clenching on the steering wheel.

It is not over. Why had she thought that? Where had the voice come from?

Oh, you're simply overwrought, Simone told herself. You just can't let go. What else could there possibly be?

But she was deeply uneasy suddenly, and for no reason she could understand, Simone found herself thinking of Thierry Rousseau.

24

THIERRY ROUSSEAU SAW the pall of smoke, black and ugly against the clear blue of the sky, as he drove along the main road in the direction of the farmhouse. A brush fire, probably – nothing to worry about it. Brush fires were not uncommon in the hot dry summers. Mostly they were brought quickly under control and there was no damage but a few acres of charred land. The destruction of the countryside which caused such distress to some people had never bothered him. It always grew back, healthier than before. And in any case, he had more important things on his mind.

He tried to execute a racing change to corner quickly and expertly as he was used to doing but the clutch and gear lever of the old car he was driving were stiff and refused to cooperate properly. Thierry grimaced. That was what came of having to buy an ancient heap for cash in an out-of-the-way garage where no one knew him or asked too many questions. He thought with regret of his beautiful Porsche. Deliberately setting fire to it and pushing it over the edge of the ravine had been one of the hardest things he'd ever had to do. But there hadn't been any choice, and he had consoled himself with the thought that there would be other cars. For the first time in his life he would be able to afford what he wanted without worrying about where the money was coming from.

Of course, he thought grimly, if everything had gone according to plan he'd have been out of the country by now, safe in the knowledge that everyone at home thought he was dead. But there had been a few unforeseen hitches. First, he'd been unable to get hold of his passport. For some reason, Hélène had taken the box file he kept it in to Le Château Gris. He couldn't believe she had been so stupid – though he supposed she had her reasons. At the time, of course, she too had thought he was dead and it wouldn't have occurred to her that he would need it. But hopefully that wouldn't be a problem much longer. When he'd finally made contact with her he'd asked her to fetch it and by now she should be back at the farmhouse where he'd been lying low, waiting for him.

Then this morning he'd had the misfortune to run into Yves Marssac. That really had been the most unbelievable piece of bad luck, yet in some ways he could almost see the poetic justice in it. He and Yves and Jean-Luc Lorrain – the Three Musketeers as they'd called themselves in the old days – thrown together by fate one last time. But he didn't think Yves would be too much of a problem. And in any case, as long as Hélène had managed to get hold of his passport, he wouldn't be around much longer.

Thierry grinned suddenly, the cheeky optimism that made even his enemies find it easy to forgive him surfacing once more. Soon he'd have all he'd ever wanted, all he'd ever dreamed of. And the best of it was he would be enjoying it at Alain Lavaur's expense.

How he hated that man! Always had, since they were children together, though he'd taken care to hide his feelings. Alain had everything – money, social standing, film-star good looks – and he'd always taken it for granted, as if it were his right. Which of course it was – well, the money and the social standing, anyway. And just to make it worse, he had always been so bloody magnanimous! They all had really, Henri and Isobelle taking him into their home when his mother had died, pretending to treat him and Hélène as no different from their own children, affecting kindness and generosity while all the time . . . A black shadow of fury crossed Thierry's face as he thought of it. But the worst of his resentment was reserved for Alain. Once, long ago, he had looked up to him, wanted to be like him. Then gradually jealousy had changed that ambition so that he no longer wanted to be like him but to have all the things that were his. Most of all he wanted Alain to know what it felt like to have to stand in the wings waiting for the crumbs that would be thrown his way and which he was supposed to feel grateful for. Most of all he wanted their roles to be reversed.

Thierry had realised very early on that if he was ever to succeed in his ambition he needed to make some money of his own. The trouble was that in the beginning he had gone the wrong way about doing it. As a young man he'd gone completely off the rails, gambling as his father had done before him and playing on the fringes of the criminal society. Those were the days when he had formed a friendship with Yves and Jean-Luc – and they had gained quite a reputation in the locality. Thierry had enjoyed the risk-taking and the drinking, the fast cars and the women. But they hadn't brought him any lasting benefits. Instead they had very nearly ruined him. The odds he had been playing for had been balanced all wrongly, of course. Too little to gain, too much to lose. For the sake of a few francs he had run the risk of going to gaol for a very long time and Thierry had made up his mind: that sort of danger could be justified only if the rewards were rich enough.

Thierry still broke out in a sweat when he remembered how close he had been to ending up in a prison cell.

It had, of course, been mostly Jean-Luc's fault – in Thierry's eyes, at least – but then it was a habit of Thierry's to blame everyone but himself for his misfortunes.

He and Jean-Luc were in Monte Carlo. Yves, for once, was not with them. He had fallen on his feet and taken off with a wealthy and still-beautiful widow who had taken a fancy to him. 'Bloody Gigolo', Thierry had called him, but he had been secretly jealous all the same, thinking of the life of luxury Yves was enjoying in exchange for pretending 'le grand passion' while satisfying the sexual whims of a lonely woman who treated him like a spoiled lapdog.

Thierry and Jean-Luc had played the casino until their money ran out and then they had begun looking for a cheaper way to recoup their losses. It had come in the shape of a party of city whizz-kids who were staying in the same hotel on a wild stag weekend. Thierry and Jean-Luc had found them running their own card school in the hotel lounge and before long they had managed to insinuate themselves into the game.

For card-sharps with Thierry and Jean-Luc's experience, the stockbrokers were an easy target. They were brash, full of themselves, and all in various stages of inebriation. Before long Thierry and Jean-Luc had recouped most of their evening's losses without arousing the slightest suspicion. But then Jean-Luc had become greedy.

During the course of the game, one of the young men had

been losing heavily and another had questioned his ability to meet his debts.

'Don't worry about it!' the young man, named Daniel, had boasted. 'I don't carry all my money in my wallet any more than you do. If I get mugged I want to be sure they only get the loose change.'

'You've got a bank in your briefcase, eh?'

'Haven't you?'

'Well, yes.'

Jean-Luc played the next game thoughtfully, actually managing to lose, and when Thierry went to the bar to buy more drinks, he followed him.

'I'll bet there's a good haul to be had in their rooms.'

'Yeah. They're loaded, the lot of 'em. Why is life so unfair? Stupid little jerks with their poncy accents and rich daddies. They don't even appreciate what they've got.'

'So why don't we do a reallocation of funds? Spread it around a bit?'

'You mean – from their pockets to ours?'

'Exactly. They'll be playing cards for hours, probably won't go to bed at all.'

'I get your drift. You stay down here with them while I . . . investigate.'

'Sure.'

There was no need to elaborate further. Thierry and Jean-Luc had worked together often enough to be able, almost, to read each other's minds.

Thierry knew the young men were all booked into adjoining rooms on the floor below the one where he and Jean-Luc were staying. He'd seen them emerging and meeting up on the landing as he'd been coming downstairs earlier in the day. He played another hand, then got up casually.

'I'm going to take a leak. I'll be back.'

No one took the slightest notice of him as he left the lounge and took the lift to the third floor. It was deserted and his feet made no sound on the thickly carpeted landing.

The locks presented him with no difficulty at all. Simple, straightforward, old-fashioned, he would have been able to pick them in his sleep. He let himself into the first room, searching it and pocketing the money and valuables he found there – gold cufflinks, a Rolex watch, a pair of Aviator sunglasses. Easy! They hadn't even bothered to hide the stuff! He slipped out of the room and moved on to the next.

He was in the third room when he heard the key in the lock. Adrenalin pumping, he dived into the en-suite bathroom, making it just in time. He could hear someone moving about – getting ready for bed? If so he was trapped. He peered through the crack in the door and saw Daniel the stockbroker opening a briefcase which he had put on the writing desk.

Thierry breathed more easily. Obviously Daniel had run out of cash and come for some of his reserve. Luckily Thierry hadn't yet had time to break into the briefcase. Inebriated or not Daniel would certainly have noticed if his 'bank' was missing!

He watched as Daniel took out a wad of notes, stuffed them into his wallet and closed the briefcase. Go – go – go! Thierry urged him. But Daniel didn't. He started towards the en-suite where Thierry was hiding. Christ – he was going to use the john! Thierry looked round wildly, saw the shower curtain surrounding the bath, and dived for it. And then his luck ran out.

There was a plastic screen as well as a curtain around the shower area of the bath and he crashed straight into it.

Thierry went cold all over. Unless he could bluff his way out – pretend he'd come into the wrong room by mistake – Daniel would very likely call hotel security and they would call the police. But Daniel didn't call security. Thierry almost wished he had.

Who would have thought it? he'd complained afterwards. Who would have thought a wimp like that would pull a knife on him? The idiot had only himself to blame for what happened. After all, what else could Thierry have done but protect himself?

Well, he'd done that all right. Thierry was fit and streetwise, Daniel out of condition and drunk. The struggle was over almost before it began and Daniel crumpled to the floor, gurgling and moaning, a patch of scarlet spreading across his white shirt. But his eyes were open, and his surprised expression told Thierry he had been recognised. In panic he grabbed the knife and stabbed again and again.

Daniel was dead. Christ, he'd killed him! Sweat broke out, cold and clammy, all over Thierry's body, then his instinct for self-preservation took over again. He had to get out of here – act normally. His hands were covered in blood and there were splashes on his evening suit but miraculously none on his white shirt. He stepped over the body, washed his hands at the sink and sponged his jacket. Then he switched off the lights, opened the door a crack and waited, listening. Silence. He slipped out into the corridor and closed the door behind him. He would go back downstairs, give himself an alibi. With any luck no one would find Daniel until morning.

He ran up one flight of stairs and into the lift on his own floor. If anyone was in the lobby they would see the indicator showing three, not two. But the lobby was deserted.

In the lounge the game was still going on. Thierry took his seat, avoiding Jean-Luc's eyes.

'What's happened to old Daniel?' someone asked.

'Called it a day I expect. He's lost enough for one night.'

You can say that again! Thierry thought and almost laughed.

'I'm ready for bed myself,' he said.

When they were alone he told Jean-Luc what had happened.

'You did *what*? You stupid bastard! We'd better get out of here!'

'No. We'd only draw attention to ourselves. We'll stay till morning and check out in the normal way.'

'But your fingerprints will be all over the bloody place!'

'Not on the knife. I wiped that clean. And the door handles. And in any case, are they going to fingerprint all the guests? Of course they're not! That's what we are, Jean-Luc, bona fide guests. No one's going to suspect us. They'll think it was a burglar he surprised.'

'It was!'

'But I'll bet my shirt no one will point a finger in our direction.'

'I hope to God you're right!'

He was. Next morning when Daniel's body was discovered, a great many worried guests checked out of the hotel and Thierry and Jean-Luc checked out with them. The moment they were away from the town they knew they were safe – the Three Musketeers never booked into hotels under their own names. It was over. They'd got away with it.

Except of course that afterwards nothing was quite the same. Jean-Luc was nervous now, he wanted to dissociate himself from Thierry in case someone, after all, came asking questions. He had taken the first legitimate job he had had in his life – as a steward on a cruise ship – and apart from the odd postcard from some exotic spot, Thierry had seen or heard nothing of him for years.

Until a few weeks ago, when he had turned up out of the blue, threatening the life which Thierry had made for himself, and all his plans for the future.

From the moment Alain had invited Thierry to work with him in the newly formed Lavaur Wine Company, Thierry had realised he was on to a good thing. Alain was an astute businessman, and backed with Lavaur money the venture had seemed certain to be a success. Thierry had looked into the future and seen a life that was very much to his taste – a good salary, a company car, and plenty of opportunity for socialising – not to mention unlimited access to the best wines in Languedoc. He had never been under any illusion about Alain's reason for taking him on – the blood-brothers bond had long since been eroded, and Thierry was well aware that Alain was championing him for Hélène's sake.

At first this did not worry him unduly, then gradually it had begun to rankle. Though he managed to hide his feelings, Thierry resented the Lavaurs' patronising attitude, and disliked feeling beholden to his brother-in-law. Most of all he was infuriated by the feeling of being on trial, of not being entirely trusted. When Alain and Hélène split up, Thierry hated Alain even more for causing his sister such unhappiness.

It was when Alain had gone to England, leaving Thierry in charge of the French end of the operation, that he had seen his chance.

Slowly and systematically he had begun milking the profits and stashing away the money in a Swiss bank account. It was, he found, surprisingly easy, for Alain had placed more trust in him that he had ever suspected. Each time he misappropriated a cheque which rightfully belonged to the company he experienced a heady triumph. A little more Lavaur money to feather the Rousseau nest – and by God, they owed it to him!

The malicious pleasure he gained from knowing he was putting one over on Alain was as great as contemplating his growing bank balance. The whole thing would come crashing down in the end, of course, but by the time it did, Thierry would have gone, disappearing into the wide blue yonder with the happy prospect of living out the rest of his life in luxury – at Alain's expense.

Only one thing concerned him – the fact that in cheating Alain he was also cheating Hélène, the one person in the world he had ever truly cared for. He did not like the idea of her being short of money, which she undoubtedly would be if Alain went bankrupt. Then the perfect solution had occurred to him. If he were to insure his life for a hefty sum, naming Hélène as beneficiary, and then proceed to fake his own death, he would be killing two birds with one stone. Hélène would not suffer financially and no one would think to look for him. Not that they would have found him, of course – he had no intention of using his own identity for his new life – but all the same, it would be tidier and safer if he was believed to be dead.

He had begun to work on different plans, gaining pleasure from each and every one of them, but he had been in no hurry. He intended to milk every single franc he could out of Lavaur Wines first.

And then Jean-Luc had turned up, and everything had begun to go wrong.

Back in France for the first time in years, Jean-Luc had looked up his old friend, and when he had discovered him in a position of responsibility at Lavaur Wines he had been as quick to grasp the possibilities as Thierry had been before him. But he didn't see why Thierry should be the only one to profit. He wanted his share of the booty too.

'I hope you're not going to forget your old friends now that your ship has come in,' he said to Thierry one night as they shared a drink in a country bistro/bar.

Thierry looked up at him sharply.

'What do you mean?'

'Well, it sounds to me as though there's plenty for both of us. Oh man, I can see it already! You and me living it up at last! Come on now, don't look at me like that! We were always the Three Musketeers, weren't we? All for one and one for all.'

Thierry was outraged.

'Yves was one of the Three Musketeers too. Surely you're not suggesting I cut him in as well?'

'No.' Jean-Luc smiled cunningly, his lips clamped around his cigarette. 'That would be pushing it a bit far.'

'So why the hell do you think you should share in my good fortune and not Yves?'

Jean-Luc removed the cigarette from his mouth, looking at Thierry through narrowed eyes.

'Well, Yves doesn't know you as well as I do, does he? He couldn't put the finger on you for a certain killing in Monte Carlo a few years back, could he? Whereas I could give them chapter and verse. Oh I wouldn't, of course. Not as long as we're friends. But if we weren't . . .'

'For Christ's sake!' Thierry said. He had broken out in a cold sweat.

'Don't look so worried, old son! I told you – see me all right and my lips are sealed.'

'That's bloody blackmail!'

'Don't call it that. Call it insurance.'

'You bastard, Jean-Luc! You were as much involved in that mess as I was!'

'But you were the one who killed him. I was downstairs like a good little boy, drinking with his friends. Come on, Thierry, play the game. I won't be too greedy. A new car, maybe? A few cases of Lavaur's best wines? And the knowledge that your secret is safe with me.'

Afterwards Thierry was never quite certain exactly when he made up his mind that Jean-Luc had to die. Perhaps there was never a precise moment and when the opportunity presented itself it just happened. But he knew that Jean-Luc's demands wouldn't stop with a car and a few cases of wine. Blackmailers always wanted more – and more. Thierry had no intention of sharing any of the money he'd salted away for himself and he knew too that while Jean-Luc was holding his secret over him he could never feel safe again.

They were heading home through the mountain roads, and because he was so angry Thierry was driving a little recklessly.

'Slow down!' Jean-Luc snapped, holding on to the dashboard as the tyres screamed around a hairpin bend where the ground fell away into nothingness only feet from the road. 'What are you trying to do – kill us both?'

And that was when Thierry knew exactly what he was going to do.

He pulled the car off the road into an escape route, feigned starting the argument again to avoid arousing Jean-Luc's suspicions, and palmed the knife he always carried with him these days. It was easy, almost unbelievably easy, to kill the unsuspecting Jean-Luc. He went for the heart and it was all over in moments. Thierry felt none of the panic he had felt when he had killed Daniel the stockbroker, and certainly no remorse. Jean-Luc had taken him for a fool and he deserved all he got. And unwittingly he had provided Thierry with the perfect cover for his own disappearance.

Coldly and systematically Thierry removed anything which might identify Jean-Luc, strapped his own watch on to his wrist and forced his rings on to Jean-Luc's fingers.

He drove to a spot where he knew the ground fell away steeply to a river gorge many hundreds of feet below, transferred Jean-Luc's body to the driving seat, finding the superhuman strength which seemed to come easily when the adrenalin was surging. Then he constructed a makeshift petrol bomb with his spare fuel can and crumpled rags, lit it, and pushed the car over the edge. His only concern was that the petrol bomb would not ignite, but he need not have worried. The jolting of the car as it hit the rocks over and over again set it off easily; by the time it reached the bottom of the ravine it was already an inferno.

The worst part of the whole exercise, Thierry thought, had been getting away from the scene. He had had to walk for miles to reach the derelict farmhouse which had once belonged to his family, with one ear constantly cocked for any traffic on the road. There was none.

Thierry had long since decided to use the farmhouse as a base when his plan was put into action and he had equipped it accordingly with food and drink, a change of clothes and enough cash to cover any emergency. He even had a cheap second-hand car hidden in the barn and filled with petrol. All he had to do, he told himself, was to bring his plan forward instead of waiting to milk the last of the funds. But he was less prepared for flight than he should have been. When he had left to meet Jean-Luc that night it had not occurred to him to take his passport with him. Now he realised he would have to risk going home in order to collect it.

For a couple of weeks he lay low, growing a beard to change

his appearance and dyeing his hair. The disguise enabled him to shop for fresh supplies in places he was not known without fear of recognition, but going back to the house was a far more dangerous prospect. Hélène would not be fooled for a moment should he bump into her. He began making phone calls to the house in order to try to ascertain when it was empty, but each time the phone was answered by Hélène, and he could tell from her voice she was getting worried that there was no one on the end of the line.

Did she never go out? He began to wish he hadn't waited so long – perhaps in the days immediately after the funeral the house would have been less likely to be occupied. But there it was – too late now. He'd just have to do the best he could.

One night, very late, he drove to within striking distance, then walked the rest of the way and hid in the bushes, keeping the house under surveillance for a while. All the lights were out, but he was a little disturbed to see Simone's car parked outside. That meant there were two of them to worry about. But he'd have to take a chance now that he was here and hope that she and Hélène were both sleeping soundly.

As quietly as possible he made for the back door. He had his keys ready, but he did not need them – the door was unlocked anyway. He crept inside and up the stairs, amused by the bizarre notion of burgling one's own home. But when he made it to the room which used to be his he was shocked to find the box file containing his passport was missing. Hélène must have moved it – though everything else seemed to be in place. By the light of the moon he searched the room; no luck. The box file was not there. He went back downstairs wondering what the hell to do now. Without his passport, the whole plan would be scuppered. In the dark he crashed into a chair. Clumsy idiot! He froze, listening, saw the landing light snap on, sending an orange glow down the stairs.

Thierry waited for nothing then. It might be Hélène, and he was certainly going to have to come clean to her if he wanted his passport, but equally it might be Simone. Even if it was Hélène she might become hysterical when she saw him, and Simone would be disturbed by the commotion. Thierry slipped silently out of the house, flattening himself to the wall outside the door and waiting.

It was Simone. He saw her clearly at the lighted window. But after a while the lights went out again and Thierry was able to creep away, back to his waiting car. He was badly shaken by the narrowness of his escape and furious that he had been unable to retrieve his passport.

What irony! he thought angrily. For the first time in his life he had enough money to keep him in luxury stashed away and waiting for him, yet he was unable to get to it!

He had no choice now but to take Hélène into his confidence, he realised, but if Simone was staying with her it might be difficult to catch her on her own. The following morning he went back to the house, parking well out of sight, and after a while Hélène came out, driving her car. He followed her, but she sped away on to the main road and headed, of all places, for Le Château Gris. Thierry waited until nightfall, but he was forced to give up when it became apparent she was staying the night there.

Next day, as he drove around wondering what to do next, he saw her old car – the Saab 96 – and set off after it. He couldn't imagine why she should be driving it – some problem with her new one perhaps? – but he followed anyway. Again the car sped off, and he tailed it, flashing his lights to attract her attention and never for one moment stopping to think that in doing so he might cause an accident.

When he saw the driver lose control Thierry went cold with horror and swore aloud. Christ almighty, Hélène, what are you doing? As if in slow motion he saw it scrape a roadside tree and run headlong into a ditch, and felt his stomach turn as it had never done for any of his other victims. He screamed to a stop, all thoughts of capture forgotten in his concern for his sister, but to his amazement he saw that the woman driver was not Hélène at all, but a perfect stranger. Puzzled and frustrated yet again, Thierry drove quickly on.

There was nothing for it now but to try to ring Hélène. Eventually he managed to get her on the line, though he thought she was going to fall apart completely when she heard his voice.

'I need your help, Hélène,' he told her when he had calmed her down a little. 'I'm at the old farmhouse. Can you meet me there?'

And she had. She had driven over, pathetically eager to see him, and they had talked so late into the night that Hélène had decided to stay.

He hadn't told her the truth, of course. He'd spun her a cock-and-bull yarn about Jean-Luc dying in an accident and that he had been afraid he would be blamed and now needed to flee the country. It was an unlikely story, but, Hélène being Hélène, she had believed him.

This morning she had set out to collect the passport. Thierry hoped she could get it without arousing suspicion. But he had stressed the need for secrecy and he had no choice but to trust her and hope for the best.

While he was waiting he drove into the village for a few things he needed – among them a razor to shave off his beard in order to satisfy the border patrols, who could sometimes prove awkward if a passport photograph was not a good enough likeness. But it was in the village that he had come close to disaster.

As he emerged from the little chemist's shop he had walked straight into one of the few people who knew him so well that no disguise on earth could prevent recognition. His old friend, Yves Marssac. Before Thierry could even think of ducking or turning away they were face to face and Yves's startled expression told Thierry he had been well and truly rumbled.

'Thierry?' Yves said incredulously. 'My God, it *is* you, isn't it? You're supposed to be dead, you cheating bastard!'

Thierry looked around sharply, terrified someone else might have overheard. But the shop assistant was busy and no one had taken notice of the exchange – yet.

'I don't believe this!' Yves said. He was grinning now, that amused grin that was his trademark. 'I followed a coffin that was supposed to have you in it! What the hell are you up to Thierry?'

He knew then that he had to do something – and fast. He was torn between making a run for it and thinking of a way to dispose of Yves as he had disposed of Jean-Luc. But making a run for it wouldn't help, and he certainly couldn't kill Yves here, in broad daylight in the middle of a village street, and get away with it. There was really only one thing for it, he thought, and that was to tell him enough of the story to satisfy him and then try to buy him off.

'Keep your voice down!' he hissed, taking Yves's arm and propelling him into the street. 'Let's go somewhere quiet for a drink and I'll explain.'

'Like hell you will! I don't know that I want to drink with a ghost!'

But he went with him anyway because his curiosity would not allow him to do otherwise.

They drove to an *auberge* just outside the village and ordered coffee and croissants, though neither of them felt in the least like eating.

'So – what's the idea of letting us all think you were dead?' Yves asked, propping his feet up on the rungs of a vacant chair.

'Haven't you ever wished you could just disappear?' Thierry countered.

'Sometimes, yes. But there's usually a reason. What's yours?'

'Money,' Thierry said truthfully.

'Money. Ah.' Behind his Ray-Bans Yves's heavy-lidded eyes narrowed speculatively. 'Would this by any chance have anything to do with the mess at Lavaur Wines?' Thierry said nothing, and he laughed softly. 'Yes, of course it has. You've been cooking the books, haven't you?'

'Maybe.'

'I did wonder. My God, you've got Alain going. He's in a tail-spin trying to sort it all out. How much have you embezzled?'

'Enough to keep me in comfort while I decide how to capitalise on it, shall we say?'

'Well, well! You old fox, Thierry. It's good, I must say. Nobody would be likely to look for the missing millions in your direction since they all think you're under a slab of concrete in the cemetery.' He chuckled. 'Who did we bury, as a matter of interest?'

'A hitch-hiker.' Thierry had no intention of telling him it was the third Musketeer.

'Poor sod. Accident, was it?' His tone was heavy with sarcasm.

'Of course.'

'Of course!' He drained his cup. 'This is my lucky day, isn't it?'

'How do you mean?'

'I'm sure you'd want to share your good fortune with an old friend. We always shared everything, remember?'

Thierry's mouth tightened. Jean-Luc had said something similar, and now Jean-Luc was dead. But there was no need for him to get rid of Yves. As soon as Hélène got back with the passport he'd be out of the country and living under an assumed name. Yves wouldn't be able to find him and nor would anyone else. He had to play for time, that was all – make sure Yves didn't shoot his mouth off before he was ready to go. And the best way to make sure of that was not to let him out of his sight.

'I've been staying out at the old farmhouse,' he said. 'Why don't we go back there now and I can give you a little something to remember me by.'

Yves grinned. 'So we still understand one another! All right, I'll follow you.'

They finished their coffee and Thierry paid the bill while Yves disappeared in search of the bathroom. Then they set off in convoy once more, Thierry leading.

As he manoeuvred the can through the lanes he was still cursing the bad luck which had made him walk straight into Yves, of all people, still wondering at the quirk of fate which had brought the Three Musketeers together again after all these years. But it scarcely mattered now. A few more hours and he'd be the other side of the border, a few hours more and Thierry Rousseau would have disappeared for good. If Yves spilled the beans then it would only make Alain realise that Thierry had made a complete fool of him. Thierry rather liked the idea. It was frustrating that no one would otherwise know how clever he had been.

He rounded a bend and saw a dark pall of smoke hanging in the clear blue sky, but paid it little attention. It was only when he had taken turn after turn and still the smoke was directly ahead of him that he felt the first qualm of alarm. Then, as he turned off the road into the track, he saw a police car blocking his way. He stopped abruptly, cold sweat breaking out all over his body, and slammed the car into reverse. Jesus Christ! Yves had already turned into the track behind him, and with no room to pass, let alone turn, Thierry felt the sick fear of a trapped animal. But the police car was empty. Thierry got out of the car and ran back to Yves.

'Something's going on.'

'Looks like a fire. It's not your farmhouse, is it?'

'I bloody well hope not! Oh my God!' Suddenly he was thinking not of his own skin, but of Hélène. She would almost certainly be back by now – unless she, too, had found the road blocked. But somehow he didn't think so.

'Yves – Hélène could be in there! For Christ's sake find out for me!'

'All right, all right – calm down.'

But he couldn't calm down. He couldn't think of anything but that Hélène might be in danger. She was the one person he cared about – had ever cared about. He'd killed twice and not lost a moment's sleep over it, but if anything happened to Hélène and it was his fault he knew he'd never forgive himself.

He paced the lane, waiting, his heart thudding, dread washing over him in cold waves. After what seemed like an eternity Yves was back.

'Yup! Your farmhouse has gone up in smoke.' He was grinning.

Thierry grabbed him by his shirt. 'You think that's funny? What about Hélène? Did you find out?'

'Stay cool, man!' Yves placed a hand in the middle of Thierry's chest, patting him. 'I talked to a policeman. She was there, you were right, but she got out. With another woman. She's in the hospital now.'

'Hospital! Is she hurt?'

'She'd inhaled smoke, by the sound of it. But they think she's going to be all right.'

'Thank God!' A rush of relief left him weak, then what Yves had said came home to him suddenly. 'Did you say there was another woman?'

'That's what I was told. Two women.'

'Simone?'

'The policeman thought she was English. A visitor.'

English! It must have been Alain's girlfriend – the one Hélène had told him about. But what was she doing there with Hélène? Did it mean that she, too, knew about him?'

'Let's get over to that hospital, Yves,' he said roughly. 'I want to make sure Hélène is all right.'

And one or two other things besides, he added silently.

Alain's car was parked outside the hospital and Thierry knew there was no way he could get inside to speak to Hélène himself.

'See what you can find out,' he said to Yves.

Yves raised an eyebrow. Thierry always had been too fond of issuing orders. But this time it was in his own interest to get as much information as he could. This morning, while pretending to use the bathroom, he'd found a telephone and made a call to the reporter who had been sniffing around. He hadn't been in, and Yves hadn't yet been able to drop the bombshell that Thierry was not dead at all but very much alive, but he guessed that the more he knew the more he would be able to screw out of the reporter.

Thierry waited for Yves in the car, sweating a little both from the hot sun and because he was afraid he might be spotted. Though they had parked in an out-of-the-way corner he was uncomfortably aware that there were people in the vicinity who would recognise him, beard or no beard, as easily as Yves had done. He slid down low in the seat, burying his face in a large road map which he found under the dash.

After ten minutes or so Yves was back, sliding into the car.

'Well?' Thierry barked.

'I think you're safe – for the moment,' Yves said. 'I talked to Alain and he didn't say anything to suggest he knows you're still alive.'

'Did you find out who the other woman at the farm was?'

'His girlfriend from England. But if she knows anything I don't think she's told him. She's gone back to Le Château Gris now.'

'What about Hélène?'

'They're keeping her in, but Alain doesn't seem to think there's any lasting damage.'

Thierry exhaled sharply.

'Thank God for that!' But another thought had occurred to him. 'I've still got a problem, though, haven't I? Hélène's the only one who knows where my passport is. Jeez, I hope it wasn't in the farmhouse. If it's been destroyed . . .'

Yves grinned, enjoying Thierry's predicament.

'Probably has.'

'Shit! That means I'm stuck here until I can get hold of another one. Have you got any contacts who might be able to help?'

'I could sort it for you, I expect – at a price.'

Thierry swore again. This whole thing, which had seemed to be running so smoothly, was suddenly a mess. It galled him to think he would have to part with yet more of his 'investment', as he chose to call it, to purchase a fake passport, but he didn't see that he had any choice. More serious was the delay it was bound to cause. His hiding place at the farmhouse had been wrecked by fire and there was an interfering English girl who may or may not know he was still alive, and may or may not decide to tell someone about it.

'What are you going to do then?' Yves asked, mock-solicitous.

'Until you can get me a passport I can't do much, can I?' Thierry grumbled. 'Take me back to my car. At least that way I'll be mobile and I'll sort out somewhere else to lie low for the time being.'

'And what if this Esther spills the beans?'

'We'll just have to hope she doesn't,' Thierry said, but he had already made up his mind. He couldn't leave a thing like that to chance.

Alain was likely to stay at the hospital with Hélène for hours yet, and probably all night. Isobelle and Henri were away. That meant Esther would be all alone at Le Château Gris.

Thierry's lips tightened to a hard, decisive line. There was only one thing for it – Esther would have to be silenced before she told anyone what she knew. It was the only way he could stay in this country for as long as it took and be safe.

In the thirty-odd years of his life, Thierry had already killed twice. He knew now that he would not shrink from doing so again.

25

ANDREW HAD EVENTUALLY managed to get hold of Yves Marssac.

'I understand you rang earlier today while I was out.'

'That's right.' There was a slight pause. 'And I understand you are interested in Thierry Rousseau for reasons you didn't mention when you came here on the pretext of buying one of Valerie's pictures.' As always there was a slightly insulting note in Yves's drawling tone, and it put Andrew on his guard.

'What exactly do you mean by that?'

'Oh come on, we both know you're not quite what you seem,' Yves countered. 'You are a reporter, looking for a story, and I think I can help you out there. In fact I could give you the goods on Thierry if I wanted to.'

Andrew felt a prickle of excitement. 'And do you want to?'

'Depends.'

'On what?'

'On whether it would be worth my while. It's a big story – worth big bucks.'

'You mean you're only prepared to tell it for financial gain.'

'That's about the size of it. I'm sure there are plenty of others who would reward me for it if you're not interested.'

'Oh, I'm interested,' Andrew said. 'But I'd have to know a bit more about what you can tell me before I made any definite offers. Can you give me some idea?'

'Not over the telephone. Can you meet me?'

'Sure. Where?'

'There's a bar . . .' Yves described it, a place in the market square of a small town, twenty kilometres or so in the direction of Perpignan. Andrew was intrigued. There must be other places, closer for both of them. He could only assume Yves had his reasons for selecting this one, and the most likely was that he didn't want to be seen talking to a reporter.

'When?' he asked.

'About an hour?'

Andrew glanced at his watch, thought ruefully of the fresh sardines he had seen in the kitchen, marinating for one of Diana's famous barbecues, and decided that there were some things that were more important than satisfying his stomach.

'I'll be there,' he said.

Simone was wandering around the rather wild garden at the rear of her cottage.

The sun was setting in a blaze of red over the Pyrenees, the dying heat drawing the last sweetness out of the huge bush roses which she seldom got around to pruning, and the swifts wheeled overhead in huge sweeping circles. This was usually her favourite time of day, when she could come out into the garden and enjoy the peace, satisfied after a productive working day, but now that safe ordered habit seemed to belong to another lifetime. She had hoped that when she reached what must surely be the end of the story she would be able to fall back into the old routine, but tonight such an idyll seemed as far away as ever.

It is not over. Why had those words come into her head when she had left Esther at Le Château Gris? *It is not over*. But it *must* be over, surely? Esther, who had once been Jeanne, had managed to avoid causing the death of her rival. What more could there possibly be?

Simone reached out and tweaked a sprig of lavender from a nearby bush, crushing it between her fingers and smelling its haunting perfume. The lavender was ready for drying; if she wanted to make some into sachets for her friends in the city now was the time to do it. But with the Simon de Montfort book still to be finished – *when* she could bring herself to get back to it – she didn't think there would be any lavender bags this year.

Simone sighed. She felt dreadfully low – exhausted by all that had happened, and also sad for Esther that she had been so badly hurt. Once, long ago, Simone had been in love and though her feelings had not been reciprocated she could remember what a broken heart felt like. But it had been inevitable really. Simone had thought from the beginning that Alain and Hélène would get back together eventually. They had been together so long and shared so much, and Simone suspected that the fact they had not divorced had been as much Alain's reluctance to take the final step as it was Hélène's.

He should never have got involved with someone else and led them on, she thought, angry with him suddenly. It simply wasn't fair. But she didn't suppose he'd meant it to happen. He'd been lonely and tired of the rows and he hadn't wanted to acknowledge how much he still cared for Hélène.

And perhaps there had been even more to it than that. The attraction between his soul and Esther's, reaching down the centuries, had been just too strong to resist. Besides, if Alain hadn't brought Esther here to Languedoc, history would not have been able to repeat itself. Some things were written – she knew that now.

The sharp pang of anxiety tugged at her again. It wasn't just that she was tired and sad – it was more, much more. Something was wrong. Something was still unresolved.

Her skin prickled suddenly with foreboding – a sense of imminent danger – and at the same moment a wind sprang up, rustling the leaves of the apricot tree and blowing up a whirlwind of dust. Some of it went into her eyes; she screwed them up instinctively, rubbing them with her fingers, but when she opened them again the air still seemed to be swirling. Giddy, disorientated, Simone reached out for the branches of the apricot tree to steady herself.

It was happening again. The past was there all around her, the dust moving to form images, shadowy at first, then gradually taking shape. She sank to her knees, twisting into a sitting position. And once again, she saw Jeanne.

In the soft spring sunshine which dappled the courtyard of Montaugure the horses stamped their feet and tossed their heads, eager to be gone. Already the men-at-arms who were to escort her were mounted and waiting, but Jeanne lingered, holding Bernard's hands in hers and feeling her heart fill with love and the grief of parting.

'Be strong, my son.'

His handsome young face was set; he was already too much of a man to allow his emotion to show.

'You know I will. But I still don't understand, Mother, why you have to go.'

Fleetingly Jeanne found herself remembering the day, so many years ago now, when Agnes had left and how she had asked much the same question. Her answer now must also be the same – though in her case it was only a part of the truth.

'There are some things which we have to do,' she said. 'Perhaps one day you will understand that.'

'Oh, I know what you are going to do, Mother. You are going to be a Cathar. What I don't understand is why.'

'Because it is the only way I can find salvation. I have sinned, grievously, and I must atone in the only way I know.'

'But you could make your confession . . .'

Oh Bernard! she thought, already a Catholic . . .

'It wouldn't be enough for me,' she said aloud, and added silently: nor for God – and certainly not for Philip. But she could not bring herself to explain to her son that it was for her part in Alazais's death that she must purge herself.

She shivered now, closing her eyes briefly as once again the images of that terrible day rose to envelop her, a nightmare from which she could never escape. They would haunt her, she knew, for the rest of her days. It was her punishment for her wickedness – that and the knowledge that Philip would never forgive her.

When he had heard what had happened, Philip had raced south and taken her home with him to Montaugure. But his inconsolable grief had told her that whatever had been between then, he had truly loved Alazais. Tormented beyond endurance, she had seen the shock and revulsion come into his face and known that he despised her.

There was only one thing for it, she had decided – and that was to follow the dictates of her conscience and return to the faith of her childhood. Only then might she find some measure of peace and hope of salvation. Bernard would be well cared for – in spite of what she had done, Philip still wished him to be his heir – and he and the rest of the Bertrands would be safer if she was no longer at Montaugure. She was, after all, a known Cathar, and who knew when she would again be summoned by the Inquisition? Her very presence in their household endangered them all.

When she had told Philip what she planned to do he had not tried to dissaude her and she knew he would prefer never to see her again. Though she had told him she did not require it he had insisted on giving her an armed escort for the journey and she wondered if he wanted to be sure she had really left. Certainly he had not come to bid her goodbye, and for that she was grateful. She did not think she could have borne the moment of parting. Bad enough to leave her son, knowing it was unlikely she would ever see him again.

Tears stung her eyes and she blinked them away, trying to smile.

'God be with you. Perhaps one day when these troubled times are over we will be together once more.'

She clasped him to her and found herself remembering the day she had brought him into the world. How long ago it seemed now! For a moment he stood stiff and awkward in her embrace, then suddenly he was hugging her back, crushing her almost, for he was now taller than she was by several inches.

Oh dear God how she loved him! Everything she had done she had done for him and now she must leave him to the future she had secured for him by her sin. How cruel life could be – what a bitter hand fate could deal out! She only prayed that Bernard would be spared the suffering she had endured.

'I must leave. A long journey lies ahead of me,' she said, swallowing her tears.

He nodded, in command of himself once more, and stood watching dry-eyed as she mounted the little mare who was to carry her to Montsegur.

At the castle gates she turned back to look at him one last time. He was standing erect, hands on hips, and it seemed to her that the morning sun was turning his hair to gold. Jeanne's heart rose in her throat. She raised her hand to him in a final farewell and urged her mare beneath the portcullis.

When they reached the edge of the Bertrand lands Jeanne dismissed the men-at-arms. They protested, but she was adamant. She preferred to make this journey alone.

For an hour or so she rode on, retracing the path she had taken so many years ago on the way to Montsegur. Her heart was heavy but she was longing now to reach the sanctuary of the Cathar stronghold and begin on the path of atonement. She did not believe that in this life she would ever forgive herself for what she had done, but at least if she was able to take the *Consolamentum* she would perhaps be making her peace with God.

In her youth, Jeanne had made the journey to Montsegur without proper food or lodging; now she was older and less resilient. When the sun began to set in the western sky she came upon an isolated hamlet and decided to seek shelter there for the night.

The people she spoke to in the main street looked at her curiously – a woman riding alone was a matter for conjecture. But one old woman offered her a bed in an *ostal* – though she would have to share it with the old woman's two daughters – and gratefully Jeanne accepted her offer. She tied up her little mare, fed and watered her, and shared her host's meagre supper before retiring to the cellar and creeping into the bed she found there beside the two resentful girls.

Tired though she was, Jeanne slept badly, but towards dawn she drifted into a deep slumber.

Footsteps on the bare stone stairs leading down to the cellar and the metallic clank of spurs roused her; she came awake with a jolt and saw two soldiers standing by the bed. The girls with whom she had shared it were gone. Jeanne sat up, then, uncomfortably aware that she was clad in nothing but her shift, pulled the thin blanket up to her chin. One of the soldiers tore it from her grasp, leering as he pulled it aside.

'Get up.' She stared at him, mute with horror, and he took her by the arm, jerking her roughly from the bed. 'There's someone who wants to see you.'

The soldiers stood watching while she wriggled into her gown, then pushed her in front of them up the stone stairs. There was no sign of the woman who had given her lodging or her daughters, but the hooded figure of a monk stood looking out of the window. As he heard her behind him in the room he turned, and with a shock Jeanne recognised her brother.

'Pons!'

'Jeanne.' He sighed, shaking his head. 'I thought that you had learned your lesson when your friend went to the stake. But that is not so, is it? It has come to my notice that you are on your way to Montsegur. You have not renounced the heresy at all, have you?'

Jeanne raised her chin, though she was trembling in the cold dawn air.

'No, Pons, I have not renounced it. My only salvation lies in making my peace with my God. I know you have turned from the faith of our childhood, but I beg you, try to understand what it means to me.'

He snorted impatiently. 'Oh, I understand that, all right. You are still a heretic. Well, I am sorry, Jeanne, but there is only one course left open to me if I am to save your eternal soul.'

She felt the blood drain from her body.

'What do you mean?' But she already knew.

'The stake, Jeanne. You must be purified by the stake.'

She swallowed at the lump of terror which had risen in her throat.

'You wouldn't . . .'

'What choice do I have? My sister – a heretic. It is my duty to save you.' He motioned to the soldiers. 'Take her!'

They stepped forward, gripping Jeanne by the arms. Briefly she struggled, then stood erect and proud. How could she defy the fate which she had seen the innocent Alazais suffer?

'Very well. If that is what you want. Only first I must receive the *Consolamentum*.'

He raised an eyebrow. 'You can't be serious.'

'Never more. I must be allowed the last rite of my faith.'

'You think that I would permit such heathen trickery? Oh no, Jeanne, if you repent you must make your confession to God in the manner prescribed by the Church of Rome.'

'Pons, please . . . !' She was terrified now, not so much by the threat of the stake, terrible as it was, as by the prospect of dying without having been allowed the *Consolamentum* to begin, at least, the cleansing of her sin. 'I beg you, allow me at least to talk with a Perfect . . .'

He turned from her, his face like stone, and gestured once more to the soldiers.

'Take her.'

The stake had been prepared, Jeanne had been tied to it. As the soldiers prepared to light the faggots, Pons climbed on to the pyre beside her. He had a sword in his hand.

'I wish to spare your suffering, my sister. Recant, and I will see that it is short.'

She shook her head, beyond words.

A strange light came into his eyes. For a moment he stared at her, then he raised the sword, placing its tip against her heart. For a moment she felt it, piercing the fabric of her gown, then he lunged. She felt no pain, only surprise that he had chosen this way to end her life. The blood gushed, scarlet in the sunshine, and her legs gave way beneath her. Only the bonds securing her to the stake held her upright. But to Jeanne it seemed that she was falling, falling, not on to the stacked faggots but into a bottomless pit. The darkness was all around, deep and impenetrable, and the cry of her pierced heart never left her lips.

'Oh God, have mercy on my soul!'

But the blackness was also silent, thick and unforgiving.

By the time the soldiers set light to the faggots, Jeanne was dead.

As the pictures faded, Simone returned to full consciousness with a jolt. The feeling of horror had intensified now, crystalised by the vision into the realisation that, as her instinct had warned her, it was not over. Esther might have prevented Hélène's death, but she was still in mortal danger herself – from the soul who had once been Pons.

Who could that be? If Aurore's theory that souls reincarnated in family groups was correct, it must be someone close to them now. But who? Simone was certain that Alain must once have been Philip, but there was no other man in their immediate family circle apart from her father, and Simone could not imagine he could pose any threat to Esther in his degenerate state. A woman, then? There was no law to say Pons must have reincarnated as a man. But she couldn't think of a woman, either, who would fit the bill.

Well, there was no point in wasting time on supposition. Esther must be warned she was in danger – and warned right away. Simone hurried back into the house.

Darkness had fallen while the final chapter in the story had been revealing itself to her and Simone was shocked to see that it was now past ten o'clock.

Had Alain returned from the hospital? she wondered. If he had, then Esther would be safe for tonight, at least. But somehow she didn't think he would have returned. If Hélène needed him, then he would almost certainly have stayed at her side.

She turned to the telephone and dialled the number of Le Château Gris.

It was a long while before the telephone was answered, and Simone was about to give up when Esther's sleepy voice came on the line.

'Esther,' Simone said urgently. 'Are you all right?'

'Yes. I'd fallen asleep in the chair, that's all.

'Oh.' Simone hesitated. 'Is Alain home?'

'No. I don't think he will be home tonight.' Her voice was flat, tightly controlled.

'Esther . . .' Simone hesitated again. No point warning her. She wouldn't take any more notice now than she had before. She didn't really know why she had rung, except to reassure herself that nothing had happened to her already. 'Look – I'm coming over,' she said.

'Tonight?' Esther sounded not only surprised but irritated. 'What on earth for?'

'It will be easier to explain face to face. But I beg you to take care until I get there . . .' She broke off, realising how peculiar that would sound to Esther. 'It really is important that I talk to you.'

'Look – I appreciate your concern, but I'm absolutely fine. Just very tired. I really don't feel up to talking to anyone tonight. As I said, I was asleep when you called, and now I'm going to bed. I've got a long day ahead of me tomorrow. I'll call you in the morning, before I leave.'

'You're definitely going home then?'

'Oh, I think so. There's no point in me staying here any longer.'

Simone hesitated, and before she could say any more, Esther went on: 'I'll talk to you again. Sleep well, Simone.'

'Esther . . .'

But the line was dead. Simone hit the redial button but got only the engaged tone in response. Esther had evidently guessed she might call again and left the phone off the hook. Simone stood for a moment feeling utterly helpless, then gave herself a little shake.

At least she knew Esther was all right. If she was going to bed now nothing could happen to her tonight – could it? And if she went home tomorrow perhaps that would be the end of it.

But the anxiety was still nagging at her and Simone couldn't shake off the dreadful certainty that it could not be that easy.

Esther put down the telephone, then removed it from its cradle, feeling a little guilty about doing so but too tired and fed up to want to take any more calls tonight. Simone might very well ring back and she couldn't face it. Besides being utterly wretched she was feeling muzzy and disorientated from being woken from a deep sleep and a little sick from drinking a good deal of Alain's whisky on an empty stomach.

She locked the door, removing the key from the lock in case Alain should come home during the night, but somehow she didn't think he would. At this very moment he was probably sitting beside Hélène's bed in the private room at the hospital, holding her hand and looking at her with that expression of love and concern which Esther had seen on his face this afternoon.

The memory made her cringe with humiliation and anguish. Esther switched off the lights and went upstairs.

The bedroom looked a little like the transit lounge at an airport, her bag packed and ready to leave, her jacket tossed across it. Esther undressed and got into bed without bothering to take off her make-up – a slovenly habit, she knew, which she would probably live to regret, but she simply could not be bothered, and in any case her toiletries were also already packed. When she closed her eyes her head spun alarmingly and she opened them quickly again, fighting the wave of nausea. Serve her right for drinking so much of Alain's whisky!

A few minutes later her eyes drooped again, and this time she felt only as if she were sinking right into the mattress. She turned her head on the pillow, hoping that her mascara would not leave smudges on it but too drowsy to care, and allowed herself to drift.

Considering her lifelong fear of fire, she had been afraid that she would lie awake for hours, reliving the experiences of the afternoon. In the past she had had nightmares just *seeing* a fire, after all, let alone having to force herself into a burning house. But strangely the phobic terror seemed to have disappeared. She could recall the way it had been, drowning all her senses in total blind panic, but now she discovered she felt subtly different, and her memories of what had happened this afternoon felt like memories of any traumatic experience – unpleasant but reasoned, the fear of real danger, not some nebulous monster.

She was on the very border of sleep when a sudden sound brought her sharply, tinglingly awake. What on earth was that? She lay, tense and motionless, listening. Another sound – the creak of a door. Someone was downstairs! Alain. It must be Alain, home from the hospital after all. What should she do? Let him think she was asleep? He wouldn't come to her room tonight, she felt sure. But then again, she was anxious to know how Hélène was. And perhaps it would be as well to get their goodbyes over tonight . . .

Wide awake now, Esther turned back the covers and got out of bed. Her own dressing gown was already packed but there was a towelling robe hanging on a hook on the door and she slipped it on. As she went out on to the landing she was surprised to find that the house still appeared to be in darkness. Hadn't Alain turned any lights on? Her stomach knotted suddenly. Supposing Hélène's condition had deteriorated – or even worse . . . Supposing Alain was sitting downstairs in the darkness because—

There was someone in the hall. She saw the shadow on the moonlit patch of wall.

'Alain?' she said. 'Is everything all right?'

No reply. She took a couple of steps down the stairs and saw him. It wasn't Alain. It was a strange man – though his face looked vaguely familiar. She froze, one hand gripping the bannisters tightly, the other pulling the robe closely around her. Her heart had begun to thud unevenly with shock and fear.

'Who the hell are you?' she asked.

He came towards her up the stairs. She tried to back away, found herself incapable of moving so much as a muscle. But her mind was working overtime, disjointed thoughts all running together. A burglar. But she had locked the door, and surely she would have heard the sounds of forced entry – breaking glass or something? And wouldn't a burglar turn and run if he was discovered? But this man was still coming towards her, slowly, deliberately, and the moonlight, shafting in through the casement window, showed that he was smiling – almost – if that fixed grimace could be called a smile. Her stomach clenched with fear.

'Who are you?' Her voice came out as a squeak.

'Don't you know?'

And suddenly she was remembering why his face looked familiar. It was the man in the car which had almost run her off the road. But what was he doing here? Why did he think she should know who he was? She moistened her dry lips with her tongue, managed to back up a couple of stairs. But he was quicker. His hand shot out, imprisoning her arm.

'I think you and I should have a little talk.'

He turned her round, propelling her back up the stairs, along the landing and through the still-open door to her room. Then he closed the door with a bang, leaning against it and looking at her with that same unnerving half-smile.

'So – you are Esther. I must say Alain has good taste. Though I could cheerfully kill the bastard for cheating on my sister.'

Your sister? She never actually spoke the words, she was too afraid to be capable of saying anything. It was simply a question in her head. And even as she asked it she knew the answer.

Thierry Rousseau. Hélène's brother. Hélène had insisted he wasn't dead and Esther had thought she was fantasising. But she hadn't been fantasising. She had been telling the truth.

The smile became a laugh, short and scornful.

'What's the matter? You look as if you'd seen a ghost.'

At last Esther found her voice. 'What do you want? What are you doing here? Hélène's in hospital . . .'

'I know. It's not her I came to see. It's you.'

'Me? Why?'

He clicked his tongue, shaking his head. 'Oh Esther, Esther, I couldn't have anyone knowing I'm alive.'

'But . . . I didn't . . .'

'Really? Well, you do now, don't you?'

She stared at him, horrified, saw the mad light in his eyes, and realised the truth. He had come here because he believed she was a danger to him. Somehow he'd known she was alone and he had come to silence her before she could tell what he thought she knew. Ironic, really, since she had known nothing. Until now.

'What a waste. What a terrible waste.' As he spoke he drew a silk scarf from his pocket, twisting it between his hands. A fresh wave of terror made her knees go weak. He was going to kill her – strangle her. She had no weapon to use against him and if she cried out there was no one to hear.

'Please!' she whispered. 'I won't tell anyone, I promise. I probably won't even *see* anyone. I'm going home tomorrow.'

He shook his head, still twisting the scarf as if he liked the feel of it between his fingers.

'That's easy to say. How would I know I could trust you?'

'You could – you could!'

'No, I don't think so, Esther. I'm afraid I've learned not to trust anyone. I couldn't even trust Hélène, could I – my own sister? She told you about me – she must have done. Why would you have been at the farm otherwise?'

'Because I followed her there.' Esther didn't know why she was telling him this, unless it was to gain time. But what use was time? She couldn't keep him talking until morning. And even then there was no guarantee that anyone would come. Simone had offered – and she'd turned her away. Dear God, the phone wouldn't even ring – she'd left it off the hook. But as long as she kept him talking there was still hope. As long as she kept him talking she was still alive, and suddenly every moment was very precious indeed.

'Everybody thinks you're dead,' she said.

'Do they? Do they really?' His grimace became a real smile, smug and self-satisfied, and suddenly Esther saw a chance of prolonging the conversation. Didn't everyone say that criminals were vain – that they loved to boast about what they had done?

'You really have been very clever,' she said.

Thierry's smile broadened.

'Yes, I have, haven't I?'

'So how did you do it? How did you fake your own death?'

He could not resist. Like her, he thought he had all night. He began to talk, telling the story, not as he had told it to Hélène or to Yves, with the facts distorted to suit what the listener wanted to hear, but as it really had been. As she listened, Esther felt the last remnants of hope slipping away. This was a desperate man, a totally ruthless man. He had killed twice before. She had no doubt that he would do so again. And this time she was to be his victim.

'So – now you know.' Thierry had reached the end of his story. 'Now you know everything, Esther Morris. What a pity you won't be able to tell anyone else! If I had my passport – if I could get away tonight – I really think I might let you live, just so that you could let them know how clever I've been. But there it is. I haven't. I'm stuck here for a few more days and I can't risk being caught. So . . .'

He drew the scarf tight between his hands and moved towards her. Esther backed away and collided with the frame of the bed. She fell backwards on to it and before she could recover herself Thierry was kneeling astride her.

'You know I think I am going to enjoy this . . .'

The sound of a car on the drive shattered the stillness of the night; headlights arced across the window in a blinding sweep. Distracted, he loosed his hold on her and she clawed desperately at his face.

'Bitch!' he snarled. His full weight came down on her stomach, squeezing the breath out of her, and she felt the scarf go around her neck. Oh dear God, dear God, there was someone out there, but they had come too late! Somehow she got her thumbs under the scarf, but it was useless . . . useless. He was pulling it tighter, tighter, and the world was going black around her . . .

With the last of her breath Esther tried to scream, but no sound came. And in the blackness, all she could see was his face, right above hers, still smiling . . .

'Esther! Esther!'

Simone's voice. The door bursting open. Two figures, mere silhouettes in the moonlight. The pressure around her neck was released all of a sudden and she was dimly aware of two men struggling. She thought that one of them was Andrew Slater. Then she heard Simone's voice again, this time a gasp of disbelief.

'Thierry!'

The room swam once more and Esther lost consciousness.

'Esther. Come on, Esther. It's all right. You're all right.'

She opened her eyes. Her neck hurt. She tried to speak but her voice came out as no more than a croak.

'Oh, Simone!'

'It's all right.' Simone was cradling her in her arms, looking down at her with tenderness. 'You're safe now. It's all over.'

Her eyes, full of fear, shimmied round. 'Where is he?'

'Gone. He's gone. He made a run for it. Andrew's gone after him.'

'He . . . just walked in . . .'

'Don't try to talk. Rest for a minute. Thank God I came over! Thank God I rang Andrew Slater . . .'

'Why . . . ? What . . . ?'

Simone shook her head. Would Esther be any more likely to believe her now if she tried to explain the certainty she had felt that Esther was in danger, felt it so strongly that she had been unable to put it aside even though Esther had told her in no uncertain terms that she did not want her assistance? Probably not. Even less would she understand the compulsion that had made Simone telephone Andrew Slater. She had spoken to Valerie earlier in the evening about Hélène's accident and Valerie had told her of the Englishman who was investigating Thierry's death. At the time she had thought nothing of it: she had had too many other things on her mind. But as she was preparing for bed, weighed down by anxiety for Esther, he had suddenly come into her mind, and without any clear idea of why she was doing it, she had rung Bob Slater's number and asked to speak to his son.

What Andrew Slater had told her had come as an enormous shock. He had been to meet Yves Marssac, who had told him that Thierry was not dead at all – that it was a hitch-hiker who had died in the accident. Suddenly Simone had realised she had a focus for her anxiety. She hadn't stopped to reason it out. She had simply known instinctively that the danger to Esther which she could sense was not imaginary but real, and the threat somehow had to do with Thierry. She had asked Andrew to meet her and together they had driven over to Le Château Gris. And thank God they had! Thank God he'd been with her, too! She would never have been able to prevent Thierry murdering Esther if she had been alone – he'd probably have murdered her too!

Had Andrew caught up with Thierry? She shivered, wondering what would happen if he did. But Andrew looked well able to take care of himself and in any case the terrible sense of impending danger had gone now. Andrew would probably call the police and they would deal with Thierry – when they found him.

Simone looked down at Esther, touching her throat gently and brushing her hair away from her face. A wave of tenderness encompassed her, the tenderness of a mother for her child.

And Simone knew without a shadow of doubt that she had lived through this moment before, long, long ago, in another lifetime.

'Don't worry, everything is going to be fine,' she said softly, and as Esther opened her eyes, half smiling at her, they shared a moment of complete love and understanding.

26

'SIMONE TELLS ME you are going home,' Alain said.

He looked weary and drawn, the bright morning sunlight emphasising the harsh lines caused by lack of sleep and the streaks of grey in his dark hair.

'Yes.' Esther, too, felt weary. She had not had much sleep either and her throat still hurt, though the doctor who had checked her over had pronounced her fit to travel. No real damage, he had said. She had been very lucky, she knew, but just at this moment she did not feel lucky. Just numb and miserable and flat. The real pain of loss would come later, she supposed, when the numbness began to wear off. 'You're not going to try to persuade me to do otherwise, I imagine.'

He rasped a hand over his as yet unshaven chin, obviously awkward and embarrassed.

'Oh Esther, I've treated you very badly, haven't I? I really don't know what to say.'

'Don't say anything then. There's no point really. We both know it's over and I don't believe in post-mortems, do you?'

'No, but all the same . . . I've hurt you, and I'm sorry. And on top of that, everything you've been through . . . I just can't believe Thierry would do something like that.'

She didn't answer. She didn't want to talk about it just now, didn't want to think about it even. She'd have to, of course. They'd almost certainly want her to come back and give evidence when Thierry's case came to trial. But for the moment all she wanted was to get home, back to some semblance of normality.

'I take it you'll be able to save the business in the light of what's happened?' she said.

'I'm hoping so. If I can get back all the money Thierry embezzled. The publicity won't do me much good, but I think people hereabouts know me well enough to overcome that . . .'

He broke off, embarrassed again. Important as the business was to him it seemed wrong, as well as insensitive, to be talking about it now.

'What about getting you to the airport?' he said, opting for safer ground.

'Andrew Slater said he'd drive me down.'

'Right. I'd take you, only— '

'I know. Best not, anyway. Let's settle for a clean break. It's much the best.'

She smiled ruefully suddenly as the irony of it occurred to her. Hadn't she said much the same to Hélène? Little realising that she would so soon be taking her own advice!

'I don't want to spoil what we had with long, drawn-out goodbyes,' she went on. 'And we did have something, didn't we, Alain? Something . . . well, I think it was special, anyway – in spite of the way it's turned out.'

'Very special.' The tenderness was back in his voice, just the way she remembered it. 'For a time I really thought . . . I wasn't making use of you – I wouldn't want you to think that. I really— '

'Don't!' she said fiercely. 'Just don't!'

'No. As you say, best not. But I want you to know . . . I'll never forget you, Esther.'

Her fingers fluttered. She wanted to reach out and touch his hand one last time. But she merely forced her lips into a stiff smile.

'I know. I hope it all turns out well for you.'

'You too.'

Her throat was aching now, not only from the trauma of last night's encounter but also from unshed tears.

'Goodbye, Alain.'

Gerona Airport was bathed in late-afternoon sunshine. She sat at one of the white plastic tables outside the sliding glass doors, her bag propped on a small trolley beside her, watching, but not really seeing, a coach disgorge a load of sunburned holidaymakers into the car park.

The glass door leading to the airport café slid open and Andrew Slater emerged carrying two Cokes. He set them down on the table, pulled out a chair and sat down beside her.

'The Bristol plane should be here soon.'

'Um.' Esther sipped the ice-cold drink, thinking how time had distorted since she had flown in. In some ways it seemed like yesterday, it others more like a lifetime – several lifetimes! 'You don't have to wait, you know. I'll be perfectly all right and I know you're busy.'

'It's OK. A couple of hours won't make much difference one way or the other.'

He did not add that he would have made time, whatever the circumstances, to take this last chance to be with her before she left for England, but she guessed it anyway, and, somewhat to her own surprise, realised she did not mind.

Such a short time ago, before she had become involved with Alain, her defences would have come up if a man had showed such obvious interest in her. Now it no longer bothered her. Because she liked Andrew and felt at ease with him, perhaps? Or for some other reason – that the almost phobic reaction had been relegated to the past along with that other overwhelming phobia: fire? She didn't know. It was too early yet to tell. She was still too numbed by all that had happened; her emotions as well as her body had taken too much of a battering But somehow, in spite of everything, there was a tiny spark of optimism trying to make itself felt beneath all the layers of hurt. She couldn't understand it – didn't even yet have the will to try – but in some inexplicable way a burden seemed to have been lifted from her shoulders. Crossing the border from France to Spain, she had felt an enormous sadness followed by a lightening of her spirit. One part of her life was over; when she got over all this another would begin. And for no apparent reason she had the strangest feeling that it would be easier than before and perhaps better.

'You realise I should have been on this flight home too if things had turned out differently,' he said.

'Should you?' She tried to ignore the unpleasant thought that if things had turned out differently she might not have been going home at all. 'How long do you think it will take for you to tie up all the ends of your story?'

'Hard to say. Another week should do it – though I'll come back out for the trial, of course. I want to see this one through.'

'What do you think will happen to Thierry?'

'He'll be found guilty. Not much doubt of that. But it's going to be a long and complicated business.'

His last words were almost drowned out by the sound of aircraft engines; looking up she saw the Britannia hanging in the sky overhead like a great silver bird.

'That looks like my plane now. I'd better go and check in.'

She stood up, he did the same.

'Can I ring you, Esther, when I get back to England?'

And to her own surprise she heard herself say, 'Yes, of course.'

She took hold of her trolley, pushing it towards the doors. They slid open soundlessly and she stepped inside. She turned. Andrew was still standing there in the sunshine, watching her go. She smiled and raised her hand to him. Then she crossed to join the queue at the check-in desk.

Esther was not the only one to experience a sense of relief, as if a load had been lifted from her shoulders. Hélène, too, was feeling more peaceful, more at ease with herself, than she could ever remember.

Everyone put her moods down to the tragic death of her mother, but Hélène knew they had begun long before that. Even when she had been a little girl there had been times when she had felt frightened for no reason, and deeply, inexplicably sad. It might be that she was playing quite happily when the dark shadow fell without warning across her sunny mood; at other times it was with her when she woke, a nameless dread that remained with her all day. She hadn't tried to understand, of course, hadn't even realised that it wasn't the same for everyone. But she had feared the times when the shadow fell and wished with all her child's heart that she need never feel this way.

Now, however, when she woke from a deep refreshing sleep, she felt a curious lightness.

Perhaps, she thought, it was because Thierry wasn't dead after all. No matter what he'd done – and he had certainly done terrible things – he was still her brother and she loved him. Or perhaps it was because Alain was here at her bedside, holding her hand and looking at her the way he used to in the days before they had begun tearing each other apart. Either of those things would have been enough to make her happy. Yet somehow she knew the sense of joy and peace went deeper than that. It was as if she had somehow lived through a metamorphosis. Perhaps the moods would still come – she could hardly believe they would not – but there was no denying she felt quite different.

She turned her head on the pillow to look at Alain, loving him as she had always loved him, and grateful that she had been given a second chance.

'Esther has gone home, has she?' she said, surprised to find she could speak the name of the woman Alain had had an affair with and feel no animosity.

'Yes. She's gone home.'

'And you and I . . . well, you're coming home too, aren't you?'

The tired lines at the corners of his eyes crinkled suddenly.

'What do you think?'

'And this time we're going to make it work.'

'It won't be my fault if we don't.'

'It wasn't your fault before,' she said. 'It was mine. I was impossible, I know. I promise I won't be like that ever again.'

His eyes crinkled again. 'We'll see.'

He obviously didn't think she'd changed that much, she thought, but he was prepared to try again anyway. Well, it was up to her to prove it to him.

'I'd like . . . well, when we've had a little time on our own first, of course . . . I'd like us to be a proper family.' He looked at her quickly, disbelievingly almost. 'I think we should try to have a baby, Alain.'

'But . . . you've always said— '

'I know. I think it was because of what happened to my mother. You do know what happened to her, don't you?'

'Hélène – you don't have to talk about it.'

'Yes, I think I do. I've bottled it up for too long. I want to tell you what happened that night.' She paused, gathering up the painful memories, finding the courage at last to face them. 'I woke up and heard her moaning. I went to her room – ran in. I was so frightened. She was . . . just lying there. White – so white. And there was blood everywhere. The sheets were soaked with it . . .' She broke off, closing her eyes for a moment, seeing once more the way it had been, yet somehow feeling the horror with the perception of an adult rather than the blind helpless panic of a child.

Alain held her hand tightly, saying nothing. A tear rolled down her cheek and he wiped it away with his thumb.

'She'd had an abortion, I think,' Hélène said at last. 'My mother died because she'd been going to have a baby. I couldn't get that out of my head. Oh – I knew it didn't make sense for me to be afraid, that it need not be the same for me, but it didn't make any difference. For me, somehow, being pregnant equated with dying. It was something . . . in *here* . . .' She pressed her hand, fingers spread, against her chest. 'I just couldn't get away from it, however hard I tried.'

'So – what's changed?' Alain asked.

'I don't know. Because I nearly died in the fire, I suppose. It's finally come to me there are other ways of dying, and since you never know what the future holds you might as well live life to the full while you have the chance.'

'Well, we'll see,' Alain said. 'When you're better, we'll talk about it again.'

She looked at him quickly. 'I thought having a child was important to you.'

'It is. But the most important thing of all is sorting ourselves out first. Making sure we don't make the same mistakes again.'

'We won't,' she said.

And wondered how it was that she could feel so sure of something.

Simone was at her desk when the telephone began to ring. She sighed, pushing her spectacles up into her hair and getting up to answer it. What now? And just as she had been getting down to Simon de Montfort for the first time in days too! But her annoyance was just that: irritation at being interrupted rather than the distracted frustration she had been experiencing recently. She felt as if a weight had been lifted from her shoulders and the eagerness to work was bubbling inside her just the way it did when she was on the point of writing something really good and worthwhile.

'Simone? It's Edith, at the library. I've had a spare minute at last and I've looked up the Bernards of Montaugure for you.'

'Edith!' Simone was surprised; she had forgotten all about her request to her friend.

'I'm sorry it's taken me so long. But you know what these

old records can be like, and as I told you, we have been very short-handed here.'

'Yes, of course . . .'

'I think you'll be pleased with what I've managed to discover, though. It really is quite fascinating. The Viscount at the time you were asking about was called Philip. At one time he was a crusader, but later he joined forces with Raymond of Toulouse and the Counts of Comminges and Foix against Simon de Montfort. And his wife, Alazais, was burned at the stake as a heretic.'

'Yes,' Simone said. 'I know.'

'You know? You mean you've been doing some research too?'

'Not exactly,' Simone hedged. 'It just confirms what I suspected.'

'So you don't know the really interesting part?'

'Interesting part? What do you mean?'

'Ah!' Edith sounded pleased with herself. 'No, I can tell you don't! Well, Philip had a son, Bernard – not by his wife, he was illegitimate from what I can gather. But Philip installed him as his heir nevertheless and he took the Bernard name along with the lands and titles. And . . .'

'Yes?'

'Well, out of interest, I went on checking the line, and do you know what I discovered? His youngest daughter moved south and married a Lavaur. One of your ancestors, Simone! Now how's that for a coincidence? Or did you have an inkling about it? Is that why you wanted to know about them in the first place?'

'No, I had no idea,' Simone said. 'That's amazing.'

But strangely she wasn't really surprised. So – there was a direct connection. She – and Alain and Valerie too – were all descendents of Philip Bernard and Jeanne Marty. In fact, if she had been Helis she had been her own ancestor . . .

The skin prickled at the nape of her neck. She would never be a disbeliever again, but some things were simply too much to take on board . . .

'Thank you very much, Edith,' she said. 'I'd like to call in some time and see the papers for myself.'

'Of course. Any time. Must go now – duty calls!'

'Well, thanks again.'

She replaced the receiver, sat thinking for a moment, then picked it up again and dialled Valerie's number.

For once, Valerie answered it almost immediately.

'Simone – I was just about to ring you!'

'Oh? What about?'

'No – you first.'

'All right.' Simone told her what Edith had said and heard Valerie's quick intake of breath.

'That is truly amazing!'

'My words exactly.'

'Those people – our ancestors! Strange though that when we all still live in the same part of the world Esther should have reincarnated in England.'

'Perhaps she'd had enough of France, after all that happened to her!' Simone said lightly.

'Mm. She thought she could escape – but she couldn't. I must ask Aurore about it when I see her – which will be quite soon. That was what I was ringing to tell you. I'm going to stay with her. All this has made me desperate to learn more about the paranormal and all it means . . . I'm leaving tomorrow and I might be gone quite some time.'

'What about Yves?'

'Oh, I thought it was time to give him the old heave-ho. I've had my wild fling, Simone – now it's time to move on to more important things. I really want to try to develop a psychic sense myself, though I don't suppose I'll ever be as good as you and Aurore.'

'Probably not, since psychic awareness calls for abstinence from alcohol, I believe,' Simone said wryly.

'Oh, you are horrible!' But Valerie laughed anyway. 'For all you know I might be prepared to give it up in a good cause.'

'For how long?'

'As long as it takes. Simone . . .' She paused for a moment. 'Do you think Maman and Papa lived in those other times too?'

'Probably.'

'So who were they?'

'I think Papa was probably Viscount Bernard and Maman was Cecile.'

'Could be. What about me? Who was I?'

Simone thought for a moment, then chuckled.

'I should think if you were any of them it's most likely you were Grazide, the lady-in-waiting who seduced poor Pons.'

'Simone – honestly! What sort of an opinion do you have of me?' But she was not displeased, Simone could tell.

'The opinion of a sister who knows you very well.'

'All right, if we're playing truth games, I'll tell you what I think. I think it's time you moved on from churning out boring old history books and wrote a novel. It could be their story – Jeanne and Philip and Alazais. It would sell a whole lot more copies and make you very rich, and I'm sure it would be absolutely riveting. After all, you've been there – you've seen it all.'

'Maybe . . .' But she couldn't help feeling that to write the story that had revealed itself to her would be a betrayal of a sacred trust. Or would it? A novel, as she had sometimes thought herself, would bring the history she cared so much for to a wider audience than her scholarly tomes could ever reach. And she could tell the world of the dangers and dilemmas, the hardships and triumphs, the poignancy and the pain and the faith of those who had died for their beliefs.

When Valerie had gone, Simone sat for a moment allowing herself to think about the events of the last week. Already there was a distant dreamlike quality in remembering them, as if they were not quite real, or had happened a very long time ago. Strange, really. A chapter had reached its conclusion and the whole episode, so real and immediate, had moved effortlessly into the annals of time.

Which, Simone thought, was exactly where it belonged. Just one tiny fragment of the universe – one set of souls who had worked out their karma after thousands of years and were now free; free to move on, free, perhaps to make other mistakes and learn other lessons, but no longer burdened by the guilt of old sins or compelled by old obsessions.

Except, of course, the soul which had once been Pons. Thierry, it seemed, had learned nothing. He had yet to pay his debts and work out his karma. Not even a lengthy spell in prison would do that for him. He would still have to face the moment when he must sit in judgement on his own misdeeds and choose a course to set his feet on the right path. But perhaps now that the chain had at last been broken he too would be able to find the way to redemption – in his next life, if not in this one.

With all her heart, Simone hoped it would be so. After all, had not Pons, with all his faults and feelings, once been her son?

A feeling of sadness cast a shadow momentarily over the sense of peace and she wondered if it would be given to her to help him too towards the light and whether she would be equal to it. Then she thrust the thought aside. Time enough to face that when, and if, it ever occurred. Once more the slate would have been wiped clean, she would be a different person then, perhaps stronger and wiser from all the aeons of accumulated wisdom and experience.

With a tiny smile Simone pulled the keyboard towards her and began to type.

It was over. The wise soul knew it and was suffused with a sense of peace which transcended her weariness. It had been a long struggle to right the wrongs of the ages and she had feared she might fail in the task to which she had been appointed. But this time the one to whom she had reached out had received her. Simone had been the perfect medium; she thought she had done nothing, but she was wrong. Without her unobtrusive influence the forces of evil would have been stronger, too strong, perhaps, for the spirit of the one who had once been Jeanne Marty, and who had once again been forced to face her imperfections while imprisoned in a weak human frame.

Without Simone the chance to right old wrongs might once more have been lost, and hundreds of earth years might have passed before it came again. Now Jeanne, at least, was safe, her feet set on the path to enlightenment, and Alazais would be freed from the old fears which had haunted her across the centuries.

Now at last the wise soul could rest. There was only one thing left to do – and that was to show her gratitude to the woman who had become her earthly medium.

A light breeze ruffled the papers on Simone's desk. She looked up. In a shaft of sunlight dust motes were dancing, swirling into a vague shadowy form. Simone stared, transfixed. She felt no alarm now, only a sense of radiant happiness and peace. The dust motes moved again, shining incandescent against the shadowy background. And for a moment Simone was certain she saw the smiling face of Agnes the Perfect.